The Critics on Erica James

'There is humour and warmth in this engaging story of love's triumphs and disappointments, with two well-realised and intriguing subplots'   *Woman & Home*

'Joanna Trollope fans, dismayed by the high gloom factor and complete absence of Agas in her latest books, will turn with relief to James' ... delightful novel about English village life ... a blend of emotion and wry social observation'
                                                  Daily Mail

'Scandal, fury, accusations and revenge are all included in Erica James' compelling novel ... this story of village life in Cheshire is told with wit and humour'   *Stirling Observer*

'An entertaining read with some wickedly well-painted cameo characters. It's a perfect read if you're in the mood for romance'   *Prima*

'This is a really sparkling novel, full of drama and laughter'
                                                  Bookcase

'A bubbling, delightful comedy which is laced with a bitter-sweet tang ... a good story, always well observed, and full of wit. The characters walk out of the pages to greet you, and you know you are in good hands from the start – a very assured comedy'   *Publishing News*

'Erica James' sensitive story ... is as sparklingly fresh as dew on the village's surrounding meadows ... thoroughly enjoy-able and fully deserving of a place in the crowded market of women's fiction'   *Sunday Express*

'Wry humour and romance ... Erica James is a breath of fresh air'   *Daily Mail*

Born in 1960, Erica James grew up in Hampshire. Since then she has lived in Oxford, Cheshire, Yorkshire and Belgium. After a series of diverse administrative jobs, in which she worked in an Oxford college and for a supplier of mining explosives, Erica decided that the best employer would be herself. There then followed several burning-the-midnight-oil years of cottage industry before she finally turned to an even harder life of toiling at the fictional coal-face of novel writing. She now lives in Cheshire with her two sons, Edward and Samuel. Her short stories have won prizes in various competitions, her first novel, *A Breath of Fresh Air*, was selected for the WH Smith's Fresh Talent promotion and *Airs & Graces* was short-listed for the 1988 RNA Romantic Novel of the Year Award.

By the same author

A Breath of Fresh Air
Time for a Change
Airs & Graces
A Sense of Belonging

Act of Faith

ERICA JAMES

An Orion paperback
First published in Great Britain by Orion in 1999
This paperback edition published in 2000 by Orion Books Ltd,
Orion House, 5 Upper St Martin's Lane, London WC2H 9EA

A CIP catalogue record for this book is available
from the British Library.

ISBN: 0 75283 417 7

Typeset by Deltatype Ltd, Birkenhead, Merseyside

Printed and bound in Great Britain by
Clays Ltd, St Ives plc

Grateful acknowledgement is made for permission to quote the lyrics from:

'All The Lies That You Told Me'
Words and music by Christie Hennessy
© Copyright 1993 Redemption Songs Ltd / Chrysalis Music Ltd
The Chrysalis Building. 13 Bramley Road, London W10 6SP
Used by permission of Music Sales Ltd
All rights reserved. International Copyright Secured

'Don't Be A Stranger' (Nevin)
© 1990 by kind permission of MCA Music Ltd

'I Will Always Love You'
Words and music by Dolly Parton
© 1973 Velvet Apple Music – All rights reserved
Lyric reproduced by kind permission of
Carlin Music Corp., London NW1 8BD

As ever, to Edward and Samuel

ACKNOWLEDGEMENTS

So many people helped create this book, but to save their blushes (and their reputations) I shan't name them all: they know what part they played and I hope they know how grateful I am.

Thanks must go to everybody at Orion for giving me another year to remember. Jane Wood, Selina Walker and Sarah Yorke need to be singled out for their extraordinary juggling skills and always having time for The Author From Hell. As does Susan Lamb for her patience and determination to get the artwork just right ... well, almost. Thanks also to everyone at the January sales conference for not eating me alive.

Last, but by no means least, thank you Mr Lloyd at Curtis Brown for the windmill, the go-karting and the freezing North Sea wind in my face. Never again!

The greatest pleasure of life is love,
The greatest treasure, contentment,
The greatest possession health,
The greatest ease is sleep,
The greatest medicine is a true friend.

Sir William Temple

Chapter One

Today of all days, Ali Anderson wasn't in the mood for empty-headed foolishness.

'Oh, get a life you silly little man,' she muttered, switching off the car radio and bringing an end to the ramblings of the out-of-his-tree caller from Redditch – a crank who had been advocating a world economy based on a system of homespun bartering. Honestly, was there anything worse than a born-again down-shifter?

She would have liked to vent her feelings further, but the opportunity to do so eluded her as, just in time, she saw the road to Great Budworth. She slowed her speed, made a sharp turn to the right, and took the narrow lane that led to the centre of the small, neat village that, up until a year ago, had been her home. Its picture-book selection of much-photo-graphed quaint houses had long since lost their charm for Ali, and as she passed each familiar pretty cottage, her heartbeat quickened and her throat tightened. She reluctantly thanked Mr Out-Of-His-Tree from Redditch for his momentary distraction and wished for a further miraculous diversion of thought.

But nothing could divert her now. She was on her own, about to come face to face with the tragedy that was made so cruelly poignant at this time of the year. As she switched off the engine, she asked herself the question for which she knew there was no easy reassuring answer: would she ever be able to make this journey without feeling the excruciating pain?

She left her car under the watchful gaze of a well-nourished ginger cat loitering in the post-office window, the panes of which were festively decorated with tinsel and sprayed-on snow, and with her footsteps echoing in the deserted street, she walked, head bowed, into the wind towards the sixteenth-century sandstone church that dominated the top end of the village with its elevated position and massive crenellated tower. It was late afternoon, cold and raw, a wintry day that was cloaked in melancholy. The unforgiving December wind stung her cheeks and snatched at the Cellophane-wrapped roses in her arms. She cradled them protectively against her chest, and breathed in their fragrant scent; a scent that was powerfully redolent of this dreadful place.

There was nobody else in the churchyard. She was glad. It was better to be alone. Last time there had been an elderly man blowing his nose but pretending self-consciously that he wasn't. She followed the path, reading the weathered tombstones that were green with a seasoned patina of lichen as she moved ever nearer to her destination. Scanning the names of Great Budworth's ancient and more recently departed was meant to be a diverting tactic: it was supposed to slow her heart, stop her stomach from coiling itself into a nauseous, tight knot, keep her from reliving the horror of that night two years ago.

But it hadn't worked before and it wasn't working now.

She passed *Robert Ashworth 1932–1990*, then *Amy Riley, 1929–1992, beloved wife of Joseph Riley*, and knew that there were only three more painful steps to take. She braced herself.

One.

Two.

Three.

And there it was.

Forever precious in our hearts, Isaac Anderson, 1995–1996, dearly loved son of Ali and Elliot Anderson.

She stood perfectly still, staring at the words, afraid to move lest she set off some uncontrollable emotion within her, but wanting more than anything to leave her flowers and run.

It was two years to the day since Isaac had died and she hated to remember him this way. This wasn't her son. This wasn't the longed-for baby she had loved from the moment she had held him against her breast in the delivery room. This wasn't the tiny fair-haired Isaac whose smile had melted her heart every morning when she went into his bedroom and picked him out of his cot. This wasn't the little boy who had tottered towards her when she came home from work, and had sat on her lap while she had read him a selection of his favourite stories before they went upstairs to have a bath together, and played at being water buffalo. This wasn't the happy eighteen-month-old boy whom she'd kissed goodbye that fateful morning and had never seen alive again.

An icy gust of wind curled itself round her neck and prompted her to move. She stooped to the small grave, unwrapped the flowers and carefully arranged them. She stuffed the Cellophane into her coat pocket, removed her leather gloves and set about picking at the weeds that were invading the rectangle of space that in theory belonged to Isaac, but in reality belonged to no one. As she worked at the weeds she thought, as she so often did, how the landscape of her life had been changed by her son's death, in particular the disastrous effect it had had on her marriage.

Where there had once been absolute unity between her and Elliot, there was now a terrible division, their lives fragmented into so many badly broken pieces that there was no hope of them being mended. They had become distant and uncommunicative. From loving one another with a passion that had seemed enduring and immutable they had quickly reached a stage where all that connected them was a wall of silent, bitter reproach. It became an insurmountable barrier that neither of them wanted to knock down. They had lived like that for a year, hiding from each other until the inevitable happened and they parted. Divorce had been her suggestion. Elliot had been against taking such a final and drastic step, but she had insisted on going through with it. She had had to.

Being with Elliot seemed only to remind her of what she'd lost, and she grew to hate him for it. Divorce seemed the only way to detach herself from all the pain. But the pain hadn't lessened. Neither had the bitterness between them.

Rigid with cold, her fingers were hurting. She stopped what she was doing and stood up, and with the backs of her hands wiped the tears from her eyes. At the sound of footsteps on the path behind her she whipped round to see who it was.

It was Elliot. He was carrying a bunch of flowers and was on a level with *Robert Ashworth*. Seeing her, he paused, but then continued on and passed *Amy Riley* in one long stride. 'You okay?' was all he said.

She lowered her hands from her face and muttered, 'It's just the wind in my eyes. It's the cold.' As though to prove the point, she pulled on her gloves, hunched her shoulders and stamped her feet on the iron-hard ground.

He glanced up at the dreary leaden sky that was rapidly darkening as the afternoon drew to a cold and bitter dusk. 'It'll probably snow,' he remarked, as though they were merely strangers discussing the weather.

'You could be right,' she responded stiffly, brushing at her eyes again and hating him for being so damnably in control. She was furious that he was here, yet more furious that he had caught her crying and that he was being considerate enough to look away while she composed herself. She didn't want his consideration, not when it reminded her of the past when he'd been so good at it: as a boss; as a lover; as a husband; and as a father. In the beginning it had been one of his attractions, at the end a torment.

She watched him bend down to place his flowers next to hers, glad at least that he was sticking to their agreement – white roses only. 'Never red,' she'd told him when they were preparing for Isaac's funeral. 'Red is too violent, too bloody, too sacrificial.'

'I'll leave you to it,' she said. She turned to go.

He straightened up quickly. 'No.' He placed a hand on her

arm. 'Please don't leave because of me. I'll wait in the car while you . . .'

She looked at his hand on her coat sleeve, then at the heavy awkwardness in his face and at the darkness that was eclipsing the natural lightness of his watchful blue eyes. 'While I what?'

'While you do what you need to do.'

She shook her head and withdrew her arm. 'The moment's gone.'

'I'm sorry, I should have timed it better.'

'I shouldn't let it worry you.' She walked away.

He returned his gaze to the flowers he'd just laid on Isaac's grave. Then, as if urged by some hidden voice, he called after her, 'Ali, will you wait for me?'

She stopped moving but she didn't look back at him. 'Why?'

'I'd like to talk to you.'

She began walking again.

'Ali?'

'I'll be in my car.'

Chapter Two

With Elliot's Jaguar XK8 headlamps following behind her, Ali drove home in the dark wondering what it was he wanted to discuss.

While sitting in her car outside the post office – the ginger cat nowhere to be seen – she had had plenty of time to ponder on Elliot's request to talk to her: twenty minutes in all. When he finally emerged from the churchyard he had asked if she would have a drink with him. Looking at his pale face in the soft light cast from the glowing street-lamp behind him, she had thought that few men had ever looked more in need of a reviving snifter. But glancing at her watch and picturing the pair of them sitting miserable-faced in the empty public bar of the George and Dragon – the scene of many a happy drinking session when it had been their local – she had suggested he came back to her place.

Now she was regretting this rash act of bonhomie and not just because she couldn't recall the state of the bathroom, or the kitchen, or indeed the sitting room – had she cleared away the remains of last night's Chinese takeaway before crashing out on the sofa some time after two and sleeping the sleep of the chronically exhausted? – but because since she and Elliot had separated they had deliberately avoided the come-back-to-my-place scenario.

And with good reason.

Neither of them was equipped to treat one another with anything more cordial than coolness edged with disparagement and crabby fault-finding. It was, she knew, their only way of coping with an impossible situation.

After she had moved out of their home in Great Budworth and had set in motion the wheels of their divorce, they had tried their best to behave in as civil a manner as they could manage. Not easy, given that they were both brimming with unresolved hurt and anger. However, by restricting their infrequent get-togethers to restaurants where it would have been unseemly to hurl abuse – or crockery – they pulled it off. For a more convincing performance, it was better if a third party was involved. Usually this was Elliot's father, Sam, who rarely objected to being caught in the occasional round of crossfire. 'White-flag time,' he would say, when she and Elliot paused for breath before reloading with fresh ammunition. 'Hold your fire.' Only once did they go too far, causing Sam to throw down his napkin and declare that he preferred his drama on the telly and would they kindly stop acting like a couple of spoilt brats. 'Now, behave yourselves, the pair of you, or I shall go home to a nice, quiet, digestibly sound plate of sausage, egg and chips.'

Indicating well in advance of the turning for Little Linton – which could be missed in the blink of an eye, and which concealed itself by merging into the environs of the sprawling neighbouring village of Holmes Chapel – Ali checked her rear-view mirror to make sure that Elliot was still following. He was and, like her, he was now indicating left.

'The boy's no fool,' she said aloud. She smiled, realising that she was relaxing . . . was beginning to be herself.

When Isaac had died she had promised herself that she would visit his grave only on the anniversary of his death. She didn't want to turn into one of those people who felt they were keeping a loved one alive by putting in a regular show of graveside attendance. No amount of tombstone weeping was ever going to bring him back, so what was the point? Since the funeral this was the second appearance she had put in at the churchyard, and it had been no easier than the first. It had the effect of turning her into somebody, or something, that wasn't the real her. It brought out the worst in her. It made her angry, self-pitying, bitter, reproachful, but mostly desperate.

Desperate to forget.

Desperate to remember.

Just desperate.

Over breakfast that morning she had considered not visiting Isaac's grave, but how could she not go? What would Elliot and everyone else think of her? That not only in life had she failed her tiny, vulnerable son but in death too?

She indicated again, this time to the right. She checked that Elliot was still on the ball and, slowing, she turned into a narrow gap in the high hedge that lined the road. This was Mill Lane and ahead of her, about a hundred yards or so, was her new home. It was clearly visible in the night sky because it was so cleverly illuminated by a special security lighting system. Windmills weren't common in this part of the country and its seventy-foot-high, brick-built tower made an impressive sight. It no longer had any sails and its tall, looming shape, and white-painted dome-capped top, reminded Ali of a very large pepper-pot. It never failed to amuse her that she was now living in such a curio.

The nasty, unforgiving part of her, that petty bit that held tenaciously on to past grievances and kept her awake at night, hoped that Elliot was impressed. He didn't need to know that this beautifully converted windmill, set in splendid isolation, didn't belong to her, that she had only been renting it for the past month from Owen, one of her expat clients now holed up in some God-awful place on the outskirts of Brussels.

She parked her Saab convertible in front of the small garage and, without waiting for Elliot, hurried to let herself in. If she could just make it up the first flight of stairs before his marathon-running legs sprinted after her, she'd be able to remove, or disguise, the worst of the potential squalor.

But she needn't have worried. As soon as she'd shouldered open the heavy studded door – it could be a devil at times, especially in damp weather – she saw that Lizzie, her priceless treasure inherited from Owen, had paid a call. Relieved, she knew that there wouldn't be so much as an atom of dust in the house, never mind a pair of knickers loitering with intent on the bathroom floor. The evidence that this was the case was on the oak table by the door where Lizzie had left a note. It read:

Out of Hoover bags and Sanilav. Chocolate cake in the tin by the kettle, a minute per slice in the microwave should do it, a pot of whipped cream in the fridge. Love Lizzie. P.S. Have strung up your Christmas cards like Owen used to . . . hope you approve.

'What an improbable place,' said Elliot, appearing in the doorway. 'How long have you lived here?'

'A few weeks,' she said. She slipped off her coat and hung it on the Edwardian coat-rack, which she could only just reach. It had been screwed to the wall by Owen who, like Elliot, was well over six foot. 'And most people wouldn't say improbable, they'd say amazing, interesting, wonderful. Spectacular, even. Close the door, you're letting the heat out.'

Elliot did as she said. He removed his coat and hung it on the hook next to where she'd placed hers. 'What was it used for originally?'

She caught the thin veneer of politeness that only just skimmed his words. 'Corn,' she answered, 'and please don't expect me to explain anything more detailed than that. I wouldn't know a grain bin from a hopper.' She opened a door and took him through to what was the largest room of the mill and where, once in a blue moon, she entertained. But it wasn't a room she cared for. It felt cold and formal. She put this down to the reclaimed slate floor of which Owen was so proud. Lizzie frequently described it as nothing but a bugger to clean.

Ignoring Elliot's look of interest in the thick beams that

spanned the low ceiling, she led the way to the next floor via a wooden spiral staircase that creaked noisily. The first floor was Ali's favourite part of the mill and, in her opinion, the best bit of the conversion. It had been designed to provide a comfortable and homely open-plan area for cooking, eating and relaxing, and it was here, when she wasn't at work or in bed, that she spent the majority of her time. The kitchen area had been built by a friend of Owen's who was a joiner and the hand-made pitch pine units and cupboards and ornately carved shelves nestled against the dark-red-painted walls perfectly, so much so that the oddity of the curve was almost lost.

She watched Elliot duck one of the beams as he moved past her to the small-paned window above the sink. She left him to peer out into the darkness and went through to the raised sitting area where she switched on two large table lamps. Soft light bounced off the polished floor and enhanced the rubescent tones in the Oriental rug in front of the fire as well as the Venetian red of the walls. She bent down to the fire, glad once more that Lizzie had chosen today to come in. Four days' worth of accumulated ashes had been cleared away and the grate now contained a fresh supply of logs and kindling, along with a couple of fire-lighters; even the empty log basket had been replenished from the woodpile beside the garage. When she stood up to replace the matches on the mantelpiece she noticed the Christmas cards that stretched from one brass picture light to another. If it weren't for their presence, nobody would have guessed from the look of the room that Christmas was only just round the corner.

'I'll get us a drink,' she said, when Elliot came through from the kitchen. 'Mind that step,' she added. 'It catches everybody. Glenlivet do you?'

He nodded and minded the step.

Chatty so-and-so, she thought, with her back to him as she rummaged in the booze cupboard next to the fridge. Pouring their drinks, she saw the tin by the kettle and remembered

Lizzie's note. She prised off the lid and licked her lips. Lunch suddenly seemed an age away. She cut two large slices of chocolate cake, bunged them in the microwave, added a dollop of cream, loaded the plates and glasses on to a tray and took it through to the sitting area, where she found Elliot looking dangerously at home in one of the high-backed armchairs nearest the fire. It was an unnerving scene, too reminiscent of their married days.

Except, she told herself firmly, while lowering the tray on to the table in front of the sofa, if they were still married, he'd have his Gieves & Hawkes suit jacket off, his silk tie slung over the back of the chair and his shoes left just where she'd trip over them.

She pushed a plate towards him, handed him his single malt and wondered whether his silence meant that mentally he was being as rude about her as she was about him. Well, if he was, it was progress of sorts. At least they weren't verbally bashing the living daylights out of each other.

'Cheers,' she said, raising her glass and choosing to sit in the corner of the sofa that was furthest from Elliot. He acknowledged her gesture and took a swallow of his whisky. He seemed quite happy to sit in the formidable silence, but Ali wasn't. 'So what did you want to talk about?' she asked, eager to be rid of him.

He looked uncomfortable, no longer at home, which, Ali noted, had the instant effect of ageing him. But Elliot wasn't old. Far from it. He was only forty-six and could pass for younger with his well-exercised body and light brown hair only faintly shot through with grey. But was that simply because she knew him so well? Wasn't it true that the people one knew best stayed the same age as one viewed oneself? When she looked in the mirror each morning, she didn't see a thirty-eight-year-old woman, she saw a girl of twenty-four. Funny that. Most people when asked how old they felt invariably responded with an age in their mid-twenties.

She watched him take another swallow of his Glenlivet

before placing the glass with extreme care on the gold-edged coaster on the table. But still he didn't answer her. He reached for his plate of chocolate cake and began eating it. She knew that these were warning signs that, whatever it was he had to say, he was choosing his words with the utmost caution. It was the way he operated; he never blundered straight in. At work it had always been one of his greatest and most effectively employed weapons. She might not love him any more, but she sure as hell still respected his professional ability and knew as well as anyone who had ever worked with him that nothing clouded his reasoning or his judgement. He had the kind of mind that could play two simultaneous games of chess and win both.

But this wasn't a work situation and she could see that despite his best endeavours to look composed he was edgy. So what was it that he had come here to talk about?

Then it struck her.

He'd met somebody, hadn't he? That's why he was here. Under the guise of wanting to be the one to break the news to her, he was really here to brag that he was getting married again. He probably wanted to rub her face in it. 'See,' he was saying beneath all that outward calm, 'I've moved on. I'm over Isaac. And I'm certainly over you.' The bloody cheek of him, sitting here drinking her expensive whisky and all the time he was trawling his mind to find the right words to boast that he'd been bonking some compliant underling at the office! Bloody, *bloody* cheek of him!

He looked up from his plate and fixed her with his serious blue eyes. 'This is very good. Did you make it yourself?'

'The hell I did. You know perfectly well that baking was never my forte. Now get on and tell me what it is you want to discuss.'

He narrowed his eyes, and she could see that he was figuring out if she'd rumbled him. He looked vaguely perturbed. 'What are you doing for Christmas?' he asked, lowering his gaze and concentrating on scraping up the last of his cake.

'Christmas?' she repeated, wrong-footed.

'Yes, that ritual we go through in the fourth week of December.'

The sarcasm in his voice was in danger of bringing out the crockery-throwing instinct in her. 'Thank you, Elliot, I'm well aware of when Christmas is. Divorce hasn't addled my brain, unlike somebody I could think of.' *Getting married again, hah!*

His gaze was back on her, and it was fierce. 'What's that supposed to mean?'

'Make of it what you will.'

He frowned. 'So *what* are you doing for Christmas?'

'I'm not sure. And I'm not sure that it's any of your business. Now, will you just get to the point and tell me what you wanted to say?'

He looked exasperated. She guessed that they were only seconds away from dispensing with the politeness forced upon them by the circumstances of the day. 'That's what I'm trying to do,' he said. His cool was definitely waning. There was even a hint of clenched teeth. 'Dad and I are going away for Christmas and . . . and, fools that we are, we wondered if you wanted to join us.'

Ali was jaw-droppingly stunned. She corralled what she could of her scattered wits and said, 'An invitation put so elegantly, I hardly know what to say.' It was true. She didn't. Nothing could have taken the wind out of her sails more succinctly. She got to her feet and went and put another log on the fire, playing for time by prodding it into place with a pair of long-handled brass tongs. An invitation to spend Christmas with her ex-husband was the last thing she'd expected to come out of the day.

She was almost touched.

Yet wholly suspicious.

Why had Elliot asked her this when he must have

concluded that she would probably repeat last year's Christmas holiday and spend it with her parents down on Hayling Island? He wasn't to know that she had decided not to do that. In fact, the only people who knew that she was planning a home-alone Christmas this year were her parents. Mm . . . she thought, and suspecting that her mother had been at work, she put the tongs down on the hearth and said, 'Have my parents been in touch with you?'

'A brief letter with a Christmas card.'

She tutted. 'And Mum just happened to bring you up to date and mention that I was being a miserable killjoy and staying here on my own, is that it?'

Gone now was his edginess and fully reinstated was his customary detached calm. He crossed one of his long legs over the other. 'Something like that, yes.'

She went back to the sofa. 'And would I be right in thinking that it was Sam's idea for you to invite me to go away with you both?'

He nodded.

'It smacks of charity, Elliot, you realise that, don't you?'

He rolled his eyes heavenwards. 'And you realise that your pig-headedness deserves a damned good smacking.'

'Good, so you'll understand perfectly that it's nothing personal, it's merely my naturally cussed nature forcing me to decline the invitation – as well-meant as Sam intended it to be.'

'So if you won't be spending Christmas with your parents or us, what will you be doing?'

Was she imagining it, or was that the orchestral sound of relief just tuning up behind his words? She could almost feel sorry for him. How shocked he must have been when Sam put that little idea to him. 'I expect I shall eat and drink myself into an exquisite state of catatonic delight,' she answered. 'What will you be doing? A hotel break of candle-lit dinners and log fires interspersed with dancing the conga like last year?'

With what was perilously close to a smile on his face, he said, 'No, I'm weaning Dad off short hotel breaks. I'm taking him to Barbados.'

Ali raised an eyebrow. 'Lucky old Sam.'

'Sure you won't change your mind?'

'You know me better than that, Elliot.'

Chapter Three

'How'd it go?'

Elliot shut the door behind him and felt that his father had been asking him that same question all his life.

First day at school: How'd it go?

Cross-country race: How'd it go?

Piano exam: How'd it go?

O levels: How'd it go?

A levels: How'd it go?

Christ Church College interview: How'd it go?

Job interview: How'd it go?

'Well?' asked Sam.

Elliot hung up his coat in silence. He went into his study and plonked his briefcase on the desk. Sam came and leaned against the door-frame. Always a patient man, he was quite happy to wait for an answer.

Elliot scanned his mail and, without raising his eyes, said, 'Which bit of the day do you want to know about? The bit when I stood by Isaac's grave blaming myself yet again for his death, or the part when I stared across the room at my son's mother and wished I could find a way of undoing all the harm I've done?'

Sam didn't say anything. He kept his gaze firmly on Elliot, regarding him with heartfelt compassion.

Elliot pulled out a Christmas card from one of the envelopes and dropped it unread on to the desk. He looked up at his father and saw the concern in his eyes. He rubbed a hand over his tired face. 'I'm sorry,' he said, 'I shouldn't have said that.'

Sam smiled kindly. 'It's okay. Come and talk to me in the kitchen while I get supper ready. I thought I'd do us one of my famous gut'n'heart-buster specials.'

Elliot followed his father to the kitchen where he could see the beginnings of one of Sam's steak-and-chip dinners taking shape: the potatoes were peeled and chipped, the onion rings were sitting in the frying-pan with half a pack of butter for company, and two enormous steaks the size of a pair of slippers were waiting to be grilled. 'What with this and the chocolate cake at Ali's, you'll be the ruin of me,' he said, forcing a lightness into his voice that he didn't feel. He took hold of one of the chairs at the table, turned it round, and sat on it astride, resting his elbows on the back.

Sam switched on the grill. 'Chocolate cake at Ali's, eh? And she didn't throw it at you?'

'She missed.'

'Now that I don't believe. If Ali meant to hit you, she'd get you all right, moving target or not. You remember that corporate hoop-la you arranged a few years back when we all got to have a go on the rifle range? She was a crack shot. Made us both look like rookies.'

Elliot remembered all too well. He recalled also how proud he'd been but, then, he'd always been proud of Ali. She had never been like the other women in the office with whom he worked. And she certainly hadn't been like the rest of the partners' wives. She had been a law unto herself. She'd called a schmuck a schmuck and hadn't given a monkey's for the consequences. Always chronically impatient and restless for a challenge, she had been one of the most sharp-witted people he knew. It had come as no surprise when eventually she had tired of the petty office politics of the big accountancy firm they both worked for and had gone it alone. She had formed her own personal taxation consultancy. It had been exactly the right move for her, though to his regret he had never said so at the time. He'd given her no real support and encouragement. But, then, he'd had none to give. All his emotional energy had been focused on trying to cope with Isaac's death.

'By the way,' he said, getting abruptly to his feet and going over to inspect the wine his father had opened, 'that particular occasion wasn't a *few* years ago, I think you'll find it was more like ten.'

Sam flicked a raw chip at him. 'Don't get smart with me, son.'

They ate their meal in the kitchen, the fittings of which Sam had designed and installed himself. When they'd moved in three months ago, the first thing he'd done was to rip out the previous owners' unworkable layout. Elliot had come home one day after a short trip to the States to find a skip on the drive and the kitchen demolished. 'I'm replacing it with something a touch more user friendly,' Sam had said. And he'd done exactly that. Out with the sterile stainless steel, and in with the natural warmth of maplewood. Out with the breakfast bar with its coiled metal stools, which had had all the comfort of barbed wire and which the previous owners had so generously left them, and in with a large farmhouse table and chairs that Sam had picked up at a local auction and had had stripped and re-waxed.

Tackling his enormous steak, Elliot told his father where Ali was now living.

'A windmill, eh? She's got style, that girl. I didn't know there were any round here. Where did you say it was?'

'Near Holmes Chapel, a tiny village called Little Linton.'

'Never heard of it.'

'Me neither.'

'So what did she say?'

'About the windmill?'

Sam finished chewing what was in his mouth. 'I told you earlier, don't get smart with me. Are we short on wine tonight?'

Elliot refilled their glasses.

'Go on, then, tell me what she said.'

'She said no.'

'You sure?'

'Look, Dad, I know the difference between yes and no.'

Sam gave him a measured stare. 'Oh, aye, I don't doubt it, but how did you phrase the invitation? The way you normally speak to her these days, Charlie Charm? Through clenched teeth?'

Elliot brought the scene to mind. His teeth had been pretty close to clenched, but his hands, for a change, hadn't been balled into tight, angry fists. 'You would have been proud of me, I was the model of diplomacy.'

'Liar! I knew I should have spoken to her. Poor girl, now she really will be all alone for Christmas.'

'Look, I tried. I did. But for all we know she might have something planned that she doesn't want me to know about. Perhaps for once she was acting with a degree of tact and sensitivity.'

'What're you saying?'

Elliot shrugged. 'Surely I don't need to spell it out.'

'Obviously you do. I'm just a working-class bloke after all. Just a thick retired builder from Yorkshire who doesn't –'

Elliot cut in quickly to stem the flow of his father's favourite wind-up. 'I'm not in the mood for the cloth-cap-and-clogs routine,' he snapped. 'What I meant was, maybe Ali's got a new man in her life and is planning on –'

'Oh, I get you. You're saying that, unlike you, she's got more than boring old Rich Tea in the biscuit barrel. That it?'

Elliot rolled his eyes. 'Exactly.'

'So why didn't you ask her if that was the case?'

'*Dad!*'

'It's a reasonable enough question.'

'Not from an ex-husband, it isn't.'

Sam smiled and pushed his finished plate away from him. 'But okay from an ex-father-in-law, I reckon. I'll speak to her tomorrow.' He sat back in his chair and patted his bulging stomach appreciatively. 'Not a bad bit of steak, even if I say so myself.'

Elliot contemplated his father. He wanted to say, 'Leave it, Dad, leave it well alone,' but he knew it would have little effect: Sam always did as he saw fit. It was last night when Sam had cooked up this stupid idea of his. In that morning's post a Christmas card had arrived from Ali's parents. Despite the divorce, Maggie and Lawrence Edwards had remained firmly in touch with him, so the card had been no surprise although its contents were, especially for Sam. 'Maggie says they won't be seeing Ali this year,' he said, as he handed the card to Elliot. 'She says she's staying up here on her own. Why do you suppose she's doing that?'

'How should I know?'

Later that evening, while Elliot was working, Sam had come into his study and said, 'I don't like the thought of Ali being all alone. It's not on. I know what it is to be on your own at this time of the year.'

'But it's hardly any of our business.'

He'd then suggested that Ali could join them in Barbados. 'Well, why not?' he'd said, in response to Elliot's openmouthed astonishment.

'Because after nine hours of being cooped up together on a plane we'll probably kill one another with our bare hands.'

'There again it might just knock the shit out of you both. Now am I going to ask her, or are you?'

'I will,' he'd said hastily. He knew that if Sam were to invite Ali she would be bound to accept and, coward that he was, he didn't think he could handle that. It was unthinkable that she would turn Sam down. Rarely did anyone refuse him. He was too nice. He was what people used to refer to as the *genuine article*. He was honest, caring and frank: you always knew where you stood with Sam Anderson. He wasn't a big man – he was only five foot five – but he seemed much larger. As Ali once said, 'There's not a lot of your dad, but every inch of him is worth getting to know.' Elliot was well aware that there had always been a special relationship between Ali and his father, and that since the divorce Sam had missed her. But inviting her to spend Christmas with them was going too far, surely?

Looking across the table at his father now, Elliot felt ashamed of himself. He wished he could be more like Sam, put the past behind him and make more of an effort to be nice to Ali. But he couldn't. It hurt too much to see her. On top of all his grief for Isaac, he'd had to cope with her walking away from him when he needed her most. But he could hardly blame her for doing that: because he'd been unable to come to terms with the horrific way in which Isaac had died, he had been of no use to Ali in helping her to deal with her grief; he'd left her to cope on her own. Quite simply she had wanted more from him than he had to give. He had let her down in so many ways and not a day passed when he didn't want to make amends for what had happened. At the time he had done the standard man stuff in the face of a personal tragedy: he'd holed himself up at work and stayed there ridiculously long hours rather than confront the awful emptiness that haunted him at home. To a lesser extent Ali had done the same, and work colleagues had thought it helpful to use their professionalism as a guide to how well they were coping with their child's death. The conclusion was that they were coping extraordinarily well. But they had merely been on the edge of survival, both of them.

Elliot had agreed to their divorce in the belief that by giving in to Ali's request and doing everything she wanted, it would help her, and that maybe they would be able to salvage something worthwhile from their shattered relationship. He had foolishly hoped that, if nothing else, they would be able to be friends. But it hadn't worked. Their separation had added to the friction between them and, like water seeking its level, their confused anger and resentment had dictated their response to each other.

He suspected that, deep within him, there was still a trace

of the love he had once felt for Ali, but too many layers of pain and bitterness covered it for it ever to show itself. And all the pain and bitterness inside him made him act as though he couldn't bear the sight of her.

In a way it was true. He found being with Ali almost intolerable. There was so much of Isaac in her face: the same compelling brown eyes; the same fair hair, even the same mouth that, in the days when he saw her smile, was identical to the welcome Isaac would give him when he came home from work and found him in the bath with Ali.

He suddenly blinked hard and cleared his throat of the lump that had formed there. In a determined voice, he said, 'Dad, if you want to speak to Ali, it's up to you, but don't be disappointed if she says no.'

'I know the score, lad, no worries there. So does that mean I have your blessing to talk to her?'

'I've never stopped you from doing that.'

Sam frowned. 'You've not made it easy, though, have you?'

Elliot kept quiet.

'Look, son, I know it's a bugger of a situation, but I still care for her. I need to know that she'll be okay when we're jetting off into the sun. I hate the idea of anyone being on their own for Christmas.'

When Elliot still didn't say anything, Sam got to his feet and said, 'Seeing as I cooked supper, you can clear away. I'm off to read the paper.'

Later that night, long after Sam had gone to bed, Elliot closed his briefcase and switched off the study light. Though it was nearly midnight, he decided to go for a swim.

When he and his father had discovered Timbersbrook House, they had seen at once that it offered them exactly what they both wanted, as well as having the bonus of an indoor swimming-pool. This Elliot now entered by means of a long corridor that led off from the hall in the main part of the house. The previous owners had shown no restraint when it came to creating the opulent and thoroughly showy pool room. They'd gone to town with mosaic tiling, mirrors, pillars, a palm tree – currently decked out by Sam with fairy-lights – and even the thoroughly ostentatious touch of a working fireplace near the shallow end. It was Sam and Elliot's favourite place to read the Sunday papers.

Elliot switched on the wall-lights and stripped off his clothes. He dived into the smooth glassy surface of the water and swam two lengths before coming up for air. He guessed Sam must have been for a swim earlier that day as the water temperature was a few degrees warmer than last night. He swam, one length after another, slowly, mechanically, each stroke as precise and rhythmic as a metronome; it helped him to think straight, which he needed to do.

It had been a hell of a day. His thoughts had alternated continually between Isaac and Ali. It was difficult sometimes to separate one from the other.

When he'd caught sight of Ali's small, hunched figure bent over Isaac's grave, her face flushed with cold and her eyes wet with tears, he'd wanted so much to comfort her.

And had he?

No.

He'd turned away to give her a few seconds to compose herself and had made some asinine comment about the weather. He had thought he was being considerate, but in all probability she would have interpreted his manner as cool and aloof. For the second time that evening, he wished he could be more like his father. Sam, for all his talk of his working-class background and lack of education, always seemed to do or say the right thing when it came to dealing with anything emotional. Sam would have put his arms around Ali and taken the edge off her pain. He would have held her and let her cry. Unlike Elliot, Sam would have been there for Ali. Just as he'd been there for the pair of them that terrible night at the hospital when Isaac died. Sam had grasped Ali to him while she had screamed and shaken with the shock of what she'd just learned, while he . . . while he had stood impotently to one side, already isolating himself from anything that might touch him.

He swam faster, pushing his arms through the water cleanly and noiselessly. He swam on and on, praying that one day there might come a time when he would lose the nightmare memory of that night. That one day the words of the poem Charles Wesley wrote on the death of his own son would cease to impinge on his brain.

> *Dead! Dead! The Child I lov'd so well!*
> *Transported to the world above!*
> *I need no more my heart conceal.*
> *I never dar'd indulge my love;*
> *But may I not indulge my grief,*
> *And seek in tears a sad relief?*
>
> *Mine earthly happiness is fled,*
> *His mother's joy, his father's hope,*
> *(O had I dy'd in Isaac's stead!)*
> *He should have liv'd, my age's prop,*
> *He should have clos'd his father's eyes,*
> *And follow'd me to paradise.*

Buying Timbersbrook House was supposed to have been a start at putting the past behind him. When he had suggested to Sam that they join forces and buy a house together, his father's reaction had taken him by surprise. He had expected hand-throwing-up-in-the-air opposition and indignant declarations of independence, along with the claim that he was only sixty-eight and didn't need anybody cramping his style. But none of this had been said. Sam had agreed readily. 'On one condition,' he'd told Elliot, 'we buy a house that has the potential for me to have my own place within it, and you don't patronise me, I pay my own way. Got that?'

'I make that two conditions,' Elliot had replied.

'Bloody accountants and their obsession with numbers.' Sam had smiled.

Timbersbrook had appealed to them both from the minute they first set eyes on it. Situated a mile from the village of Prestbury, with views across to the Peak District yet within easy driving distance of Manchester where Elliot worked, it was set in an acre and a half of garden with two large outbuildings that had once been stables. One of the outbuildings was the obvious choice to convert into what Sam jokingly referred to as his Lurve Nest, and the other would suit them perfectly as a workshop, where they would be able to indulge their hobby of restoring left-for-dead classic cars. Within twenty-four hours of viewing the property they had made an offer and subsequently moved in three months ago, with Sam keen to get to work on the Lurve Nest. He prepared plans, checked out materials and local suppliers, then lost interest in the project.

It was ironic. They'd bought the house on the clear understanding that they were both to have their own space, but it soon became evident that they needed the opposite: one another's company.

Elliot hauled himself out of the water. He looked at his watch. He'd been swimming for almost an hour – another hour and he might have got close to working off the excesses of his father's cooking.

He went over to a mirror-fronted cupboard where they kept a supply of towels and old bathrobes. He wrapped himself in a robe, and just as he was about to switch off the lights, a flicker of movement through one of the patio doors caught his attention. He leaned against the glass and cupped his hands around his eyes.

It was snowing, just as he'd predicted.

One of Ali's classic put-down lines came to mind: 'What's it like, Elliot, always being right?'

Chapter Four

Fifty miles away, in the village of Astley Hope, Sarah Donovan stood at the sitting-room window in Smithy Cottage and listened to her husband coaxing the engine of their tired old car into life. In the still, snow-muffled night, it sounded as glum and ill-disposed as she herself felt. Eventually the engine submitted to Trevor's determined will and the reluctant Ford Sierra disappeared sulkily down the lane, its tyres following in the slushy tracks already made in the snow. Sarah hoped that he would drive carefully, that his current state of near apoplexy wouldn't distract him. She also hoped that he wouldn't embarrass and humiliate Hannah too much when he found her.

She moved away from the window and glanced at her watch. It was twenty-five past twelve. To Trevor's knowledge, Hannah, their eighteen-year-old daughter had never been out this late before on her own. What he didn't realise was that, behind his back, Hannah's social life wasn't the safe, dull routine he imagined it to be. Aided and abetted by Sarah, Hannah had recently, and in secret, started to enjoy a greater degree of freedom than her father would ever allow. As on previous occasions he had thought that Hannah was staying the night with her friend Emily to help each other with their school work. Tonight it was supposed to be a session on Molière's *Le Malade imaginaire*. In reality Hannah and Emily had been in Chester at a nightclub.

Poor Trevor, he just wasn't in tune with the world Hannah lived in. He hadn't realised that he could no longer play the part of omnipotent father to a small hero-worshipping daughter. He had no idea that his role now was to be a middle-aged saddo, who was only to speak when spoken to and was expected to stay in the shadows of his daughter's fast-changing life. He had no comprehension why his authority wasn't respected any more, or why his opinions weren't wanted and the advice he offered went unheeded. It was standard procedure in most households and most fathers went along with it, treating these strange, surly beings as an alien life form temporarily exchanged for their precious little darlings. They knew that they had no choice but to go along with the derision and the tantrums and that, before long, if they played their part accordingly, their loving, sweet-natured daughters would be returned to them.

But Trevor didn't understand any of this and he was fighting Hannah every step of the way towards her becoming a woman. He couldn't see that the struggle was futile – he might just as well have been trying to hold back the tide.

Perhaps if Hannah had been more troublesome when she'd been younger, Trevor might have been prepared for the change in her now, but Hannah had never been a difficult child. Biddable, hard-working and affectionate, she'd adored her father and he'd doted on her. Compared to a lot of girls her age, she had been a late developer, which was probably why they were now experiencing such a radical change in her. Before now she'd never been interested in boys or parties, preferring instead to pursue her musical interests. She'd played the flute since the age of twelve and had recently passed her grade eight exam with distinction. Until the summer she had sung in the school and church choirs. Her teachers had nothing but praise for her. Their only negative comment, which had been made some years ago, was that they thought she ought to make more of an effort to mix with the other girls at school. She wasn't a solitary child, but she took after her mother in that she'd always been happily self-contained and quite content with her own company. But this had changed last year in the lower sixth, when Emily had joined the school. Hannah had been assigned to show the new girl the ropes and, though their characters were very different, they instantly became friends.

The first time Sarah met Emily she had been reminded of her and Ali. They'd been friends since the age of ten, and in the way that Hannah and Emily were chalk and cheese, so were she and Ali. And just as Ali had shown Sarah that another world existed beyond the boundaries of the sheltered one she'd hitherto experienced, Emily had done the same for Hannah.

Which was why, at half past midnight, Trevor was now driving through several inches of snow on a rescue mission to find his daughter.

The plan was always the same, and usually it worked, but this time it hadn't. The arrangement was that whenever Hannah wanted to be out for longer than Trevor would allow she stayed the night with Emily, whose parents had a much more relaxed attitude towards teenage daughters than Trevor, though this was a detail of which he had been kept in ignorance. Sarah had gone to great lengths to ensure that Trevor never met Emily's parents – she knew he would never approve of them: 'Heavens,' she could imagine him saying, 'they don't even go to church!'

Sarah didn't want to lie to Trevor, but if they were to avoid a huge scene every time Hannah wanted to stay out late, which wasn't often, it was the only solution to ensure that Sarah could give her daughter the freedom she felt she deserved. She herself had grown up in a strict, dictatorial, curfew-driven home and had hated it. All the freedom she had ever experienced as a child had been given to her by Ali and her parents. Maggie and Lawrence Edwards had been wonderful to her, including her in their family as if she were one of their own. They still treated her in much the same fashion. Every year they sent her birthday and Christmas gifts, as well as something for Hannah.

It was funny to witness history repeating itself, in that

Sarah had had Ali, and Hannah had Emily. Though she sincerely hoped that Hannah's life would turn out differently from hers. She didn't want Hannah to be married to the kind of man from whom she had to hide things. Deceit was no basis for a happy marriage. Too often it had a nasty habit of backfiring, just as it had tonight. Their carefully constructed plan had gone completely wrong. Hannah had telephoned a few moments ago to say that she and Emily were stuck in Chester. Emily was blind drunk and had given away their taxi money to a homeless man whom they'd met outside the nightclub and, to make matters worse, Emily's parents were in London – which Emily had kept quiet about – and they had no way of getting home.

'I'll be there as quickly as I can,' Sarah had told Hannah. 'Don't let Emily out of your sight. And, for goodness sake, don't let her drink any more.'

But the telephone had disturbed Trevor, who had gone to bed for an early night. He had come downstairs bleary-eyed to find her in her coat. 'What's going on?' he'd asked. There was no avoiding the truth now, so she'd told him. He'd flown into an immediate and predictable rage, demanding to know the details.

'Chester! At this time of night! A *nightclub*!'

He'd then insisted on going to Chester himself. 'I'm not having you driving so late and certainly not in this weather.'

She'd pleaded with him that it would be best if she fetched the girls. But he'd refused to listen, dashing upstairs, throwing on the first clothes to hand and rushing out of the house to start the car.

Poor Hannah, thought Sarah. All her recently acquired street cred would be blown away when her father rolled into town in their rusting D-reg Sierra, dressed in what she called his Sad Old Man At C & A clothes.

She bent down to the floor and tidied away the Christmas presents she'd been wrapping before Hannah had phoned. She put the carrier-bags in the cupboard under the stairs and wondered what to do next. The bed in the spare room was already made, so at least Emily would have somewhere to sleep, but a couple of hot-water bottles seemed a good idea. She went into the kitchen and filled the kettle, and while she waited for it to boil she decided to ring Ali. As well as wanting to make sure that her friend was all right, she needed to talk to somebody about the impending disaster in the Donovan household.

Ali had been on Sarah's mind for most of that day, and not just because it was the anniversary of Isaac's death: she'd received a card from Maggie and Lawrence that morning. She had wanted to ring Ali earlier, while Trevor was out at a church meeting, but at the last minute the meeting had been cancelled owing to the snow. It was ridiculously late to be ringing anyone, but Sarah knew that Ali hardly ever went to bed before midnight and that in the last two years she'd become even more of a night owl.

The phone was answered almost immediately.

'Ali, it's me, Sarah. You're not in bed, are you?'

'Course not. Hours of fun to get through yet. It's a bit late for you, though, isn't it? What's wrong? A case of insomnia?'

'I'll tell you in a minute. But first, how was your day?'

'It was bloody, bloody, *bloody* awful.'

'I'm sorry.'

'And to make it a hundred times worse, Elliot turned up while I was at Isaac's grave.'

'Oh, Ali, what does that matter?'

'Believe me, it matters.'

'How did he seem?'

'Stiff. Polite. Angry. The usual.'

'A mirror image of yourself, you could say.'

'Look, if I wanted to hear clever-dick comments I'd pay good money to have someone more qualified than you analyse me.'

'More qualified than your oldest friend? You've got be

joking. Did you manage to exchange a few kind words with one another?'

'Put it this way, I was kind enough to invite him back here.'

'Brave as well as kind. And?'

'He'd obviously been instructed by Sam to invite me to spend Christmas with them. Which thoughtful invitation I naturally refused.'

'Naturally.'

'Oh, come on, Sarah. You're not seriously suggesting that I should have considered it?'

'Why not?'

'Because, you fool of a girl, it would be a disaster. Elliot and I can't stand to be near one another, you know that.'

'Maybe you're right. But if I ask you to come and spend Christmas here with us, will you turn me down as well?'

There was a pause.

'Ali?'

'Have you had a Christmas card from my parents?'

'I might have. Why?'

'Because your card probably said the same as Sam and Elliot's. Honestly, how many other people has my mother enlisted in –'

'So why are you planning to spend Christmas alone?' Sarah interrupted. 'Is this just another step down the road of self-inflicted punishment? Because if it is, I think it's high time—'

'Sarah—'

'I haven't finished.'

'Oh, yes, you have. I'll come.'

'I beg your pardon?'

'I said I'd spend Christmas with you. Anything to get you off my case – though God knows how I'll survive Trevor.'

'You'll manage.'

'That remains to be seen. Now tell me what you've been up to.'

Sarah told her about Hannah and Emily and the deception

31

that had been going on behind Trevor's back. 'I can't begin to think how he's going to react when he knows the full story.'

'I can. He'll totally overreact. Just as well I'm coming for Christmas, then. My heathen comments will take the heat off you and poor Hannah. He'll be so busy trying to save my heretical soul from being tossed into the fiery furnace of hell and the devil's awaiting pleasure that he won't have time to be cross with you.'

'Ali, if there was any such thing as the fiery furnace of hell and the devil, he'd toss you right back whence you came and we'd have to put up with you for a bit longer.'

'Funny ha-ha.'

'Oh, heavens, Ali, I can hear a car. It's probably Trevor with the girls. Wish me luck.'

'Buckets of it. Give my love to the wayward god-daughter. Tell her I'm proud of her. I'll ring you tomorrow from the office to see how you got on. 'Bye.'

Sarah put down the phone and went out to the hall. She opened the front door and was met by a furious, red-faced Trevor, a tearful Hannah and Emily vomiting copiously into the snow-covered shrubbery.

Chapter Five

Not surprisingly, the girls slept late.

Just as predictably, from the moment he was out of bed and dressed, Trevor had been pacing the small kitchen like a caged animal in a zoo, although as Sarah tidied away the remains of their breakfast she wasn't sure that this was quite the right analogy: there was nothing of the majestic lion about Trevor.

Nor the sleek panther.

Nor even a hint of the prowling tiger.

A disoriented gerbil was more the mark.

'But what really disturbs me is that you knew,' he said. Sarah had lost count of how many times he'd thrown this line at her. 'You knew,' he said again, and for added emphasis – just in case she'd missed the point – he slapped his hand down on the worktop and rattled the cutlery in the drawer beneath. 'You knew all along what she was doing. You were even party to the deception.'

She turned on the hot tap and squirted a streak of vivid green washing-up liquid into the sink. Above the rising steam she stared out of the window and took in the serene beauty of the morning. The sky was the clearest of blues with not a cloud to be seen, and the long, thin garden, which had been the recipient of so much of her care and attention in the ten years they had lived at Smithy Cottage, lay hidden beneath a smooth, perfectly formed blanket of snow. A few feet away from the kitchen window, a robin had the wooden bird table to himself and was happily breakfasting on the first-class selection of nuts and seeds on offer. He was a regular visitor to the garden and Sarah called him Gomez. He was such a happy-looking little thing, his only apparent concern being the search for his next meal, which in this neck of the woods wasn't arduous. Sarah envied him the simplicity of his existence.

After she'd settled Hannah and Emily last night, having told Trevor to leave everything to her, she'd put off going to bed for as long as she could. She had hoped that Trevor would go to sleep without her. He hadn't. He'd been waiting for her, sitting bolt upright, his arms folded tightly across his chest, his face grim, his eyes cold and steely. It was the same expression he wore whenever he felt she was challenging him. The last time she'd seen it was in September when, yet again, she had hinted that she would like a job. 'We're fine as we are,' he'd said, his arms slipping into place across his chest in a gesture of first-line defences being erected. 'And anyway,' he'd gone on, 'you have a very important job in running the house. It wouldn't be fair to Hannah if you went out to work. She needs you here at home.' Sarah had countered that it wasn't fair to Hannah that she'd had to miss out on the school classics trip to Italy because they couldn't afford it.

For the most part of their marriage they had always been desperate for the money that another income could provide, but Trevor had resolutely denied that this was the case, claiming that they had sufficient to meet their needs. 'Sarah,' he would say, quoting a well-worn line of scripture, '"Life is more than food, and the body more than clothes."' Every time he said this she felt inclined to say, 'I'll remind you of that next time you're hungry or you're hunting for a clean pair of underpants.'

As guilty and disloyal as it sounded, Sarah had to admit that she found Trevor to be that uncomfortable variety of red-hot Christian who gave religion a bad name. He hadn't always been this fervent. When she had first known him as a student teacher, he had been a regular, straightforward churchgoer, but these days he seemed dangerously fired up on an excess of faith. It drove Ali, a passionate, card-carrying atheist, to distraction, especially when he tried to flaunt his spiritual superiority over her. It incensed Sarah too, but in contrast to Ali she kept her thoughts to herself. She didn't think it was right to shake anyone out of their religious beliefs. Not when she had enough doubts and failings of her own. And, besides, there really wasn't any arguing with Trevor: when he had a viewpoint, he stuck limpet-fast to it. As he did whenever the subject of her going out to work raised its head. His old standby of camels, eyes of needles and rich men was usually tossed into the arena of the going-nowhere discussion. His final word was always the same: 'Our Lord's example is very clear on the matter, Sarah. Spiritual wealth is what we seek, not secular riches.'

But Sarah guessed that the real reason behind Trevor not wanting her to work had little to do with scriptural teaching and a lot more to do with his insecurity. As infuriating and absurdly outmoded as it was, he needed her at home so that he could bask in the glory of being the family's sole provider: his position as head of the house had to be maintained. If she were ever to earn more than him, where would that leave him?

But in the end, and employing a huge amount of compromise on her part, she had, at last, got her way. It wasn't a brilliant job, it didn't really pay that well, but it was a job and one that posed no threat to Trevor. For the past six weeks she had been working for an interior-design shop. She'd always been good with her hands and had made all the soft furnishings in Smithy Cottage. Now she was being paid to do the same for other people's homes. She worked upstairs in the spare bedroom and, though the work wasn't stimulating, she enjoyed it. More importantly, it brought in a little more money, which she was putting by for Hannah when she went to university. Trevor had begrudgingly given his approval to what Sarah was doing and had left her to it.

But there had been nothing begrudging or approving about him last night when she had joined him in bed.

'I can't believe that Hannah went to that – that *nightclub*.'

He'd said the word nightclub as though it were foreign to him. Which, of course, it was. To Trevor the word represented another world: a wicked, salacious world frequented only by wicked, salacious people.

The low-life of Chester.

The drug-pushers.

The pimps.

The prostitutes.

It wasn't at all the place where a daughter of his should show her face.

Sarah had wanted to say, 'It's probably just the kind of environment in which Christ would have hung out,' but, coward that she was, she hadn't. Instead, she'd said, 'Please, Trevor, it's very late. Can we discuss this in the morning?'

His response had been to look pointedly at the digital alarm clock on his bedside table, his arms still rigidly folded, and say, 'In case you hadn't noticed, Sarah, it's been morning for some hours. You don't seem very shocked by what Hannah's done. You sound almost as if you don't care that she lied to us.'

'That's because I'm not shocked and she hasn't been lying – at least, not as you think she has.'

And out of some kind of defensive anger and wanting to protect Hannah, who had flatly refused to explain anything to her father, she had gone on to tell Trevor the truth. But not the whole truth.

She turned now to where he was breathing like a knight-hungry dragon. 'Why don't you put some of your excess energy into drying the dishes for me? Stomping about the place won't help.'

'I haven't got time,' he snapped, giving his beard a sharp little tug. 'I need to get on.'

'Well, nobody's stopping you.' Really, he was acting in

such a ridiculous manner. Anyone would think they were discussing a thirteen-year-old child and not the adult Hannah practically was.

'You know perfectly well I can't, not until we've sorted out this dreadful mess. How can I be creative when things haven't been resolved?'

'There's nothing to resolve.'

He stared at her uncomprehendingly. 'Sarah, you and Hannah both tricked me into believing that she was staying the night with Emily and her parents, where they would be doing nothing more dangerous than their French homework, when all along you knew that they were planning to get themselves dressed like – like a couple of tarts and go into Chester where anything could have happened to them. Did you see how much *makeup* they had on?'

Sarah pulled off her rubber gloves and looked patiently at him. 'Trevor,' she said, with just a trace of firmness, at the same time placing a hand on his arm, 'neither Hannah nor Emily bore any resemblance to women of questionable repute. They were wearing clothes and makeup that make them feel good about themselves, that was all.'

He shrugged away her hand. 'But look at the trouble they got themselves into.'

'That had nothing to do with what they were wearing. Admittedly Emily was silly to have drunk so much, but didn't you ever do that when you were their age?'

He gave what Hannah would call a grade A snort. 'That's an absurd line of argument,' he said. 'You know very well that it's different for boys.'

'Well, it shouldn't be!'

He ignored her heated tone and said. 'None of this excuses you and Hannah for lying to me. Your behaviour is, at best, irresponsible, and at worst –'

'Trevor, please, I did it because it's important that Hannah learns to be more independent. You give her no freedom, none whatsoever. How on earth do you expect her to cope with going away to university next year if she hasn't made any mistakes? She has to make the odd one so that she can learn from it. And, if you want the real truth, she and Emily have done this before. This is the first time the arrangement has gone wrong. You should be proud of her for doing exactly the right thing when she phoned us for help. Far better that than her turning to a stranger for a lift home.'

A stupefied expression covered Trevor's face. He backed away from her. She wouldn't have been at all surprised if he'd held up two crossed fingers to her in a gesture of get-thee-behind-me-Satan. It was a few seconds before he could speak. 'I don't believe I'm hearing this. As Christian parents it's our duty to raise our daughter in a manner pleasing to—'

'Please,' Sarah interrupted, 'don't bring God into this. You do it whenever we have to discuss anything of importance.'

'Sarah,' he said sharply, 'I'm not sure I like your tone of voice. And, what's more, if you'd brought God into your thinking in the first place, none of this would have happened.'

Sarah sighed. All hope of a logical debate was now lost. That was the trouble with Trevor: when he suspected he was losing the fight, he would run home to fetch God to play the part of big, bullying brother. She let his accusation go and reached for a tea-towel to dry the breakfast dishes. A few moments later the kitchen door crashed shut and Trevor was gone. She pictured him in his workshop taking out his frustration on an innocent piece of wood, slamming it on to his lathe and attacking it with one of his lethally sharp chisels.

Oh, well, better that than taking it out on me, she thought, glad that he was no longer hovering at her side like an angry bee. And not for the first time she was grateful that, although Trevor worked from home, the nature of his work kept him firmly out of the house.

Nine months ago, Trevor had given up his teaching job to become what he rather grandly referred to as 'a craftsman'. When Sarah had told Ali what he was planning, she had burst out laughing. 'Oh, that's a good one. Trevor the carpenter, just like Christ.'

Sarah had wanted to laugh too, but loyalty wouldn't let her. She'd chided her friend instead: 'Please don't make fun of him, Ali.'

After years of teaching basic woodwork skills to adults with learning difficulties, Trevor was finally doing what he'd always wanted to do and that was to down-shift and work for himself. He'd been a good teacher but never a happy one, and now, in what had once been the village blacksmith's workshop, he was like a dog with two tails. For a long time, he'd been making gifts for friends at church and his skill at woodturning had been much admired. Knocking out candlesticks, little pots with lids, apples, mushrooms, pot-pourri holders and large fruit bowls for church fund-raising events had become a speciality and several people had remarked that he ought to sell his work on a more enterprising scale. But even Trevor had known that giving up a steady teaching job to join the precarious craft-fair circuit was a risk. But the Lord works in mysterious ways, as Trevor would say, and when Sarah's mother had died last June, two years after her father, Sarah had been left enough money to pay off their mortgage. Trevor had announced then that he'd been called by the Holy Spirit to quit the world of teaching.

Business was not what one would call brisk, but it seemed to be picking up, although that was probably due to the season. The proof of Trevor's success would come once they were into the New Year. For now, though, he was busy enough to be happy, supplying a few arty-crafty shops in the area, as well as hawking his wares round the pre-Christmas fairs. His only problem with any of this, and it did cause a genuine moral dilemma for him, was that the fairs sometimes covered an entire weekend, and Sunday, after all, was a day of rest. But, after much prayer, he concluded that he'd been led to do this work so therefore it must be all right.

The kitchen now clean and tidy, and still no sign of the

girls, Sarah decided to take Trevor a peace-offering cup of tea. She knew that his anger and silliness stemmed from his love for Hannah and that he would go to any lengths to keep her safe. It was sad, but he would probably prefer her not to blossom into adulthood. He'd been such a good father to her when she was little. He hadn't been, as most other fathers, too busy with his career to participate fully in his child's life. He'd never missed a single concert at which she'd either sung or played in the orchestra, or a performance of a play in which she'd acted, no matter how small the role. Not one parents' evening had gone by without him being there to keep tabs on Hannah's progress.

Yes, he'd been a good father, there was no denying it.

Which was why it was such a shame that he was now spoiling all the good work he'd put into parenthood.

He had to learn to stand back and let her go. He was also going to have to let her make up her own mind about going to church. Hannah had confided in Sarah that she no longer wanted to go to St Cuthbert's, the local church at which she'd been an active member since the age of eight; where she'd played Mary in the Nativity play no fewer than four times; where she'd pretended to be a pumpkin during harvest festival and where more recently she'd helped out with the dwindling Sunday school.

'How can I go, Mum,' she had said, only last week, 'when I don't believe in any of it now? It's real to you and Dad, it makes sense for you. It's not ringing my bell any more. I reckon Buddhism's got more going for it. I think I'll become the first Buddhist in Astley Hope. I'll shave off my hair and go chanting up and down the lanes in an enlightened manner, preaching the four Noble Truths. That should give everyone something to talk about.'

They had laughed together at the idea, even though Sarah was disappointed to hear Hannah talk in such a way. Spiritual faith wasn't to be mocked. It was what underpinned society. It was the fulcrum of one's being. When all else was gone, including hope, it was only faith that shone through the darkness.

And, as Sarah poured Trevor's mug of tea, she hoped that he would understand that Hannah had to discover for herself what did and did not make sense.

Chapter Six

Sam handed his coat to the waiter and took his seat at the table he'd reserved over the phone that morning. He was early and knowing that punctuality wasn't one of Ali's strong suits, he settled himself in for a minimum wait of ten minutes.

Last night when he had told Elliot that he would speak to Ali, he had known all too well that he was skating on the thinnest of ice, and though he didn't want to do anything to upset his son, he couldn't ignore his feelings for Ali. He missed her keenly: she'd been more to him than just a daughter-in-law. In the days before Isaac's death, and when Elliot had been away on business, as he frequently was, he had often taken Ali out for dinner. Their evenings together were always fun, especially when they were mistaken for a couple, and he and Ali hammed up his supposed role as a sugar daddy. They would howl with laughter after they had left the restaurant and Sam would drive her home high on machismo pride that people thought a short, dumpy old fellow such as he could pull an attractive young woman.

But those evenings no longer existed. Since Isaac had been snatched from them, it seemed that there had been little for any of them to laugh about. Though his own reaction to the death of his young grandson could come nowhere near what Ali and Elliot must have experienced – and still were experiencing – it had had a profound effect on him: the death of a child was never easy to accept. But he'd been through the grieving process before, when Connie, his wife, had died more than twenty years ago, and he knew that although the pain never entirely went away, it did lessen.

He knew also that in some cases grief could separate the bereaved from those closest to them, and that was what had happened to Ali and Elliot. In the immediate aftermath of Isaac's death, he had watched two people who had loved one another with the strongest of passion erect a barrier of bewildered confusion to keep the other out, along with everyone else. Unable to help or stop what they were doing, Sam had seen how difficult it was for them to relate to anything but the pain within themselves and project that hurt on to the other. In the months that followed they turned away from each other and focused what was left of their energy into the routine of work, letting their minds be absorbed by the mechanics of the mundane. Now all that was left between Ali and Elliot was the currency of their disappointment in life itself, which they exercised by attacking the other in the belief that it was the best form of defence.

All Sam could hope for was that this stage in their lives would soon pass, that they would eventually find a way to transcend their grief and anger. His greatest wish was that, at the very least, they could be friends.

Realising that he'd now been waiting for a quarter of an hour, Sam glanced round the smart French restaurant, hoping to catch sight of Ali. He took in a couple of small tables in the arched window that looked out on to the busy street. They were occupied by two pairs of elegantly dressed women who, judging from the carrier-bags at their feet, were having a quiet lunch after a hard morning of Christmas shopping. The rest of the diners made up a large, noisy party of exuberant office workers who were presumably enjoying their annual Christmas binge; their faces were rosy-red from the intake of midday booze, their heads decorated with ill-fitting paper hats. Then, out of the corner of his eye, Sam saw the restaurant door open, and a wave of what other men his age and background would have called unmanly sentiment came over him.

The sight of Ali brought home to him just how much he'd

43

missed her all these months and how very fond of her he was. It also reminded him that if anyone were to judge Ali purely on her appearance, they would be in danger of committing the cardinal sin of underestimating her. She was only a fraction over five foot and, with her slight build and delicate features, she looked years younger than thirty-eight. Sam knew that Ali's youthful looks had often been a hindrance to her career and that she hated it when people did not take her seriously and treated her as if she could only be trusted to work the photocopier. Even from this distance across the restaurant, Sam could see the darkness of her eyes – brown eyes that were made to look darker still by the fairness of her skin and her short, slightly wavy blonde hair, which Sam guessed was as genuine as the woman herself. He didn't know anyone else like her. She was sassy, steely and, at times, too full of chutzpah for her own good. He had always known why his son had fallen in love with Ali – hell, he'd have done the same thing if his age hadn't been against him! – and it hadn't been the exterior packing that had attracted Elliot, as delightful as it was. No, it had been deeper than that: Ali had the same tough, incisive mind as Elliot, and he'd respected and admired her for it, seeing her as his soulmate.

When she came over, Sam rose to his feet and they greeted each other with a warm embrace. He let her go and said, 'When was the last time you ate? There's nowt of you. You're much too thin.'

She smiled affectionately at him. 'I'm in training.'

He pulled out a chair for her. 'What the hell for? The one-hundred-metre slipping-between-the-cracks event?'

'Six-pack-Sam, you've lost none of your cheek, have you? Are you going to be as rude as this to me all lunch?'

'Not rude, love, just concerned.' He attracted the attention of a passing waiter and ordered a carafe of Château Maison. 'That okay with you?' he asked, when the waiter had left them.

'It's fine. So what's with all the concern, Sam? Invitations to spend Christmas with you, and now lunch. What's going on?'

He leaned back in his seat; bulls and horns came to mind. 'We've had lunch before, nothing odd in that.'

'But on those occasions I was married to Elliot.'

'Oh, aye, so you were.'

Ali contemplated Sam's round, smiling face. He reminded her of Bob Hoskins with a bit of the dark-eyed Danny DeVito thrown in. Ever since he'd phoned her first thing that morning at work, she'd been speculating as to what he was up to. However, she'd agreed to meet him for lunch, not just to satisfy her curiosity but because she was keen to see him. It was ages since they'd talked on their own and it pained her to think that he had witnessed her and Elliot at their worst, that their divorce and appalling behaviour had put him in an impossible situation, and that he had done his best to make the best of a bad job. She admired him for it. She knew also that there were boundaries that could never be crossed. She could never, for instance, be openly critical of Elliot to Sam. Sam could be as rude as he cared to be about his son, but woe betide anyone else who tried it. As paternal love went, Sam's knew no bounds. In his light-hearted fashion he was fiercely protective of Elliot. Which made the fact that they were having lunch here on their own something of a surprise. Did Elliot know about this? Or had Sam gone behind his back?

She wondered now if Sam's protectiveness went as far as trying to get her and Elliot back together. 'Sam,' she said, fixing him with a penetrating gaze, 'do I have to come right out with it and accuse you of being interfering and devious?'

He laughed heartily. 'If the cap fits, love.'

She laughed too. 'It bloody well fits all right and you know it does.'

'Good, that's settled, then. We've agreed that I'm a sneaky, meddling bugger, so come on, choose your lunch, my stomach's thinking of packing up and going home.'

They ordered their food, and when their wine arrived Sam raised his glass. 'Here's to Christmas and . . .' He hesitated.

'Barbados?' she suggested, with a half-smile.

He lowered his glass. 'A straight answer for a straight question, Ali. Why the hair shirt this year? Why aren't you going down to your parents?'

She shrugged.

He reached for her hand across the table and looked at her with loving eyes. 'I hate the thought of you being on your lonesome for Christmas.'

She squeezed his strong square hand. 'But I shan't be alone,' she said brightly. 'I just had a better invitation than yours, that's all.'

'Better than Barbados?'

'Yep.'

'Oh,' he said. Ali heard the flat tone of disappointment in his voice. 'So Elliot was right,' he added.

'In what way?'

Sam stared at her with a clear, frank gaze. 'The Boy Wonder reckoned that might be the case.'

'Reckoned what might be the case?'

'That you'd gone and got yourself a boyfriend and were—'

'Got myself a boyfriend?' Ali laughed. 'What a joke! And just what the hell would I want with one of those? They're untidy, time-consuming and, like Saturday night curry stains, awkward to shift, and that's just their finer points.'

'There's nothing of the cynic in you, is there?' Sam chuckled. He caught sight of their waiter on the horizon and said, 'Mm . . . at last, our food.'

When the plates and side dishes of vegetables had been settled on the table and they were left alone again, Ali said, 'Don't think I'm not grateful for the offer, Sam. I am. But you must have realised that I could never accept it. It would never work. Elliot and I have experienced too much pain at one another's expense to be anything but horribly polite to each other. You must believe me when I say that any kind of reconciliation is out of the question.'

He looked at her, his countenance serious and, with a bolt of what she could only describe as pain, she was reminded of Elliot. Elliot bore practically no resemblance to his father, but there in Sam's face was the same serious expression that had attracted her to Elliot when she'd first met him.

She'd just started as a graduate trainee working for what was then, back in the early eighties, the biggest accountancy firm in Manchester. Eight years her senior, well established in the organisation, and already branded a high flyer – the company's rising star – Elliot hadn't been like the crowd of graduates with whom she was supposed to socialise; thirty of them in total, all of whom still hadn't shaken off their student mores, and without intending to, she had found herself gravitating to his more mature attitude. While her contemporaries were happy to spend their evenings swilling beer before, during and after a vindaloo curry in Rusholme, she was happier to be in Elliot's more thoughtful, sophisticated company. There was an aura of composed calm about him that was enormously appealing. He was a man of few words, claiming that he'd rather speak the right ones than waste his breath on the wrong ones. His taciturn nature made him a good listener and he would fix his candid blue eyes on her and listen intently to whatever she had to say. In the early stages of their relationship, she'd had no way of knowing if he was aware of the devastating effect he had on her, that his subtle but wholly powerful sex appeal was so totally compelling. This was a new phenomenon for Ali. During her time up at Oxford she had been the one firmly in control of her feelings, giving a long line in badly treated boyfriends the runaround. But suddenly she was no longer in control. This man, with his low-key charm and generally acknowledged intellectual brilliance, had taken her heart in one swift movement and was in danger of keeping it.

There was so much in his character that drew her to him,

but if she had to name one thing that did it, it was his tendency to look solemn. Even when he was enjoying himself, he rarely smiled. She became fascinated with the man behind the face, and those clear blue eyes, wanting to know what it was that made him tick. The first time he took her back to his house – after several months of discreet dating, neither of them wanting to attract the attention of every busybody at work – she had told him that he was the most understated man she knew. 'You're laconic, droll and about as buttoned-down as a guy could be.' His response had been to kiss her and take her upstairs where he had proved to her for the next two hours that his approach to sex was anything but laconic. Afterwards she'd said, 'Elliot, there's an interesting dichotomy to your character. Beneath that rigidly contained coolness is quite another man.' He'd smiled one of his rare smiles and she'd known from that moment that she loved him.

'I'm really sorry that you feel that way, Ali,' she heard Sam saying. She dispelled the memory of his son lying naked and exhausted beside her, and forced herself to concentrate on what Sam was telling her. 'It would mean a lot to a poor old man to know that you and Elliot could at least be friends.'

She scowled at him. 'Less of the poor-old-man routine, Sam. Any more talk like that and you'll lose all my respect.'

The Elliot-like seriousness was instantly gone and Sam's eyes twinkled with their usual warmth and humour. 'It was worth a try.' He grinned.

'No, it wasn't. It was a cheap shot grounded in sentimentality that wasn't worth an airing. Now, tell me how it's going, you and Elliot living in domestic harmony. I haven't seen you since you cast yourselves as *The Odd Couple*.'

'Not so fast, lass. You're not off the hook yet. You've still not told me how you're spending Christmas.'

'Gracious, everybody's obsessed with my private life.'

'That's because we care about you.'

'Rubbish! You're all a bunch of nosy-parkers. If you must know, I'm going to Sarah's.'

The relief on Sam's face was plainly visible. 'I'm delighted to hear it. How is she?'

'Oh, the usual, a saint for still putting up with Trevor.'

'Didn't he leave his teaching job to try his hand at earning a living from woodturning?'

'Yes, and it makes me mad every time I think of it. When Sarah's mother died and left her that money it should have been used to make their lives financially easier, to give them a few luxuries in life. It should not have been used to give Trevor the excuse to jack in his job. An inheritance, no matter how small, should serve a worthwhile purpose.'

'Just as I've always suspected,' Sam observed. 'We parents are at our most useful and loved when we're six foot under and the will's being read.'

It was Ali's turn to look serious. 'I don't think Elliot, or I, will ever think that of you, Sam.'

He caught the sincerity in her words. He placed his screwed-up napkin beside his finished plate and said, 'Don't go getting sentimental on me, love. Got room for a pud?'

They left the restaurant an hour later. Sam insisted that he walked Ali back to her office. It was a cold, wet, wintry afternoon, and although it was only two thirty, the light was losing its hold and yesterday's fall of snow, like old news, wasn't worth having around. They made their way slowly through the slush and hordes of Christmas shoppers. The main street was decked out in pseudo-Dickensian style and piped carols tinkled merrily. In the square in front of Marks and Spencer, a small crowd was gathered round a thickly padded Santa. At his side was his pixie helper – a young girl, who in the stiff December wind looked frozen to death in a pair of skimpy, red, fake-fur hot-pants and a pointy hat complete with brass bell; the sleety rain had made her mascara run and she looked thoroughly disenchanted. They

49

were handing out balloons and flyers advertising a new cut-price drugstore that had just opened in town. At the front of the crowd was a small boy in a pushchair, his cold-reddened face a picture of anxious delight as he waited patiently for a balloon. A ghostly shiver went through Ali and, as chilling as an icy hand, it gripped and twisted at her heart. Her whole body froze. Sam put his arm around her shoulder and steered her away. 'Done your shopping, yet?' he asked, by way of distraction.

She shook her head, unable to speak.

'Me neither. Haven't a clue what to buy the Boy Wonder.'

They walked on in silence. 'It's a real bugger, grief, isn't it?' Sam said gruffly, when at last they came to a stop outside the renovated Georgian building where Ali's office was situated on the first floor.

She agreed with a slight tilt of her head, quickly kissed his cheek, wished him a happy Caribbean Christmas and shot inside. She took the stairs two at a time and fled to the toilets where she shut herself inside one of the cubicles. She leaned against the door and sank slowly to the floor. She covered her face with her hands and wept.

Chapter Seven

'I'm fine,' Ali told herself, 'I'm absolutely *fine*.'

She splashed cold water on to her face, looked at her ruined makeup in the mirror above the basin and knew that this was far from the truth. Outwardly the tears had stopped, so had the shaking, but inwardly the choking pain was still there.

She dried her face and hands on a rough paper towel and thought of Sam's words: *It's a real bugger, grief, isn't it?*

Oh, how right he was.

There was nothing so dark, so painful as the agonising torture of bereavement. Losing Isaac had made her realise the extent of love itself, that what she had expressed for her son when he was alive had been only the tip of the iceberg. It was what she felt in her heart, deep below the surface, that caused the pain and tore her apart when she was least expecting it.

There were days when the memory of Isaac was manageable, when she could almost meet her grief head on, confront it, reason with it and accept it. On other days she could work herself into such a state of exhaustion she didn't have a moment to dwell on what had been snatched from her. But then there were the times when, like a stalker hiding in the shadows waiting for its opportunity, the torment of grief would leap out of the darkness and strike her down.

This was what had taken place just now. That little boy in the pushchair with his smiling face had caught her off-guard and razed her defences to the ground.

She closed her eyes and saw Isaac so clearly. He was wrapped from head to toe in his all-in-one quilted suit, his mittens pulled off – she never could get him to keep them on – and his eyes shining with delight. The three of them were Christmas shopping in Manchester. It was a bitterly cold day. The shops were crowded and hectic. They'd just bought Isaac a present – a toy garage complete with cars and trucks – and Elliot was carrying it under his arm while she pushed the buggy through the crowded streets. They were waiting to cross the road to go into Waterstone's when Isaac's eyes rested on two little girls each with a balloon. He was smiling that heart-melting smile of his, the one that was so irresistible. They had tracked down the balloon-seller, who turned out to be a young man with a nose-ring, dressed half-heartedly as Santa – he'd managed a hat and a tuft of cotton wool on his chin, which was in danger of catching light from the cigarette dangling out of his mouth.

The balloon lasted a week, until it wrinkled and shrivelled itself into a flaccid nothingness. She threw it away one evening while Isaac was sleeping.

Two days later, he was dead.

Ali opened her eyes, screwed the paper towel that was still in her hands into a tight, hard ball, then tossed it into the bin. She took a determined breath. She would beat *it*. For Isaac's sake she would not let *it* get the better of her.

Daniel, her business partner, confidant and, after Sarah, her closest friend, was on the phone when she entered the office. He pointed to the pile of messages for her on the corner of his desk where his feet were resting on a file. She picked up the bits of paper and went over to her own. She was glad to discover that one of the messages was from a client cancelling their four-thirty meeting. Good, she now had the rest of the day free to finish the report she'd started that morning.

She heard Daniel trying to wind down his conversation, and from his look of concern as he glanced her way she could see that he knew she'd been crying.

She and Daniel had known one another since their

graduate-trainee days, when together they had rented a damp, carpetless flat in Flixton. By day they had worked in the centre of Manchester surrounded by the lavish corporate glamour of the office, and by night they had slummed it like students, surviving on black coffee and takeaway pizzas while getting to grips with the study-load expected of them. Happy days!

When they'd completed their three-year training contracts and qualified they'd looked to the future with enthusiasm. For each of them came a steady, encouraging succession of promotions, but by the time they had reached their early thirties they both realised that, for different reasons, they had reached an immovable glass ceiling. Ali was never going to get the ultimate promotion she desired because she was a woman, and Daniel's future within the organisation was blighted because he was gay. Nothing was ever said, but there had never been a gay senior partner, and the chance of there ever being one was about as probable as hell freezing over. The firm might be riddled with divorce as a result of office affairs, it might be run by lecherous men who couldn't resist sampling younger girls, but perish the thought that a decent, morally minded man who had lived with his partner for more than ten years – longer than a lot of marriages lasted – could manage seven hundred employees without the empire tumbling down because of his sexuality.

Daniel came off the phone and said, 'You okay, Babe?'

She stared at his anxious face and thought how unfair life was for him. There was nothing in his manner or style of dress to hint that Daniel was gay – there was none of the moustachioed, earringed, tight-jeaned extrovert about him. He resembled any straight man she knew who took an above-average interest and pride in his appearance. With his gold-card good looks, and lean, long-limbed frame he made a striking sight in his expensive designer suits, which suggested, rather than flaunted, that he spent a good deal of money on his clothes. Armani and Gucci came as naturally to him as St

Michael underwear did to Ali. He wore his hair short, but not buzz-cut short, and *faux*-tortoiseshell-framed glasses gave his clean-cut features an academic look that was pure Ivy League. His silk ties were never loud and often favoured the sombreness of a man paying his last respects. His voice held no camp timbre and, indeed, for some years now he and his partner, Richard, had sung in their local choral society – they jokingly referred to themselves as the Two Queer Tenors. In Ali's opinion, Daniel couldn't be further from the stereotypical image of a gay man. He once said of himself that he represented what to many was the acceptable face of homosexuality. As cynical as it sounded, it was probably true.

'Babe, you've a face on you like thunder. What's wrong?'

'I'm sorry,' she said. 'I was letting my anger get the better of me. I was thinking of the big bullyboys of corporate accountancy who forced us out of their poxy power games.'

He smiled. 'We weren't forced. And, anyway, they were silly games they played. I much prefer our own.'

She frowned. 'Don't you ever feel bitter?'

He got to his feet and went over to the photocopier. 'No,' he said simply. He set the machine in action, then turned his back on it, leaned with his shoulder against a filing cabinet and said, 'You and I were never cut out for that particular ball-crushing fest. We were, and still are, too independent, too round for the squareness of the peg on offer. Of course, we could have tried our luck at sleeping our respective ways to the top but – I don't know about you – I never fancied any of those overweight, overpaid guys.'

She gave him a wry smile. 'You're forgetting Elliot. He wasn't overweight.'

He lowered his glasses and peered at her over the top. 'I was deliberately forgetting him, Babe. He was always the exception.'

She feigned a look of shock. 'Dan Divine, you're not telling me you fancied him, are you?'

He laughed. 'Too much competition from you, kid. I couldn't get a look in.'

A curious expression worked its way across her face. She sat back in her chair and swivelled in it. 'I've no idea how it happened, but during lunch with Sam I was remembering the first time I ever went to bed with Elliot.'

'And?'

She hesitated.

'Come on, I'm all agog, hanging on your every word.'

She shook her head with finality. 'And nothing.'

Daniel rolled his eyes. 'Well, I clearly recall a young woman returning to the flat experiencing a certain difficulty in walking after she'd spent a weekend with the man in question.'

'I had vertigo.'

'Rubbish! You'd overdosed on Elliot's physical attributes. God knows what kind of state you'd left him in. He was probably a stretcher case.'

She laughed and, as ever, felt enormous gratitude to Daniel for always being able to lift her spirits – a talent that, in recent times, had been frequently put to use. He was one of the most warm-hearted people she knew. He was tolerant too, and although over the years he had been confronted with varying degrees of prejudice in one form or another, he had never allowed it to spoil his easy-going disposition. 'I wish I could be more like you, Daniel,' she said. 'You're one of the nicest people I know. You have such a forgiving nature.'

He gathered his papers from the photocopier and returned to his desk. 'It's a gift,' he said, 'I'll get you one for Christmas. Now, are you going to do any work today, or is it just me running this place?'

It wasn't until Ali was at home that evening, in front of the television and munching the last of Lizzie's chocolate cake, that she remembered she hadn't called Sarah, as she'd promised. Too lazy to move to the kitchen for the phone, she turned the sound down on Kirsty Young – the intelligent face of newsroom drama – and reached for her mobile, which was in her briefcase at the other end of the sofa. She listened to the ringing tone and hoped that Trevor wouldn't answer it.

She was in luck. It was Hannah's voice that greeted her.

'So your father's let you out of the doghouse to answer the phone, has he?'

'He's at a meeting.'

'Which means you and your mother can breathe a sigh or two of relief.'

Hannah laughed. 'Something along those lines. I'll fetch Mum for you. By the way, I'm really glad you're coming for Christmas. It should liven things up no end.'

'Hey, if I'm to be the cabaret turn, I shall expect to be paid. And, I'll warn you now, I don't come cheap.'

'I'll put an extra-specially nice present for you under the tree. One of those tins of gin and tonic do you?'

'Nah, that's a girlie drink. A good single malt's more my style.'

'I prefer vodka and Coke myself. 'Bye.'

While Ali waited for Sarah to come to the phone, she wondered how it was that, in such an impossibly short time, her conversations with Hannah had progressed from vague toddler ramblings to alcohol preferences. Just as well that dear old Trevor wasn't around to hear what had been said: he would have choked on his disapproval and probably accused Ali of leading his daughter astray.

'Hello, Ali.' Sarah sounded breathless, as if she'd been running. 'Sorry to keep you, I was upstairs stripping the spare bed, getting it ready for you.'

'That's what I like to hear. I'm expecting best-quality Egyptian cotton sheets, the covers turned back and a heart-shaped chocolate on the pillow.'

'You can expect all you want, but you'll have to make do with see-through cotton and polyester and a nail-varnish stain on the pillowcase.'

'Sounds just like home. Now, tell me, how did last night pan out? Did Trevor hit the roof and ground you and Hannah for the rest of time?'

'Not exactly.'

'Go on, what did he do?'

There was a pause.

'Sarah?'

'You'll have to talk about something else. He's back, I can hear him putting the key in the lock. Tell me when you're arriving.'

Ali wanted to ignore her friend and demand to be told all the details about what the silly man was up to now, but she knew better. Sarah was ridiculously loyal to Trevor and would never do or say anything to annoy or disparage him. 'Okay, Sarah,' she said, 'I'll go along with you, but I want you to understand that if I get the chance over Christmas to ram home the message to Trevor that I think he's overreacted to this thing with you and Hannah, I will. I'll be there on Monday evening. That okay with you?'

'Christmas Eve, that's great,' Sarah said, in an excessively bright voice. As a cryptic afterthought, she said, 'And there'll certainly be no need for any messages, no need at all. I'd better go now. See you Monday, lots of love.'

Ali switched off her mobile and stared at Kirsty Young, who was still mouthing the news while perched side-saddle fashion on the corner of a desk. She felt angry and wondered, as she so often had over the years, why her friend stayed with Trevor. It never ceased to amaze her that Sarah, an intelligent and attractive woman, could settle for a life that was so appallingly second-rate. Whenever Ali had said as much to her, her friend's reply was invariably the same: 'You're too judgemental, Ali. You refuse to open your eyes to Trevor's good points, you choose only to see his faults, of which you and I both have our own fair share.'

Ali had once admitted to Elliot that she'd never forgiven Sarah for marrying Trevor. 'But, Ali,' he'd said, 'we can't dictate to others how we think they should live their lives. And have you ever considered the possibility that Sarah loves Trevor?'

How anybody could love Trevor was a mystery to Ali. A complete and utter mystery.

Chapter Eight

There was silence. The stony variety that was as portentous as the look on Trevor's face – a face that Ali saw as a cold, unappetising collation of thin, pale lips, beaky nose and beady eyes, which peered at the world through a permanently furrowed brow, an excess of facial fuzz, and seventies-student collar-length hair, which was showing its age by thinning and greying. It was Christmas Eve and Trevor had just raised the inevitable subject of Ali joining the Donovan family at church for the midnight service; he was waiting for her response.

She had only been at Smithy Cottage for two hours but already he was threatening her resolve to be nice to him – made for Sarah's sake. Nothing provoked her more than his supercilious manner; it worked on her with the speed of a class A amphetamine, coursing through her blood and heading straight for her brain where it triggered the desire to shoot down in flames whatever he uttered. When he'd opened the door to her on her arrival, the first thing he'd said was, 'Now, Ali, I know what an independent little soul you are, so what's it to be? Do I help you with your luggage, or do I let you struggle in with it?' She would have preferred a third option, that of her beating him round the head with it. And, not content with patronising her, he went on to lecture and bore her on a subject that was currently close to his heart. 'What I want to know,' he pondered, to nobody in particular as they sat down to eat, 'is why today's clergy are so anti the devil? There's a modern theory that the devil doesn't exist, but he most certainly does and the sooner we pin the tail on the donkey and face up to him, the better we'll all be. Why be so wet and talk in terms of shadows and darkness when what we're really dealing with is a very real personification of evil?'

'I couldn't agree more, Trevor,' Ali had said, giving him an ingenuous smile. 'You give me the pin and I'll gladly stick it where it belongs.'

Hannah had sniggered into her glass of orange juice and Sarah had shot them both a behave-yourself-or-I'll-send-you-to-your-room glance across the table. But Trevor, absorbed by the sound of his own voice as he carried on to the next point in his lecture, missed her not so subtle gibe.

And now he was giving her one of his tiresome wheedling looks in the hope of tempting her to go to church. She wasn't the slightest bit tired but she faked an enormous yawn, stretched her arms above her head and said, 'Oh, Trevor, much as I'd enjoy that, I think an early night is all I'm good for.'

He cocked a deprecatory eye in her direction. She smiled back at him and, adopting the I'm-pretending-I-like-and-respect-you-but-really-I-think-you're-a-rattle-head expression she invariably used when dealing with a pernickety tax inspector, she said, 'Yes, a bath followed by an early night is just what I need.' His eye grew chilly. It was very nearly frosty. 'But only if there's enough hot water,' she added sweetly.

'I'll go and check that the immersion heater's on for you,' Hannah said, springing out of the sofa and making for the door.

'There's no need for that, Hannah,' Trevor said lightly. 'I think we'll find that Ali is having another of her little jokes at my expense.'

Perception from old Mutton-chops, thought Ali. Whatever next?

'Your auntie Ali knows full well that our Christmas Eve itinerary wouldn't be complete without going to church.' He laughed one of his mirthless chuckles.

Ali cringed, and not just because she found Trevor such a

barrel of unfunny laughs: she hated being called *auntie*. It made her sound wrinkled and dry-boned. Trevor was the only one who insisted on referring to her in this inaccurate way. It was as though he was making her less of the woman she was, that by giving her this title he was taking away her true status. There was something oddly sexless about *auntie*: it had connotations of floral-scented bath cubes, powdery faces and hand-knitted cardies. Elliot had once commented that he suspected Trevor was threatened by her, and not just intellectually. He reckoned that she challenged Trevor sexually and this was his way of making her less of a threat. By turning her into a nice, safe auntie figure, he was protecting himself. Naturally she had scoffed at such a ridiculous far-fetched notion, saying that the only person Trevor was turned on by was Trevor the Almighty.

'I don't think Ali's having a joke,' Hannah said, matter-of-factly. 'I think she's trying very politely to tell you that she doesn't want to go to church tonight.'

Trevor swivelled his beady eyes from Ali to his daughter and gave another of his unamused laughs. 'Nonsense, your auntie Ali is trying one of her intellectual games on me. She loves nothing better than to tease me into a religious debate. We've been doing it for years, haven't we, Ali?' His voice was syrupy with condescension.

'Sure have, Trev.' If he was going to insist on calling her *auntie*, he could have a taste of his own medicine – she knew how he hated his name being abbreviated.

'And she knows perfectly well that we'd like nothing better than for her to accompany us to church.'

'But you're forcing her and it's wrong, Dad.'

Another tight little laugh. 'Goodness, I'd never force anyone to go to church against their will, Hannah. That wasn't how our Lord operated.'

Hannah shrugged. 'Good, so you won't be offended if I don't go tonight.'

Fair play to the girl, thought Ali, with quiet admiration.

Trevor's eyes suddenly fixed on Hannah. Gone was his syrupy tone. Now his voice was sharp and overbearing. 'Now, hold it right there, young lady—'

'No, Dad, I'm not going. And I might just as well tell you what I've wanted to say for some time. I've decided not to go to church any more. I know you won't approve, but that's how I feel.' She opened the door and left the sitting room.

Another silence ensued. It was even stonier than the one before.

Ali wondered whether Trevor would notice her sliding out of her chair and slithering across the threadbare carpet to sound the alarm that would warn Sarah there was trouble at t'mill.

From his chair beside the Christmas tree, Trevor slowly rose to his feet, his lanky, wire-thin body making the room feel claustrophobic. It always surprised Ali that he was so tall: she generally thought of him as being a small, insignificant man. He went and stood with his back to the gas fire and folded his arms across his chest. 'I sense dissension in the troops,' he said, in a low voice.

'I guess you just have to accept that Hannah's old enough to form her own opinions.'

He disregarded her comment with a loud sniff. 'She's at an impressionable age, an age when she could be easily swayed.'

A nice rip-roaring debate on the Church's dubious record of indoctrination was an appealing prospect, but Ali gritted her teeth and resisted the urge to slaughter Trevor with a no-holds-barred row. Thinking that she had probably caused enough trouble for one evening, she slipped out of her chair and went to find Sarah. She was in the kitchen listening to the radio while putting the finishing touches to the Christmas cake. Ali was about to explain what had been going on when Trevor came in and switched off the boy soprano who was giving his all to 'Silent Night' – oh, if only! – and put in his two penn'orth, implying that Ali had been the instigator of Hannah's latest act of insubordination. Ali marvelled at her

62

friend's concentration as she apparently ignored Trevor and, with a steady hand, continued to guide the piping bag across the cake, forming a tracery of green holly leaves. She didn't look up from what she was doing until the last leaf was in place. She wiped her hands on a cloth and said, 'I'm sorry, Trevor, but you can't blame Ali for influencing Hannah. This has been on the cards for some weeks.'

He drew in his breath then exhaled slowly. 'But why is she doing this? We've done everything to ensure that this wouldn't happen.' He sounded genuinely baffled and Ali almost felt sorry for him. It couldn't be easy being a parent when you'd invested so much time and energy into mapping out your child's future and she effectively told you to shove it.

Sarah smiled kindly at him. 'You mustn't blame yourself, Trevor.'

'I wasn't going to,' he said haughtily. 'It's not me who's been encouraging her to throw away all the values we've given her.'

Ali saw Sarah flinch – this was clearly a reference to the nightclub débâcle – and any momentary sympathy she had felt for Trevor was gone. She opened her mouth to stick up for Sarah, but changed her mind when she saw the pleading look on her friend's face. Oh, hell, she thought, and for the sake of damage limitation, she said, 'So, what time's kick-off at St Cuth's? I think I might join you, after all.'

Grateful eyes rested on her, as did a cold, unforgiving pair, the like of which she'd only ever seen in a fish shop.

Ali didn't know how Sarah had persuaded Hannah to don her coat and accompany them in the biting cold for the short walk along the lane to Astley Hope's small sandstone church, but as they leaned into the wind in the amber glow of the street-lamps, she was full of admiration for her. But, then, she'd always admired Sarah, right from the beginning of their friendship. They'd met in the playground at junior school when Sarah had come to her rescue. In compensating for her lack of stature, Ali had spent a good deal of her childhood being a real pain in the backside by continually trying to prove herself, especially with her older brother, Alastair. She was always getting herself into scrapes with her peers, boasting that she could outrun, outjump and generally outclass them in anything and everything. On this occasion she had taken on Caroline 'Woof-Woof' Rothwell whose authority was never challenged on account of her being the biggest and most spiteful girl in the school. She was a year older than Ali and that day she hadn't taken kindly to Ali's boasting that she could outrun her and had decided to teach her a lesson. Sarah had come across Ali as Woof-Woof was sitting on top of her forcing her to eat handfuls of grass. Very quietly, Sarah had asked Woof-Woof what she thought she was doing. When she didn't get a reply she had knelt on the ground and stared thoughtfully at the older girl as she continued to stuff grass into Ali's mouth. 'I really don't think you should be doing that,' she'd said. 'She doesn't look as if she's enjoying it.' There had been something so grown-up in the way Sarah had uttered the words that Woof-Woof had stopped and raised her eyes to see who was speaking. It was all the breathing space Ali had needed. Immediately she was on her feet, lip curled, fists raised, her blood well and truly up. But the moment had been defused and Woof-Woof had sauntered away.

For a few seconds Ali had been at a loss as to what to say. It annoyed her that she hadn't been allowed to fight her own battle, she wasn't used to relying on other people for help, and certainly not a girl who was smaller than herself and whom she didn't even know.

'So what's your name?' she asked reluctantly, spitting blades of grass out of her mouth.

'Sarah. What's yours?'

'Alison, but I prefer Ali.'

A few awkward seconds passed. Ali spent the time dusting herself down and running a finger inside her mouth to check for any damage. She hoped that this strange, quiet girl with her enviable head of long dark hair would leave her alone. When she realised that the girl had no intention of moving, she said, 'I didn't need any help just then. I was waiting to catch her off-guard.' Her ungrateful words were met with a smile. A smile that, even at the age of ten, Ali recognised as knowing. It was the way her mother looked at her sometimes. 'How come I haven't seen you here before?' she asked.

'I'm new. This is my first day.'

This piece of information further irritated Ali and, taking in the pristine uniform, she said, 'Do you normally go poking your nose into other people's business on your first day in a new school?'

She shook her head.

Ali frowned. She couldn't make out this girl. She wouldn't make any friends if she carried on being so quiet. She'd probably get picked on. Which meant she would need an eye keeping on her. If Woof-Woof Rothwell decided to come looking for her, she wouldn't stand a chance. 'Tell you what,' she said, 'seeing as you're new, why don't you stick around me, just until you've got the hang of the place?'

Sarah smiled that annoying knowing smile again. 'You mean you could be my guardian angel?'

'Something like that, yes.'

It wasn't until she was a lot older that Ali realised the irony of her friend's words. For ever since that day Sarah had been *her* guardian angel. In her quiet, undemonstrative way she'd always been there for Ali. With her extraordinary gift for defusing moments of cliff-hanging drama – just as she had tonight – she was exactly the friend Ali needed by her side. While she was hot-tempered and impetuous and would incite Armageddon if she thought it would help her cause, Sarah was loving and gentle, patience personified.

It wasn't a big turn-out at St Cuthbert's, and when heads were lowered in prayer, Ali glanced along the Victorian pew towards Trevor. He was the only one in their row who was kneeling, and with his forehead resting on his clasped hands in front of him she was pretty damn sure she was witnessing an excess of reverential zeal. He was red-hot on the liturgy as well and at times raced ahead of the young rector, who seemed to lose the plot every now and then. Poor bloke, thought Ali, as she watched him mumbling his words into his robed chest. He looked washed out with tiredness and was probably sick of the whole concept of Christmas. Trevor, though, was positively getting off on it. Without once referring to his prayer sheet his voice resonated above the mutterings of the rest of the meagre congregation. Now he was declaring himself unfit so much as to gather up the crumbs from under the Lord's table. Hah! What a joke! Trevor Donovan was one of the most swollen-headed people she knew. She didn't know anyone more puffed up with his own self-importance. She felt a nudge in her side. It was Hannah, and she was grinning at her. 'I spy with my little eye,' she whispered, 'something beginning with OG.'

'Obscene Godmother?' Ali whispered back.

'No.'

Ali looked around the church for inspiration, taking in the dried hydrangea flower heads that had been sprayed gold and fixed to the stone pillars; the holly and ivy decorations hanging from the pulpit, and the cobbled-together Nativity scene in the side chapel. Gaining no illumination from her surroundings, she said, 'Obnoxious Gasbags?'

Hannah sniggered and shook her head.

'Opinionated Gibberish?'

'*Ssh!*' It was Trevor, taking a break from bending God's ear and giving Ali the frosty-eye treatment.

'Sorry,' she murmured to Sarah, on her immediate right, when he'd turned away, 'I'll be good from now on. I promise.'

Sarah smiled. 'Don't make promises you can't keep, Ali.'

*

When they let themselves into Smithy Cottage, Trevor announced that there was something he needed to do in his workshop. 'You won't mind me leaving you girls to have a late-night gossip, will you?'

'Santa's got to see if the elves have finished all the toys, has he?' Ali joked to Sarah and Hannah when they were alone.

Hannah laughed, settled herself on the chair nearest the boiler and warmed her back against it. She drew her long legs to her chest and wrapped her arms around them. 'Seeing as it's Christmas, Mum, any chance of a drink? I could murder a vodka and Coke.'

'And your father would murder you if he found you knocking back that stuff. Don't you think he's had enough shocks for one week?'

'Yes,' joined in Ali. 'Discovering that his precious daughter is hitting the drinks cabinet like Boris Yeltsin would send him completely over the edge. And, apart from anything else, he'd blame me and I'm in enough trouble as it is.'

'In that case I'll go to bed and sulk,' said Hannah good-humouredly. She got to her feet and kissed her mother goodnight.

She was almost out of the kitchen when Ali said, 'Hey, what do you think you're doing scooting off without kissing me?' Hannah came back and hugged her. 'And you'd better put me out of my misery with OG,' Ali added. 'What the hell was it?'

'Old Gits,' said Hannah over her shoulder, as she closed the door.

'She's getting worse,' sighed Sarah. 'Whatever shall I do with her?'

'Absolutely nothing. She's perfect, cast from the same mould as her godmother.'

Sarah raised an eyebrow. 'And would that paragon of modesty like a drink?'

'Mm . . . please.'

Sarah opened the fridge and pulled out one of the bottles of

Chablis Ali had brought with her. She gave it to Ali to deal with while she arranged two plates of mince-pies and put them on the table.

'Home-made?' enquired Ali.

'Of course.'

'Including mincemeat?'

'Naturally.'

Ali bit into the light, buttery pastry and closed her eyes. 'Exquisite,' she said, when she'd finished the first mouthful, and opened her eyes. 'Now I know why I accepted your invitation to spend Christmas with you.'

'Which is as good a cue as any for me to ask you why—'

'No,' interrupted Ali, 'don't spoil it. Like good sex or a good bottle of wine, this pastry should be allowed to have its moment.'

But Sarah wasn't letting her off the hook so easily and, with the quickest of movements, she whipped Ali's plate away from her. 'Now,' she said firmly, 'not another morsel of hedonistic delight until you've explained to me what's going on. I want to know why you were preparing to put yourself through the misery of spending Christmas alone, why, when you're lucky enough to have the best parents in the world, you were choosing not to stay with them. What are you trying to prove to yourself, Ali?'

In the stark brightness from the overhead fluorescent strip-light, Sarah's small, pensive face suddenly looked stern. Her perfectly defined eyebrows were slightly knitted and her pursed lips accentuated her elegant cheekbones; dark, determined eyes stared at Ali. 'Well?' she said, pushing back her thick, charcoal-black hair in a graceful flick of her thin wrist.

'I could ask you the same question,' Ali said defensively.

'And what's that supposed to mean?'

Ali looked away.

'Oh, come on, Ali, you can do better than that. It's not in your repertoire to turn down the opportunity to have your say.'

Ali returned her gaze. 'All right, then, I will have my say. I'm talking about Trevor, as well you know. What the hell do you think *you're* trying to prove by staying with him?'

Sarah passed Ali's plate back to her and thought how easy it was for them to slip into the routine of this familiar, but unwelcome, exchange. It was a bit like wearing a mohair sweater: it always irritated in the end. 'I know you've never taken to Trevor, but he is my husband and I'd rather you didn't speak about him in that way.'

Ali dismissed this gentle rebuke with an impatient wave of her hand. 'Oh, please, I've heard it all before. For more than eighteen years I've listened to you trotting out the same loyal line, but tell me this, does he make you happy? Does he make you laugh? Does he make you want to chew great chunks out of the mattress when you have sex? In short, Sarah, does he do it for you?'

Sarah frowned and fiddled with the service sheet that Trevor had left on the table on their return from St Cuthbert's. 'You make marriage sound so one-sided. There's more to it than what's-in-it-for-me?'

'I wasn't implying anything of the kind,' Ali said hotly. 'Marriage should be an equal partnership or it's nothing but a submission of will. No, second thoughts, make that a violation of will. But satisfy my curiosity. What is it you see in him that I don't?'

Sarah ripped the service sheet in half, then in half again and pushed it aside. She reached for her glass of wine and said, 'I don't expect you to understand this, but I've always felt sorry for Trevor. I feel that . . . I just feel that I have to protect him.'

'Protect him? From whom?'

Sarah shook her head sadly. 'From people like you, but mostly from himself.'

Chapter Nine

As usual, Sarah was up first on Christmas Day. She crept quietly downstairs. The house was icy cold and she switched on the boiler, silently cursing the faulty timer. She should have insisted that it was serviced in the autumn as she'd wanted and not listened to Trevor's claims that another year wouldn't do any harm. She filled the kettle, plugged it in, then opened the fridge to tackle the turkey. The sight of the lump of pale, puckered flesh squatting in the old enamel roasting-tin brought to mind the disturbing dream that had nudged her out of her sleep. She'd been dreaming of a much older Trevor: he was in bed with her, naked and fully aroused but his decrepit, loose and ill-fitting body had repelled her.

She knew what had induced the dream: it had been Ali's absurd reference to whether Trevor could make her chew chunks out of the mattress in their more intimate moments.

Trust Ali to be so graphic.

But the truth was they didn't have any intimate moments. There hadn't been any since Trevor had grown worried that Hannah might hear them. She very much doubted if things would change when Hannah left home next year to go off to college. Sarah had long accepted that, first and foremost, Trevor was a father. It was incidental that he was a husband.

She had tried to explain this to Ali last night.

'Feeling sorry for a person and wanting to protect them is no basis for a real marriage,' Ali had argued.

'It's given us a marriage that's lasted eighteen years,' Sarah had countered, 'and has provided a happy and loving environment for Hannah.'

'But at what cost?'

'Ah, well, that's the accountant in you talking.'

'Don't give me any of that, Sarah. You're my closest friend, there's no one I care about more, but ever since you married Trevor I've watched you continually sacrifice and compromise yourself to him. I just want to understand why.'

'Oh, Ali, I wish I had a pound for every one of these conversations we've had.'

'Yes, and I wish I had a pound for every time you've sidestepped the issue. You've always given me the same guff that you were attracted to Trevor because you recognised in him a similar upbringing to your own.'

'I resent the word guff. It's the truth.'

'Okay, so you both had cold, uncaring parents, and I'll go along with the theory that that might be sufficient to spark off a degree of empathy between you, but marriage?'

'There was the small matter of me being pregnant with Hannah, don't forget.'

'But you didn't have to marry him.'

'I wanted her to have stability. And that's what she's had. Trevor's been the best of fathers.'

'And what about the best of husbands?'

'It doesn't always cut both ways. I've been happy with my lot. Have you ever heard me complain?'

'No, but that's because you're a saint. Don't you ever feel the strain of being so damned good?'

Sarah had been on the verge of telling Ali never to call her a saint when the back door had opened and Trevor had joined them in the kitchen, bringing with him a blast of freezing night air. 'Still here, girls?' he'd said. 'There's no stopping you two when you get together, is there?'

Their conversation had ended then, and after they'd locked up, turned out the lights and gone to bed, Sarah had been only too aware that Ali had done her own bit of sidestepping. By attacking Trevor, she had smoothly deflected the question about her wanting to be on her own for Christmas this year.

'Morning, Sarah.' It was Ali. She plodded across the cork-tiled floor in a pair of woolly socks and her thickest winter pyjamas – she knew of old how arctic Smithy Cottage could be. She gave Sarah a hug. 'Happy Christmas. How long have you been toiling away down here?'

'Only a short while.'

'Anything I can help with? Potatoes, sprouts, cranberries, parsnips?'

'Later. For now you can make a pot of tea. The kettle's just boiled.'

While she waited for the tea to brew, Ali went over to the boiler and sat on the chair Hannah had used last night, and as Hannah had, Ali drew her knees up under her chin for extra warmth. She watched Sarah across the cramped kitchen as she chopped a large onion followed by a bunch of fresh sage. There was something intrinsically reassuring and comforting in watching somebody else cook. As a small child she had loved to sit in the big airy kitchen at Sanderling and chat to her grandmother while she worked. Physically her mother's mother had been tiny, but in character she'd been huge: spirited, intrepid, forceful and totally uncompromising. When she was little, Ali had thought there wasn't anything her grandmother couldn't do. 'I want to be like you when I grow up,' she'd told her. 'I want to be able to hold back the waves, just as you can.' It was a family joke that Grandma Hayling, as she was known, was such an indomitable character that she was called upon by the local coastguards to go down to the water's edge and keep the potentially dangerous spring tides at bay. The rest of her family now claimed that Ali's wish had been granted, that she was indeed a carbon copy of her grandmother.

It had been Grandma Hayling who, during the long summer holidays that Ali spent with her, had taught her to swim, to sail, to cook – but, more important than any of this, she had also taught Ali to set her sights on the highest of goals. 'Second best is not an option, Ali,' she had told her.

'Take second best and you'll make do with third, fourth and fifth. Then where will you be? At the bottom of the heap, that's where.' And when Sarah had joined the family trips down to Hayling Island, she also had been taken in hand.

'You look deep in thought,' Sarah said. 'Not regretting coming, are you?'

Ali laughed. 'Not yet.' She uncurled her legs and went and poured their tea. She passed her friend a Forever Friends Christmas mug, a stocking-filler present she'd bought for Sarah more years ago than she cared to recall. 'I was thinking of my grandmother,' she said. 'You were a bit scared of her at first, weren't you?'

'I was terrified of her.'

'But not as terrified as those boys who called round for us late one night. She gave them a right roasting. Do you remember?'

'Not particularly. There were too many of them. They were like driftwood – they came in on the tide each morning.'

'And went out on the evening tide, thank goodness. My ghastly brother was put in charge of keeping an eye on us in the end, wasn't he?'

'I think he rather enjoyed himself, despite having to fend off the rude comments you made in the hope that he would take offence and leave us alone. He was very sweet.'

'Get away. There was nothing sweet about my big bruv. There still isn't.'

'How is he?'

'Still languishing in Singapore, convincing people he's God's gift to the world of finance. If his Christmas card is to be believed, it looks as if he's heading for the altar.'

'After all this time?'

'Exactly.'

'And while we're on the subject of your family, and please don't think you can deflect me as you did last night, would you care to explain why you've ended up here for Christmas?'

Ali resumed her position by the boiler and cradled her hot

mug in her hands. She stared into it and said, 'Everyone's made too much of my wanting to be alone. I just felt that it was time I stood on my own two feet. I didn't want people being extra nice to me just because of Isaac and the time of year it was.'

Sarah stopped what she was doing. She lifted her mug, drank from it and peered at Ali over the rim. Very softly she said, 'Why don't you want people to be nice to you?'

Ali shrugged.

'Is it because you feel you don't deserve it?'

'Whoa now, don't start going all deep and meaningful on me.'

Sarah ignored her. 'You wouldn't be the first to feel the need to punish yourself.'

Without looking at Sarah, Ali said, 'I'm not consciously punishing myself.'

'No, you don't need to. Your subconscious is doing far too good a job on its own. But you have to stop it, Ali, and stop it now before it gets out of control. Otherwise we'll be having this same conversation in ten years' time.' She smiled. 'And I really don't think you're cut out for spending too many Christmases with the Donovan household.'

'It'd be all right if it was just you and Hannah,' Ali said grumpily.

Sarah put down her mug and returned her attention to the finely chopped onion that was softening in the frying-pan on the hob. She gave it a stir and added some salt and pepper, followed by the sage. 'I ought to warn you,' she said. 'Trevor will be expecting another full turn-out at church this morning.'

'What? But we were there only a few hours ago.'

'It's what we do, Ali. And I think after last night's little confrontation I'd be grateful if you didn't rock the boat too much.'

'But if Hannah doesn't want to go, she shouldn't be press-ganged into it.'

74

'I know that and you know that, but for the sake of a peaceful Christmas, I'd rather we didn't go out of our way to annoy Trevor.'

Ali groaned and thought, It's always about Trevor. Trevor this. Trevor that. Well, Trevor could stick it up his bum.

'Ali?'

'Mm?'

'You will try, won't you?'

'On one condition.'

'It's not another question about my marriage, is it?'

'Nah, I'll just have to put that down as one of life's great mysteries. But while I have you in the hot seat, tell me what got you into all this God stuff. I've never dared to have a heart-to-heart with you about it before in case you roped me in for a quick conversion. Did it all start with you having an Audrey Hepburn crush when you were little and dreaming of being a nun?'

Sarah carefully added a bowl of breadcrumbs to the frying-pan, stirred the mixture a few times, took it off the heat and said, 'Ali, before you completely trivialise everything in my life, consider the words of that famous Quaker, William Penn: "O God, help us not to despise or oppose what we do not understand."'

'Hey, I wasn't trivialising your—'

'Yes, you were.'

'No, honestly, Sarah, it's more a matter of not having the right vocabulary. You know what we atheists are like when you God-squaddie Christians start babbling about Jesus as if he's a best pal! We get all squeamish and hot and bothered and have to resort to the language of profanity.'

Sarah smiled. And then she laughed. 'Ali Anderson, you sit here in my kitchen on Christmas morning with your bare-faced creedless cheek imagining you can talk your way out of anything and everything.'

Ali smiled too. 'That's me.'

'And I want it understood that I would never take it upon

myself to convert you. Anyone with an ounce of sense would leave that to God.' She returned her attention to the frying-pan and tipped its contents into a shallow Pyrex dish. Ali watched her and thought how strange it was that she had known Sarah since they were ten years old but there was so much about her that she didn't understand. Ali had never been able to get to grips with this God lark of Sarah's. As far as she was aware it had started when they were up at Oxford, and while Ali had frequently wondered what fulfilment her friend was gaining each time she visited the University Church of St Mary the Virgin in the High, she had been careful not to pry too deeply into Sarah's other life for fear of being sucked in.

Or, worse, of losing Sarah.

But she had made it her business to observe Sarah closely, watching for the first sign of a change in her, dreading the appearance of ropy sandals and a beatific expression similar to the one on the gormless face of the first-year linguist in the room next door; a starry-eyed girl who seemed to think that Jesus loved her more if she left off shaving her legs and wore an old greatcoat that stank of wet dogs. But Sarah didn't undergo some dramatic road-to-dementia experience, and whatever heavenly delight it was that she was pursuing, she kept it very private. Just as she still did. Not once had she ever inflicted her views on Ali.

Which could never be said of Trevor.

Put Trevor and religion together and what you ended up with was something similar to herpes – an annoying disorder that would never go away. When Hannah was born and Sarah had said that she wanted Ali to be godmother, Trevor had very nearly suffered a paroxysm of disgust. 'But she's an atheist,' he'd said, staring at Ali as she held the tiny two-week-old Hannah in her arms, and probably thinking that she was already tainting his daughter's pliable soul. 'What kind of spiritual guidance would she ever be able to offer?'

'Well, we'll just have to wait and see,' had been Sarah's rather oblique reply.

Watching Sarah expertly push a large dollop of sausage-meat into the turkey's bottom, she said, 'So what is the deal with God, then, Sarah? How did he catch you?'

'That's sounds alarmingly like an agnostic talking, not the atheist I know and love. Are you now saying there is a God?'

'Certainly not. I'm merely trying to understand what it is that makes you believe in something you can't prove.'

'That's the whole point of faith. It's having the courage to trust in the unseen.'

'But isn't that the great universal cop-out?'

Sarah moved over to the sink and washed her hands. 'It might be, but I'm happier with it than without it.'

Trevor ran a tight ship when it came to Christmas. Breakfast was a paltry affair of a bowl of cereal – 'We don't want to eat too much and spoil our lunch, do we, girls?' – and there was to be no frenzied stocking-and-present opening until they were back from church. 'The exchanging of gifts should not be allowed to become the focus of the day,' he intoned, as he frogmarched them down to St Cuthbert's in the raw, blustery wind and rain.

'So why were the three wise men fannying around with those expensive gifts?' Ali shouted above the wind that was slapping her in the face.

He banged a big bony hand down on her shoulder and laughed one of his unfunny laughs. 'God bless you, Ali, I swear you've been put on this earth as a personal challenge for me.'

'Yeah,' she muttered under her breath, as she hurried on ahead to walk with Sarah, 'and I swear that you're the scratchy thorn in my side.'

St Cuthbert's was as exciting as it had been on their last visit, with much talk in the sermon of babies being symbols of hope and new life. Owing to the effectiveness of the sound system there was no avoiding what the rector – who at one stage in the service actually yawned – was saying, and Ali tried in vain not to think of Isaac. Sarah's hand reached out to hers and squeezed it gently. 'Soon be over,' she said. 'Hang on in there.'

Finally the service came to an end, but any hopes Ali had harboured of them making a speedy getaway were dashed by a small segment of the congregation advancing towards Trevor and Sarah to wish them a Happy Christmas.

'AHW,' whispered Hannah in Ali's ear.

'Arse Hole Wankers?' suggested Ali, out of the corner of her mouth.

Hannah laughed loudly. 'Astley Hope's Worthies, but yours is better. Much more accurate. Oh, no, I don't believe it, Dad's inviting them for tea.' She groaned. 'Ali, believe me, this'll be one Christmas you'll never forget.'

Ali suddenly looked grim. 'I've had worse, I assure you.'

Hannah's innocent young face flushed crimson. 'I'm sorry,' she said, 'I was forgetting. I'm really sorry.'

Ali recovered herself and grinned. 'Don't worry. Just help me survive the rest of the day. Do you have a house key?'

'Yes.'

'Well, then, what are we waiting for? Let's leave your mum and dad to socialise and head for home. And, I don't care what your father says, it's time to hit the booze.'

As they walked back to Smithy Cottage, leaning into the squally wind, Ali asked Hannah how the nightclub débâcle had been resolved. 'I haven't had a chance to ask your mother about it, but I guess if it had been truly horrendous she would have told me by now.'

'It sort of just fizzled out,' Hannah said, 'I was expecting Dad to really flip, but he didn't.'

'What, no stern words at all?'

'Oh, there were plenty of those.' She imitated her father's worst pulpit-preaching voice. '"How could you have lied to me? How could you have gone to such a dreadful place? How could you have got dressed up like that?" I think Mum copped more than I did, though. Poor old Mum.'

'Poor old Mum indeed.'

It wasn't long before Trevor and Sarah arrived back and found Ali attending to a green net of Brussels sprouts and Hannah surreptitiously hiding her glass of vodka on the window-sill behind the curtain. The kitchen was comfortably warm and humid with so much cooking going on: the Christmas pudding was inside a large steamer that was gently bubbling on the hob, and coming from the oven was an appetising smell of roasting turkey. It almost felt like Christmas. So much so that Trevor appeared to lose control of himself. 'I think we might open one or two of the smaller presents,' he announced, rubbing his bony hands together in what he probably thought was an expansive gesture of festive good will to all men, but actually made him look like Uriah Heep. 'We'll save the sharing of the bigger gifts until after the Queen,' he added, just in case there was a danger of anybody getting overexcited.

Ali deliberately ignored his instructions and gave Sarah and Hannah her main presents to them. Hannah loved her black Diesel jacket and immediately tried it on. It fitted perfectly. She checked the label and said, 'Is it the real thing?'

'My life, my life, you think I'd buy you fake schmutter?'

In her delight Hannah did a little pirouette and nearly knocked over the Christmas tree. She came and hugged Ali. 'Thanks,' she said. 'It's great.'

Sarah carefully unwrapped her present and opened her eyes wide when she saw the gold chain Ali had given her. 'It's beautiful,' she said, in a small voice. Ali waited for Sarah to go all boring on her and say that it was much too expensive, that she couldn't possibly accept it, blah, blah, blah. To her relief, Sarah said no such thing. 'Help me put it on,' she said excitedly. 'I'll wear it now.' And as she admired herself in the mirror above the gas fire, Ali handed Trevor his present.

'Oh,' he said, when he saw that she'd bought him Billy Graham's autobiography. 'Thank you, Ali. You've been very thoughtful and most generous.'

Generosity had had nothing to do with it when she'd chosen Trevor's present. She'd been far more devious than that. The idea was that Billy Graham's life story would keep Trevor quiet for most of Christmas.

They sat down to eat at half past one, but though the meal was delicious, it was a sombre affair, a far cry from what Ali was used to. If she were at Sanderling with her parents, things would be very different. For a start, nobody would have been up before nine – having overindulged the night before. Her father would have staggered downstairs first and made tea for everybody. He'd have brought the tray of mugs upstairs and gone knocking on all the bedroom doors telling everyone to rendezvous in five minutes in his and Mum's room for the ceremonial stocking opening. Rubbing the sleep from her eyes, Ali would have crossed the landing and climbed into bed beside her mother, and when Dad had given the word they would have delved into their overstuffed stockings. Even when she was married and she and Elliot had taken Sam to Sanderling for Christmas, this same ritual had continued. Everyone joined in, nobody was excluded. She and her mother would sit in bed spraying themselves with their favourite perfume and munching chocolates, while the men, including Alastair if he was in the country and had honoured them with his presence, would stand around comparing socks and miniatures of malt, the latter invariably being sunk within seconds. 'It's important that we line our stomachs,' they would claim, like the silly boys they were.

It was always Dad's job to take charge in the kitchen at Christmas and every year he threw himself into the task with happy enthusiasm. Breakfast was scrambled eggs on toast with strips of Irish smoked salmon, liberally covered with coarsely ground black pepper, accompanied by a flute of perfectly chilled champagne. A round of present-opening would follow and eventually Dad, armed with a new bottle of eighteen-year-old Glenmorangie – a present from Mum – would retreat to the kitchen where he'd do battle with the beast of a turkey he would have insisted on buying. 'Unless it's big enough to stand up and look me in the eye, it's not worth having,' he'd say each year when he went along to the butcher to place his order. And on Christmas Eve when he came home with the turkey strapped into the passenger seat of his car he would proudly introduce his new friend. 'I met him at the pub,' he'd joke. 'Say hello to Fred, everyone.' By the time they sat down to eat on Christmas Day it would be late afternoon and they'd be so happily pickled that they wouldn't have noticed if Fred had appeared at the head of the table dressed in a jacket and tie with a cigar sticking out of some suitable orifice.

Ali groaned inwardly as she took in the chilly atmosphere of Smithy Cottage – or Coal Scuttle Cottage, as she often referred to it. This was definitely a far cry from what she was used to. In all the years that she had been coming here, she had never once felt comfortable. Come to think of it, she'd never even been warm. She didn't know how Sarah survived it. It was a strange house. From the outside it held great promise: white-painted walls, a slate roof, small-paned windows, a canopy porch and two chimney-pots at each gable end – it had the charming look of a classic hundred-year-old cottage. But inside, and despite Sarah's best efforts, it was charmless and characterless. There were no quaint beams, no funny little nooks and crannies, no original fireplaces, no exposed brickwork and no stripped-pine doors, just a relentless abundance of woodchip and anaglypta and uninspiring square rooms that had had their original features ripped out by the previous owners. Certainly from what she recalled of the family from whom Sarah and Trevor had bought the house, they were not the kind of people to be interested in period restoration. She remembered Sarah bringing her to have a look at the house before Trevor made an offer on it. The garden had been no better, but it was difficult now, after Sarah's green-fingered touch had transformed it, to conceive how it had formerly been a dumping-ground for wooden pallets, discarded furniture and a battered old caravan minus its roof – all of which had appealed to Astley Hope's more discerning rat population. Ali wouldn't have given the owners twopence for it, but Sarah had said, 'Ali, it's cheap, it's all we can afford. We'll do it up, gradually, when we have the money.' All credit to Sarah, she had done her best by trying to brighten the place with superficial touches of paint and cheerful fabrics, but what the house needed was a serious injection of cash to make a real difference.

And money was what they'd never had. Until, that was, Sarah's miserable old parents had popped their clogs. It still rankled with Ali that the money that had been left expressly to Sarah hadn't been used for her benefit. She had tried to advise Sarah on how best to invest or safeguard it, but it had been to no avail. Trevor had seized upon the opportunity it offered him to become a born-again down-shifter, just like that stupid man on the radio last week.

As though picking up on her thoughts, she heard Trevor saying how pleased he was these day to be out of the rat-race. Helping himself to a spoonful of cranberry sauce, he said, 'We need more people brave enough to throw away the rule book as I did.' Ali knew well enough that the trick with Trevor was to let him have his say, to let him run down his battery. But the temptation to disagree with him was too great. It was all she could do to stop herself howling with derision, then taking him by the slack of his smug self-importance and booting him up the backside. 'Now, Trevor,' she said, in her silkiest voice, 'just how long do you think it would be before the entire country ground to a shuddering halt if everyone stopped what they were doing? What if every nurse and doctor in Britain decided to wave goodbye to reason and took to growing mung beans?'

'Perhaps if we all took to eating healthier stuff such as beansprouts we wouldn't need conventional doctors and nurses.'

'Hah! That's no argument. No argument at all. That's the trouble with people like you, Trevor. There's no real substance to what you say.'

'Did you know,' said Hannah, skilfully hijacking the conversation, 'that Buddha's disciples, in their search for truth, renounced all worldly goods and begged for their food, and in return people benefited from their wisdom and teaching?'

They all looked at her.

'Just thought you might like to know that,' she said reasonably.

'St Paul and the early Christians did much the same thing,' Sarah said.

'But what I find particularly interesting about Zen Buddhism,' Hannah continued, 'is that it's all about contemplation. Enlightenment comes from disciplined meditation, not from doing good, studying or—'

'You seem very well informed in all this faddish nonsense, Hannah,' Trevor interrupted, with a sharp tone.

'Trevor, please don't insult Hannah's intelligence,' said Sarah. 'Buddhism is not a fad. More turkey, anyone?'

A nice bit of Jack Daniel's-induced nirvana to get through the rest of the day would have suited Ali perfectly. But life just couldn't be that sweet. And at six o'clock that evening, her day got seriously worse.

The AHWs arrived.

Sarah had tried to warn her in advance what to expect. But it was clear within a few minutes of their arrival that she had painted a less than candid picture. They arrived as one, stood on the doorstep and sang the opening verse of 'O Come All Ye Faithful', then proceeded to stand around in the hall chit-chatting while removing their outdoor shoes and exchanging them for slippers, which they'd thoughtfully brought along in carrier-bags – though one enterprising man had his stuffed into the pockets of his anorak. They seemed inordinately fond of the cold, draughty hall and in no hurry to leave it, but eventually they trickled through to the sitting room where Ali was introduced. A scary-looking overweight woman in a full flowery skirt with a drawstring waist and frilled hem-line, a large enamelled cross hanging round her neck, sidled up to Ali and, in a waft of Deep Heat fumes, asked her if she was saved.

Ali would have been less shocked if she had asked her if she was into sadomasochism. She stood staring at the woman and frisked her stunned brain for a suitable riposte. 'No, fatso, I ain't,' was not going to cut the mustard of *agape* fellowship that this cranky lot were probably into. But before she had a chance to open her mouth, Sarah tactfully said, 'Ali is partial to playing devil's advocate, Shirley. She hasn't made up her mind yet. How's your back? Any better?'

One look at the salvationist expression on the woman's face and Ali knew that Shirley wasn't interested in her back, not when there was a soul to be saved. Well, she'd have to catch her first, and with a nimble shimmy, she was across the crowded sitting room and by the door offering to put the kettle on. Hannah joined her in the kitchen. 'HB,' she said, as she watched Ali tip spoonfuls of coffee into a long row of mugs.

'Horny Beast?' replied Ali, when she'd finished.

'Nope. Happy Brethren.'

Ali put the lid back on the coffee jar and went to stand by the boiler. 'Are they as cranky as I suspect they are?'

'And some. They're thinking of forming a prayer group with Dad as their leader.'

'What's one of those when it's at home?'

'A gossip and spiritual get-together. We used to have them with our old rector, but since Gordon's been here things haven't worked in quite the same way.'

'Was it Gordon we saw last night and this morning?'

'Yep.'

'He struck me as being dead on his feet.'

'*Aha!* So this is where you're hiding.'

Both Hannah and Ali turned to see Shirley's broad-beamed figure looming in the doorway. To Ali's horror, she came straight towards her, laid a hand on her shoulder and said, 'Ali, I want you to know that I feel called by the Lord to pray for you.'

Ali looked her straight in the eye and said, 'You'll have to excuse me, but I feel called to go to the loo.'

Late that night, when Ali was in bed warming her feet on the hot-water bottle Sarah had just brought in for her, she said, 'Thank you for the quilt you made me. It's beautiful, far more imaginative and creative than the present I gave you.'

Sarah fingered the gold chain around her slender neck. She smiled. 'We each gave the other what we knew they'd appreciate most. I can't remember the last time I received anything so remotely frivolous.'

Ali stared at her friend. 'There's not been a lot of frivolity in your life, has there?'

Sarah frowned. 'There was plenty of that when I was with you at Sanderling. They were happy, carefree days and I treasure the memories.'

'That's a terribly sad thing to say.'

'No, it isn't. Now, come on, I must love you and leave you. Trevor will be wondering where I've got to.'

But as her hand reached for the door handle, Ali said, 'Sarah, those people who came here today, you won't . . . you won't ever become one of them, will you?'

'Not a hope!'

Ali looked relieved. 'You want to watch that Shirley, she's a seriously weird case.'

'Oh, don't let her worry you. She's always going up to people and saying that she's been called to pray for them. It's just something she does.'

'And it doesn't scare the hell out of you?'

'There are worse things in life than that. Now, come on, I want to go to bed. I'm shattered.'

The door closed and Ali lay back against the pillows. She could hear the wind gusting in the trees outside. She could also feel a cold draught whistling through the badly rotting window-frame above the bed. She shivered and tugged at the duvet and the patchwork quilt Sarah had made for her. She thought of the many hours her friend had patiently spent on it and, quite unexpectedly, she began to cry: for the awful life that Sarah led; for not being with her family at Christmas; for Isaac and for the break-up of her marriage. She wondered what Elliot and Sam were doing right now. She had a sudden mental picture of Sam limbo-dancing with some lithe, scantily clad exotic dancer. The thought instantly cheered her. She switched off the bedside lamp and slipped her hand under the duvet feeling for Mr Squeezy, Isaac's teddy: she always slept with him.

Chapter Ten

Elliot closed the door quietly behind him and followed the immaculately swept path down to the palm-fringed beach. Other than a member of the hotel staff raking the sand, it appeared that he had the immediate stretch of coastline to himself. The young black man stopped what he was doing and raised his hand. Elliot returned his greeting and set off. He was aware that he looked downright pretentious as he jogged along the soft golden sand in his running gear and sunglasses, but he didn't give a damn: there were standards to maintain and one of those was that he didn't allow himself to get like the other senior partners at work. Ali used to joke that it was only a matter of time before he became a clone of the men she despised – the fat-faced, chauvinistic lard-lumps, as she had referred to the people he now presided over as partner-in-charge.

He turned up the speed and increased the distance between him and the hotel. It wasn't long before he was beginning to feel the heat from the sun's rays, despite the early hour. He flicked at the sweat working its way into his eyes and pushed himself on. Jogging for him was the same as swimming: it was an act of self-mastery through which he could test his endurance with a ruthless, iron-willed single-mindedness. In other words, he could physically punish himself as no other person could. He occasionally played squash, but after Isaac's death he'd found the pace too sedentary and his opponents had grown thin on the ground, having tired of the silent but ferociously aggressive rallies to which he subjected them. But jogging suited him perfectly. He could run and run, until the blood pounded in his head and he was almost sick he was so breathless.

After thirty minutes he turned round and retraced his steps. When he reached the hotel he saw that, as on previous days, a row of prime waterfront sun-loungers had been claimed with beach towels. According to one of the waiters with whom Sam was now pally, it was always the wives who slipped down in their nightwear first thing in the morning to commandeer the best ones and the umbrellas.

He paused to steady his breathing, sitting on the low wall that separated the beach from the hotel pool area, and stared out to sea. He noticed a woman swimming towards the shore – so he wasn't the only one benefiting from an early start to the day. She emerged from the water, squeezing her long dark hair with each step she took. He watched her bend down to the sand and pick up a multi-coloured sarong, which she tied around her slim waist. She was an attractive woman, nearly as tall as himself with long, straight legs. He decided that she was younger than him, but not as young as Ali. When she drew level, she said, 'Happy Boxing Day. Bit different from home, isn't it?'

He politely returned the greeting and agreed.

'Have you stayed here before?' she asked.

'No.' And, conscious that he sounded curt and unforthcoming, he forced himself to ask how long she'd been at the hotel – judging from her tan, a lot longer than he and Sam had.

'This is our second week,' she said. 'We leave on Saturday. How about you?'

'We arrived on Sunday and leave next Sunday.'

'Too bad you can't stay another week, it's a great place to unwind. You'll have to make the most of it while you can. You're here with your father, aren't you?'

He nodded, not surprised by her question. Sam was one of the most sociable men he knew: in the short space of time that they'd been here, he had established himself on first-name terms with several of the waiters and waitresses, and was hanging out with a number of other guests, including an Irish couple from Dun Laoghaire with whom he'd played cards into the early hours of this morning after the Christmas party had ended. It wasn't beyond the realms of possibility that by now every guest at the hotel knew Sam and Elliot's life history. Not that he was accusing his father of being a gossip. He wasn't. For Sam, striking up conversation with a stranger came as naturally as breathing.

'I'm in the same situation as you,' the woman said. 'I'm here with my mother – maybe we could get them together.' When he didn't say anything, she said, 'I'm going for breakfast now. Perhaps I'll see you around.'

Sam was sitting on the balcony of their ocean-view suite when Elliot let himself in. He was washed, shaved and dressed in a pair of Bermuda shorts with an open-necked shirt. He was reading a Dick Francis novel but hadn't got very far with it – unlike Elliot who was already on his second book.

'Who's the piece with the legs and sarong?' he asked casually, without raising his eyes.

'I've no idea,' Elliot answered, 'but I should watch out, she's got plans to hitch you up with Mother.'

Sam lowered his book. 'What kind of *mother*? The Sophia Loren variety or Vera Duckworth?'

'Not a clue, but I'm sure you'll find out soon enough. I'm going to have a shower.' He stripped off his sweat-stained T-shirt and slung it over his shoulder.

'Yes, please do. I was wondering what the awful pong was. But don't be ages, breakfast beckons.'

'Go on ahead, if you want.'

'You don't mind?'

'Of course not. I shan't be long anyway. Ten minutes at most. Time for you to suss out *Mother*.'

*

In the open-air restaurant, and without Elliot's kill-joy scrutinising eye watching over him, Sam helped himself to four spicy sausages, a few rashers of crispy bacon, a couple of eggs and some fried plantain. He loved these buffet breakfasts: they really set a man up for the day. He knew the Boy Wonder meant well with all his talk of fresh vegetables and white meat, but he'd got this far eating the way he did, and was still as fit as a butcher's dog, so he might as well risk it a bit longer. He poured himself a glass of pineapple juice, exchanged a few good mornings with some of the other guests, then took his plate to their usual table overlooking one of the hotel pools with the twinkling sea beyond. The tape of calypso carols was on again and, to the sound of 'Joy to the World' hammered out on a steel drum, he settled into the comfortably padded wicker chair and made a start on his breakfast. He chewed a mouthful of sausage with relish and took in the view. It was one hell of a spot that Elliot had chosen for them, one hell of a spot. A grand way to spend Christmas, if you wanted to get away from all that tradition and convention. It was certainly a million miles from any Christmas he'd ever known.

He smiled and wondered what dear old Connie would have made of all this. 'Sam,' she would have said, 'pull your stomach in and behave yourself. You're with the smart set now.'

Poor Connie, she'd never felt comfortable with anyone who didn't have the same broad Yorkshire accent as herself.

Other than the Boy Wonder, of course.

Strange, but even from when he was a young lad, his accent had been softer, less noticeable than his mates'. They'd jeered at him for it initially, but after he'd given them a damn good pasting they'd seen the sense in leaving him alone. Connie hadn't approved of the fights Elliot got himself into – which he always won – but Sam had backed his son, saying that sometimes it was the only way.

It was when Elliot was three that they gained an inkling

that their only child was loft-extension bright. He was already able to read and soon his head was permanently stuck in any book he could lay his hands on. They had next to no money in those days and couldn't afford to keep him in reading matter, so Connie took him religiously to the library every Saturday morning. By the age of seven he was reading Tolkien and by the time he was nine he'd done with the children's section and was bringing home Charles Dickens. It was one of the women Connie cleaned for who suggested that Elliot should sit the entrance exam for Bradford Grammar. She and Sam had refused to give the suggestion so much as an inch of house room, knowing that they couldn't afford the fees, but when his teachers started making encouraging noises about Elliot being scholarship material, they thought it was worth a try. To this day, Sam could still see Connie's face when she opened that letter from the headmaster to say they were offering Elliot a place. And not just any old place: he'd got a full scholarship. Connie's heart had been near to bursting with pride and she had spent the rest of the day crying. But that night she paced the bedroom floor, wringing her hands, chewing her lip. 'What's up?' he'd said. 'The boy's done it, he's got himself in, just as we hoped he would.'

'Yes, but now he might stop loving us. He might think we're not good enough for him. Oh, Sam, what've we done?'

'There's just no damn pleasing some folk,' he'd said. He'd pulled her into bed and held her tightly, knowing all too well what she'd been agonising over: he'd been doing the same, worrying himself sick for weeks that Elliot would grow away from them, that he'd be educated out of their lives.

But worst fears seldom happen and Elliot didn't change. He remained the same, quiet, introspective and considerate lad he'd always been, gliding effortlessly through the next seven years of school, before going on to Oxford to study economics and surprising no one when he left with a first. Yep, as the football pundits would say, 'The boy done good.'

It was a shame that Connie had never seen the success

Elliot had made of himself. Or, for that matter, the success that Sam had made of his own life. He sometimes felt guilty that she had only ever known the tough, lean times. She hadn't lived long enough to see his building business prosper. Even he had been astonished when he retired a few years ago and realised the extent of his ill-gotten gains. Back in the early eighties, and as a sideline to his main business, he'd dabbled in doing up dilapidated terraced houses in Leeds and, instead of selling them on for a quick, easy buck, he'd let them. It proved to be a lucrative venture and one that he enjoyed. He quickly acquired a reputation as a fair-minded landlord who cared about the quality of his properties as much as he cared about the tenants who occupied them. They were mostly young students and found him a refreshing change from the usual cowboy rent collectors. He'd kept on a few houses, just to keep his eye in, but the bulk of his business was now sold and he was reaping the rewards of a lifetime's hard graft. He was determined to bloody well enjoy himself. No point in having a bit of brass and not enjoying it, now, was there?

'How are you this morning, Sam?'

He turned and looked up into the smiling face of Justin, the friendly young waiter who always made sure that this particular table was kept free for Sam and Elliot. 'I'm doing fine, Justin, and yourself?'

'A bit out of it.'

'Late night again at some wild party or other?'

'No, man, it was a family get-together. They're always the worst.'

Sam laughed. 'Depends on the family, Justin, depends on the family.'

'So, what can I get you? Tea or coffee?'

'Tea for me, and if you can throw another bag in the pot, so much the better. I like to see a bit of colour in a brew. Elliot will probably have coffee.'

'He's sleeping in this morning?'

'No, lad. Elliot isn't one for taking it easy.'

Justin looked about himself and said, in his lazy drawl, 'Then what's he doing here, man?'

'Running away,' Sam muttered, under his breath, when Justin had left him. Running away, just as he'd been doing for the past two years.

Elliot appeared a few minutes later. He eyed his father's plate and said, 'Another gut'n'heart-buster?'

'No worries. I'll sweat the calories off later by the pool.'

Elliot tutted. 'I've told you before, Dad, calories need to be burned off.'

'Then I'd best watch myself in this heat or there'll be nowt left of me when we fly home. I ordered you coffee, by the way. Justin only brought it a few seconds ago so it'll still be good and hot.'

'Thanks. I'll go and get something to eat. Can I get you anything? Something with a hint of vitamin C?'

Sam chinked his knife against his untouched glass of pineapple juice. 'This'll do for me, lad.'

When Elliot returned with a large bowl of sliced melon, paw-paw and mango, he said, 'Any sign of *Mother*?'

Sam smiled. 'I'd forgotten all about her.' They both turned their heads and slowly glanced around the restaurant. 'Easy does it,' Sam said, 'I've spotted *Sarong*. To your right, two o'clock by the palm. I can't see if she's sitting with anyone – there's a pillar in the way.'

Elliot followed his father's directions. He raised an eyebrow.

'Does that mean she's in the Sophia Loren category?' asked Sam hopefully. 'Is she hot?'

'How can I best put this, Dad?'

Sam groaned. 'Just my luck. Are we talking Bride of Frankenstein she's had that much surgery, or tight pinky perm and the makings of a moustache?'

'See for yourself, they're coming over.'

Chapter Eleven

Ali used to say, 'Never trust a woman with loose skin and gold shoes, especially if she's carrying a matching shoulder-bag. And, whatever you do, approach with extreme care if there's an abundance of red nails and lipstick.'

The swiftest of glances revealed to Elliot that *Mother* had scored a hat-trick and, according to Ali's brief, should be given as wide a berth as possible. But it was her hair that really did it for Elliot: he couldn't take his eyes off its staggeringly rigid auburn form as she and her daughter approached their table.

Both he and Sam rose to their feet. Introductions were made – *Mother* was Pamela and *Sarong* was Rosalind – chairs were pulled out and assertions made that the women had already had their breakfast and were in need of no further sustenance, although another cup of coffee would be nice. Sam immediately assumed the role of genial host, attracted Justin's attention and a fresh pot was fetched.

'Well, isn't this lovely?' said Pamela, curling her long fingernails round her cup and focusing her attention on Sam. 'And what a coincidence you being here with your son and me with my daughter. Have you been to this part of the world before?'

'No, this is my first time and I'm enjoying every minute of it.'

'What about you?' Rosalind asked Elliot.

'Oh, he's been around that one.' Sam laughed. 'You name it, he's been there – Tobago, St Lucia, Antigua. Ask him where he's not been.'

'That's a slight exaggeration,' Elliot murmured, 'but this is my first visit to Barbados.'

'How does it compare with Antigua?' Pamela asked. 'We're toying with the idea of going there next year.'

'Favourably,' was all he said. What else could he say? It was where he and Ali had spent their honeymoon. It had been a fortnight of unimaginable pleasure, when they had experienced nothing but the blissful self-sufficiency of their love. There had been no formal order to their days and nights: the sun and moon had simply dissolved into each other while they ate, swam, slept and made love as the mood took them. Often they would go for a moonlit swim and on one occasion, at two in the morning, they had gone for a long walk along the deserted beach. It had still been warm and the night air thick with the hum of insects and water lapping on the soft white sand. They had taken their clothes off and gone for a swim, and afterwards they'd returned to their hotel room and made love. There had never been any awkwardness between them when it came to sex, and he was a man who enjoyed taking his time over it. Ali had often teased him that he was as meticulous in bed as he was at work. 'You're the most thorough man I know,' she'd said that particular night, as he massaged her neck and shoulders in a way she loved.

'That sounds suspiciously as if you're accusing me of being boring,' he'd replied, turning her on to her back and kissing her warm salty lips. She'd smiled and said, 'No woman who's ever been to bed with you would ever accuse you of being boring. I've told you before, Elliot, you're the sexiest man on the planet . . .'

It was inevitable. Sam proposed that they should all meet for lunch. Pamela accepted at once. 'What a lovely idea,' she said, hitching her gold bag on to her padded shoulder. 'Rosalind and I are going into Bridgetown on a little shopping expedition. You're welcome to join us if you wish, though I know how you boys react at the merest mention of the word shopping.'

'I think we'll leave Bridgetown in your capable hands,' Sam said. 'Elliot and I are going to take a dekko at one of the distilleries. If we've time and haven't tasted too much rum we might fit in a drive along the coast.'

She wagged a sharply pointed finger at them. 'Well, you make sure you behave yourselves.'

'Nice woman,' Sam said, when they were alone. 'Daughter's not bad either.'

Elliot eyed him warily and poured another cup of coffee. He saw a slow but predictable smile spread over Sam's face. 'Forget it,' he said. 'I'm not interested.'

'I could help. I could keep Pamela amused leaving you to have the fair Rosalind all to yourself.'

'You'd do that for me?' Elliot responded, in a voice heavy with mock gratitude.

'Come on, son. Didn't you notice the way her eyes were working you over?'

'Frankly, no, I didn't.'

'Then you're more out of touch than I thought you were. Go for it, Elliot. What harm a little holiday romance, eh?'

Elliot drained his coffee-cup and stared at the sea. He squinted against the strong sun and said, 'I told you, I'm not interested.'

Sam frowned. 'Look,' he said, his tone placatory, 'I know that the memory of Ali is powerful and she's one hell of an act to follow, but you have to look to the future. You can't go on living in the past. You've told me many times that there's no hope of you two getting together again, so you've got to start living once more. Self-containment isn't healthy if it goes on too long. Have some fun. Who knows? A bit of a fling might do you the power of good. It might just put the brakes on you running away from yourself.'

Elliot was furious. Bad enough that Sam was playing Cupid, but worse that his father should say he was running away from himself.

It was true, of course, and that was the real source of Elliot's anger. Nobody ever enjoyed hearing an unpalatable truth about themselves. And, like the recurrent pain of toothache, Sam's words had continually jibbed at him during the guided tour round the distillery. Not even the heady sweet smell or taste of the island's most famous rum could take the edge off the bitterness of his self-loathing.

He crunched the gears on their hired open-top Mini Moke and slammed his foot to the floor. The diminutive engine whined its disapproval at being treated like a formula-one car, but Elliot didn't care: he kept up the pressure ruthlessly and pushed the car on. Going much too fast, they sped along the narrow lane that cut through the fields of sugar-cane either side of them, the warm tropical wind whipping at their hair and faces as they headed towards Cherry Tree Hill and the east coast of the island. Having climbed higher and higher, they were now bucketing downhill, and as they veered to the left the cane was at its tallest, towering over them and reducing their visibility. Without warning, the road turned sharply to the right, then back to the left. Elliot misjudged it, lost control and, what seemed for ever, they zigzagged perilously across the dusty potholed track. Gripping the wheel with all his strength and praying that no other vehicle would appear, Elliot brought the car under control and they skidded to an abrupt, undignified stop alongside a shallow ditch.

For a few seconds neither man spoke. Sam straightened his Panama and said, 'Well, I certainly hope that's made you feel better.'

Elliot snatched off his sunglasses and raked a shaking hand through his hair. He didn't know what to say. He got out of the car and stalked away. He came to a clearing in the sugar-cane, and from his elevated vantage-point, shielding his eyes from the glare of the midday sun, he looked towards the unspoilt rugged coastline, which in places was treacherous for swimming but in others was perfect for surfing. Knowing the difference was crucial.

As was knowing the right and wrong time to be angry. Now wasn't the right time. He could so very nearly have killed his father. He shuddered at his selfish stupidity. It was reprehensible what he'd done. How many deaths did he need on his conscience? He heard footsteps behind him.

'What maddened you most?' asked Sam, when he joined him and took in the stunning view. 'That I was trying to fix you up with a good-looking woman or that I accused you of running away?'

'Neither,' lied Elliot. 'It was the thought of you and Pamela.' He couldn't bring himself to tell his father that his anger was all to do with his growing conviction that he would never break free of the past. Ali and Isaac weren't just his past, they were his present and his future, and there didn't seem to be a thing he could do to change that.

Sam took off his hat and mopped his forehead with a handkerchief from his shirt pocket. 'Don't you worry about me,' he said. 'I can handle the likes of our Pamela. She's not so bad, I've had worse.'

Slowly Elliot turned his head.

'Don't look so shocked, lad. The celibate life doesn't suit me . . . not like it does you.'

Elliot returned his gaze to the view and pushed his hands into the pockets of his shorts. 'I don't know where you've got this notion from that I enjoy living like a bloody monk.'

'Must be summat to do with the way you refuse to let go of the past and haven't done anything about finding yourself a girl—'

'So a mindless bonk is the answer, is it?' cut in Elliot. 'A quick exchange of bodily fluids and I'll be a new man?'

They fell silent. Until Sam said, 'Don't you miss it . . . you know, the sex?'

Of course I sodding well do, Elliot wanted to shout. After what I had with Ali, don't you think I bloody well miss it?

But instead he said, 'Come on, it's hot standing here, we'd better get going.'

They went back to the car, and as Elliot started the engine he thought of their narrow escape from the potential clutches of death. He shook inwardly. Something had to be done. He had to get a grip on himself. He couldn't go on as he was. He said, 'Perhaps you're right, Dad. Maybe it is time for me to take a positive step towards the future.'

'Does that mean a mindless bonk with the fair Rosalind?'

He gave Sam what Ali would have called one of his inscrutable stares.

By the time they arrived back at the hotel, had washed the dusty road off themselves and were being shown to their table by Justin, Elliot had decided that if there was any chance his father was right, there would be no harm in pursuing a transient moment of sexual pleasure if it meant he could be free from the ghosts of the past.

Then, right on cue, he caught sight of Rosalind coming towards them from the other side of the restaurant.

Chapter Twelve

A group of local lads were playing a wild and impassioned game of makeshift cricket on the water's edge, and from his seat in the thatched beach bar, Sam watched the spirited goings-on with amusement. He sucked at the straw in his rum punch and waved at the woman who came here every day to set out her stall of locally made knick-knackery. It was the tail end of the afternoon and she was packing her screen-printed T-shirts, leather sandals, bead and shell necklaces and batik sarongs into a couple of tatty cardboard boxes. Next to her was another woman, who spent each day listening to a small radio while braiding tourists' hair. She, too, was packing up to go home.

Sam ordered another drink and continued his wait for Pamela, who had gone to her room to fetch her camera – she and Rosalind were leaving the following morning and it was her last opportunity to photograph a Caribbean sunset. Just as their holiday was coming rapidly to an end, Sam was conscious of his and Elliot's return to a cold wet England drawing ever nearer. He'd be sorry to go. He'd enjoyed himself immensely and was grateful to Elliot for arranging their trip. He could quite understand why so many guests came back year after year. At breakfast yesterday, he'd been talking to a couple who said they'd got married here five years ago and had returned every year to celebrate their anniversary. There'd been a wedding in the hotel only this morning, a big American do, the full works: the young bride done up like a meringue; the groom as pale and rigid as a corpse in his John Travolta suit, and the bridesmaids bouncing about the place knocking over flower arrangements, while the rest of the guests sweltered in the heat and guzzled champagne. After all the expense, Sam hoped that the marriage would last and, rather tactlessly, had said as much to Elliot. Poor devil. His face had dropped and he'd said, 'Just as well Ali and I insisted on a small cheapskate affair, then.'

'I'm sorry,' Sam had said, 'I didn't mean it that way. It's all the sun and rum punch – my tongue's worked itself loose.'

Thinking of Elliot now, Sam wondered how he was getting on. He and Rosalind had taken out a catamaran and so far had been gone for over three hours. 'Don't they make a nice couple?' Pamela had said archly, as they'd watched them go. 'They seem to have hit it off splendidly.' Though Sam wasn't sure that this was the case, he'd agreed politely.

Since their roadside adventure on Boxing Day, Elliot had done a fair impression of a man enjoying Rosalind's company, but Sam knew his son's heart wasn't in it. It had been difficult for him to encourage Elliot into a holiday fling when he secretly still harboured a hope – forlorn as it was – that his son and Ali could put the past behind them and make a go of things again. But Ali had been so adamant that day over lunch that even he had to admit that there was only one realistic option left on the table and that was for them all to move on.

Including Elliot.

Especially Elliot.

But Sam knew that an 'exchange of bodily fluids' was never going to be a long-term answer to Elliot's problems. At best, a dalliance would take his mind off the past for a few brief moments. And Sam should know: he'd been in a similar situation himself. Most men he knew who had been widowed or divorced had remarried as soon as possible, but after Connie's long-drawn-out battle with breast cancer, which had finally claimed her, nothing could have been further from his mind. For a while the thought of being with another woman had horrified him, but gradually he had come to view things differently, and had found himself seeking out the company of the fairer sex. There was no avoiding it: he was a man who enjoyed the physical aspect of a relationship and saw no reason to go without. But as to marriage, well, he just wasn't interested in that. The way he ran his life suited him perfectly. Admittedly it was haphazard and perhaps a little shallow, but it ticked over pleasantly enough.

But it would never suit a man like Elliot.

Elliot wasn't cut out for such a casual hit-and-miss approach to life. He didn't deal in tombola come-what-may probabilities. He dealt in blueprinted specifics. He'd never had the happy-go-lucky attitude or demeanour that could leave things to chance; his *modus operandi* was to have a goal and work tirelessly towards achieving it.

And he'd done exactly that.

With the foundations set firmly in place, he had ventured into the arena of adulthood with some pretty clear objectives in mind and, to this end, and with meticulous care, he had slowly and steadily built a superstructure of certainty around himself that was meant to be durable and invincible. By carving out the challenging career he wanted, by marrying the woman he desired and by fathering the child he'd hoped for, he must have thought that he had succeeded in masterminding his life down to the very last detail. He had left nothing to chance. All his bases had been covered.

Or so he had thought.

The events of the past two years had proved that even his meticulous approach was fallible. To have lost so much in so short a time was devastating enough, but to blame himself as well was doubly so. It didn't matter how many times Sam told Elliot that it hadn't been his fault, he wouldn't listen. Even the doctors had told him that, given the circumstances, there was nothing anyone could have done. The inquest had spelled out the same message too. But Elliot had refused to believe any of it. He'd also refused to tell anyone in any detail, especially Ali, exactly what had happened that night.

'I'm trying to protect her,' he'd said, when Sam had pressed him on the point, 'I don't want her to remember Isaac that way. She's never to know.' While Sam had applauded Elliot for wanting to protect his wife, he wasn't so sure that it had been the right thing to do. He had tried on numerous occasions to get Elliot to tell him about those last moments with Isaac, but he wouldn't, and Sam could only wonder at what horrors he was keeping to himself.

'You look like the glummest man in the whole of the Caribbean,' said a chirpy voice. Sam looked up to see Pamela, camera in hand and pointing it in his direction.

'Sorry, love,' he said. 'How's this for you?' He put on his best cheery grin and raised his drink.

'Perfect,' she said. 'That's just how I shall remember you. Now, then, where's that sunset?'

Less than a mile away, Elliot and Rosalind were sitting on a deserted stretch of beach beneath a semi-circle of coconut trees watching the sun slowly sink.

'Thanks for this afternoon,' Rosalind said, breaking the silence that had settled on them for the past few minutes. 'I've really enjoyed myself.'

'Good,' he said, 'so have I.' To a degree it was true. Since their initial meeting he'd found Rosalind's company more agreeable than he'd expected. She was a solicitor from a large practice in Guildford and specialised in family law. 'I doubt I shall ever marry,' she'd told him over dinner last night, when they'd left Sam and Pamela to enjoy the calypso extravaganza at the hotel and had taken a taxi along the coast to St Lawrence Gap. 'I've worked for too long at the sticky end of marriage to be convinced that it could ever be a workable arrangement. I've also had the benefit of experiencing at close quarters my parents' divorce, as well as that of two of my closest friends, and it's not been a pretty sight. Monogamy doesn't stand a chance, these days.' He'd told her about his own divorce, glossing over the details. He hadn't mentioned Isaac. But, then, he rarely did.

He stared at the darkening expanse of sea, and at the sky, which was a luminous mixture of flame-red orange, lilac and inky blue where gossamer strands of cloud had formed. A small sailing-boat was inching its way across the setting sun, which was now within seconds of touching the hard line of the horizon.

'You don't talk much, do you?' he heard Rosalind say.

He caught his breath. It could have been Ali speaking – that day in his office when she'd been assigned to him to work on a big audit. It had been her first day in his department and she'd been standing next to him at his desk going through a client file. She'd paused suddenly in what she was doing and said, 'Are you always this quiet?'

'Yes,' he'd replied, amused at her candour.

She'd smiled and said, 'Good – don't ever change, it suits you.'

He turned and looked at Rosalind, her skin glowing in the reflected luminescent light from the sky. He wanted desperately to dispel the taunting memory of Ali's smiling face so he leaned across and kissed her parted lips. She didn't seem surprised and kissed him back with considerable conviction and urgency. So this is it, he thought, tilting her down on to the soft sand and pressing his mouth against hers. This is the solution. But almost immediately he realised, with shattering disappointment, that no matter how intensely they kissed he couldn't bring himself to touch her, not as she was touching him. He forced himself to clamp a hand on her thigh and gave it an experimental squeeze. He tried to imagine that it meant something. That any second he'd feel a spark of desire for her – she was, after all, attractive and apparently willing. But as her tongue slid into his mouth he knew he had to stop what they were doing. But how, without offending her? He closed his eyes as if the answer would come to him, and suddenly – suddenly it was Ali in his arms. Instantly he relaxed.

Instinctively he moved his hand, gently stroking the warm, smooth skin beneath his fingertips and slowing the pace of their kissing. He was aware of her shifting beneath him and of the change in her breathing. His own breathing had intensified and his body was miraculously alive to the explosion of desire within him. He opened his eyes to stare into Ali's face to tell her how much he loved her, to tell her that –

Horrified, he pulled away.

He didn't know what shocked him more, that his state of mind was unstable enough to have created this situation, or that he still loved Ali. Mortified he sat up and pushed both his hands through his hair.

Beside him, Rosalind righted herself. 'What is it? What's wrong?' Understandably she sounded put out.

Overcome with embarrassment, he mumbled, 'I'm sorry, I – I shouldn't have done that.'

'Oh,' she said flatly. 'Care to talk about it?'

He shook his head.

'Has this happened before, Elliot?' Her voice sounded less cool now.

Again he shook his head.

She touched his arm lightly. 'You wouldn't be the first man to find post-divorce relationships difficult to handle.'

He was about to say, 'And what the hell would you know?' when he remembered what she did for a living: she must have seen plenty of wrecks like him passing through her office.

'Perhaps you need to give yourself more time,' she said.

'Maybe there'll never be enough time,' he said bleakly.

'Do you still love her?'

He swallowed, taken aback by the perceptiveness of her question. 'I didn't think I did, but now . . .' His words trailed away.

'But now you're not so sure?'

Afraid to admit, even to himself, what he might feel, he shrugged his shoulders.

'Have you tried talking to her?'

'There'd be no point. She thinks I hate her as much as she hates me.'

'Hate is such an overused word.'

'Substitute it for despise, then. It all comes down to the same thing.'

'Then prove to her she's wrong.'

He almost laughed. 'That would be fatal. Ali doesn't like to be wrong.'

'Nobody does. It's one of the many uncomfortable truths and challenges we sometimes have to face.'

He sighed. 'I feel as if we've both had enough challenges to last us several lifetimes over.'

She squeezed his arm. 'You don't strike me as a man who would give up easily on anything. Didn't you get help when you suspected your marriage was failing?'

He scooped up a handful of sun-warmed sand and let it trickle slowly through his fingers. 'No,' he murmured, 'it was too complicated for that.' It wasn't much of an explanation, but he wasn't prepared to go into any more detail. How could he expect a relative stranger to understand what he and Ali had gone through? That the hell of Isaac's death had thrust them into what he could only describe as a vortex of self-loathing, which they had systematically projected on to each other, and that the presence of a third party prodding their most raw and tender hurts would have served no helpful purpose.

'What are you like on New Year resolutions?'

He turned and looked at her. 'Sorry?'

She smiled. 'The majority of people don't stick to resolutions made in the heat of a booze-filled moment. It's something to do with loss of memory due to a hangover the next morning, which is why I like to make them when I'm stone-cold sober.' She got to her feet. 'Come on, we need some symbolism.'

He followed her to the water's edge and, in the fading light, he watched her bend down to the sand. She picked up a tiny pearly-pink shell. She handed it to him. 'When you're back at home,' she said, 'put this on the shelf in your bathroom. Then, every time you wash or shave, you'll remember the resolution you made on the beach in Barbados with a woman who, if she were given the opportunity again, wouldn't let you get away so easily.'

He raised a questioning eyebrow. 'And the resolution?'

She tutted. 'Don't play silly buggers with me, Elliot. I'm going to leave you to it while I get the boat ready. We ought to be getting back before the light goes completely.'

With all the hesitancy of a small but hopeful child making a wish, Elliot turned his face towards the vastness of the sea, closed his eyes and promised himself that some time in the coming year – he didn't know how or when – he'd try to tell Ali what she still meant to him.

Chapter Thirteen

It was late March and it was a glorious morning, the air sweet with the scent of a mild spring day. Pale sunlight washed over the rooftops of Astley Hope and cast a tenuous warmth on Sarah's face as she closed the gate of Smithy Cottage behind her. The bitterness of winter had dragged on for too long; it had been unrelentingly cold, wet and windy and it was a heartening thought that they might have seen the back of it. As she set off along the lane, listening to the symphony of birdsong, breathing in the fresh smell of soft damp earth and noticing that the leaf buds in the hawthorn hedge were fatter than when she'd last looked, Sarah was filled with a satisfying sense of well-being. She even slowed her pace to admire the rows of golden yellow daffodils that lined both sides of the road.

Four years ago, the then rector of St Cuthbert's, Christopher Llewellyn, a man of considerable energy, had instigated a campaign called *Plant a Bulb to Light the World* – an initiative that called upon as many villagers who were physically able to get busy with a trowel. It had taken them three backbreaking weekends to work their way through the village planting hundreds of King Alfred bulbs in the verges and hedgerows, but their efforts had paid off: now, the main road through Astley Hope was not only a focal point of achievement for its inhabitants, giving them roughly four weeks of pleasure each year, but it had also featured several times on the front cover of the Easter issue of *Cheshire Life*.

As claims to fame went, it was all Astley Hope was ever going to be known for: excluding the show of daffodils, it was a remarkably uninspiring place to live. There was no real heart to the village; there was no post office or row of dressed-up little shops; no pub decorated with hanging baskets and ye olde reproduction coach lamps; not even a red-brick Victorian-built infant's school, where the sound of happy laughter could be heard from the playground.

All the village could boast was a selection of houses of varying age and architectural styles ranging from pretty white-painted double-fronted Georgian cottages to 1930s bay-windowed semis and, on the site of what had once been the village dairy, there was a medium-sized housing estate that offered a range of countrified starter homes. That was the extent of Astley Hope, so it was hardly surprising that, in the absence of anywhere better for locals to congregate and gossip, St Cuthbert's, and its shambling wooden-built church hall, was the nerve centre for anything newsworthy going on. As Sarah passed the small church and the path that led to the grey pebble-dashed rectory, which she'd always thought dauntingly austere, she wondered what terrible stories were currently doing the rounds regarding their recently departed rector.

Gordon Watkins, who had been saddled with the predecessor who'd been behind the Plant a Bulb campaign, had not yet made his own mark on St Cuthbert's. Or, more precisely, he hadn't been allowed to. The few changes he had wanted to make since coming to the village back in October – such as overhauling the choir and doing away with all the genuflecting – had been met with a wall of disapproval. It didn't help either that he was such a plain-looking man or that, according to Trevor, he was a little wishy-washy on certain points of scripture. Nostalgic references to the physically robust and spiritually dynamic Christopher Llewellyn had frequently been made within Gordon's hearing. Since Christopher's departure from St Cuthbert's, when he had taken with him his splendidly organised and efficient wife and their two perfectly behaved children, he'd all but been canonised and deified by the heartbroken parishioners he'd left behind. He was a man who had served them well, they maintained, with longing smiles, despite letting them down by moving on to pastures new. Seated staunchly in the right wing fold of the Church of England, where there was little room for doubt or uncertainty, his sermons had had a pulling-no-punches style. Telling it radically how it was in an age of political correctness had surprisingly won him many friends and much support, and if his success was to be measured in bums on pews, he was on his way to being a bishop. But Sarah hadn't always been comfortable with his pulpit dogmatism, and while watching his handsome face playing to the crowd as he delivered his sermons, she had wondered quietly how he would fare if he ever had a crisis of faith.

If Astley Hope had lapped up Christopher Llewellyn and greedily asked for more, they had chewed reluctantly at Gordon Watkins, found him not to their taste and had duly spat him out. They hadn't appreciated his unclear views. Surely homosexuality was wrong? Surely women priests were wrong? And as for purporting to be a fan of that dreadful one-time Bishop of Durham, David Jenkins, well, really! Whereas Christopher had managed to accommodate the various camps within St Cuthbert's, Gordon had not. With his liberal views he had displeased both the fundamentalists as well as the old diehards of traditional Anglicanism.

Before coming to Astley Hope, Gordon's previous church had been in a tough, inner-city parish where he'd presumably tackled more things under heaven and earth than Astley's self-righteous, complacent dwellers could ever dream of. And it was probably this that had been his undoing. The poor man had had a nervous breakdown in the middle of January and, from then on, the rectory had stood empty.

As a consequence tales had been reverberating around the village that he'd been drinking himself into a state of depression.

There was talk of a woman.

There was talk of a man.

There was talk of him losing his faith.

But none of this scaremongering was true. He had simply worn himself out in his last parish. Perhaps the powers that be had thought he could recover his spiritual and physical strength by taking it easy in a cushy, well-behaved parish such as Astley Hope. What a shock he must have had when he'd realised what he was up against. The apathy, the disapproval and criticism that had met him on his arrival must have daily chipped away at his exhausted psyche. Perhaps if he had been married, and had had a wife in whom he could have confided, he might have survived. In the circumstances it was a wonder that he had lasted as long as he had. Would any of them have coped any better in his shoes?

But that was the terrible thing: nobody in the village had been inclined to picture themselves in Gordon's shoes and, though Sarah had thought he looked more and more tired each time she saw him, she was ashamed to admit that she had been too preoccupied with her own life to realise what he was going through.

The sad truth was that each and every one of them had failed him.

Perhaps it was something she should mention at Audrey's coffee morning, which was where she was on her way now. Oh, to be brave enough to say, 'Where were we when our rector was all alone and suffering?' If she had real courage, she'd want to add, 'If Gordon had been the hidden face of Christ, then we all failed to carry out the faith by which we claim to live.'

Yes, that would stir them up.

She mentally rebuked herself. She really shouldn't want to sound such a discordant note. This new prayer group that Trevor had formed in January was, in his words, supposed to be a 'melodic and harmonious blend of spiritual communion and togetherness'. A petulant, dissenting voice was not what was needed.

But it was so difficult to be in full accord with what Trevor believed in: he was so inclined to get overexcited about these things. 'In the absence of a rector, there's the danger that our church could run dry of its vital spiritual water,' he'd said, on the day Gordon had left St Cuthbert's to cope with its period of interregnum, 'so what we need is a hands-on working prayer group.' And after the tiny fledgling group had met in its new official capacity in their sitting room at Smithy Cottage, he'd said, 'It's as if it's meant to be. Who's to say where the Holy Spirit is leading us?'

Who indeed?

And while Trevor had talked enthusiastically about the semantics of timing and the potential power the group could generate in the name of the Lord, a faint warning voice in Sarah's head whispered that Trevor was taking advantage of a situation. She suspected that, while the hierarchy of the Church of England went through the laborious process of finding them a new rector, he would steal his own little bit of limelight while he could. Without a permanent steady hand at the helm of St Cuthbert's, Trevor was employing his own – and he was enjoying every second of it.

Though he had never said as much, Sarah knew that it had always irked Trevor that he hadn't been able to play a key role in the running of the parish. The chosen few on the PCC were a body of men and women whom Trevor described as the Sunday Socialites, who viewed the taking of sacraments as an extension to their golf-club membership and expected to be able to run their village church along similar lines – the more exclusive and élite the better. And while Sarah agreed with Trevor that this was wrong, she couldn't entirely go along with his theory that the PCC actively looked down its collective nose at him because he didn't know a birdie from an eagle. She didn't have the heart to tell him that it was the waving of his hands in church that had blackballed him.

But now, in the absence of a substantial figurehead at St Cuthbert's, Trevor was in his element. Having gathered together a group of misfits from the congregation, he had set himself up as their leader and was maddeningly intent on putting a spiritual spin on the everyday and exerting a worrying amount of fundamentalist muscle-power. Initially Sarah had seen the group as a bit of a hobby for Trevor, something to take his mind off losing his daughter to adulthood, but now she was worried about where it was all going and had shared her concerns with Ali.

'I warned you, girl,' Ali had said last week, on the phone, 'I told you at Christmas that Trevor was only one step away from trailing clouds of his own glory. Has he decided on a name for the group, yet? I hope you told him what my suggestion was, the Slipper Gang.'

As appropriate as this name was – as a sign of fellowship respect for their hosts' carpets the members of the group were never without their slippers – Sarah hadn't mentioned it to Trevor. 'He's settled on the Disciples,' Sarah had told Ali.

'How ghastly. And are all disciples equal, with the notable exception of one being more equal than the rest?'

Sarah had now arrived at Woodside House, an unprepossessing thirties semi, the home of Audrey and Maurice Taylor. Audrey greeted Sarah with a plate of shortbread. Sarah's heart sank. She'd clean forgotten that she had offered to bring a cake for Audrey's coffee morning.

'Not to worry,' Audrey said brightly, when Sarah apologised. 'I'm sure I can rustle up something else from my storecupboard.' Sarah didn't doubt it for a minute: Audrey was one of those bracing evangelical types whose talent in the loaves and fishes department was legendary, she would have been able to cater for the Last Supper at a moment's notice. Wartime rationing was held accountable for this singular resourcefulness and she was the only person Sarah knew who still darned socks and stockings, and proudly saved her husband's worn-out Y-fronts to use as dusters.

Audrey led her through to the sitting room, where everyone was already gathered. As the female contingent of the

Disciples, the usual faces were there. Squashed on the sofa was Beryl Wade, sporting her Bobby Crush haircut, with Valerie Thompson and Elaine Stewart on either side of her. Sitting in the draught of an open window, with her shoulders hunched, was Brenda Perry, who wouldn't dream of complaining that she was cold although she was shivering in her short-sleeved blouse with its Peter Pan collar. In the most comfortable chair, the furthest from the open window, was Shirley Makepeace, she of the bad back. Propped up with several cushions, she was dressed in bishop's purple – a colour that couldn't have suited her less.

'Sorry I'm late,' Sarah said, despite knowing that she wasn't and that everybody else had arrived early. They paused in their gossip and acknowledged her presence. Audrey pressed a cup of coffee into her hand and she scanned the room for an empty chair. No such luck. Being last to arrive meant she'd landed the piano stool, which was far too high for her short legs and would ensure a gruelling hour of strained calf muscles as her toes skimmed the surface of Audrey's Scotchgarded carpet.

'We were just talking about Anna,' Beryl said loudly, holding her cup out for more coffee from Audrey as she passed – Beryl was one of those infuriating people who specialised in the art of mispronunciation: she continually got Hannah's name wrong and insisted on emphasising certain words in her own annoyingly unique fashion; she drove a red Per-*jo* and she and Martin went away for weekends in their cara-*van*. 'Shirley was saying that we haven't seen her in church for some weeks. Is she busy studying?'

'Very busy,' Sarah said noncommittally.

'One should never be too busy for the Lord,' said Shirley, her countenance po-faced with piety.

But one could go off him, Sarah wanted to say. Wisely she held her tongue: a comment like that would invite Shirley to pray for her. Oh dear, she thought, I'm beginning to sound as cynical as Hannah. Since Christmas, when Hannah had told

Trevor she didn't want to go to church any more, the tension between them had increased, as had the rows over free will and the dangers of indoctrination, and as usual Sarah had been the one to mediate and play peacemaker. She had persuaded Hannah that an occasional appearance at St Cuthbert's would go a long way to easing the situation, if not for Trevor's sake, or Hannah's, then for Sarah's. Perhaps it was wrong of her to manipulate her daughter's loyalty in such a crude way, but it was the best she could do in keeping the peace. Unfortunately, though, Hannah still needed to rebel and recently she'd been driving Trevor to distraction by threatening to have her nose pierced. 'And while I'm about it, I might have my belly-button done,' she'd said, revelling in the horror on his face. She was also deliberately shocking him in what she wore, and he would visibly pale when she paraded round the house in what she and Emily called their urban-chic look: a skimpy top that might have fitted her better when she was ten years old, together with a pair of combat trousers that hung off her slim hips and flaunted her enviably flat stomach. He had tried to stop her leaving the house when she was dressed like this, but it had been useless. She had met his disapproving gaze and said, 'If you won't let me go out, I won't revise for my exams, and when I've failed them I'll have to go on the dole, and to make my tedious existence worth living I'll become a heroin addict, and to feed my five-hundred-pound a day habit I'll be forced into a life of petty crime and prostitution, and I'll live unhappily ever after in a squat with my drug-crazed pimp. And all because you wouldn't let me go out.' Trevor had never sent Hannah to her bedroom as a punishment, and now, the first time when he wanted to do exactly that, he couldn't for fear of her openly laughing at him. Poor Trevor. He really couldn't cope with the new Hannah.

When her father wasn't around, Hannah dropped her stroppy, belligerent act and behaved quite normally. Sarah had begged her not to treat Trevor so cruelly, but Hannah had said, 'I can't help it, Mum, he makes me do it. He doesn't see that I'm grown-up. He's still treating me as if I was at primary school.'

Sarah had tried reasoning with him, but he wouldn't listen. One day when he'd lost yet another argument with Hannah he'd shouted at Sarah, 'It's all your fault! If you hadn't encouraged her to lie to me, I'd still have some hold over her. You've turned her against her own father.'

Sarah had stared at him, aghast. 'A hold over her?' she'd repeated. 'Is that how you see your relationship with Hannah?'

He'd seen his mistake and tried to bluster his way out of it. 'You know perfectly well I didn't mean it like that. You're – you're twisting my words.'

But that slip of the tongue revealed so much about Trevor. He was trying to control Hannah just as his parents had controlled him. Sarah had never met Trevor's mother and father: they had refused to have anything to do with him after he had told them that he and Sarah were getting married because she was pregnant. As strict old-style Methodists they had been appalled at their son's nefarious behaviour. 'You've let us down,' his father wrote to him. 'You've danced with the devil. Now you must pay for the consequences.' If Sarah had felt sorry for Trevor before, her heart had ached for him after reading that letter. To be so easily discarded was a terrible thing. She had felt so responsible, but had hoped that, in time, his parents' attitude would mellow. It hadn't. They had stuck rigidly to their resolve and had died ten years ago, never having met their only grandchild. From what Trevor had told her of his upbringing, it had sounded remarkably similar to her own, the only difference being that her parents hadn't been religious. He had been an isolated child with no brothers or sisters, and he had learned from a very young age that if he was to please his parents, by doing exactly what they told him to do, he would go up in their estimation. It was the nearest to love he ever came.

Until he met her.

It was his upbringing of which Sarah continually reminded herself when she found him overbearing and unlovable.

Be patient with him, she would tell herself.

Be understanding.

Try to love him unconditionally.

Be the one to make the difference in his life.

He needs you.

But she was fast tiring of being so patient. She wasn't even sure she could go on understanding Trevor. She'd spent nearly twenty years trying to make the difference and it seemed that, so far, it had got her nowhere. She was growing ever more worried that he would exhaust her supply of patience and that, if pushed, years of tolerance might explode in her and she'd end up doing something she would regret. When her mind had first started wandering down this dangerous avenue just a few days ago, she had recalled the childhood game she and Ali used to play. It had been of Ali's grandmother's invention that the two girls should have an *alter ego*: they were called Sarah the Impudent and Ali the Angel. Ali the Angel was supposed to cool her hot-headedness, and Sarah the Impudent was supposed to develop a sense of daring boldness.

Maybe, Sarah now reflected, it was time to resurrect that second self and see if it would help, if only by amusing her and lightening the effect Trevor had on her. It would be an outlet of sorts through which she might be able to channel the rising bubble of discontent within her.

If all this wasn't enough to worry about, Sarah had become convinced that Trevor was turning to the group for the rewards he felt he wasn't getting at home. Without a doubt the Slipper Gang held his thoughts and opinions in higher regard than either she or Hannah did. In fact, if she hadn't known better, she thought a touch of hero-worship was going on. Women of a particular age invariably had a soft spot for a man with strong, unequivocal views, and Shirley's curly-haired head never tired of bobbing up and down in agreement every time Trevor opened his mouth.

Sarah finished her coffee, looked across Audrey's sitting room, and saw Shirley staring straight at her. She probably had been for some time. Oh, Lord, thought Sarah, with a sinking feeling. She's got that I've-been-called-to-pray-for-you expression on her face. 'Anyone heard how Gordon's getting on?' she asked, knowing that it was a distraction that couldn't fail. But nobody knew anything about Gordon's road to recovery and, with a cold, blatant disrespect for his welfare, they went on to discuss the series of visiting preachers that had graced St Cuthbert's since January. They then lapsed predictably into a period of reminiscence for St Christopher Llewellyn. 'Oh, if only we could be lucky enough to have another Christopher,' Elaine said, with a wistful sigh.

'I disagree,' ventured Sarah, who felt that Elaine's sigh of nostalgia had nothing to do with Christopher's pastoral skills and everything to do with menopausal desire. She also felt that if she didn't defend Gordon she would never forgive herself.

'Oh?' said Valerie, from her end of the crowded sofa. 'What do you mean, Sarah?'

'I think we should have somebody just like Gordon again,' Sarah said. Her words provoked a spontaneous lowering of cups into saucers. 'It would be interesting to see if we all repeated the mistake of showing so little concern.'

In the ensuing silence Shirley, with what Sarah thought was a pointed look in her direction, suggested that they finish the morning with a moment of prayer.

Conversing with one's Maker had always been a personal, solitary matter for Sarah. She wasn't any good at this communal let's-throw-it-to-the-crowd form of worship, but as Shirley began to mutter her way through a shopping list of demands on God's time and attention, Sarah dutifully lowered her head. A lock of her thick hair fell in front of her face and, winding it tightly around her finger, she prayed that she could find the courage to extract herself from any more of these ghastly coffee mornings, wishing with hindsight that she had given them up for Lent along with chocolate. Then, struggling with her Christian conscience, she reminded herself that not only was she meant to like these women she was supposed to love them. They mean well, she told herself. Really they do.

Even Shirley.

She squeezed her eyes shut and did her best to think nice thoughts about everybody, but it didn't work, so she let her mind roam the darkening corridors of her faith and thought how the essence of prayer should be about connecting with a better world . . . and a better self. But too often, these days, she found herself on the wrong side of the fence of this better world. It was as if she was there with her face pressed against the chain links waiting for somebody to notice her.

She walked home with a heavy heart, her earlier mood of spring cheerfulness completely gone. Not even the splendour of the Plant-a-Bulb-to-Light-the-World daffodils lifted her weary spirits, and as she neared Smithy Cottage she found herself unwilling to go inside. She decided to pay a call on Astley Hope's newest inhabitant. She had planned several times to visit the lady who, last week, had moved into the tiny bungalow that was the nearest house to theirs, but somehow the time had never been right.

Today it was.

She pushed open the gate and walked up the concrete path, which was cracked in places with shallow-rooted weeds growing in the fissures. The small front garden had recently been tended – the grass had just been mown, judging by the lovely sweet smell, and the flower-beds, though devoid of any colour had been carefully dug over. Sarah could see a long fat worm wriggling about in the rich soil. She reached for the doorbell and hardly had to wait before the glass-paned door was opened. She was expecting an elderly, white-haired woman – a widow, according to the couple who had sold the bungalow to move down to Cornwall – but the sight of a tall man in his late forties, dressed in an O'Neill T-shirt and faded jeans, with dried mud on the knees, made her hesitate. Her expression must have betrayed her confusion for he said, 'You're probably wanting my mother. Hang on a tick and I'll fetch her.'

A few seconds passed, then the woman of Sarah's expectations appeared in the doorway, though she wasn't as elderly as she'd imagined. Sarah explained who she was.

'In that case you must come on in,' said the lady, whose name was Grace – a name that suited her perfectly, Sarah reflected, as she took in the smooth grey hair pushed elegantly back from a face that was only finely lined and brightened by a pair of strong blue eyes, which had not faded with age. 'Callum's just finished doing the garden for me and we were about to have an early lunch. Would you care to join us?'

Sarah hovered awkwardly on the doorstep, held by the clear blue gaze, which was both sure and beguiling. 'I only meant to stop by and say hello. I didn't –'

'It won't be anything fancy, a glass of wine and a bit of bread and cheese, that's all. We thought we'd sit in the conservatory in the sun. It's such a lovely day.'

It sounded heavenly. But still Sarah hesitated.

'Don't overdo it, Mum,' Callum said, from behind his mother. 'Maybe she's got something better to do than have lunch with a couple of strangers.'

'Oh, be quiet, Callum. You'll frighten her away. Please, Sarah, won't you come in? I'd like to get to know the only person in the village who's taken the trouble to call on me.'

Sarah thought of the cold, empty house awaiting her return and of the curtains she was half-way through making. She smiled back at the kind, gentle face before her and, feeling irresistibly drawn to her warm-hearted new neighbour, she gladly stepped over the threshold.

Chapter Fourteen

Sarah was working in the spare bedroom when Hannah arrived home that afternoon from school. It was impossible not to notice the smile on her daughter's face when she came in.

'Good day?' asked Sarah, switching off the sewing-machine and casting aside a swathe of expensive blue and gold Italian brocade.

'Not bad.' Hannah sighed. She went over to the small mirror above the dressing-table where Sarah kept her threads and offcuts. She pushed back her long, dark hair, so obviously inherited from her mother, and studied her face, tilting her head from side to side as if to make a thorough and impartial inspection of herself.

Suppressing the urge to laugh, Sarah said, 'So what's his name?'

Hannah turned and faced her, her cheeks suddenly a charming and delicate shade of pink. 'I don't know what you mean.'

Sarah laughed. 'From what I saw of him I'd say he was quite an attractive proposition.'

'*Mum!* Were you spying on me?'

'Of course I wasn't. I heard voices, glanced out of the window, and saw the pair of you talking at the gate. Who is he?'

Hannah came and sat on the bed. For all her supposed umbrage, Sarah could see that she was itching to talk. She felt glad that her daughter was still prepared to confide in her. 'I met him when I got off the school bus. He was lost and wandering about looking for where his grandmother's just moved to. He was supposed to be meeting his dad there.'

'Is his name Jamie?'

Hannah looked amazed. 'How did you know?'

Sarah smiled. 'Because I'm extraordinarily clever.' She told Hannah where she'd had lunch that day. 'His grandmother and father were very nice. I've offered to make some curtains for Grace. I think we'll being seeing quite a bit of each other.'

Hannah smiled too. 'I'm hoping to see quite a bit of Jamie as well. He's asked me out tonight – he's hoping to borrow his father's car and take me to the Cholmondely Arms. Is that okay?'

Sarah opened her eyes wide. 'You're asking my permission? What's happened to Little-Miss-Bolshy-You're-Doing-My-Head-In?'

'Just trying to keep you sweet.'

'More like you want me to keep your father sweet.'

'You will, though, won't you? I don't want him spoiling this.'

'So what do you want me to tell him?'

Hannah shrugged her shoulders and went back to the mirror to examine her face for spots. 'You could say I'm seeing Emily.'

'I'd sooner tell the truth.'

'But then we'll have the most awful scene. Remember, we're talking about an evening to be spent in the company of a member of the opposite sex. It'll completely freak him out.'

'And, conversely, we'll have the most awful scene if he discovers that we've lied to him again.'

Hannah seemed to consider this. Then, satisfied that no unsightly blemishes were lurking in her perfect complexion, she faced her mother and said, 'You spend your whole life protecting people, Mum. Don't you ever get tired of it?'

Yes, I do, Sarah said to herself, when Hannah had left her alone. I'm extremely tired of it.

*

After tea, and while Hannah was upstairs washing her hair, Sarah told Trevor that Hannah was getting ready to go out on a date. It was a scene they hadn't previously performed, but definitely one that Sarah felt she was as well rehearsed for as she'd ever be. She'd known that it was only a matter of time before this moment came and, of course, in most households this would have been an issue long since dealt with. But until now Hannah's interest in boys had restricted itself to a crude level of critical analysis; never had she shown an inclination towards singling one out for close-up scrutiny. But now she had. And Sarah couldn't help but admire her choice.

'What kind of a date?' Trevor said sharply, lowering his newspaper a couple of inches.

It was such an absurd question that, from nowhere, Sarah was seized with the mercurial and mischievous nature of her *alter ego* Sarah the Impudent who, with a frantically nodding head and a heated, vociferous voice, was urging her to say, 'Oh, you know, the sort we eat at Christmas, darling. Our daughter's going to ride off into the sunset on the back of a marzipan-stuffed one.' She banished Sarah the Impudent to her bedroom – for some uncanny reason she had not aged a dot from her original creation as a teenager. The ever-restrained Sarah wiped a damp cloth over the kitchen table and said, 'She's having an evening out with a young man she met this afternoon. He's the grandson of the woman I had lunch with.' Sarah the Impudent poked her head round her bedroom door and shouted down the stairs, 'And he probably snogs like a dream!' *Homework, young lady!*

'Precisely what do we know about this *young man*?' Trevor uttered the last two words as if he were dangling them between his thumb and forefinger and keeping them at a healthy arm's distance.

'Hardly anything,' admitted Sarah, 'but if he's anything like his father and grandmother I'd say he'll be both gentlemanly and gracious.'

'What if he's nothing like them? Supposing he's—'

'Then I suggest we cross our fingers and hope for the best.'

He gave her one of his how-can-you-be-so-flippant? stares. 'What time is he coming for Hannah?'

Sarah was suspicious. He was taking it much too calmly. Why wasn't he pacing the floor? Why wasn't he muttering about imminent exams and threatening to shackle Hannah to her desk? 'He's not calling here for Hannah,' she said. 'She's meeting him at Grace's.'

'So much for being a gentleman.' A few seconds passed. Then, after discarding the partially read newspaper, he sat back in his chair and folded his arms across his chest; he resembled a well-behaved schoolboy at the front of the class, smug in the knowledge that he alone had all the right answers. 'In that case, I'll walk down there with her and check him out.'

'Trevor, you can't do that.'

'Sarah, just because you seem to have taken leave of your senses and decided to let Hannah make every mistake possible, don't think for one minute that I'm prepared to do the same.'

Up on the landing, Sarah the Impudent had sneaked out of her bedroom again and was champing at the bit to have her say, but her thunder was stolen by Hannah's appearance in the kitchen. Sarah groaned inwardly when she saw what Hannah had elected to wear for her night out with Jamie. Did skirts really come that small? And wouldn't she freeze to death in that tiny little top? And oh, Lord, look at that those long, long legs. Where had they suddenly come from?

'I'll be off, then,' Hannah said, happily, deliberately ignoring her father's fiercely disapproving stare. She casually threw her black Diesel jacket over her shoulder.

'Not so fast,' said Trevor. He got slowly to his feet and stared at her. 'I suggest you put on the rest of your outfit, which you seem to have forgotten in your hurry, and when

124

you've done that I'll escort you down the road and you can make the necessary introductions.'

Hannah backed away from him. She shoved her fists on to her hips and said, 'No way, Dad. No way. No way.'

'The choice is yours. It's that or nothing.' He sounded horribly distant, not at all the loving father he'd always been.

But Hannah was having none of it. She turned her back on him and headed for the hall. Trevor chased after her. 'You'll do as you're told,' he said, 'or I'll –'

She whirled round on him, her carefully made-up eyes flashing furiously. 'Or you'll what?' she challenged.

Sarah felt scared: scared for Hannah, in case Trevor hit her; scared for Trevor, because if he did raise a hand to his daughter he'd never forgive himself; and scared for herself, because goodness knows what blame would be in store for her.

For that split second while nobody said anything, Hannah opened the front door and slipped outside. Watching her retreating figure, Trevor stood inert and superfluous, as the cold evening air swept into the house like a malevolent spirit.

'You have to let her go,' Sarah said softly, as she closed the door. 'She's an adult now. You have to start treating her as one.'

He turned his head and levelled his bewildered gaze on her. For a moment Sarah thought he was going to admit that she was right. She reached out a gentle, conciliatory hand and rested it on his arm. But his whole body stiffened and he jerked away from her.

'I don't have time for this,' he snapped, 'I need to pray before the group arrives.'

The Slipper Gang was as punctual as ever and arrived together. Sarah didn't know how they did it. Did they ring round and co-ordinate their watches? 'Rendezvous will take place at twenty hundred hours. The time now is nineteen forty-three . . .'

'No, I think you'll find it's nineteen forty-five . . .'

'Sorry but according to my trusty timepiece, which is never wrong, it's exactly nineteen forty-six and thirty seconds.'

'Oh dear, the twenty-four-hour clock always confuses me, what time is it, really?'

Sarah could imagine them twitching for hours over their watches. If there was one aspect of the group that amused her it was its ability to sidetrack itself, which was probably why they were so happy for Trevor to be in charge. They needed somebody to boss them about. 'Leadership is a vital element in evangelism,' Maurice Taylor had said several weeks ago. And there was no doubting Trevor's willingness and commitment to taking command of the 'Lord's soldiers' as he sometimes called them.

As the group filtered through from the hall, outdoor shoes now exchanged for slippers, Sarah glanced at Trevor as he steered them towards their seats. He seemed impatient to get things moving. She wondered how on earth he'd managed to calm himself down after the brief but upsetting altercation with Hannah.

The power of prayer, she told herself wryly.

'Right, then,' he said loudly, when everybody was finally in place but was still intent on wasting vital minutes in chatter. He clapped his hands for good measure.

'Goodness, Trevor,' exclaimed a startled Audrey, 'you quite made me jump.'

Murmurs of agreement were voiced and quickly gave rise to a Mexican-wave of rerouted banter until Trevor held up his hands in a gesture of 'Enough'. 'Five minutes of quiet time,' he announced, 'to get us in the right frame of mind.'

It sounded as if he were putting them under starter's orders. A few seconds of shuffling and clearing of throats followed, then at last eyes were closed and minds supposedly cleared of all unnecessary trivia. Sarah's quiet times usually followed the same unnerving pattern: she'd start off confidently enough, strolling effortlessly through the sunny, buttercupped meadows of her thoughts, but very soon she'd find herself stumbling into the nettles and brambles of her criticism of Trevor and the group. She would spend the rest of the time allocated to meaningful contemplation guiltily dodging God and his thought police.

To help them clear their minds, they were meant to focus on a pertinent image and exclude all other thoughts. Sarah's image, when she bothered to use it, was Holman Hunt's famous painting *The Light of the World*. Its track record was quite good for emptying her head of its hotch-potch of confusion, but this evening, as she tried to focus on its composition, it felt worryingly as if the candle in the lantern Christ carried had been snuffed out. The details of the picture, which were normally so clear and luminous, were now dark and fuzzy. She squeezed her eyes as though to accustom herself to the shadowy darkness of the painting. But the harder she tried to focus on Hunt's figure of Christ, the more it slipped away from her until eventually it was gone.

She flicked open her eyes and checked the room to see if anybody else was having trouble concentrating. On her left Audrey and Maurice were both fully absorbed in whatever it was they had zeroed in on. Maurice's recycled Y-fronts came to Sarah's mind and she quickly moved her gaze to Trevor, who could have been in a coma he was so still and lost in thought. To his left was Martin Wade, whipcord thin and shifting uncomfortably in his seat – he was a rather silly man who believed that anything enjoyable was a sin and of the devil, which was why he'd opted for the puritanically hard kitchen chair. His wife Beryl was more comfortably posi- tioned, and not just because she professed to have God in her pocket, but because she was on the sofa with Elaine and Tom. And if Sarah was any judge of the angle of that slumped and slightly balding head, Tom was well on his way to dozing nicely. To Tom's left, and seated in a generously cushioned armchair, was Shirley; she was adopting her habitual eyes-closed-palms-up-for-Jesus posture. The recently resurrected Sarah the Impudent whispered in Sarah's ear, 'Hey, wouldn't it be a laugh to drop something cold and slimy into those expectant hands?' *Behave!* And sitting in front of the window were Valerie and her husband Stan. They were wearing a matching pair of whimsical puppy-dog slippers, whose canine heads were bowed, just like their owners', in a perfect composition of his-and-hers unity. And lastly, the newest and youngest – and, in Sarah's opinion, the nicest members of the group – Brenda and Dave Perry with their zip-up Bibles, which were as new and unsullied as their faith. Sarah thought they brought a much-needed breath of fresh air to the proceedings – and more often than not they grasped the wrong end of the stick. Without meaning to, they invariably punctured Trevor's pedantic, inflated views.

Sarah was about to close her eyes and see if *The Light of the World* had resumed normal service, when she noticed Brenda check her watch, then pass a Polo mint to Dave. She smiled to herself, heartened to know that she wasn't the only one struggling to concentrate.

Eventually, Trevor decided that the meter on their quiet time had run into the red, cleared his throat and began to rustle the pages of his notepad. Everyone, except Tom, looked up. Elaine gave her husband a surreptitious nudge in the ribs. 'I'm afraid I'm changing tonight's topic,' said Trevor.

Disappointed, Sarah wondered what he was up to. She'd been looking forward to discussing Gideon, that wonderful Old Testament example of a hero of faith who repeatedly dithered between relying on God's power and his own.

Trevor got to his feet and started handing round pencils and bits of A4 paper. 'We're going to play a little game,' he said. 'I want you to write your name at the top of this paper, then pass it on to your neighbour –'

'Would that be to the right or to the left, Trevor?'

'To the right, Dave.'

'So I give my piece of paper to Brenda?'

'Exactly. Now, as I was saying –'

'And Brenda gives hers to Stan?'

'Yes.'

Brenda giggled. 'It sounds like a game of consequences, doesn't it? Is there a prize?'

Trevor tugged at his beard. 'The prize is enlightenment, Brenda,' he said sternly. 'Right, then, have you all done that? Good. Now, I want you to write underneath that name and, using just the one word, describe that person.' He flashed a look in Dave's direction. 'Is that clear?'

'Clear as daylight, Trevor. You want me to think of a word that best describes Brenda.'

'No! The piece of paper you now have in your hand has Sarah's name on it, doesn't it? It's her you have to describe.'

Dave looked apologetically at Sarah. 'Whoops,' he said. 'I was about to say that you were cuddly. Not that you're not, of course, but that's for Trevor to say, isn't it, not me?'

'Please,' said an exasperated Trevor, 'can we get on? When you've done that, fold the paper so that only the name shows at the top, then pass it on and repeat the exercise until we each end up with our own piece of paper returned to us. And if everybody has done what they should have done,' he flashed another look at the Perry camp, 'we should each have a list of thirteen words that should help us to understand our own personality that little bit better. And I should point out that this only has any merit if we're all honest towards our brothers and sisters in Christ. It also helps not to read what the previous person has written.'

The game got under way.

'Resourceful' wrote Sarah for Audrey. 'Coward,' whispered Sarah the Impudent, '"Show off" is much nearer the mark. That whole Mrs Beeton act is her way of grabbing herself a slice of acclamation pie.'

For Maurice she put down 'Uninhibited'. Glory! She was thinking of those wretched underpants again.

Then it was Trevor's name on her lap. Sarah the Impudent

was hurriedly bustled upstairs to her room before she had a chance to open her mouth. *And stay there this time!* Sarah tapped her pencil against her teeth and wondered what to write. She caught Trevor giving her an odd look and was panicked into writing the first risk-free word that came into her head: 'single-minded'. She hoped that hyphenated words were allowed.

So it went on. The only other person she had trouble with was Shirley.

'Misguided.'

'Deluded.'

'Weird.'

They were all possibilities.

'*Crackpot!*' yelled a voice from upstairs.

'Intense' seemed a safer bet.

'There, now,' Trevor said, when they were at last in possession of their original piece of paper. 'Read through the comments and ask for God's guidance if there's anything that particularly challenges you.'

Sarah read through her list starting from the top so that she could work out who had said what about her. Audrey's neat economical handwriting said that she was 'Thoughtful'. Well, that was fair enough. Maurice had put down 'Pensive'. Okay, so there was a theme developing here. She then read what Trevor had written.

But Trevor had cheated and had used three words to describe her: 'Disobedient lost sheep'.

She stared stricken, her mind numb with shock. Then she wanted to laugh out loud, but she knew she mustn't. A horrible realisation dawned: this whole exercise had been nothing but a cowardly and not-so-subtle way of telling her exactly what he thought of her behaviour of late. He must have been notching up all the times she had backed Hannah and not him; now he obviously meant to do something about it.

She folded the piece of paper over and over wondering how

many people had seen what he'd written. She looked across the room and caught Shirley and Trevor exchanging a furtive but knowing glance. And knew that he must have confided in her at some time. 'She's going off the altar rails, Shirley,' she imagined him saying. 'Whatever shall I do with her?' 'Pray, Trevor,' she would have advised. 'Get down on your knees and pray.'

And, oh, my God, thought Sarah, that's exactly what the dreadful woman's planning on doing right now. Bad back or not, Shirley was hauling herself out of her armchair and making her way towards Sarah.

Chapter Fifteen

It was Ali's turn to make the coffee. She took Margaret's Save the Rainforest mug through to the outer office. Margaret enjoyed a reputation for believing that she was the only one who knew what was what, and to a degree it was true. She wasn't only Ali and Daniel's secretary and receptionist, she was also their link to the lurid goings-on in the rest of the building; life would be dull without her. Renting their office space from a trio of whiz-kids, who ran an impressive financial investment outfit and employed a rapidly expanding workforce, had provided Ali and Daniel with continuous soap-opera drama. It was difficult at times to keep abreast of all the dating, hating and slating that went on. But Margaret did her best to keep them informed.

She was on the phone making short work of a delivery company who for the second time in as many weeks had failed to meet its contractual promises. Glad that it wasn't a client on the receiving end of such a vitriolic barrage of abuse, Ali left Margaret's coffee for her and went back to the main office, where she found Daniel with his feet up on his desk studying a set of overhead transparencies – their visual-cum-sexual aids as he referred to them. She gave him his National Trust 'His Lordship' mug.

'What? No biscuits?' he asked.

'Sorry, I ate the last one while I was waiting for the kettle to boil. I didn't want you and Margaret fighting over it.'

'There'd have been no contest. I'd have gladly given it to her. A guy should always know when to do the honourable thing.'

Ali laughed. 'You're nothing but a big girl's blouse.'

'Nonsense. There's something very unseemly about a man and a woman tussling over the last Hob-Nob.'

'Especially when she'd make mincemeat of you.'

'There is that, I'll grant you. Now to business. Our sexual aids are looking a tad jaded. They're losing their integrity. I think we should either tart them up or start again. Any thoughts?'

Ali perched on the corner of his desk and flicked her eyes over the transparencies. 'For now, let's go for the tarting routine.'

At this stage of the year it was their relatively quiet stretch. The tax returns were all done and dusted, and while they were doing some of the straightforward planning work on their clients' files, they took advantage of the lull to promote themselves. They did this by giving a series of presentations, usually to other accountants who felt the need to brush up on expat tax issues. Ali had never intended to specialise in this area, but as a senior manager in Manchester she had been offered the chance to run a new department that was to concentrate entirely on expatriate work. An extra incentive had been thrown in: if she could really make something of the department there was every chance that soon she would join the partnership track. She had leaped at the opportunity, but as the months turned into years and she was no nearer a partnership, she realised that she'd been conned. The incentive had been nothing more than an old trick employed by the senior partners to get the most out of the lower orders, especially women, who were so keen to please and further their careers. By exploiting her ambition and keeping her nose firmly against the grindstone, and claiming at each assessment stage that the time wasn't yet right to promote her, they had got exactly what they wanted from her: an impressively turned-round department that could knock spots off most others and all without any extra effort on their part. She really shouldn't have been so surprised by their deviousness.

It was widely known that this was how every male-dominated industry worked. But it still irritated her that she'd been so gullible.

On the other hand, the experience had taught her everything there was to know about expat tax and the law, and it was currently standing her in good stead for their series of forthcoming presentations. This morning they were preparing a talk for the personnel department of a large electronics company which was increasing its number of overseas secondments.

For the next couple of hours she and Daniel worked on rejigging the transparencies with the latest updated information from the Inland Revenue. 'Right, then,' said Daniel, when they were satisfied. 'How about we run through the spiel?'

Ali hated this bit. She wasn't a natural performer in the way Daniel was: she was conscious that whenever she was in front of an audience she sounded stilted and slightly aggressive, and if she allowed her nerves to get the better of her, her voice reached notes a boy treble would have been proud of. Often Daniel would signal to her to slow down and take a deep calming breath under the guise of drinking from the glass of water he made her have beside her notes.

'Do we have to?' she asked, knowing the answer Daniel would give.

He treated her to one of his headmasterly stares over the top of his glasses. 'Babe,' he said, 'you know it makes sense. It's like safe sex. Preparation is all.'

'Well, you go first, then. You need more practice than me.'

'And what colour is the sun in your world?'

'Oh, get on with it, or I'll tell Margaret that it was you who ate the last of the Hob-Nobs.'

'Bitch!'

Daniel gave an effortless performance. He was laid back, he was eloquent, he was to the point, he was funny. He was everything Ali would never be when it came to stand-up delivery.

'Damn you, Dan Divine. Why do you have to be so good?'

'To make you look terrible. Now come on. Up on your feet. Remember, body language is all.'

'I thought you said preparation was all.'

'That too. Now, for heaven's sake, don't stand like that. You resemble a woman who hasn't had a bowel movement for a fortnight. Relax, shoulders back, and give it some of the old Ali sex appeal.'

'Oh, please. Now you're being silly.'

'No, I'm not. Trust me. Sit on the corner of your desk and give me those foxy come-hither eyes.'

'I'd rather eat my own spleen.'

'And if you don't do as I say I'll personally remove it for you. Think sexy, Ali. Be provocative.'

'I can't!' she cried. 'I've forgotten how. I'm all tense.'

He threw his hands in the air. 'Honestly, the things I have to do in the name of work.' Removing his glasses, he crossed the room, grabbed Ali by the shoulders and pushed her down on to the desk. His movements were so quick and deft that she didn't have time to resist. He stared seductively into her eyes, trailed a finger over her lips and said, in his best theatrically camp voice, 'Kiss me, Hardy.'

Her body disintegrated with laughter beneath his and she tried to wriggle away from him. 'No,' he said, pinning her arms either side of her, 'you're not going anywhere until you've snogged me.'

'But you're gay, Daniel!'

He grinned wickedly. 'Then prove to me I'm not.'

As his mouth hovered over hers and their lips made contact, she decided to call his bluff and kissed him long and lingeringly. She expected him to back off, but he didn't and, to her consternation, her heart began to pound faster than it should have. Shocked, she clamped her mouth shut and turned her head. Daniel stared into her eyes and said, in a low voice, 'Darling, I don't know how to break this to you, but it's not working. I'm still gay.'

She laughed and pushed him away. 'God, you're awful – and what's more, I'm going to tell Richard what a terrible little strumpet you are.'

He struck his forehead with his hand. 'Oh, please, anything but that!'

'You're completely mad, Daniel, completely off piste. I don't know why I have anything to do with an old slapper like you.'

'It's because you love me to bits.'

'True.'

'And because I've just successfully managed to relax you.'

'Truer still.'

'Good. So get back to perching on the desk and being provocative.'

She did as he said, struck an over-the-top wanton-woman pose, hitching up her skirt and pouting. 'How am I doing, big boy?'

'Perhaps this isn't the most convenient time to call,' said a voice at the door.

It was Elliot.

Ali sprang off the desk, scattering files, pens, pencils and paperclips. Of all the people to catch her in such a mortifying position it had to be Elliot, didn't it? And just what the hell was he doing here?

After a few polite exchanges, including an explanation for what Ali had been doing – as implausible as it sounded – Daniel made himself scarce under the pretext of needing something from the printer room.

When they were alone, Ali said, 'You're looking well, Elliot.' Even though it was several months since Christmas, she could see that his week in the sun still showed: he looked fit and vaguely bronzed.

'So are you.'

'Well, then,' she said, moving away from him and tidying the mess on her desk, 'we must have nearly exhausted our supply of pleasantries. What can I do for you? Not so short on clients that you've come here to poach some of mine, have you?'

Elliot willed himself not to react to Ali's brusque offhand manner. It's habit, he told himself. Habit that she can't be nice to you. He swallowed hard and threw himself off the cliff edge. 'I wondered whether you'd have lunch with me.'

She stopped what she was doing. 'Lunch?'

'Yes. Lunch.'

'You mean, *lunch*?'

'I mean something to eat in the middle part of the day.'

She narrowed her eyes. 'When were you thinking?'

He looked at his watch. 'How about now?'

They walked the short distance to the restaurant where Ali and Sam had eaten the week before Christmas. Then the weather had been bitingly cold and the sky grey. Today it was clear and blue, and the sun was shining. A few hardy souls were pretending it was warmer than it really was and were wearing T-shirts; one young girl, sitting next to a litter bin in the square and eating from a bag of chips, was bravely displaying a pair of winter white legs.

'I've never been here before,' Elliot said, as he held open the restaurant door for Ali. 'Is the food any good?'

'Of course it is, or why else would I bother with it?'

Her words were as good as a slap in the face and he wondered why he was bothering. But then he heard her say, 'I'm sorry. That was uncalled-for.' It was a minuscule scrap of hope and perhaps all he was entitled to.

Ali watched Elliot hang up their coats on the row of hooks and waited for somebody to come and show them to a table. She was terrifyingly on edge and couldn't believe that she had actually agreed to have lunch with him. She could so easily have said no, she was too busy. Any amount of excuses would have done, but she'd stood there as though she were an idiot, nodding and saying that it would have to be quick.

They were shown to a discreet corner table, and when they were sitting opposite one another, in a familiar awkward silence, Ali felt her nerve going. 'This isn't going to work,' she said. 'Couldn't we just have a drink and leave it at that?'

'Please,' he said, 'for once, let's try and have a normal conversation.'

'But why?'

'Can we order first, then talk?'

'Sure.' Typical Elliot, she thought, further rattled by his calm detachment. How typical of him to be so systematic, so prioritised. She turned her head to her right and scanned the chalkboard menu. She quickly made her choice and switched her thoughts to why he had taken the time and trouble to turn up at her office in the way he had. Why hadn't he phoned? Probably because he knew she would have been better able to fob him off. He would have planned it precisely this way. He'd have wanted to catch her with her guard down, hoping to render her sufficiently witless to be unable to put him off.

But why had he gone to all that effort?

They ordered their meal and when they were alone again Elliot was sensitive to Ali's quick brown eyes darting nervously over him, around him – anywhere, in fact, but actually *on* him. He longed to put her at ease. He made his opening move. 'Ali, I want to apologise.'

With all the hesitancy of a butterfly landing on a flower, her gaze finally came to a quivering rest. She stared at him over the top of her glass of fizzy water. 'Really? What for?' She sounded remote. Hostile.

Good question. Where should he start? There was so much to be sorry for – they'd be here all day if he had to apologise for every wrong thing he'd done. Pinpointing the trivial seemed as good a way as any. 'I'm sorry I didn't make a better job of inviting you to spend Christmas with Dad and me.'

She shrugged. 'Given the circumstances, I thought you did pretty well. How was Barbados? Did Sam enjoy himself?'

There was a glimpse of one of Elliot's rare smiles. But it faded so fast she wondered if she'd imagined it. 'He had a great time. Even fitted in a little romance.'

'Good for him. How about you? Not that it's any of my business.'

'I was my usual boring self, head in a book mostly. How was your Christmas? Dad told me you were going to Sarah's.'

'That's right.' She picked up a roll of bread from the basket in the centre of the table and pulled it apart with her hands. She chewed on a small piece thoughtfully. If she were honest, Christmas at Coal Scuttle Cottage had been unutterably depressing, but loyalty to Sarah would never allow her to admit that.

Their food arrived, and when the waiter left them, Elliot was acutely aware that the conversation had stalled. He seized on a topic that was guaranteed to get Ali talking. 'How did you get on with Trevor when you stayed with them?'

Ali grimaced. 'As badly as ever. The man's become even more of an insufferable fool, if that's possible.'

'And how was Hannah?'

'Growing up fast. She's quite the young lady now. All set for Oxford if her exams go as planned. Brasenose has given her an offer of –' she broke off suddenly and stared blankly at her plate.

'What is it?' he asked. 'Something wrong with your meal?'

She dropped her knife and fork and reached for her napkin. She screwed it into a tight ball. 'It's no good,' she murmured, 'I can't do this. I can't sit here indulging in this mindless small-talk.'

'I don't understand.' It was the wrong thing to say.

'You wouldn't,' she said, with scathing bitterness. 'You wouldn't understand how difficult it is for me to be here.'

'You think it's any easier for me?'

She looked up at him, her eyes flashing angrily. Accusingly. 'It was you who wanted this.'

Another slap in the face.

He let out his breath. Would they ever get beyond this? 'Please, Ali, I don't want to fight with you.'

'So what do you want?'

He stared at her reflectively. I want to tell you that . . . that I still love you. I want you to know that I wish we were still married, that I regret all the pain I've caused you. But he didn't say any of this. He couldn't risk that much honesty. It was too soon. There was still too much he didn't understand himself. He said, 'I want us to prove to ourselves, just once, that we can act as normal human beings having a quiet meal together.'

She frowned, unconvinced, but then very slowly, and in a rare act of acquiescence, she picked up her knife and fork.

He sighed inwardly, knowing that he'd come within an inch of being flayed alive by her anger. He'd known from that instant on the beach in Barbados with Rosalind, when he'd been made to confront what he still felt for Ali, that it wasn't going to be easy to talk to her. But this morning while he'd been shaving, and after weeks of ignoring the little pink shell he'd placed on his bathroom shelf, just as Rosalind had suggested, he had decided that today he would do something about his resolution. It had to be a spur-of-the-moment thing, he'd concluded. He would simply appear in Ali's office without warning, offer to take her out for lunch and get her to talk. It would be a start.

What he hadn't bargained on was surprising Ali to the extent that he had: the timing and manner of his appearance had seriously unnerved her, which hadn't been his intention. When he'd climbed the stairs to Ali and Daniel's office there had been no one in the small reception area, so he had decided to announce himself. On the verge of knocking at their door he'd found it slightly ajar and, for a few extraordinary seconds, he'd been treated to the sight of Ali lying temptingly across her desk. He wished now that he had the courage to tell her how fantastically desirable she'd looked.

He risked a glance at her across the table, taking in the softly layered hair, the dark eyes, the small, elegant hands and the close-fitting silvery-grey jacket that matched her short skirt, which just over an hour ago had revealed the full length of her lovely legs. At the memory of her on that desk again, he lowered his gaze lest she could read his thoughts from the expression on his face.

Up until Christmas he'd had no idea how he really felt about Ali. When Isaac had died, he had thought that every other emotion within him had also died. It had been a time of paradox: when he'd most needed the warmth of another human being, he'd made it impossible for anyone to be near him. He had wanted to be isolated. He'd wanted to feel the pain of it. To be comforted was out of the question. He didn't deserve it. And he'd gone to such lengths to punish himself, even denying himself the love of his wife.

It wasn't until he'd been lying on the beach with Rosalind and he had imagined that it was Ali in his arms that he had realised how his feelings towards Ali had changed. Instead of wanting to push away her memory, he wanted to draw it closer to him. More than anything, he wanted her back in his life. That night in the hotel in Barbados, as he'd listened to the water lapping at the sand a few yards from his room, he'd pondered on the irony that the only woman he had ever truly desired was the one who cared least for him . . . and that it was of his own doing. Nobody but he had made Ali hate him. The following day when he'd said goodbye to Rosalind as she was leaving for the airport with her mother, she'd said, 'Don't go back on your resolution, Elliot. If Ali means as much to you as I think she does, be patient with her. But, most of all, be patient with yourself.'

But it hadn't been patience that had made him wait nearly

a full three months before getting in touch with Ali: it had been fear. Fear that she'd reject out of hand even the remotest possibility of there ever being some kind of friendship between them.

Determined to banish this fear, he said, 'This hasn't been so bad, has it?' He waited for her reply, searching her face for an honest, unguarded response. But her countenance remained impassive. Her eyes were distant and gave nothing away. She didn't say anything either.

'Do you think you'd risk it again?' he pushed.

'Would there be any point?' Her tone was less acerbic than it had been. Now there was a ring of finality to it.

'There might be.'

'Elliot, I think we can both be satisfied that we've made it through to the end of a meal with a full complement of limbs intact. Sam would be proud of us. But you have to realise that when I'm with you all the pain of Isaac's death comes flooding back . . . and I'm sorry, but it's too much for me to cope with. Can you understand that?'

He nodded sadly. Oh, yes, he could understand that all right. But could she understand that he'd felt exactly the same until now? Now when he looked at her, or thought of her, the worst of the pain of Isaac's death was miraculously kept at bay and, for a few precious seconds, the darkness that he had lived through showed signs of lifting.

Chapter Sixteen

Ali was a firm believer that, like shoes, houses gave away a lot about their owners and, as she lay back in the enormous, enamel clawfooted bath that took for ever to fill, she thanked Owen for his impeccable taste and for stamping it so effectively on this one particular room. The exquisite décor and characterful fittings spoke volumes of a man who clearly enjoyed dallying over his ablutions, for this was no ordinary bathroom. Owen must have had it tailor-made to suit his own special needs, which presumably extended beyond the perfunctory routine of washing and shaving.

The tiles that covered the sloping walls were predominantly white but were interspersed with a random pattern of blue and white Delft tiles – genuine handmade Delft tiles that Owen himself had chosen when he'd visited the factory on one of his working trips to Holland. Opposite the bath there was a tub-sized marble sink, above which hung a brightly lit gilt-framed mirror with an unruly bunch of chubby cherubs tumbling all over it. Either side of this was a pair of brass sconces, which were wildly and ostentatiously Gothic in their design; the floor was made of polished cherrywood and glowed with the richness of warm honey. At the head-resting end of the bath, within arm's reach, was a low-level built-in cupboard: instead of it being a discreet hidey-hole for the obligatory loo rolls and toilet brush, as one might have expected, it was a drinks cabinet. And when Owen's selection of wines and spirits had been shipped over to Brussels along with the rest of his belongings, Ali had moved in her own supply. She fancied a drink now, and leaning over the rolled edge of the cold enamel, she opened the panelled door of the cupboard and poured herself a large glass of Jack Daniel's. Then she reached for the remote control of the CD player in her adjoining bedroom and activated Bach's *Goldberg Variations*. From the two speakers on the bracketed shelf above the bath, the restrained, smoothly flowing music washed over her. She closed her eyes and began to relax.

It had been quite a day.

She cast her mind back to the morning when Daniel had kissed her.

Or was it she who had kissed him?

Well, whatever. It wasn't that they'd kissed that concerned her, it was her reaction to it. Not since before Isaac's death had she experienced that kind of physical contact and it had awakened in her something she thought she had lost.

Desire.

She knew that she wasn't sexually attracted to Daniel, or he to her. What had taken place was just a silly case of larking around, but there was no getting away from it: the feel of his lips on hers had sparked off arousal in her. She hoped he hadn't realised that and misinterpreted it. It would ruin their relationship if he thought she was lusting after him. But at least she had proved to herself that, if the right man ever came along, she needn't be frightened of not feeling anything for him. This was not something that preyed on her mind, but there had been occasions when she'd doubted she would ever feel for a man as she once had. The combination of bereavement and Elliot's rejection had knocked on the head the very thought of a sex drive. Add to that the fact that she spent the majority of her time on the edge of exhaustion – deliberately so – it was only natural that she didn't squander her energy reserves on anything as superfluous as a sexual encounter.

But now . . . well, now sex might not be such a bad idea, just in the way of recreational therapy, of course.

She took a sip of her drink and sighed. Who was she

kidding? Who, this side of full-moon, wolf-howling insanity, would ever want to get entangled with an emotional wreck such as her? No. It would be a whole lot simpler if she could remain uninterested in sex; it would be far easier to be frigidly dispassionate than trying to keep the lid on a revitalised jack-in-a-box libido that would probably spring out at the most inopportune moments.

She smiled at this analogy, set down her glass on the side of the bath and reached for the phone on top of the drinks cabinet. When she had got in from work there had been a message on the answerphone. It had been from Sarah and it had worried her: her friend hadn't sounded at all as she usually did.

It was a while before she heard Sarah's voice at the other end of the line. Her suspicion that something was wrong was confirmed straight away.

'Ali,' said Sarah quietly, 'I need to come and see you.'

'Why? What's wrong?'

'I don't want to talk about it now. Can we meet for lunch?'

'Oh, Sarah, I'd love to, but it's crazy this week at work. Daniel and I are giving –'

'What about Saturday?'

'Yes, that's fine. But what's the urgency?'

'I just need someone to talk to.'

'Has something happened?'

'You could say that.'

Ali had never heard her friend so tense on the phone before. Sarah's voice was always gentle and warm, never terse and tight as it was now. 'Sarah, I know from the sound of you that it must be something serious. Can't you tell me?'

'No. Just let me come and see you.'

'Okay. But why don't you stop over? Let's make a weekend of it. We so rarely get any time to ourselves these days. Leave Hannah in charge of Trevor and stay the night. We'll get a takeaway and have a bottle of –'

'All right, I'll see what Trevor –'

'Never mind what he says, just do it.'

'Ali, please don't tell me what to do. I get enough of that from Trevor. Now, goodnight, I'll see you on Saturday, about three.'

When Sarah had rung off, Ali slipped back into the hot, fragrant water and reached for her drink. She felt curiously hurt by what Sarah had said. *Please don't tell me what to do.* It wasn't so much the words that stung her, it was the way they'd been said. Sarah, so mild-mannered – so reliably mild-mannered – had never spoken so harshly to her. What the hell was going on? Or, more to the point, what the hell had Trevor been up to?

One way or another, the day was getting stranger and stranger.

She still hadn't recovered from the shock of Elliot appearing so unexpectedly in her office. She had wanted to discuss this with Sarah and, while acknowledging how selfish she was being, she felt disappointed that she hadn't been able to offload her thoughts on to her friend.

When she had said goodbye to Elliot, she'd rushed back to the office hoping to catch Daniel before he left for his afternoon appointment with a new client – who was, of all things, a romantic novelist. Trust Daniel to acquire such a kitsch client! But she'd been too late, he'd already gone, and she'd spent the rest of the day trying to rehearse for their series of talks. She hadn't done very well, though: her thoughts had inevitably strayed from the latest changes in taxation law to Elliot. She cringed now as she recalled his face when he had seen her sprawled across her desk. Well, thank God he hadn't arrived any earlier and copped the sight of Daniel on top of her.

She shuddered and groaned out loud. Then the phone rang. It made her jump and she slopped Jack Daniel's down her neck and chest.

'Yes,' she snapped bad-temperedly into the receiver.

'I'm sorry, I must have misdialled.'

'Daniel, is that you?'

'It's me, but is it *you*, Babe?'

'Of course it's me.'

'Then why the harridan act?'

'You made me spill my drink.'

'Does that mean you should be rushing about putting clothes into cold water?'

'There's no need, I'm in the bath. What do you want?'

'All the details about your lunch with Elliot.'

'Oh, that,' she said airily, her tone suggesting that she'd all but forgotten the episode. And just to be deliberately and annoyingly obstructive she asked, 'How did you get on with Jessica Lloyd? Was she a vision in pink with a couple of fluffy pooches under each arm?'

'I shall tell her you said that. She was extremely nice. She reminded me of you, razor sharp and very much to the point.'

'And, like me, did she see right through your fatal charm?'

'Oh, to the bone I should think. She has great taste in men, by the way.'

'I know what a babe magnet you are, Dan Divine, but are you saying she tried to hit on you?'

He laughed. 'I'm saying she's got a class act of a husband. Photographs of him all over her study, including one of him –'

'Yes, all right, all right, I'm getting the message loud and clear that you thought he was a regular sex god. Don't you think of anything else?'

'Ooh-er, touchy, Madam!'

'I'm not being touchy.'

'Yes, you are. You're not cross because I kissed you this morning, are you?'

Ali gulped back the last of her drink. 'Um . . . well, seeing as you've brought that up, there is something I wanted to mention in connection with –'

'Aha, you want an appraisal, do you? Well, your technique is perhaps a little rusty – you didn't quite get all the raspberry pips out of my back teeth – but on the whole, and given the dynamics of the situation, it wasn't a bad kiss. Not bad at all.'

'Daniel, you arrogant pig, stop making fun of me.'

'*Moi?*'

'Yes, you. Now, be quiet and let me speak.'

'I ought to warn you, one word of criticism about my technique and I'll never talk to you again.'

'And what a mercy that would be!'

'Are you pre-menstrual?'

'No, I'm not!'

'Then you're probably ovulating. It must be that that's making you overheat.'

'Daniel.'

'Yes?'

'Shut up. Just shut up long enough for me to say that because we kissed . . . you know, in the way that we did . . . well, it doesn't mean that I fancy you. I wouldn't want you to think that –'

'Ali, please, stop, you're embarrassing me.'

'I'm embarrassing myself.'

'Then quit while you're ahead. I knew precisely what was going through that pretty little head of yours when I had you pinned to the desk.'

'You did?'

'Yeah, you were thinking, Great kisser, shame it's not the right bloke.'

'Mm . . . not exactly. But it'll do, you're close enough.'

There was a pause.

'Are you going to tell me about lunch with Elliot now?' asked Daniel. 'Seeing as you've led me all round the houses, down the garden path and on to the motorway of diversion in the hope that I would forget why I'd phoned you.'

Ali gave him the details. 'It was horrible,' she said. 'It was so unreal. He was trying to make me chat as if it was quite normal for us to be having lunch together. He even suggested that we do it again.'

'What did you say?'

'I told him no, that it would be too painful. Oh, Daniel, I don't want all that shallow let's-be-friends stuff, I need to try and get on with my life as if Elliot and Isaac had never been in it.'

'But, Babe, you can't pretend that you weren't married to Elliot, and you certainly can't pretend that you didn't have the most gorgeous son.'

She sighed. 'I know that. It's not that I want to forget Isaac, I don't . . . and I never will. I don't have any choice, he's still a huge part of me. But it is my choice whether I choose to be hurt by seeing Elliot.'

There was another pause.

'Daniel?'

'Ali, I'm going to ask you something so earth-shatteringly obvious you'll probably spill your drink again, so put it down. Why do you think Elliot wanted to see you today? Why do you think he asked if you'd have lunch with him some other time in the future?'

'I don't know. Perhaps he's got nothing better to do. Maybe he's bored and needs a hobby to take his mind off the dull life he leads.'

A long silence ensued.

'Say something, Daniel.'

'I'm waiting for you to say something sensible. Come on, just say the words.'

'What words?'

'Why can't you admit that the man still cares about you? And, if I'm any judge of male lust, I'd say the look on his face when he saw you on the desk with your skirt hitched half-way up to your neck was a fair indication that his feelings for you run deep, as they say. But, there again, I'm gay, and what would I know about heterosexual desire?'

'That's not funny, Daniel.'

'It wasn't meant to be.'

'Oh, this is absurd.'

'Is it? Is it really? I'd say you're scared. You're scared that by seeing Elliot again and actually being mutually nice to one another it might remind you of what you once had.'

'And why would I be scared of that?'

'Because then you'd be in danger of having to admit that you were wrong to divorce him.'

Chapter Seventeen

Invariably there was a disagreement over which music they should listen to while they were in the workshop: this evening Sam had advocated *South Pacific* and Elliot had wanted one of his Leonard Cohen tapes.

Leonard Cohen was a bad sign.

Sam knew that when this particular songster flexed his vocal cords, with his unique ability to make his lyrics sound as if they were being put through the coffee grinder, things were far from good. Which was why he had stuck to his guns and insisted on an hour of inoffensive crowd-pleasing numbers to hum along with. He didn't know what was wrong with Elliot, but he'd been quieter than normal since he got in from work.

While *South Pacific* moved on to 'There is Nothing Like a Dame', Sam lovingly stroked the curvaceous wheel arch of the 1963 Morris Minor four-door saloon that he and Elliot were restoring. They'd bought it as a sad, abandoned heap of rusting metal and had been working on it whenever they could. They'd made templates out of cardboard and tin-plate for some of the repair sections, but for the really tricky structural bits they'd got hold of premanufactured parts. The welding had taken them for ever and had been the worst part, but patience and perseverance had won out. Luckily the engine had been in fine fettle, and with only eighty-five thousand on the clock, Sam reckoned it would be good for at least that again. The next big job they had lined up for Tilly – as they affectionately called the car – was to have her professionally painted. They'd tried doing it themselves:

they'd bought a compressor, some primer and five litres of dove-grey paint, but because they'd been stupid enough to spray the car outside, they had ended up with the bodywork covered in hundreds of dead flies. They'd had to strip down their ruined paint job and resign themselves to handing Tilly over to a professional refinisher. That day was fast approaching: only a couple more weeks of work and Sam would arrange to take the car to the Morris Minor specialist in Flint for her final makeover.

When that was done, he and Elliot would have to find another project to work on. Ever since he could remember, the pair of them had messed around with cars. While his peers had been chasing honour and glory on the rugby pitch, Elliot – when he wasn't in his room studying or practising the piano – had been with Sam getting covered in engine oil and grease. By the age of fifteen he had known how to strip down a gearbox and could refit a disc brake calliper without too much trouble. Connie had always been on at him for messing up the Boy Wonder's clothes or, worse, his hands. 'His piano teacher would have a fit if she saw all that oil under his nails,' she'd say in horror, when they came in from the garage so filthy that she made them stand on sheets of newspaper while they washed at the kitchen sink.

Though he didn't hold out much hope of it happening, Sam harboured a very real wish that their next project might be the present he'd planned to give Elliot the Christmas Isaac had died. He'd spent months organising the surprise for his son – getting in touch with the Jaguar Enthusiasts' Club and following leads that took him all over the country until, at last, he had tracked down a viable proposition to restore: a 1964 3.8-litre E-type. The car had been kept in a cowshed for nearly twenty years by the sister of the deceased owner. As it had had nothing done to it in the way of bodged tinkering, it was a real find. More importantly, it was realistically affordable – being a true canny Yorkshireman, Sam wasn't one to be hoodwinked into parting with more money than was necessary. His intention had been that he and Elliot would work on the car and then, ultimately, they would pass it on to Isaac on his eighteenth birthday – Sam had cherished the thought that he would live long enough to see that day. It had never occurred to him that his grandson might not. Not surprisingly, neither of them had had the heart to remove the tarpaulin that, since Isaac's death, had shrouded the car. Looking to the far end of the workshop, where it now rested on bricks, ignored and unwanted, Sam told himself that sooner or later they would have to bite the bullet. If nothing else, they ought to restore it in Isaac's memory.

'Do we have to listen to this drivel?' Elliot asked, from the back of the Morris Minor where he was rubbing down the boot area. Nellie was singing in her determined voice that she was gonna wash that man right out of her hair.

'Hey, bud,' said Sam, affecting the casual air of a US Marine, 'you gotta problem you need to discuss?'

'Not particularly.'

Sam moved round to the rear of Tilly and looked down at Elliot, who was on his knees. 'You sure?' he asked.

A few seconds passed as Elliot apparently applied all his concentration to the area he was working on around the shiny chrome boot hinge. Then, without raising his eyes, he said, 'I had lunch with Ali today.'

So that was it, thought Sam. He switched off the cassette player and, rationing himself to the most restrained response he could manage, said, 'Oh, aye? How was she?'

Elliot got to his feet and wiped his hands on the legs of his overalls. 'She's well and sends her love.'

'That's good. And, um . . . how did all this come about? Did you just happen to run into each other?'

Elliot heard the painfully forced nonchalance in his father's question and decided to be straight with him. 'It was of my doing,' he said. 'I called on her this morning to ask her if she'd have lunch with me.'

Sam couldn't disguise his surprise. Or his delight. Not only had Elliot taken the initiative, but Ali had taken him up on it. 'So has a reciprocal arrangement been made, then? Will there be a return match?'

Elliot knew the conclusion Sam had instantly reached. He didn't want his father to get carried away on a wave of optimism only to have his hopes dashed, so he said, 'It turned out to be a once-only event.' He went over to the workbench and began pulling off his overalls.

'What happened?' Sam's disappointment was as conspicuous as his earlier delight. 'Oh, don't tell me, you blew it. Did you get all defensive and start patronising her? You know how she hates that.'

'I wasn't aware of being defensive or patronising. If you must know, she said it would cause her too much pain to see me again. Are you coming in now? It's getting late.'

Sam sensed that Elliot had made the assumption that he'd just terminated their conversation, but he had other ideas. He wriggled out of his tatty, oil-stained overalls, threw them on the workbench and hurried after his son, who was already switching off the fluorescent strip-lighting. When they were inside the house, washing their hands in the utility room, he said, 'So what brought on this sudden change of heart? What made you want to see Ali?'

Elliot moved away from the sink and picked up a clean towel from the folded pile of washing on top of the tumble-dryer. He looked thoughtfully at the back of his father's head. He knew that, by offering partial truths and explanations, he was being unfair to Sam, and though his natural inclination was not to take the conversation any further, he forced himself to say, 'I'd been thinking about seeing her for some time.'

Sam kept his back to Elliot. He suspected that he'd get more from him by avoiding direct eye-contact. Despite the close relationship they had, he'd never been much good at prising information out of his reserved son. Connie had sometimes managed it. Like that time when Elliot hadn't told them about the school trip to Normandy. 'I didn't fancy going,' he'd said, when they'd found out about it and asked him why he hadn't put his name down for it. In the end Connie had got him to admit that he'd been worried that they couldn't afford for him to go. Sam reached for the nailbrush behind the mixer tap and pretended that his hands needed an in-depth scrubbing session. He said, 'Some time, eh?'

Understanding exactly what his father was doing, and why, Elliot said, 'Dad, if we're going to pursue this conversation, do you think we could do it face to face and over a drink?'

The sitting room was dark, and while Sam switched on lamps and drew the curtains, Elliot poured two glasses of Scotch from the tray of decanters on the table behind the sofa. He handed Sam his crystal tumbler, but instead of sitting in the armchair opposite him, he went and sat at the piano. He lifted the lid of the baby grand and stroked the keys ruefully. He played a languid melancholy scale, then let it grow until his hands were sweeping the full length of the keyboard. He stopped abruptly and listened to the swell of notes echoing in the hush.

He rarely played, these days, and when he did it was for release. In happier times he'd played for Ali: Rachmaninov, Chopin, Haydn, Mozart. One of her favourite pieces had been the *Presto agitato* from Beethoven's Moonlight Sonata. 'That namby-pamby *adagio* stuff at the beginning is all very well,' she'd say provocatively, 'but it's so bloody gloomy. Give me the heart-stirring passionate bit any day. It's so sexy.' It was a game of Ali's to make out that she knew next to nothing about classical music, but it was all a front: she loved it when somebody made the fatal error of being musically pretentious. It was a mistake they never repeated. Sometimes when he played she would creep up behind him and join him on the piano stool. She would sit in rapt silence, sometimes with her eyes shut, but more usually they would be open and fixed on his hands. Often her enjoyment of the music would be a prelude to them making love. She would

155

joke afterwards that the combination of watching his hands moving over the keys of the piano and the expression of intense concentration in his face was the fastest and most effective way to arouse her. What his long-suffering piano teacher would have thought of all those lessons serving the rather pleasurable purpose of getting the woman Elliot loved into bed was anybody's guess. Just think how much extra practice he would have put in if he'd been told as a teenager what the rewards might be!

Suddenly he closed the lid of the piano and got to his feet. He crossed the room and joined his father, and took a sip of his Scotch then told him what had led him to see Ali. He even spoke of the humiliating incident on the beach in Barbados with Rosalind. When he'd finished, Sam said, 'So what's to be done? If you still love her, don't diddle about, tell her how you feel.'

Elliot shook his head. 'But how, if she won't see me? She made it very clear that another lunch, or any similar arrangement, isn't going to take place. And don't suggest that I write to her. It wouldn't work – I'd never get the right words down on paper.'

'Do you want me to speak to her?'

'No. Definitely not. Please don't go behind my back either. God knows how, but this is something I have to sort out myself.'

Chapter Eighteen

Daniel left for the office earlier than usual. He shut the door behind him quietly, envious of Richard who was still lying in bed – he wasn't in court today and was planning to work from home before going to his chambers in Manchester that afternoon. Barristers, thought Daniel, with a smile. Cushy life or what?

It was a beautiful, magical morning: the air was cool and fresh, and from the dew-washed fields that bordered their land came the plaintive bleating of sheep and new-born lambs. Way off in the distance, Daniel could see a scrawny black-legged one gambolling after its mother; it looked so vulnerable and insubstantial he hoped that the current spell of warm spring weather would not revert to a wintry coldness.

But there didn't seem to be any chance of that happening: despite it being so early, the sun was already shining, resembling a highly polished white disc in the clear sky. It was also very low, and after placing his suit jacket and briefcase on the back seat of his Audi A3, Daniel put on his sunglasses – not to pose, as Richard was so quick to imply, but because at this time of year, and at this hour when the sun was hardly above tree level, its blinding brightness could make his cross-country route to work deceptively treacherous.

He switched on the engine and Handel's *Messiah* burst forth, carrying on from where it had left off yesterday evening when he'd driven home after his appointment with Jessica Lloyd. 'For unto us a child is born,' sang the Huddersfield Choral Society, and joining in with more gusto than skill,

Daniel turned the car round and set off down the long, sweeping driveway. It had been on a morning such as this five years ago when he and Richard had first clapped eyes on Lane End Farmhouse. And Lane End was exactly what it was. Situated in a dip in the valley between the Cheshire Peak villages of Rainow and Kerridge, and with breathtaking views across to the monument of White Nancy, their nearest neighbours – as the proverbial crow flew – were three-quarters of a mile away.

When he and Richard had decided it was time to buy a place where they could put down roots, they had deliberately only viewed properties that were remote and secluded – they were astute enough to know that not everybody wanted a gay couple living on the other side of the respectable suburban fence. Of course, there would always be those who would say that they had taken the cowardly approach, that they should have moved into a house centre-stage of some backward-thinking homophobic community and flaunted who and what they were. But as far as they were concerned their sexuality was their own business; it wasn't something they needed to prove, share with or justify to anybody else. Neither of them felt inclined to turn their relationship into a crusade for gay rights.

As it turned out, living at Lane End Farmhouse – a modest two-hundred-year-old stone-built gentleman's residence – had given them the best of both worlds: they had all the remoteness and seclusion they desired, including being occa-sionally cut off by three-foot snowdrifts in winter, but had the benefit of a friendly village a short drive away. It was at the village pub that Richard had made his own inimitable impression on the locals. As a self-confessed news-holic and general-knowledge freak, he was in high demand whenever it was quiz night at the Weary Traveller – his presence usually ensured an easy victory for his team.

As he drove past Adlington Hall and joined the B5358, Daniel turned his thoughts from his hitherto relatively trouble-free life to last night's kamikaze skirmish with Ali. When he'd come off the phone he'd warned Richard that it might be in order to start putting together a guest list for his funeral – just close friends and family, no flowers.

Not surprisingly, Ali had been furious with him for what he'd said. It was just as well domestic hi-tech videophones were still a thing of the future because he really wouldn't have wanted to see the expression on her face when he'd accused her of having made a mistake in divorcing Elliot. He knew that it was either a very brave or very stupid man who told Ali that she was wrong, but the compulsion to do so last night had far outweighed his fear of the consequences. They'd been friends for too long for him to hold back what he truly believed needed saying.

He didn't underestimate what Ali had gone through, and what she was still going through, but seeing her daily as he did, he felt better equipped than anyone else to know that she was no nearer to putting the awful tragedy behind her than she had been this time last year.

He'd actually been with her when it had happened, when she'd received the call from Elliot. They'd been in Frankfurt, on business, visiting a merchant bank in need of specialist expatriate tax advice. There had been no real reason why the pair of them should have been asked to go: as the senior manager of the department and Daniel's immediate boss, Ali was more than able to deal with the matter on her own, but one or two of the partners had said that a man's presence was required – ironically, even a gay man's presence. They had only just arrived at the hotel – their flight had been delayed several hours – and were in the process of reviving themselves from the mini-bar in Ali's room when the phone had rung. He had seen at once the alarm in her face when she'd answered it. She'd been clutching a small bottle of Jack Daniel's and seeing how tightly she was holding it, he'd taken it from her, worried in case she crushed it in her hand. There was no need to ask what was wrong. Her responses to what

Elliot was saying were sufficient to let him know that Isaac was seriously ill. 'I'll be on the first plane there is,' she said. 'I'll go straight to the hospital.'

When she came off the phone he called for a taxi for the airport. He went with her and, not wanting her to be alone, tried to insist that he flew back to Manchester as well, saying that they could cancel the meeting with the bank, that everyone would understand. But she refused to listen. 'No,' she said, 'there's no need. You must stay here. I'll phone you as soon as I know what's going on.'

He'd hugged her taut body, wiped away her frightened tears, and waved her goodbye. He had no idea how she fared during the flight and could only guess at the thoughts that must have gone through her mind. As for him, he'd taken a taxi back to the hotel and willed little Isaac to beat whatever it was that had struck him down so virulently, and so suddenly.

But his efforts had been in vain.

What he and Ali didn't know, was that Isaac was already dead.

Elliot had deliberately lied on the phone to Ali to spare her the ordeal of travelling all that way knowing that her son had just died. He had told her that Isaac was desperately ill and that she had to come back. His motive had been understandable, but Ali never forgave him for that lie. She had never seen it for what it was – a man simply wanting to protect the woman he loved. To this day, Daniel still didn't know what dreadful scene Ali must have walked into when she arrived at the hospital. He couldn't conceive of the courage it must have taken for Elliot to break the news.

And it was courage, admittedly of a much lesser sort, that Daniel was going to need this morning when he confronted Ali. This was why he had left home earlier than usual; he wanted to make sure that he reached the office before she did so that he could greet her with a cup of coffee and a white flag. He'd even raided the cupboard in the kitchen at home and pinched a packet of Richard's favourite almond and chocolate chip cookies as a peace-offering. And though he very much wanted to continue last night's conversation with her when he'd tried to persuade her to consider Elliot in a more favourable light, he knew that it wouldn't help if he did. And, besides, he had a far more pressing objective to fulfil: he had to ensure that she was calm, that she was no longer angry with him. If he failed to do this, then she'd never make it through their presentation this morning. If she was still stoked up with the blind fury he suspected her to be firing on, this morning would be a disaster.

But when Ali breezed into the office at eight thirty-five and dropped her briefcase on the floor by the side of her desk, she appeared to be anything but furious. 'Morning,' she said brightly. Her airy mood made Daniel suspicious and he watched her closely as she removed her suit jacket and slipped it over the back of her chair. He left her to open her mail while he went and made the coffee. When he returned and had cautiously settled her mug on the desk along with a plate of Richard's biscuits, she said, 'Daniel, it's quite all right, I'm not going to bite you.'

Despite her innocent tone, he retreated to the safety of his own desk before saying, 'And why would I think that you would want to bite me?'

She opened another envelope. 'I don't know, you tell me.'

Oh, shit, thought Daniel. This cat-and-mouse routine is much worse than outright anger. A blazing row would be far healthier. He decided to take the light-hearted approach. 'Babe, you're scaring me. I know that somewhere there'll be a sting in the tail. You've not hired a hit-man to take me out, have you?'

'I don't know what you're talking about,' she said uninterestedly, not even bothering to look up from the document in her hand.

Her indifference was too much for Daniel. He threw away

his attempt at jocularity and moved on to poker-faced severity. 'Ali,' he said sharply, 'put that down and talk to me.'

She did as he said. 'Well, as you can see, I'm all yours. Now, what is it I'm supposed to be talking to you about?'

He frowned, not sure what he did want her to say. 'I want you to talk about last night,' he said, hoping that if nothing else it would be a good opener.

She turned away. 'There's nothing to discuss.'

'I disagree. We need to clear the air.'

She ignored him and began tearing open another envelope.

Daniel had never seen her act so coolly towards him. 'Look,' he said, realising that it was down to him to make the first move towards apologising, 'I'm sorry for what I said. You probably think I went too far, but I want you to know that I did it for –'

She looked up at him and the directness of her gaze cut him dead. 'You were expressing a point of view, Daniel. A point of view you're perfectly entitled to have.'

'But I never intended to hurt you by giving it –'

'Hurt me?' she interrupted. 'Is that what you think you've done?'

'Well, I can't think why else we'd be having this arctic-temperature conversation if I hadn't upset you.'

She set aside the letter that was in her hand. 'Daniel, let's get this straight once and for all, shall we? You didn't hurt me.'

'I didn't? Are you sure?'

She nodded. 'Very sure.'

'Thank goodness for that.' He relaxed. But he shouldn't have.

'To be fair to you I've put a lot of thought into what you said and I'm going to prove to you that you've got it all wrong.'

He stared at her steadily, sensing that the sting in the tail was looming on the horizon. 'You mean you're going to prove that you're right?'

'Smart boy, Daniel.'

'But what good will that do? I only said what I did to try to make you see things more clearly. It was to help you.'

'And I told you on the phone that I don't need any help. I'm okay. I just wish that everyone else would accept that small but very significant fact. Perhaps we should put out a message on the Internet: "Ali Anderson is fine. Ali Anderson is coping just fine with her grief. It's a slow old process, but she's managing it to the best of her ability." There, how does that sound?'

Daniel thought it sounded a classic case of self-deception. 'So how do you intend to prove me wrong?' he asked.

She gave him chilling smile. Then, flicking through her Rolodex, she reached for her phone. 'Good morning,' she said, when a few seconds had passed. 'I'd like to speak to Elliot Anderson, please. No, he's not expecting my call, and yes, I know he's busy, he always was. Tell him it's Ali, I'm sure he'll spare me a couple of his valuable minutes.'

Daniel watched in rising horror. What the devil was she doing?

'Elliot, yes, it's me, quite a surprise I know. I just wanted to thank you for lunch yesterday and to say that maybe I was a little hasty in what I said about not wanting to see you again. Are you free for dinner later this week? You are? That's great. How about you come to me and I'll cook. Eight o'clock suit you? Good. I'll see you then.'

She put down the phone and turned to face Daniel. 'There,' she said. 'What do you think of that?'

Daniel got to his feet and went over to her. He leaned forward on to her desk and rested his hands either side of him. He looked her in the eye and said, 'I think the question is more what do *you* think of that?'

She backed away from him, but only an inch or two. She said, 'I'm going to prove to you that I can be pleasant to Elliot without once considering that I was wrong to divorce him. I shall be as nice as pie to him and not regret what I did.'

Daniel stared at Ali in dismay. He didn't want to hear the coldness in her words or see the flinty hardness in her face. He was horrified at what she was doing, but blamed himself. If only he'd kept his great big mouth shut last night. But he'd genuinely thought he was helping her. His intentions had been all for the good. He'd always suspected that Elliot had never really stopped loving Ali, and when yesterday he'd seen the evidence to confirm this in the man's face, he had thought that a nudge or two of common sense might help to set the wheels of a much-needed peace treaty in motion.

But now look at the mess he'd caused. If Ali was cold-heartedly going to use Elliot as a means to prove to the world that she was never wrong, then heaven help the poor guy.

Chapter Nineteen

Sarah was alone in the kitchen at Smithy Cottage, thinking that she would go quietly mad if she didn't talk to somebody. Trevor had just left to go over to Buxton to collect an order of ebonywood for a set of candlesticks he wanted to make and had left her with the washing-up and specific instructions to open her heart to the Lord. 'Don't tempt me,' she had wanted to say nastily, when he'd driven away in a cloud of burning oil coming from the back of their spluttering Sierra.

Never mind a gentle outpouring of penitent communion with God, what she wanted to do was give Him a piece of her mind. And not the well-behaved bit she normally offered Him. What did He think He was doing by sending Trevor off on this crazy crusade of obsessive evangelism?

The events of Monday night – and subsequent conversations with Trevor – had more than proved to Sarah that spiritual common sense flies out of the window when fanaticism bursts through the door. She was sure that what was happening to the group was a clear case of biblical principles being woefully misapplied, that through blind faith and ignorance they were misusing scripture to suit their own prejudices.

In the past she'd heard terrible cringe-making stories of house churches and breakaway groups getting wildly out of hand; of individuals who started out with an enthusiastic zeal for serving Christ, but who in the end did nothing but serve their own egotistical needs and diminish the God they proclaimed. But could this really be happening to Trevor and the Slipper Gang? Or was she overreacting? Trevor would say that subconsciously she wanted to destroy what they had and she didn't have. And hadn't she said as much to Ali at Christmas when she'd quoted William Penn to her – 'O God, help us not to despise or oppose what we do not understand.'

But this was different.

Surely it was.

It had to be.

When Trevor had played that sly trick on her with that stupid game and had pronounced her a disobedient lost sheep, Shirley had tried to menace her with one of her I've-been-called-to-pray-for-you sessions. Sarah had jumped to her feet and pushed the horrible woman away. She'd tried to make a run for it by saying she'd make the coffee, but Trevor wouldn't let her. He'd stopped her passing him as she'd made for the door and said, in a low voice, 'Perhaps you'd like us to pray for you, Sarah.'

She'd looked at him in astonished disbelief. 'What on earth for?'

He'd lowered his gaze to the Bible on his lap and said, 'Ephesians, chapter five, verse twenty-two.'

She'd wanted to shout, Oh, no, not that old chestnut about wives submitting to their husbands, can't you do better than that? But she'd forced herself to laugh and say lightly, 'I don't think this is the time to air our domestic differences, Trevor. It wouldn't be fair to our friends to bore or embarrass them.'

'As a sister in Christ you could never bore or embarrass us,' Shirley had said, still on her feet and probably hoping to perform a quick laying-on of hands.

'Shirley's right,' Martin Wade intoned. 'Domestic disharmony is one of the devil's favourite weapons. It should never be allowed too great a foothold.'

'Amen to that,' Stan joined in, crossing his legs and making one of his puppy-dog slippers look as if it were nodding in agreement.

'Have you thought of fasting?'

Sarah turned to Beryl and thought, No, but have you ever

considered minding your own business? 'Not ever,' she'd said, with strained dignity. 'I'm not sure that it serves any real kind of purpose . . . other than help one to lose weight.'

Her flippancy had galvanised Trevor and he'd said, in his especially pious voice, 'Sarah, I'm very worried about you. You don't seem to be in step with the rest of us . . . You're not losing your faith, are you?'

An audible hush fell on the room, and while everyone waited for her response she had stood motionless, almost able to believe that it was a bad dream she was experiencing, that she could say whatever she wanted and it wouldn't matter, there would be no comeback. Then from nowhere, Sarah the Impudent, who until now had been noticeably silent, suddenly came crashing through the door and blurted out, 'My faith is my own affair and it's not up for discussion. But I'll tell you this, the God I pray to isn't the one that you have tucked into your smug-lined pockets.'

Then, horror upon horrors, she'd realised that it hadn't been her *alter ego* speaking it had been *her*. Shocked, she'd fled from the room to the kitchen. A soft pattering of spirit-filled slippered feet had followed her, and the next thing she'd known she was caught in an all-female rugby scrum of evangelical concern. Audrey was praying for her to be renewed, Beryl was calling on her to die to herself and be reborn, and Shirley was asking for the sin that had separated her from God to be removed. And, worst of all, Trevor was hovering by the fridge, tugging at his beard and muttering something about casting out demons.

She hadn't the energy to fight them off.

Even if she'd had the strength she was too scared to do anything about them.

It seemed easier to let them be convinced of their spiritual muscle-power. Let them believe that they had scored a triumphal victory over the dark satanic forces of doubt and evil.

'That better?' enquired Beryl, when at last they let her go.

She nodded and, overcome with the need to be alone, she said, 'I think I'll just go and lie down, I'm feeling a little strange.'

'Aha,' said a smiling Audrey, 'that would be the Holy Spirit working in you.'

'Would you like one of us to come and sit with you?' asked Shirley.

'That's very kind, but no, thank you. I'll be okay on my own.'

She had gone upstairs and stayed there until she'd heard them all leave an hour and a half later.

The next morning Trevor had treated her with a deference she'd never known in him before. He had brought her a cup of tea in bed and insisted that she take it easy. 'You've obviously been under a lot of strain recently,' he said, patting her hand on top of the duvet, 'but you'll be all right from now on. I'm sorry that I had to resort to such drastic measures. But it was worth it, wasn't it? You do feel better, don't you?'

He never actually said the words, but it was terrifyingly clear that he believed she'd been an instrument of the devil for the past few months. And even clearer was his belief that the power of prayer had chased the devil away from Smithy Cottage.

She didn't know whether to laugh at him or be angry, so she kept quiet. But when later in the day he had given her a Christian paperback entitled *The Devil and All His Cunning Ways* she'd known for sure that one of them was in dire need of help. That was when she'd left a message on Ali's answerphone.

The washing-up now finished, Sarah wrung out the dishcloth and draped it over the leaking tap that Trevor kept meaning to do something about but never did – he was probably waiting for an angel of the Lord to stop by with a bag of tools and washers. Taking a discarded crust of toast with her, she went outside to the garden where she crumbled it on to the bird table. As soon as she was back inside the kitchen, Gomez appeared. She smiled at the sight of his trim little body and felt marginally better than she had a few minutes ago. She let out a long sigh, realising with sadness how tense and overwrought she was becoming. She really had to find a more effective way of coping with Trevor and the Slipper Gang. Suggesting that they were doing more harm than good would only have them on their knees praying for her confused soul. Going along with them seemed the safest thing to do. At least then she could be the occasional voice of reason. But if she was to do that, she would have to put a gag on Sarah the Impudent. Another outburst such as the one the other night and she'd be done for.

She wondered now about what she had said: 'My faith is my own affair, and it's not up for discussion.'

And what exactly was her faith, these days?

Not so long ago she would have known exactly how to answer that question. But now she wasn't so sure. As with *The Light of the World* painting, which she had tried to focus on on Monday evening, the firm edges of her faith were growing worryingly blurred and fuzzy. Where once it had filled the void in her life, it now added to the vacuous echo of it, resounding like a tolling bell in the growing hollow emptiness.

Another weary sigh.

Oh, where would it all end? And how much more energy was she going to need to keep everything together? Knowing she had no answer to this, she got out the ironing-board and began ironing Hannah's school shirts, grateful at least that her daughter was so preoccupied with her approaching exams that she was blissfully unaware of what had been going on. Her attention had also been conveniently diverted by the appearance of Jamie on the scene.

The inevitable reprimand from Trevor when Hannah had arrived back after her evening with Jamie was met with a casual, 'Sorry, Dad, but you really shouldn't have shouted at me in the way that you did. There was no need, not now that I'm eighteen.' She had sauntered up to her bedroom, leaving Trevor impotent with parental frustration at the foot of the stairs. But perhaps he'd been too exhausted to argue with her. He had, after all, had a busy evening exorcising his wife.

Though it was only two days since she had met Jamie, Hannah was full of him. 'He's really nice,' she'd said yesterday morning, when she came down for breakfast, and while Trevor was still in the shower. 'He lives with his father the other side of Nantwich and he's on a gap year before going to Bristol to read law. He's spending most of the summer travelling round France. God, what I wouldn't do to be able to do that.'

'And how's he funding his little jaunt round France?' Sarah had asked, despising herself for asking the question, but wanting, like all parents, to categorise the poor lad.

'He's spent his year off working for his dad's law firm in Chester. He's just passed his driving test and his father's helping him to buy a car in a few weeks' time.'

'Doesn't sound as if he's short on motivation, does it?' Sarah had said.

Hannah had smiled. 'Believe me, Mum, he's not short on anything.'

'So we'll be seeing more of him, will we?'

'I hope so. He said he'd ring tonight.'

True to his word, Jamie had indeed called last night and they had chatted for nearly half an hour, much to Trevor's concern.

'A boyfriend's out of the question,' he'd said to Sarah in the kitchen, while peering through the crack in the door at Hannah on the phone. 'She's on the brink of her A levels and this is a distraction she can do without.'

Sarah agreed with him: in part, she didn't want anything to get in the way of Hannah fulfilling her potential either, but she also knew that Trevor's condemnation of Jamie was really about him not wanting his hugely important role in his daughter's life being superseded by a mere boy.

The ironing finished, Sarah wondered what to do next. For once she had a free day. Should she open her heart to the Lord, as Trevor had instructed, or should she call on Grace and discuss the bedroom curtains she'd offered to make for her? It would be somebody to talk to; somebody to stop her going quietly mad.

Grace was delighted to see her. 'How extraordinary, I was thinking of calling on you myself,' she said.

'I've brought you this,' Sarah said, as she was shown through to the sitting room, not the conservatory as on Monday. She handed Grace a tin of home-made fruitcake. 'As a thank-you for lunch the other day.'

'How very kind of you. I'll put the kettle on and cut us a couple of slices, shall I? Tea or coffee?'

'Tea, please.'

When Sarah was alone she took the opportunity to survey her surroundings. What struck her first about the room was its immense tidiness. Oh dear, she thought with disappointment, was her new neighbour obsessively house-proud? If so, she'd get a nasty surprise when she visited Smithy Cottage. The contrast between the two houses couldn't have been greater. No matter how hard Sarah tried to keep order it never seemed to work. Between Trevor and Hannah, the house was always a mess, albeit a clean mess. When she took a closer look at Grace's belongings, she realised that it was the lack of them that presented such an orderly effect. There were a couple of framed photographs on the mantelpiece and one or two nice bits of furniture, a dainty satinwood desk, a rosewood pie-crust table and a glass-fronted mahogany bookcase, all of which appeared a bit out of kilter in a modern bungalow with UPVC window-frames and swirly patterned Artexed ceiling. There were no pictures on the walls; nor were there any china bits and bobs of questionable taste. Maybe she hadn't unpacked everything yet.

'There,' said Grace, coming came back into the room and lowering the tray of tea and cake on to the rosewood table. 'Now we're all set for a cosy gossip. Tell me, Sarah, how did Hannah take to Jamie?'

Sarah smiled. 'She liked him a lot.'

'How splendid. I had the distinct feeling when he came here after dropping her off that he'd thoroughly enjoyed himself. There was a smile on his face that hadn't been there before. He's a lucky young man.'

'I don't know about that,' said Sarah.

'Now, then, no false modesty. Jamie brought Hannah in when she called for him and I saw for myself that she's a remarkably pretty girl. I wish I'd had her legs when I was that age.'

Sarah pulled a face. 'I'm afraid her skirt was very short. I hope you weren't shocked.'

Grace laughed. 'I was nothing of the kind. Though I must admit that Callum was rather taken aback. I think it came as a surprise to him that his son could attract such a lovely girl. That's the trouble with being a parent, we so badly underestimate our children.'

'Perhaps that's more true of fathers.'

'Yes,' said Grace thoughtfully. 'You may be right. Generally mothers are more in tune with their children's development, whereas the vast majority of fathers, bless them, come home from work one day and realise that their son or daughter is not only looking them in the eye, but they're on the verge of leaving home. Does Hannah's father fit into that category?'

'In many ways, yes, and he's not doing awfully well at coping with the reality of Hannah not being his little girl any more. He isn't terribly keen on Jamie being around either – her A levels start in May.'

'Jamie mentioned that. He also said that she's hoping to go to Oxford.'

'Yes, that's right,' and, unable to keep the pride out of her voice, Sarah added, 'She's been offered a place at my old college.'

'How wonderful. You must be so proud of her. Does she take after you in all things?'

'Goodness, I hope not,' Sarah said, with a hesitant smile. And as she took the cup of tea Grace had just poured for her she had the feeling that her new neighbour was one of those cleverly intuitive people, whose questions were a lot more probing than they first appeared.

It wasn't until nearly lunch-time that Elliot had a chance to reflect on his telephone conversation with Ali first thing that morning.

As soon as he'd put down the receiver he'd wanted to ring his father and find out what the hell he'd been playing at. He'd expressly told him not to go behind his back – and that was exactly what he must have done, for what else could have made Ali change her mind so suddenly? But there hadn't been a free moment for him to speak to Sam: he'd had to sit through a three-hour meeting with his senior partners, which was only now showing signs of coming to an end.

It was part of Elliot's job to keep everybody in line and, as he stared round the table and observed the egotistical oneupmanship that was rife between his colleagues, he felt that on days like this his position was little more than that of an unpopular teacher trying to control a class of dysfunctional teenagers.

He'd known when he was promoted to partner-in-charge that the decision would not be well received in certain quarters – in particular, by Gervase Merchant-Taylor and Scott Hunt who had been the two front runners for the job – both considerably older than Elliot, each convinced of their own suitability for the job. Neither had taken kindly to the news from London that Elliot was to run the Manchester office. When the announcement had been made, Elliot had known that London expected him to be the one to defuse the resentment caused by his appointment. It had come at a time when he needed a distraction from the chaos of his personal life, when whipping this lot into shape had seemed a blessing. It had provided him with a much-needed focus, as well as a convenient excuse to work at a blistering pace, thereby minimising the number of hours spent alone dwelling on Isaac.

Mostly, he derived enormous satisfaction from the job and thrived on the challenge of the work, but there were aspects of it that appalled him. The situation of his office didn't help either. Large and ostentatious, situated at the top of the nine-floor building, it rendered him practically inaccessible. But what irritated him more than anything was the skin-crawling sycophancy that went on. He could cope with Gervase and Scott, who disliked each other as much as they disliked him, but what he couldn't tolerate was the constant toadying from the rest of the senior partners who, with the exception of Howard Jenkins, who kept himself to himself, sucked up to him whenever they could. And if that wasn't bad enough, Gervase was constantly pumping him for confidential information about the rest of the partners and what was going on in the firm; he hated the idea that Elliot knew anything before he did. Elliot had quickly learned that he had to make sure he never left any important documents from London lying around in his office. He'd made that mistake once and had caught Gervase snooping through the files on his desk late one evening.

It was a lonely job and made more so by not having a fellow-worker in whom he could put his trust. But he couldn't complain: it was, after all, one of the accepted and inevitable consequences of having achieved so much so young. Being fast-tracked throughout his career from the day he'd started his training contract meant that it had been difficult to form any lasting friendships with his colleagues. He'd always envied Ali that she'd had Daniel's friendship at work; there'd never been any shortage of trust between them. And it was probably this that had been at the root of his proposition to his father that they join forces. Working with embittered rivals and arse-lickers and having no one to talk to at home, was it any wonder that he'd sought out the company of somebody on whom he could rely 100 per cent?

And still the meeting was droning on and on, with Gervase and Scott doing their best to outmanoeuvre each other at every possible turn in the conversation. But at last Elliot had had enough. He mentioned the time pointedly, closed his file, snapped the lid on his fountain-pen and alerted everyone to the fact that he considered their long-winded discussion over. Everyone got up from the table and drifted away to their own offices.

All except Gervase, who seemed to be spending an unnecessary amount of time putting his file in order. 'I wonder if I might have a word,' he said, when they were alone and the door had been shut.

Despite wanting to be rid of everyone so that he could ring his father, Elliot said, 'Sure.' He went and sat behind his desk and regarded the repellent porcine man before him with deep suspicion. 'What is it?' he asked.

'I thought you ought to know that we might have a problem with Scott.'

'Oh?' said Elliot impassively.

Gervase stared back at him with lazy watchfulness. 'It appears that he's keeping more than a weather eye on the job market.' His whole demeanour as he spoke smacked of oily, conspiratorial wanker. 'Just thought you ought to be informed,' he added, 'knowing how difficult it must be for you to keep your ear to the ground stuck up here in your ivory tower, as it were.'

'Thank you, Gervase. I'll bear that in mind. Now, was there anything else?'

A look of annoyance stamped itself across Gervase's fat-jowled face. Obviously this was not the response he had wanted. 'My dear chap,' he drawled, 'you are going to do something about the matter, aren't you? Divided loyalty just isn't on. We can't have it, we really can't.'

Elliot could have struck him to the ground. The man's pompous, monstrously affected pratness had never got up his nose so much as it was now. Every atom of Gervase's refined over-privileged upbringing was bringing out the back-street fighter in him. He'd come out on top of enough childhood brawls to know that he could knock the shit out of this posturing prig if he wanted to.

And did he ever want to!

'As I said, Gervase, I'll bear in mind what you've told me. If there really isn't anything else, I have an important phone call to make. Would you excuse me?' He waited for Gervase to get to his feet and cross the office before delivering a well-aimed warning shot across his bows. 'By the way, how's Jim Collins? I believe you had lunch with him last month.'

Gervase's hand fell away from the door handle and his blubbery face reddened all the way to his receding hairline. 'He's very well,' was all he said.

When Elliot was alone he allowed himself a small, wry smile. Jim Collins was his opposite number with a rival firm of accountants in Manchester, and clearly Gervase wasn't privy to the knowledge that they played squash together now and then. Jim had told Elliot over a drink in the bar after their latest game that Gervase had invited him out for lunch, had not so subtly hinted that he might be looking to switch horses – and did Jim know of any likely thoroughbreds in need of a decent jockey?

Gervase might like to labour under the misapprehension that Elliot didn't have his finger on the pulse, but it would take more than a supposed ivory tower to dull his awareness of what was going on around him. Just as he already knew that Scott was looking for another job, he had also heard rumours that Gervase was making himself more unpopular than he already was with some of the women in his department. Elliot was convinced that it was only a matter of time before a formal complaint was made.

He made a note to do something about this, then phoned Sam.

'Hi, it's me,' he said, when his father answered the phone at Timbersbrook; he could hear *The World at One* in the background.

'Hello, son, what can I do for you? Did you forget something?'

'No, nothing like that. But tell me the truth, and no bullshit, did you speak to Ali first thing this morning?'

'No. You made it very clear that I wasn't to do that.'

Elliot heard the indignation in Sam's voice and knew that he was speaking the truth. So if his father hadn't talked Ali into seeing him again, who, or what, had changed her mind?

Chapter Twenty

Ali had regretted her actions from the moment she'd told Daniel on Wednesday morning what she planned to do, and not because she thought there was a grain of truth in what he'd said but because she had, so very plainly, upset him. Though they hadn't actually rowed with an all-out guns-blazing ferocity, there had been a subsequent atmosphere of strained coolness between them, especially in the car when, an hour later, she'd driven them to Macclesfield where they were to give the first of their presentations that week.

How they'd got through it, she didn't know. As the acknowledged ice-breaker of the duo, Daniel had gone first, but she'd been keenly aware that his performance had lacked its usual smooth-paced sparkle; at one point he seemed even to lose the thread of what he was saying. Seeing him unprecedentedly distracted, and knowing that she was the probable cause, she had been unable to concentrate when it came to her turn. Her nerves kicked in and when, half-way through her talk, she couldn't work the overhead projector she'd panicked. In her agitation she'd knocked over her glass of water and ruined her notes.

All in all, it had been an unprofessional turn-out on their part. She had hinted as much in the car afterwards when they were on their way back to the office.

'I agree,' he'd said tersely. 'We'd better make sure we do better on Friday when we perform our next freak show.'

'We weren't that bad.'

'Burlesque comes to mind.'

'You don't reckon they'll ask us back for an encore, then?'

Her tone had been light, almost throw-away, in an attempt to lift his mood. But it hadn't worked.

He turned slowly and gave her a long, hard stare. Glad that she was driving and didn't have to meet his gaze, she focused on the road ahead. After a few minutes he took her by surprise when he said, 'Please don't do it, Ali. Elliot's had enough to cope with without being made to think that there's a chance of being reconciled with you, only then to have his hopes dashed.'

'Oh, don't exaggerate,' she said hotly. 'One dinner does not a reconciliation make. And, anyway, I know for sure that Elliot isn't interested in me in the way you think he is.'

'Oh, and how do you work that out?'

'It's obvious. I'm simply his ticket to easing his conscience. He now feels guilty for the break-up of our marriage and wants to square things so that he can sleep at night. If it'll make you feel better I'll cancel Friday night. I'll ring Elliot and say –'

'Yeah, right, as if this has anything to do with me needing to feel better.'

They'd driven the rest of the journey in silence. It was fortunate that Ali was out of the office meeting several clients the following day, as she had no idea how to handle Daniel in his current frame of mind, or how to deal with what she felt towards him. She felt annoyingly betrayed that he seemed so intent on taking Elliot's side. Why the sympathy for Elliot all of a sudden? *Elliot's had enough to cope with.*

Men!

Straight or gay, they all sided with one another no matter what.

Her anger had stayed with her throughout yesterday as she kept thinking of everything Daniel had accused her of. What he had said of course, was complete rubbish, a lot of absurd nonsense generated by an over-vivid imagination. It was outrageous that he had suggested that her refusal to see Elliot was because she was scared of feeling anything for him again.

And, as she'd told Daniel, she genuinely believed that if Elliot wanted to carry out a post-battle campaign of patch-up-our-differences, it was purely down to his need to use her as a means of softening the sharp edges of his grief. So if anyone was being used it was her.

But it didn't matter how strongly committed to this view she was, it didn't make things right between her and Daniel. She was worried that if their marked difference of opinion was left to its own devices for too long it could force an unbridgeable gap between them. And that was something she wasn't prepared to let happen: Daniel meant the world to her. Which meant she had to do something in the way of climbing down from her precarious position. Sadly, though, she had to admit that self-effacement wasn't something she was terribly well acquainted with.

It was this thought that was with her now on Friday morning as she drove through Stockport's rush-hour traffic to meet up with Daniel at the electronics company where they were giving another presentation. She found him in the prestigious marble-floored, pot-planted foyer chatting to one of the receptionists. He came over when he saw her.

'Can we have a word before we kick off?' she asked. Apart from desperately wanting to re-establish their friendship, Ali knew that in view of the shambles they'd made of their last presentation they had to regain their happy equilibrium as soon as possible, or they would be in danger of giving a repeat performance of Wednesday's fiasco.

They went and sat on a massive sofa that had a proportionately sized glass and steel table in front of it, the surface of which was covered in an artfully fanned display of that morning's newspapers. Every paper carried the same story that Ali had caught on the news on the car radio, and pictures of a flood-devastated area in Bangladesh stared back at her. Headlines claimed that the floods were the worst in living memory with more than fifteen hundred reported dead and three times that number now homeless, facing poverty and disease. Every paper had its own photograph to portray the disaster but the story behind each grim composition was the same: this was death on a vast, unimaginable scale.

'What is it, Ali?' asked Daniel. 'We don't have much time.'

Suddenly everything Ali had wanted to say wedged itself in her throat in a log-jam of emotionally charged confusion. It had been her determined intention to clear the air with Daniel, but the sight of such mass human suffering so explicitly spread before her stripped her of all her carefully thought-out words and made her realise the shallowness of what she'd really had in mind. In her arrogance she hadn't doubted for a single second her ability to reaffirm what she had already told Daniel and as a consequence extract from *him* the necessary apology to set them on an even keel. So much for a climb-down on her part. This clarity of thought also made her see the truly vindictive nature of her actions towards Elliot when she'd invited him for dinner. Appalled at what she'd done, she continued to sit in mute shame.

'Ali,' Daniel pressed, 'we're supposed to be upstairs in the conference room in five minutes. We ought to go.'

She tore her eyes away from the nearest paper, which showed a distraught young mother crouched in mud, cradling the body of her dead baby. She looks no more than a child herself, Ali reflected, with heartfelt anguish. 'I ... I just wanted to say that I'm sorry,' she murmured, finding her voice at last. She looked up into Daniel's concerned face. 'I've behaved horribly, haven't I?'

Knowing exactly which photograph would have disturbed Ali most from the selection in front of them, Daniel took one of her hands and held it gently. 'Have you? When was that? I must have missed it.'

'Don't joke with me, Daniel. Not now.'

'I'm sorry. And I'm sorry for some of the things I said to you.'

'Only some?'

'Yes. I'll leave you to figure out which.'

'Well, that won't be too difficult. As soon as we have a spare minute, I'll ring Elliot and cancel tonight. I don't know what could have made me do such a calculating thing. It was very cruel.'

He smiled. 'It was your heavy-handed way of telling me to mind my own business.'

'And to teach you a lesson.'

'That too. And talking of lessons, are you admitting that one of us – a person who is extremely dear to me but who shall remain nameless – was wrong?'

She gave a little nod. 'But I'm only admitting to being wrong in wanting to manipulate Elliot to prove a point. The rest still stands.'

'So why don't you risk dinner with him anyway . . . just for old times' sake?'

She shook her head. 'No, I mustn't. If you're right about Elliot, then it would be unfair to give him the wrong signals.'

'As you wish, Babe. Now, come on, it's show-time. Give me your best Norma Desmond face and let's hit them with one of our Oscar-winning performances.'

The day flew by and it wasn't until a quarter to four when they stopped for a short tea-break that Ali found a slot in their busy schedule to excuse herself and ring Elliot's office. When she got through, an overly officious woman told her that Mr Anderson was unavailable.

'But it's extremely important that I speak to him,' Ali said.

'I'm sure it is, but he's not in today.'

'Is he at home?'

'Who is this?'

The question implied that, depending on the answer received, a *pro rata* amount of information would be forthcoming.

Incensed, Ali said, 'Oh, go shove yourself!' cut off her mobile – very probably her nose too – and tossed it into her bag.

'Problem?' asked Daniel, appearing with a cup of tea for her.

'Yes. Elliot isn't in the office today and his dumb secretary was not what we'd call user friendly.'

Daniel deposited the cup of tea on the table that Ali was leaning against, held out a hand and said, 'Give. It's time for our old friend Bob Schlock III to throw his weight around.'

She gave him her mobile and watched him press the redial button. 'Elliot Anderson,' he barked, in a grossly exaggerated American accent which brought a smile to her face. Bob Schlock III was a long-standing device who, every now and again, came in handy when Daniel needed to bypass the occasional annoying obstacle. When he'd been put through to Elliot's unhelpful secretary he slipped even further into character. 'This is Bob Schlock of Texas Incorporates,' he drawled, 'I'm returning Elliot's call. What do you mean, he's not there? Well, where is he? Now you stop right there, little missy, no point in giving me the runaround, I'm not calling for the good of my health, y' know. So just go right ahead and give me a number where I can contact him. No. No message, honey. Now, you be sure to have a nice day.'

Daniel returned Ali's phone to her. 'Nothing to it, honey. You just gotta show them who's boss.'

Ali rolled her eyes affectionately. 'So what's the deal, Schlock III? Where is Elliot?'

'Strategy meeting in London. He's booked on the five-fifteen shuttle out of Heathrow.' He glanced at his watch. 'He's probably already at the airport.'

Ali groaned. 'Now what do I do?'

'Sweetpea, it looks as if you'll just have to don your pinny and entertain him as originally planned.'

'Oh, Daniel, I can't. There has to be a way round it.' She thought for a minute, then said, 'I know, I'll ring Sam and leave a message with him.'

But there was no answer from the phone at Timbersbrook.

Not even an irritating message telling her that nobody was there to take her call.

Elliot knew that he was cutting it fine, but he calculated that as long as his flight wasn't delayed, he just had time to make it home for a quick shower and change of clothes before driving to Ali's for eight o'clock. And while he prepared to wait patiently in the executive lounge for the Manchester shuttle to be called, he helped himself to a drink and a copy of the London *Evening Standard*.

Luck was with him and he was shortly stowing his coat and briefcase in the overhead locker, along with the flowers and chocolates he'd bought for Ali, then taking his seat. On average, he made this journey to and from London every other week and was as familiar with the routine as he was with the nature of the head-office meetings he attended on each of his visits – it was the favourite old ploy of attack and defend. The commonly held view in London was that, out of all the regional offices, Manchester was the most efficiently run; it was also known to be the hottest bed of personal ambition. Nothing had ever been said directly, but Elliot was astute enough to know that his promotion had been a carefully orchestrated piece of divide and conquer – London had selected him in the belief that his appointment would clear out some of the dead wood. But twelve months into the job Gervase was still hanging in there, probably hoping that if he made life difficult enough for Elliot he would be the one to clear off. But Elliot was a darned sight more tenacious than that. If there was one single thing he was grateful his father had taught him it was 'You don't get owt for nowt, son.' It had been a favourite axiom of Sam's and had often been punctuated with further encouraging mantras such as 'Stick with it, lad' or 'Make sure you go the distance' and 'Don't let the bastards grind you down.' Sam had never been a pushy parent – he'd never needed to be, not with Elliot being as driven as he was – but he had been a stickler for seeing things through, and Elliot suspected that out of all his father's many qualities this was one of the few he'd inherited. He had often wondered whether he'd been a disappointment to his father when he was growing up. He must have been a boring kid, always reading, always studying, and even when he was at Oxford he hadn't changed. What leisure time he'd allowed himself he'd spent jogging round Christ Church Meadow and along the Cherwell or listening to music in his room, rather than hanging around the college bar seeing how much he could drink before falling down blind drunk. During his second term, one of his tutors had tactfully suggested that he might like to participate in college life a little more enthusiastically. Reluctantly he had made a token gesture to sociability by showing his face in the Junior Common Room once a week and extending his breakfast in hall by five minutes each day. He quickly acquired the sobriquet TSB – That Solitary Bugger – but by the middle of the Trinity term, much to his annoyance and embarrassment, his nearest neighbour's extensive circle of airheaded girlfriends had changed it to QBD: Quiet But Divine. This was after one had missed her footing on the stairs and fallen into his arms as he'd been following her after an hour running in the rain down by the river. Afterwards, when he'd carried her safely to his neighbour, having been taken in by her claim that she'd twisted her ankle, he had heard her giggling through the wall that she'd gladly part with a year's clothing allowance for a night in bed with him. 'Never mind you uncouth, beer-guzzling, rugby louts,' she'd shrieked, at the top of her voice. 'Give me a strong, silent man in a wet T-shirt any day.'

When they landed at Manchester, Elliot made his way through the busy arrivals hall, paid his parking ticket and hurried to the third floor where he'd left his car at half past six that morning. He was home by ten past seven, and after reading Sam's note that he wouldn't be back until late that night, he was in the shower by seven sixteen. He washed, shaved, cleaned his teeth, dressed and was in the car again by twenty to eight. It was a masterpiece of timing and it was only now as he headed south on the A535 that he allowed himself to think of the evening ahead. So far that day he'd done everything in his power not to imagine what had led Ali to invite him to dinner. He'd convinced himself that, at best, she wanted to apologise for being so curt earlier in the week.

And at worst?

Oh, that was easy.

At worst she wanted to spell out on her own territory, syllable by syllable, exactly why she never wanted to see him again.

'This isn't happening,' Ali muttered to herself, 'it's a bad dream. Any minute now and I'll wake up and find it's morning and I'll be able to ring Elliot to put him off. Or, better still, I'll realise that this whole week has been one long dream sequence.'

She slugged back another mouthful of wine and glanced at the clock again. It was ten minutes to eight. She groaned and wished that she didn't know Elliot as well as she did. It would be futile to hope that he would be late, or that he would fail to show. Elliot was the most punctilious man she knew. He was never late. He'd always managed to make time work in his favour. She didn't know anyone like him. In the days when they used to work together, and there was a big job on that would throw everyone into a maelstrom of frantic activity, he had never once worried about the deadline hanging over them. Instead he had quietly applied himself to the task in hand and had been the epitome of unruffled efficiency. He'd been the same in meetings. No matter the temperature around the table, his body language was always that of inscrutable calm. It was a compelling technique he had cultivated, which had on one occasion, during a lively, heated debate, caught her out. It was in the early days of her training and she had been so mesmerised by the impassive expression on his face that she'd stopped listening to what was being said. When he'd suddenly asked her opinion, Daniel had had to step in and rescue her.

It was not something she had allowed to happen in the workplace again. From then on she had kept her desire for him firmly under control.

But at least that was something she wasn't going to have to concern herself with tonight. There were many things she felt for Elliot now, but desire wasn't one of them. And despite what Daniel thought about Elliot's feelings for her, she was convinced that lust wasn't on his mind either.

When she and Daniel had finally got away from Stockport late that afternoon, they had headed back to the office for a quick catch-up session with Margaret. After they'd gone through their e-mails, returned several clients' calls, were turning out lights and setting the security system, Daniel had said, 'Go easy on Elliot tonight, won't you, Babe? It takes too much energy to keep fighting another person. Give yourselves a break.'

'Hah! Go easy, indeed,' she said, as she brushed egg-yolk on to the puff pastry of the haddock and prawn pie she'd cobbled together when she'd arrived home from work – knowing how particular Elliot was about what he ate, she had decided not to antagonise him by confronting him with a plate of red meat and saturated fats, and had gone for the safe option of fish.

Now, was that going easy enough?

Or would she still be accused of serving him a nice little fricassée of harboured bitterness on a bed of reproachful blame?

She heard the ominous sound of an approaching car, threw back another mouthful of wine and crossed the kitchen to the small window that looked out on to Mill Lane. Sure enough, there in the darkness she could see the headlights of Elliot's distinctive XK8 coming slowly towards the mill. A glance at her watch showed that he was exactly on time.

Damn the man! Would he never surprise her? Would he never defy his own gravitational force of perfection?

She took a deep, steadying breath and braced herself for the evening ahead.

Chapter Twenty-One

Elliot saw at once how uptight Ali was when she opened the door.

'Exactly on time, Elliot,' she said. 'No change there, then.' She banged the door shut with a crash that was so loud and sudden it made him start. 'Sorry about that, don't know my own strength. Overcompensating for the warped wood. No coat? You'll regret that when you go home.'

Seeing the dreadful effect he had on her, Elliot's heart sank with heavy sadness. 'Look,' he wanted to say, 'I know this is difficult, but slow down, relax.' However, a comment such as that would do more harm than good: it would put her on the attack and make her more agitated than she already was.

A friendly kiss on the cheek was plainly out of the question so he handed her the flowers and chocolates. They were received with polite thanks and she led the way up the spiral staircase to the first floor of the mill, to where they'd sat on his only other visit. It looked exactly as before, but minus the cards that had been strung between the brass picture lights. These were switched on, as were two silk-shaded table lamps; soft light reflected off the rich red walls.

'What would you like to drink?' she asked. 'I've made a start on some white wine, but feel free to have what you want.'

'Wine would be nice. Thanks.'

He followed her to the kitchen area and saw that she'd set the table for dinner. He noted that there were no intimate touches of candles and flowers. To the right of the cooker, and waiting to be baked, he saw what he took to be their supper: it had been one of his favourite meals that Ali used to make for them. She handed him his glass of wine and caught him looking at the pie. She opened the oven door and put it inside and said, 'Sorry to be so dull, but my culinary repertoire hasn't had much of an opportunity to move on, since . . .' She trailed off.

He waited awkwardly for her to finish the sentence. When she didn't, he said, 'Since we separated, is that what you were going to say?'

'No,' she said, with an indignant frown. 'I was going to say since work has been so busy and I haven't had time to fiddle around in the kitchen as I used to.'

Rebuffed, he went back to the sitting area and strolled over to a large old black-and-white photograph of the mill, taken in the days when it still had its sails. While sipping his wine and apparently studying the picture, he figured out his best chance of changing the course of the evening. As things stood, he'd be shown the door before long. Then, sensing that Ali was standing behind him, he turned and said, 'Any chance of a guided tour?'

She put down her glass. 'If you want, though there's not an awful lot to see.'

Once again Ali took the lead and as they climbed the narrow wooden staircase, she said, 'We'll go right to the top and work our way down.'

A few steps behind her Elliot tried to keep his eyes on something other than Ali's legs and the shortness of her skirt, which barely showed itself beneath the silk blouse she was wearing. She'd flay you alive if she knew what you were thinking, he told himself sharply. 'How many floors are there?' he asked, endeavouring to keep his thoughts on safer lines.

'Five.'

'Any idea how high the mill is?'

'*Exactly* seventy feet,' she said pointedly. They reached the top floor and, slightly out of breath, she stopped and pushed open a stripped-pine door. 'This is supposed to be my study, but I don't use it often. I always seem to end up working on my laptop at the kitchen table.'

Elliot took in the small circular room with its white-painted walls and two tiny windows: it reminded him of a cell. Its diameter was about fourteen feet and its only furniture a desk and chair and two bookcases, which contained several rows of lever-arch files and a selection of standard accounting textbooks. There was a computer, a compact Canon printer, a phone on the desk and nothing else.

They went down to the next floor where there was a bedroom and a small adjoining shower room. The bedroom looked as if it was waiting for a guest: it was meticulously tidy; the double bed was made up with three cushions placed decoratively against the headboard, and on the dressing-table beneath one of the three windows was a pastel-coloured tissue box and a cut-glass vase of daffodils.

'Somebody coming to stay?' he asked.

'Yes. Sarah.'

'With or without Trevor?'

'Without. It's going to be a strictly girls-only weekend.'

When they reached the floor below, Ali paused. 'My room,' she said, after a moment's hesitation. She pushed open the door and let him go in first. They stood side by side a few feet away from the corner of the bed. A painful thump of jealousy hit Elliot – had she ever brought a man back here? He willed himself not to picture the scene. But he couldn't stop himself and all too easily he saw her climaxing in the arms of some stranger. He thrust his hands into his trouser pockets, cleared his throat and moved away. 'Cleverly built-in wardrobes,' he said, going over to take a closer look at the workmanship that had ingeniously accommodated the slope and curve of the wall.

'Yes,' she agreed, to his back.

He turned a few degrees to his right and for the first time

noticed the bedside table, or rather, he noticed what was on it: a framed photograph of Ali sitting on the beach with their son on her lap. Isaac was wearing the New York Yankees baseball cap that Elliot had bought for him on a recent trip to the States. Much too big for his little head, it had slipped to one side and had given him a cute, jaunty look. With instant recall Elliot could remember the day he had taken the photograph. They'd been down at Hayling, staying with Ali's parents. It had been the most perfect of summer days, hot and sunny with a refreshing breeze blowing in from the sea. They'd spent the afternoon on the beach paddling and building sandcastles and hunting for razor shells. They'd bought ice creams and Isaac had insisted on holding his own, and in the heat of the August sun it had melted and dribbled all over his hands before he'd had a chance to eat any of it. Ali had taken him down to the water's edge to wash him while Elliot had fetched a replacement. The tableau of them all together was so clear and so very real in Elliot's mind that for a split second he was convinced that if he closed his eyes he'd be there on the beach, breathing in the smell of the sea air and hearing the happy sound of Isaac's squealing laughter as the rushing waves whooshed over his tiny feet dragging the grains of sand from under his toes.

He wrenched his eyes from the photograph but then saw something else that brought back another haunting echo of the past. There, almost hidden beneath the duvet, was Mr Squeezy. Without thinking, he went to the bed and picked up the small bear. He held it lovingly in his hands, reacquainting himself with the crooked nose, the long, dangly arms and legs and the soft well-cuddled body. He swallowed and his jaw tightened as he thought how limp and lifeless the teddy felt . . . limp and lifeless just as Isaac had felt at the end. 'I didn't know you'd kept this,' he murmured, almost inaudibly.

Ali opened her mouth to speak but found that she couldn't. She was completely paralysed with the desperate need to make Elliot put Mr Squeezy back in the bed. She didn't want him touching that small precious bear. It was practically all she had left of Isaac. Irrationally, she knew that she was on the verge of tears and, despising herself for her weakness, she whispered, 'Please, put him down.'

Elliot raised his eyes and saw the agony in Ali's face. Shocked, he immediately did as she said. 'I'm sorry, I didn't mean to—'

She held up a hand to stop him. 'No, don't say anything. Not a word.' Then, turning towards the door, she said stiffly, 'We'd better go downstairs. Supper should be ready by now.'

Ali served the meal while Elliot, at her suggestion, selected a CD. The thought occurred to him as he ran his gaze along the row of CDs that she might be testing him: choose something they both used to be fond of and he'd be accused of cloying sentimentality. His fingers hovered over *Eric Clapton Unplugged*, then flicked away – 'Tears in Heaven' was on that album and he didn't know about Ali but he could never make it through to the end of that song without a colossal amount of desensitising alcohol. He trailed his hand further along the shelf, instinctively bypassing all the classical stuff – Rachmaninov, Brahms, Beethoven and Chopin were dangerously evocative and would dredge up too many poignant, erotic memories. His hand stopped at an album by an artist called Frances Black. He hadn't heard of the singer or the CD. It was called *Talk To Me*. Well, it was appropriate enough. He removed the disc that was already in the hi-fi and looked around for its box. Ali had never been any good at putting things back in their proper place. After extending his search to a wider area, he eventually found it hidden beneath that month's copy of *Taxation*.

'How long does it take for an accountant to put on a CD?' called Ali from the kitchen, where she was refilling their glasses and observing his progress.

'I don't know,' he answered. 'How long *does* it take for an accountant to put on a CD?'

'Apparently twice as long as anybody else.'

He adjusted the volume and, catching the opening lyric of the first track – 'All the lies that you told me, all the tears that I've cried' – hoped he wasn't going to regret his choice. He joined Ali at the table, sat in the chair opposite her and, after he'd complimented her on the meal, to which she made no comment, he asked the question he'd wanted to ask since Wednesday morning when she'd phoned him. 'What made you change your mind about seeing me again?' he said.

Oh, hell, thought Ali. What am I supposed to tell him? That he's only here because I was so mad with Daniel? 'I don't really know,' she lied.

'Oh,' he said flatly. It wasn't a very satisfactory answer. It still left him wondering where he stood with her. Another silence followed and Elliot turned his attention to the CD. The singer had moved on to another track and was now dishing out lyrics with sledgehammer subtlety – 'I wish you would tell me what I'm doing wrong, we could talk it over and try to get along . . .' Inwardly recoiling from its hamfisted appropriateness, he put down his knife and fork and reached for his wine, wishing that the singer would get to the end without bludgeoning them any harder with the poignancy of the words. But his hope was in vain. She blundered on, regardless of his discomfort: 'So be my friend or my enemy, be whatever you have to be, but don't, don't be a stranger . . .'

Ali was listening to the lyrics too. Puzzled, she couldn't recall buying the album. Nor did she have any recollection of ever hearing it before. But she couldn't deny how apt the words were. She and Elliot had become like strangers to one another. Daniel had told her earlier that day that he thought their divorce had been as senseless a tragedy as Isaac's death. In her heart she knew that he was right. But it didn't help. It didn't change the need she had to keep the distance between her and Elliot. 'But what if there was a way to change some of what's happened?' Daniel had asked. She hadn't answered him because she couldn't bring herself to admit that part of her didn't want her wounds to be healed. Not yet. She wasn't ready. She still needed to kick against the hurt of her grief.

The track came to an end and Ali remembered that Daniel had given her the CD. She recalled what he'd said to her at the time. 'Put it on loud, Babe, and listen to it closely.' She hadn't, of course. But, then, she so rarely did what people told her to do.

Conscious that nobody had spoken for some minutes, Ali looked up from her plate and caught Elliot staring at her. In the lamplight the solemnity of his face was startlingly profound and his eyes, normally so clear and blue, were faded with sadness. Oh, God, she thought, with genuine remorse, he doesn't deserve this. Why had he agreed to come here and put himself through this dreadful misery? Had it been to punish himself? Had she mistaken his motives for using her? Having thought that he wanted to be friends to assuage his guilt, was he in fact here to torture himself by remembering how it had once been? Filled with the need to dispel the mood of gloom that had settled on them, she said, 'How did your day in London go?'

His eyes narrowed fractionally. 'How did you know I was in London?'

She realised her error. If she told him the truth that she'd tried to phone him to cancel this evening, it would lead to him asking why. 'I called your office this afternoon to check that you were still on for dinner,' she lied once more. 'Who's the unhelpful woman you've got masquerading as a secretary, these days?'

He raised an eyebrow. 'Her name's Dawn, and in polite circles she's what one would describe as an acquired taste.'

'And is she your acquired taste?'

'No. I can't stand the woman.'

'Then get rid of her.'

'Other than objecting to her offhand manner, I don't have any real grounds to do so. She's surprisingly good at her job.'

'Historically that's never stopped a partner-in-charge from wielding the great axe of power.'

'True, but misguided as I might be, I pride myself on not being one of those industrial dinosaurs.'

If any other man had said this, Ali would have condemned him for fishing for a compliment, but coming from Elliot she knew better. He'd never been one of those idiots who needed to roll on to his back to have the under-belly of his egotism rubbed. 'So what's this Dawn like? I've money on her being a right old witch.'

He put down his knife and fork and carefully wiped his mouth with his napkin. 'There are some who think she's a vision to behold.'

'Really? With anyone in particular? Or is she not choosy? Perhaps she has a display case of trophy scalps at home?'

'That wouldn't surprise me at all. But for a time it was rumoured that she and Scott had a thing going.'

Ali reached for the bottle of wine. She offered it to Elliot but he shook his head. When she'd refilled her own glass, she said, 'And does this Dawn the Porn have designs on the ultimate prize in the office?'

'Who? Gervase?'

She rolled her eyes. 'I think we can both safely assume that never in a million years would either of us consider Gervase as an ultimate prize. I was referring to the boss. Has she tried to hit on *you*?'

Elliot looked indignant. 'Certainly not.'

Ali smiled to herself. *He really doesn't have a clue how attractive he is*, she thought, *or what an easy target it makes him.* 'So how is Gervase?' she asked. 'Still grinding people underfoot if they've dared to get in his way?'

'More or less.'

She groaned. 'The destruction derby of big office politics, nothing else compares with it. How the hell do you stick it, Elliot?

He shrugged. 'It's just a job.'

'Oh, come off it. Your career means more to you than that.'

He tapped his fingers lightly on the table and almost smiled. 'You're right. Perhaps it's the power struggle I enjoy so much.'

'What? Knowing you've made it and the others haven't?'

'No. It's watching them all fighting with each other and knowing that it's pointless. The real sense of power is accepting that at the end of the day none of it matters.'

'Easy to say when you're sitting comfortably in the coveted office on the ninth floor.'

'Will that be my epitaph? "He made it to the ninth floor."'

'It could be worse. It could be "He only made it to the third floor."'

'Or how about "He cheated and took the lift"?'

'That's not cheating, that's good lateral thinking. Of which I strongly approve.'

'What about you? Do you feel comfortable in your empowered position these days? After all, you're the boss as well.'

'Ah, but a different kind of boss.'

'More human? More caring?'

'Of course, that's real girl power for you.'

'So it all comes down to power, then?'

'I suppose it does when you believe it's something you've been deliberately denied through years of male-dominated prejudice.'

'Does Daniel feel the same way?'

Ali laughed. 'God, no. Not Daniel. He's far too tolerant for his own good.'

Elliot sipped his wine reflectively. After a bit, he said, 'Tolerance is a quality we despise at our peril.'

'Is that what passes through your mind when you're head to head with Gervase?'

He leaned back in his chair and stroked the long, slender stem of his glass. 'I'm afraid there's only the one thought that comes into my mind when I'm with that man and that's to knock the hell out of him.'

Ali pretended to be shocked. 'I'm not at all sure that that's the correct way for a partner-in-charge to talk.'

'Then it confirms what Gervase has probably always thought about me.'

'What's that?'

'That I'm the wrong man for the job. My background and credentials are not at all suitable.'

'Aye, lad, as Sam would say. You're a crest short on t' family silver.'

They both laughed.

But then quickly fell silent as they realised what had happened: they'd allowed themselves a brief respite of light-heartedness. They each looked around for a distraction: Ali poked at the few remaining rocket leaves in the salad bowl and Elliot folded his napkin carefully then laid it beside his plate. He wanted to tell Ali how much he was enjoying her company now that she'd relaxed, that chatting with her about the Guano of the Big Practice, as they used to refer to it, seemed the most natural thing in the world to him. He was about to open his mouth to speak when she rose from her chair and began to gather up the dishes. 'I'll get the next course,' she said. 'Why don't you choose another CD?'

Dumping the crockery with a clatter on the draining-board, Ali tried to assimilate the rampant confusion of her thoughts. Only a few hours ago she had been utterly convinced of her distrust for Elliot and his motives for wanting to see her, but now she wasn't so sure. What had passed between them just now was, in essence, little more than an exchange of cordial dinner-party chat, but it made her realise for the first time since they had grown apart what it could be like if the fighting stopped. It tempted her to consider the viability of Daniel's long-held claim that by calling a truce with Elliot, the worst and most debilitating pain of Isaac's death could be disarmed.

Could he be right?

Could it really be that simple?

And was it worth a try?

'Yes,' whispered a faint voice inside her. 'Let it go. Let the past go. Stop fighting him.'

But a more strident, familiar voice asserted itself: 'Why should either of you know peace of mind when you don't deserve it?'

She shook the voices from her head and lifted the cover from the plate of cheese she'd put together earlier in the evening. She placed it on a tray with a basket of wholewheat crackers and took it to the table. Elliot was over by the bookcase behind the sofa inspecting the cover of the CD Daniel had given her, and while he had his back to her, Ali took the opportunity to assess his appearance, which so far that evening she hadn't noticed. He was casually dressed in an open-necked cream shirt, tucked into a pair of sage green linen trousers with a belt that matched the soft brown leather of his Deck shoes. His hair was shorter than she approved of and made him look a little severe, but for all that, it did nothing to diminish his attractiveness. Then just as she'd reached this conclusion he turned, saw that she'd been quietly studying him and, very slowly, very hesitantly, he gave her one of his rare smiles.

He could have fired no deadlier a shot. It was as direct and powerful as a cruise missile and caught her thoroughly off-guard.

Holy Moses, she thought, when she'd regained the power of coherent reasoning, where the hell did that come from?

Chapter Twenty-Two

It came as no surprise to Ali that her waking thought should be of Elliot. Not that she'd slept much. And when she had it had been fitful and restless.

It was Saturday morning, and instead of being able to enjoy the luxury of a lie-in, her unsettled mind was forcing her to get out of bed. She pushed back the duvet and went downstairs to make a pot of tea. While the kettle boiled, she peered out of the window into the grey half-light of a disappointingly dull and dreary day. The sun was a ghostly orb in the sky and a thin layer of mist covered the surrounding flatness of ploughed fields. In the tall alder trees at the end of the lane she could see the hunched figures of three large crows high up in the tracery of branches that were yet to burst into their spring greenery. There was a sinister and portentous when-shall-we-three-meet-again look about the birds as they surveyed their territory of exposed farmland.

She shivered, left the window and made two rounds of peanut-butter wholemeal toast. She put her breakfast on to a tray, went upstairs, and climbed back into bed. She poured herself a large mug of Rose Pouchong and took a bite out of one of the pieces of toast. She chewed thoughtfully, savouring the taste of what had to be at least a hundred calories per square inch.

Now it was time to think about Elliot.

Elliot.

Elliot.

Elliot.

It didn't matter how many times she said his name, it didn't straighten the tangle of knotted thoughts that had kept her awake for most of the night. Impartiality told her that the evening had gone better than she could have hoped for. Apart from that terrible moment here in her bedroom with Mr Squeezy, it really hadn't been too awful. The mood between them might have been wary, but it had certainly been a lot less hostile than on previous meetings.

But there was no denying how relieved she'd felt when Elliot had said that he ought to be going. She had made no attempt to detain him by offering another cup of coffee, but had risen from the sofa and said, 'Give my love to Sam, won't you?'

In return, he'd said, 'And mine to Sarah when you see her tomorrow.'

Neither of them had suggested, 'This was fun, we should do it again,' and it was left that he would call her. There had followed a tricky few seconds downstairs at the front door when they both realised that somehow they had to bring the evening to a close, but on what note?

A formal handshake?

A see-you-around-sometime nod?

Or a cheek-brushing kiss?

She'd stood numb with indecision as the night air had swirled in through the open door and nipped at her ankles like a small snappy dog. But she saw in Elliot's eyes that he had made a decision and with only the merest hint of hesitancy in his movements he reached out a hand, rested it on her arm and bent his head to kiss her. But she'd panicked. Stepping back from him, she'd said, 'Brrr . . . it's cold out there. I said you'd regret not bringing a coat.'

She hadn't stayed at the door politely waving him off as he drove away, but had turned the key in the lock, shot the bolt and scuttled back upstairs in a state of red-faced, hackles-up shock.

He'd tried to kiss her!

The bloody cheek of him!

One fish-pie supper and he thought he could make free and bloody easy with her!

The nerve of the man!

These were the thoughts that had passed through her mind as she'd tried in vain to sleep. But now as she finished the last of the toast, she wondered if she hadn't overreacted. The evening may have been a little chilly in places, but there had been one or two tangible flashes of warmth in the conversation, mainly when they'd been discussing work. That had certainly provided them with a conveniently fertile patch of common ground, especially when it came to their mutual dislike of Gervase Merchant-Taylor.

But what about her response when Elliot had given her the benefit of one of his smiles? Was she going to dismiss that as nothing more than a 'flash of warmth'? And wasn't that the real cause of her sleepless night? Hadn't it scared her rigid to know that after everything they'd gone through he could still have the same high-charged effect on her? And that was why she'd panicked when he'd tried to kiss her, wasn't it? She hadn't trusted herself. Go down that road, she'd thought, and goodness knows where she would end up.

She smiled, thinking of Daniel's probable contribution to the conversation if he were here. He'd be smirking and saying, 'Told you so, told you so.'

That afternoon, when what little light there had been during the day had almost faded, Ali banked up the fire with some logs from the wood basket then went over to the window to see if there was any sign of Sarah. It was almost four o'clock; she should have arrived an hour ago.

It wasn't like Sarah to be late and Ali hoped that she hadn't broken down on the way. She knew that Sarah was a slow driver, but even allowing for an extra fifteen minutes on her journey time, she should have been here by now. Ali had already tried ringing Smithy Cottage, but there had been no reply so all she could do was stare into the distance, hoping for a glimpse of her friend's ancient Sierra in the dwindling light. The fields were still shrouded in mist, which Ali had felt, as the day wore on, had seeped its cold, melancholy dampness through the thick walls of the mill and wrapped itself around her.

She'd spent the morning catching up on the tedium of domestic paperwork, a job she hated and which she always put off as long as she could. She'd reluctantly given two hours of her time to sorting through the pile of mail that lived between the fruit bowl and the microwave.

Finally, when she'd finished answering letters, writing cheques for her credit cards and gone through her bank statements, she had decided to go upstairs and see what she could find for Sarah. Sarah rarely spent money on herself, least of all on clothes, but as she and Ali were the same size, Ali had always passed on to her anything she no longer wanted. There was never a feeling of misplaced charity in the gesture and Sarah accepted the clothes in the spirit they were offered. Only once had Ali overstepped the mark when she had deliberately bought a MaxMara outfit with Sarah's beautiful dark hair and much darker complexion in mind. She'd given it to her casually and said, 'One of those impulse buys I should never have made. It looks dreadful on me.' But Sarah had seen right through her. 'Ali,' she'd said sternly – well, sternly for Sarah, 'I want your genuine hand-me-downs. Don't ever do this to me again.' She had refused the outfit and forced Ali to take it back to the shop.

It was while she had been sorting through her wardrobe for clothes she could pass off as genuine 'hand-me-downs' that she had come across the shoebox. She should never have opened it, but an urge far stronger than common sense made her carry it to the bed and take off the lid to look at its contents. Carefully wrapped in white tissue paper was one of Isaac's first Babygros, along with a photograph of him wearing it. The picture showed him fast asleep in her arms, his face pale and relaxed, his top lip slightly overlapping the lower one; he was only a week old but unknowingly his tiny being had held the key to what made her complete. She placed the soft fabric comfortingly against her face. She closed her eyes and, just as she knew it would, she let the familiar ache of grief work its way through her body. She stayed like that until tears, unbidden, slowly slid down her cheeks and she dropped to her knees, leaned against the bed and wept loudly and without restraint. And just as freely as her tears flowed, so did the stream of unanswerable questions. Why did Isaac have to die? Why him? Why her child? Why her little boy?

When she was all cried out, she rewrapped the Babygro and photograph and returned the box to the back of the wardrobe. She went into the bathroom and washed her face. She couldn't bring herself to glance in the mirror – she knew that she looked awful and didn't need to have it confirmed. She reached for a freshly laundered hand towel and as she rubbed at her face she breathed in the sweet, fragrant smell of fabric conditioner. Instantly she was reminded of a similar aroma, and of another occasion when she had lost control. It was two months after Isaac's death and she'd been shopping in Sainsbury's. She was pushing the trolley past the shelves of breakfast cereals and as she turned the corner expecting to find household cleaning products she discovered that the supermarket had swapped things about: she was face to face with an aisle of baby products. In previous weeks she'd planned her route to eschew the shelves of nappies and baby foods. But there was no avoiding it that day, and as she forced herself forward the sweet smell of infant hygiene engulfed her – nappies, shampoo, bubble bath, wipes, talc. The sickly smell filled her nostrils making her feel violently ill. She abandoned the trolley, rushed outside to her car and drove home, unable to stop herself shaking or sobbing. Elliot had been so worried about her he'd called the doctor, who prescribed a cocktail of sleeping pills and tranquillisers. But she had refused to take them and had stuffed the packets unopened into her bedside table.

There was still no sign of Sarah and, moving away from the window, Ali thought of the desolation and bitterness she had felt earlier that afternoon when she'd been crying for Isaac. She had never told anyone this, but it was when she was at her most wretched that she felt closest to Isaac. It was as if she gained a perverse sense of comfort from putting herself through the agony of crying for him. Only when she was in pain could she feel that her love for Isaac was still real, that *he* was still real. Some of her memories of Isaac were already fading – worn out like a treasured photograph with too much handling – and she was worried that if she ever came to terms with his death it would not only be a betrayal of his short life but she would have nothing left of him.

So the pain had to go on. It was her only real source of comfort.

When she arrived and dropped her overnight bag to the floor, Sarah's first words were, 'Please may I have an enormous glass of wine, and after I've gulped it down will you give me another?'

Bemused, Ali opened a bottle of chilled Sauvignon *blanc* and watched, in astonished silence, as her friend plonked herself on the sofa, drained the glass in one go, then held it out for a refill. Ali obliged and when that, too, had disappeared she said, 'And how long do I have to wait before I get an explanation for why my normally sober-as-a-judge friend is suddenly resembling Oliver Reed on an all-out bender?'

'Quite a while,' Sarah replied. 'I want to get drunk. Completely drunk. Then I'll talk. Not before.'

'Has this got something to do with Trevor?'

Sarah said obstinately, 'More wine, please.'

Another glassful disappeared and Ali grew concerned. She

moved the bottle away from her friend's field of vision and said, 'Ready to talk yet?'

'No. I want to keep on drinking until everything bad in my life is no longer there.'

'Sarah,' Ali said gently, 'if it were possible to drink one's problems away, don't you think I might have tried it? Now, no more booze until I've had some sense out of you. In fact, I'm going to go and put the kettle on because by the time it's boiled you're going to be feeling the effect of all that wine you've knocked back and in dire need of several mugs of strong black coffee.'

'But I don't want to be sober,' Sarah said, leaping up from the sofa, her cheeks flushed, her voice thick with the onset of tears. 'I've come here to get drunk. Don't you understand? I've come here to be different. I'm tired of being who I am. I don't want to be the Sarah you know, or think you know. I want to be the Sarah I was meant to be.' Her shoulders shook and she sobbed.

Ali went to Sarah and put her arms around her. 'Whatever is it? What's been going on that you've kept from me?'

It was some minutes before Sarah could speak and when she did she realised that Ali had been correct about the effect of all the wine she'd drunk. 'Could I have that coffee now, please?' she said, slightly shamefaced. 'My head feels as if it's floating a couple of inches above my shoulders.'

Ali hurriedly made a large cafetière of coffee, tucked a box of tissues under her arm, went back into the sitting area and joined Sarah on the sofa. 'You were right about this being to do with Trevor,' Sarah said, her composure reinstated once more. 'It is.'

Ali wanted to say, 'Well, of course it is. Who else could push you to this breaking point?' but she wisely held her tongue. This was not the moment for a litany of hatred against the man she held responsible for everything miserable in Sarah's life.

'Trouble is, I'm not sure where or how to begin,' said Sarah, taking a cautious sip of her coffee.

Again Ali wanted to chip in: 'You could go back to when you agreed to marry the stupid man. That's when all your problems started, surely.' But with great restraint she said, 'Why don't you tell me what made you call me on Tuesday evening? You didn't sound at all like you. Had something happened then?'

Without being able to look Ali in the eye Sarah told her what had been going on at Smithy Cottage. She told her of the extent of Trevor's preoccupation with the Slipper Gang and what it was doing to him. Then she told Ali what had gone on at their Tuesday night prayer-group meeting and the pathetic game Trevor had played.

Ali's face blazed with anger. 'Bloody hell!' she thundered. 'This is appalling. The man's stark staring bonkers.'

'It gets worse,' murmured Sarah.

Ali stared at her anxiously. 'He's not hurt you, has he? Because if he's so much as looked at you with intent, I'll—'

Sarah shook her head. 'No. Nothing like that.'

'What, then?'

She told Ali about Jamie.

'Don't tell me, Trevor doesn't approve.'

'That's putting it mildly.'

'But how does that compare with imagining that you're in league with my old mate Beelzebub?'

'This morning he . . . he went into Hannah's bedroom and found her diary and—'

'Hold on a moment,' cut in Ali. 'What do you mean by "found"?'

Sarah looked uncomfortable. She put down her mug, took a long lock of her hair and twisted it round her finger.

Ali recognised straight away what she was doing: it was a sign that Sarah was struggling with her conscience. Other people chewed their lip, bit their nails or clasped their hands, but Sarah fiddled with her hair. It amazed Ali that even now, after everything Sarah had just told her, her friend was still torn with loyalty towards Trevor.

At last Sarah spoke. 'While Hannah was out in Chester this morning he searched her room until he found where she'd hidden it. Oh, Ali, she'd written about Jamie and what she felt for him. He's her first boyfriend. It was so innocent, so sweet and touching. But Trevor turned it into something sordid and shameful.'

Ali was furious. 'He's got no right to do that,' she roared. 'What kind of father is he?'

'A scared father,' Sarah said quietly.

'You sound almost as if you're defending him.'

'I'm not. It's just that I can understand what drove him to it. He's desperately trying to control something that's no longer within his power. He wants his little girl back. It's as simple as that.'

Ali got up from the sofa to throw another log on the fire. 'Well, he'll lose her for ever if he carries on behaving the way he is. Does Hannah know what he did?'

'Yes. He confronted her with the diary when she came home. I've never seen her so upset or so angry. She burst into tears and screamed and screamed at him. She said some terrible things.'

There's not a living soul who would criticise her for doing that. You've not left her on her own with him, have you?'

'No. I decided we would all benefit from some time out from one another. I took her to stay with Emily, which was why I was so late coming to you.'

Ali came back to the sofa and sat with her legs tucked underneath her. 'And in what state did you leave Trevor? On his knees praying for both your mortal souls?'

'Not exactly. He was in his workshop taking out his temper on a piece of wood. I've no idea what I'll return to tomorrow.'

'Then don't go back.'

The words hung in the air provocatively.

Sarah raised her eyes to Ali's and knew that she wasn't talking in the short term. 'I have to,' she said softly.

'No, you don't.'

'Ali, I know what you're suggesting, but it's not in me.'

'And it's in you to stay with a man who's unhinged?'

'He's not unhinged,' Sarah said, with a frown. 'I'm sure this is just some kind of mid-life crisis he's going through. He's using the Slipper Gang to replace the relationship Hannah is withdrawing from him. If I can be patient and wait for him to work it out of his system, everything will come right in the end.'

'Oh, Sarah, listen to yourself. You keep on defending him. Why?'

'Because he's my husband.'

'Bugger that for a game of soldiers! No decent husband publicly humiliates his wife and makes out that she's consumed by an evil force that needs exorcising. You have to face up to it. He's hurting and abusing you and will continue to do so for as long as you let him. Just leave him. When Hannah's done her exams come and move in with me. There's plenty of room. We'd have a great time, we'd—'

'Stop it, Ali. Please stop. None of that is possible.'

'Why not?'

'I told you before, he's my husband. I could never leave him.'

'Which means you could never be truly happy. How can you live with that?'

Sarah's face was serious and she gazed across the room at the flickering flames in the fire. 'Because I couldn't live with the knowledge that I'd broken my marriage vows,' she said quietly.

Ali let these words sink in. She had the nasty feeling that Sarah was about to start waving the banner of her religious beliefs as a reason for staying in her incomprehensible marriage. Stalling for time to reassess the situation, she said,

'Sarah, let me ask you a question. Could you ever conceive of living on your own and being happy?'

Sarah returned her gaze to Ali and very slowly a tentative smile appeared on her face, until finally it broke into a radiant expression of happiness. Then she threw back her head and laughed. 'Oh, yes,' she said, her laughter echoing round the room, 'I believe I could be extremely happy without Trevor.'

Chapter Twenty-Three

The bright, carefree laughter that had so unexpectedly filled the room came to an abrupt end, and in an altogether more subdued tone, Sarah said, 'You've no idea how good that was, actually to hear myself say what I've thought so many times, but never dared to voice. Are you very shocked?'

Ali *was* shocked. But not for the reason her friend was thinking. She couldn't get over the intense change in Sarah's face as she'd uttered those words: *I believe I could be extremely happy without Trevor.* Not for years had she seen or heard Sarah express herself with such heartfelt joy. Or with such passion.

'Ali?'

Ali kicked herself out of her thoughts. 'Of course I'm not shocked, Sarah, it's more a matter of being stunned that you know how different and infinitely better your life could be but you're not prepared to do anything about it.'

'It's not as simple as that.'

'It could be.'

Sarah shook her head resolutely. 'No. Divorce is not an option for me.' Then she said, 'I'm sorry that I arrived here in such a hysterical state.'

'Given the circumstances, I'd say you've behaved as you always do, with admirable self-control. If it had been me in your shoes I wouldn't be drinking cups of coffee with a friend, I'd be out there searching for a suitable hiding-place for the recognisable bits of Trevor's dismembered body. Isn't there anything I can say to make you see sense?'

Leaning forward to place her empty mug on the table,

Sarah said, 'No, there isn't. I meant it when I said that divorce isn't an option for me.'

Ali drew a knee up to her chest, rested an elbow on it, and gave Sarah one of her no-holds-barred penetrating stares. 'Okay, so give it to me straight. God's lurking at the bottom of all this, isn't he? The God who so graciously dumped Trevor on you expects you to stay with him, no matter what. Even if it makes a mockery of your own existence and robs it of its worth. How am I doing? Am I close?'

'As always, and in your inimitable fashion, you've entirely missed the point,' Sarah said wearily.

'Oh, I know what the point is, all right,' Ali said hotly. 'You expect the wrathful hand of God to strike you down in a fit of retributional malice if you don't do as he commands.'

'Goodness, for an atheist you've got an awful lot to say about something you don't believe exists,' countered Sarah.

'That's because there's so much propaganda put about one can't help but absorb some of it. And while we're on the subject, and I accept full responsibility for the lack of originality to the question, but humour me with a credible answer. If your faith hangs on the belief that God is all-powerful and that nothing's too insignificant or too great for him to handle, why do we spend most of our lives having to cope with so many appalling atrocities? Or is that because we get what we deserve? The punishment fits the crime. You're such a bloody awful sinner God gave you Trevor and, of course, it makes perfect sense that all those poor devils in Bangladesh must have been so inherently bad that they've been given a flood just to make them appreciate the squalor and poverty they already live with. And as for me, well, that's bloody obvious, isn't it? My crimes against humanity were so great I had . . . I had –' But her words fell away and, her face suffused with colour, she stared miserably into the middle distance of her anger.

'And you had Isaac taken away from you just to teach you a lesson in humility,' Sarah murmured softly.

'Yeah,' Ali muttered, her eyes dark with bitterness, 'so I did.' She blew her nose, then threw the tissue at the fire but missed. 'I guess in your book that stupid outburst makes me a sodding agnostic, doesn't it?'

Sarah looked at her kindly. 'Chance would be a fine thing. But I have to say, from a theological point of view, you're all over the place with that theory. Isaac didn't die to serve you right, any more than the people of Bangladesh deserved what they're currently experiencing. The question we should ask ourselves is not what sort of God allows thousands of innocent people to die in a disaster, but what kind of person stands by while his neighbour suffers? Our reaction should always be, what can I do to help?'

Ali returned her gaze and said, 'That's what I'm trying to do with you. I want to help you but you won't let me.'

'But, Ali, you are. Right now you're helping me by giving me the opportunity to speak my mind. I'm sure that once I've got everything off my chest and I've calmed down I'll go back home tomorrow and everything will be all right.'

Ali looked at her doubtfully. 'You don't really believe that, do you?'

'I have to believe it.'

'But what if Trevor gets worse? What if he's undergoing some sort of delusory disorder? What if he starts trying to exorcise Hannah?'

'He won't,' Sarah said firmly. 'I'm sure that deep down he thinks she's just going through a typical teenage stage of rebellion.'

'Well, if he thinks that, why can't he adopt the appropriate role of quietly bemused father, instead of going off his head with all this fanatical everything's-of-the-devil baloney?'

'I don't know the answer to that. I wish I did.'

'And I wish I could understand why you're sacrificing your happiness for the sake of your beliefs. Divorce has been going on in the Church of England long enough for even a saint such as you not to feel guilty about resorting to it.'

Sarah smiled patiently. 'All my adult life I've lived according to my faith,' she raised a hand to stop Ali interrupting, 'and yes, I'm well aware that you'd like to throw in a quick, below-the-belt and-look-where-it's-got-you, but I happen to believe that without it I would have been very much the poorer. I know that when we were at Oxford you suspected that I'd taken up with all that "religious nonsense", as you not so intellectually referred to it, because I was searching for some kind of mental crutch to make—'

'Yes,' Ali was unable to keep quiet any longer, 'you're right, that's exactly what I thought. What's more, I reckon you've hung on to that crutch in the mistaken hope that it would fill the void a loving husband should have filled.'

Sarah opened her eyes wide. 'Ali, I can't believe you just said that! You, the red-hot archetypal independent woman who beats her chest every morning to the chant "Men, who needs them?"'

'Funny ha-ha. But I notice you've avoided answering my question.'

'I was coming to that before you stepped in so rudely.'

'I'm sorry. Go on.'

'How one views religion, spirituality, faith – call it what you will – is very personal, but for me it doesn't provide one iota of certainty, not even guaranteed peace of mind—'

'So what's the point in it, then?'

Sarah smiled with amused tolerance at yet another inter-ruption. 'It provides the courage to face what we think is beyond us,' she said patiently.

Ali thought about this. 'Are you telling me that it's your faith that's kept you sane throughout your marriage and that it's faith that will keep you there?'

Sarah nodded.

Ali let out her breath. 'Hellfire, that's some act of faith.'

'Marriage is.'

'But . . . but you can still believe in Christ and all his merry apostles and be divorced. Surely the one doesn't preclude the other. Why can't you simply play the Christian trump card of confessing, repenting and moving on? I thought that's what the Resurrection was all about?'

'One has to abide by the basic principles of one's beliefs. I'm afraid I can't subscribe to the view that one can pick and choose from the Bible. If we did that it would fall apart and there'd be nothing left of any value.'

'No leeway, then?'

'No. To disregard a basic tenet of scripture just because it doesn't suit one's current situation is a flagrant breach of faith. If you recall, I did it once before back in Oxford and that's why I'm now married to Trevor.'

'But the bulk of what the Bible says is open to conjecture and how we interpret it. It was written centuries ago and for a very different culture.'

'And to quote something you said to me at Christmas, isn't that the great universal cop-out? Now, if we could drop the subject, I'd love something to eat. I missed lunch and I'm starving.'

They cooked supper together, and while Ali prodded at the lamb chops under the grill, she watched Sarah out of the corner of her eye as she added milk and butter to the potatoes she was mashing. She looked as though she hadn't a care in the world and Ali marvelled at her restored calm. Was it possible that only a few hours ago she had been distraught with frustrated unhappiness?

But wasn't it what they all did? Hadn't she, herself, been on her knees that afternoon consumed by the worst misery? The masks we wear, that's what it was all about. It was always easier to keep the mask in place than let it slip to reveal one's true self. And she should know: she'd been doing it for more than two years now.

'Elliot was here last night,' she said, as casually as she could, deciding that Sarah deserved a break from being under the spotlight. 'He came for dinner, at my invitation.'

'Did he indeed?' said Sarah, joining her at the cooker and putting the saucepan of mashed potatoes on the ring.

'Indeed he did. And afterwards we made love till dawn.'

'Yes, dear, and was that before or after you danced naked around the maypole?'

Ali laughed. 'Why can't I ever make you rise to the bait? If I'd thrown Daniel that line he would have been panting for the sexually explicit details.'

'That's because he's the same as you, incorrigibly nosy.' Without taking her eyes off what she was doing, Sarah went on, 'And did the thought of making love till dawn go through your mind when Elliot was here?'

'Sarah!'

She smiled. 'So it did cross your mind.'

'For no more than a second, I swear.' Ali was part-horrified to hear herself admitting to it but also part-relieved.

Sarah appeared to read her thoughts. 'Come on, Ali,' she said, 'confession is good for the soul. Why don't you tell me what else you thought while he was here? But before that, put me in the picture as to why you invited him for dinner in the first place.'

'I'm afraid you won't approve of my motives.'

'Have I ever approved of any of your motives?'

'But this one was particular unpleasant. Even I'm ashamed of it.'

They served their supper and carried it over to the table. Ali opened another bottle of wine and told Sarah about her week: of Elliot surprising her in the office when she'd been sprawled on her desk showing her all; of him taking her out for lunch; and of Daniel's words of interfering wisdom, which had led her to wanting to prove him wrong.

'And who exactly did you prove wrong in the end?' asked Sarah, when Ali had finished.

'Heaven only knows. Just as I think I've got the answer to all this mess, I realise I haven't. I'm so bloody confused. I thought I had Elliot all neatly buttoned up. I thought I had him sussed. But after last night I'm not so sure. I was dreading him coming here and certainly to begin with my fears were confirmed. We were horribly distant and cold to each other, but then gradually we got talking about work and we seemed to relax. There were moments when it was almost enjoyable.'

'So when did the idea of sex enter your mind?'

'When I was getting the cheese and biscuits. I was sneaking a good long look at him while he had his back to me, then suddenly he turned and . . . Oh, God, this is so embarrassing.' She hung her head.

'Go on, what did he say?'

Ali raised her head. 'It wasn't what he said, it was what he did. He flashed me one of his rare-as-gold-dust smiles and I was a goner. *Phwoar* factor big-time.'

'And then?'

Ali grinned. 'Then I ripped off my clothes, threw myself at his feet and said, "It's a wholewheat cracker or me. Make your choice!"'

Sarah didn't return the smile. She sipped her wine and looked serious. 'When you start joking, Ali Anderson, that's when I know I'm getting close. Tell me honestly, how did it make you feel knowing that he could still have that effect on you?'

Ali scowled. 'Confused. Then later, when he tried to kiss me goodnight, I felt cross. Furious.'

'And was that a kiss on the lips or the cheek?'

'It didn't get that far. I ducked out of the way just in time.'

'How fortunate,' Sarah said drily. 'So if he treated you to one of his sexy smiles, which I recall only too well, *and* tried to kiss you, what do you suppose Elliot feels for you, Ali?'

'If you were to ask Daniel, he'd tell you that Elliot—'

'I'm not asking Daniel, I'm asking *you*.'

'Then you're asking the wrong person. I've no idea what Elliot thinks about me.'

'But you're more than capable of making an educated guess.'

Ali reached for the bottle of wine and topped up her glass. 'Are you trying to push me into a corner?'

'Is that how you see it?'

Ali rolled her eyes. 'It's what it bloody well feels like. And if you intend on wheedling away until you get an answer, I'll save you the trouble. Elliot could be doing either of two things. It's possible that he's deliberately trying to punish himself by seeing me, or he could be wanting to use me as a means of assuaging his guilt. Personally, I'd go with the second option.'

Sarah set her glass down on the table and said, 'And that's the last thing you'd want to help him with, isn't it?'

There was a tense pause while Sarah waited for Ali to explode. But she didn't. Neatly changing the subject, she said, 'Oh, I nearly forgot, Elliot sends his love.'

It was tempting to say, 'Give him mine when you see him next,' but Sarah didn't want to antagonise Ali any further. She let her thoughts linger on Elliot and pondered on her own personal loss at not seeing him since the divorce. He was a kind, thoughtful man who had always shown great tact when confronted by Trevor in one of his less than endearing moods. 'Accountants,' Trevor would joke, 'little more than parasites making good on the backs of somebody else's hard graft.' It was quite obvious why Trevor said what he did: it was his way of handling being the odd one out of the foursome. She, Ali and Elliot had all made it to Oxford but Trevor had not: he'd studied at the polytechnic at Headington and had never let anyone forget it. 'Elitist groves of academia are all very well,' he'd pontificate, 'but it's the polytechnics that provide the sound, practical education that industry is after.' The more he went on, the more he made himself the social and academic inferior. It was so embarrassing. Ali would frequently lose her temper with him and tell him not to be such a pig-headed fool, but Elliot would listen patiently then turn the conversation to a subject that showed Trevor in a better light. 'How's Hannah getting on with her music?' he'd ask, and off Trevor would go, happy as Larry to boast of his daughter's skill on the flute. Trevor's pride in Hannah, with his hopes and aspirations for her, was one of those strange but perfectly understandable paradoxes. While he openly disparaged the system that had educated Ali, Elliot and his wife, it was quite within the rules of his prejudice for his daughter to go there. 'Of course, it's different nowadays,' he had said, when Hannah first talked of applying. 'They've had to move with the times and change the whole ethos of what they stand for. It's no longer acceptable to be so élitist.'

It was a not-so-subtle moving of the goal-posts but Sarah was more than willing to let him get away with it. Conceding was, after all, something she was good at.

Unlike Ali.

Ali had probably never conceded a point in her life. It was as alien to her nature as it was to forgive and forget. And if only she could do that, thought Sarah, with sadness, as she glanced at her friend across the table, she would be so much happier. From what Ali had told her about Elliot, it sounded very much as if he was ready to move on, that he was now wanting to put Isaac's tragic death behind him, and that, for whatever reason, he saw Ali as a crucial part of that process.

As if she'd picked up on the dangerous direction Sarah's thoughts were heading, Ali pushed away her empty plate, rested her elbows on the table and said, 'So let's get back to this divorce thing. I still don't get it. There has to be a way round it.'

She might just as well have rolled up her sleeves, thought Sarah, with a wry smile. Well, two could play at that game. 'Before you subject me to a further onslaught of interrogation,' she said, 'I have a question for you. How much longer do you intend to use Elliot as a focus for your pain and anger?'

Chapter Twenty-Four

Ali gave a short contemptuous laugh. 'What is it with everyone?' she asked. 'Suddenly you all fancy yourselves as armchair psychotherapists, first Daniel, now you.'

Undaunted, Sarah said, 'Ten out of ten for a typically defensive response to a question you don't want to answer. Is there any chance of me having some of that wine, or are you going to hog the bottle for the rest of the night?'

Ali pushed it across the table and reflected on why it was that her two closest friends had taken to questioning her. They never had before, so why had they chosen now to start shining the light in her eyes, and giving her the third degree? She decided to be direct. 'Before I submit to your cack-handed grilling technique,' she said, 'am I allowed to ask why the sudden interest in what I do, say or think? What have I done that warrants this special scrutiny?'

Sarah heard the sharpness in Ali's voice. Should she risk all and pursue the conversation in the hope that Ali would finally admit the truth, or should she keep quiet? A true friend would want to help, she told herself. And ignoring Ali's question, she bravely made herself say, 'Knowing you as well as Elliot does, can you imagine the courage it must have taken for him to turn up at your office unexpectedly and ask you out to lunch?'

Ali shrugged indifferently. 'Give him his due, Elliot was never a coward. So where's your point leading?'

'Where it should be leading you.'

'Which is?'

'It strikes me that Elliot is ready to move on. Perhaps he's doing his best to put Isaac's tragic death behind him. I want to know if you're prepared to do the same.'

Ali studied the half-empty glass in her hand. Holding it by the stem, she slowly turned it round and round, the base of the glass scraping on the table. 'Well, bully for him,' she said, without looking up.

'But isn't that what you should be striving for?'

Still fiddling with the glass, Ali didn't say anything.

Sarah knew what Ali was withholding from her and believed that it was the key to unlocking the prison her friend had made for herself. 'Ali,' she said gently, 'look at me and tell me why you don't want to move on?'

Reluctantly Ali raised her eyes. 'Because it would be a betrayal.'

'Of whom?'

'Isaac, of course.'

'So punishing yourself is the way to keep Isaac alive, is that what you're saying?'

'I'm not punishing myself.'

'Oh, but, Ali, you are. And not just you.'

Ali's face darkened. She let go of her glass and shifted uncomfortably in her chair. 'Now you're really scraping the bottom of the trick-cyclist's barrel,' she said airily, letting out her breath as though she was tired of the subject.

Undeceived by Ali's air of dismissive boredom, Sarah took a metaphorical deep breath and pressed on in the unshake-able belief that what she was doing was right. It had to be done. She'd brought Ali this far, she wasn't going to let her slip away. 'I'm talking about your need to punish Elliot,' she said fearlessly. 'By not forgiving him for his rejection of you, you're keeping him in the same hell that you're in. You need his company there because you can't cope with the thought of being all alone in that miserable place. With nobody there to abuse, you'll end up punishing yourself even harder. And, as we all know, nobody punishes us more than ourselves.'

The colour drained slowly from Ali's face. She went very

pale. Her hands reached out for her wine-glass, then as if thinking better of it she pushed it away. 'I hate it when you get clever,' she said quietly. 'Why couldn't I have chosen a friend who was as dumb as me?'

Sarah smiled at her fondly, relieved that her words hadn't invoked a rage of hot denial. She understood that Ali's flippancy was her way of accepting what she'd just said and lightened the mood by saying, 'You didn't choose me. I chose you. The moment I saw you in the playground with Caroline Rothwell on top of you I thought, Now, there's somebody who goes about everything the wrong way.'

'I haven't changed much, then, have I?' Ali said despondently.

'Strange as it may seem, that's part of your charm. It's why Daniel and I love you as much as we do.'

'Well, I don't feel very charming. I should be more like you, virtuous and perceptively wise.' She smiled awkwardly. 'Do you remember my grandmother making us have an *alter ego*? I was supposed to learn from you how to be more thoughtful and you were supposed to take a leaf out of my book and be more assertive.'

'I think we'd both be the first to admit that we failed that little exercise. But it's funny that you should have mentioned our *alter egos*. After years of not thinking of her, Sarah the Impudent showed up the other day.'

'My God, I'd forgotten we'd given them names. What was mine called?'

'Ali the Angel.'

Ali groaned. 'So it was. Much good she's done me.'

'Perhaps you ought to resurrect her.'

'What, and have her confirm what a terrible person I've become?'

'Don't be too hard on yourself. What you've been through hasn't been easy. Given the extent of your loss, the mistakes you've made are quite understandable.' After a slight pause, she said, 'Why don't you tell me the rest?'

'The rest?'

'Yes. What really drove you to push Elliot away from you?'

Ali frowned with exasperation and chewed her lip. 'But, you know, it wasn't like that. It was *him* who froze me out. He wouldn't let me near him, he –'

Sarah reached across the table and touched Ali's hand lightly. 'In the beginning that's what happened, but what then? Did you talk to him? Did you try to help him, or did you deliberately provoke Elliot by being as cold and unforgiving as you knew how?'

With a sudden, quick-tempered movement, Ali snatched away her hand.

'And isn't it true,' continued Sarah, undeterred, 'that you kept on hurting him until you were convinced that he was in as much pain as you, if not more?'

'That's a terrible thing to say,' hissed Ali, her face blanched with both anger and distress. 'I – I didn't do that. How could you even think that of me?' But her lip trembled and betrayed her. She lowered her head and a painful hush engulfed them. When eventually Ali looked up there were tears in her eyes. 'Oh, Sarah,' she said, all sign of her rancorous denial now gone, 'I didn't mean to do it, I was mad with grief. I couldn't accept that Isaac was dead, it just wasn't possible. And when Elliot turned away from me, I felt – I felt that I had nothing left, that I'd lost everything. I was so angry . . . Then once I'd started hurting him I couldn't stop myself. It was . . . it was like a drug and I kept on going for his jugular until I was sure he hated me. It was the ultimate punishment I could inflict on him – to destroy the love we'd once had. To put him through the hell I was experiencing.'

'Did you never think he was already in hell?'

Ali shuddered. 'I wasn't in any fit state to think logically. All I knew was that if we were both damned, it meant in some crazy way we were connected.'

'Have you ever tried to explain this to Elliot?'

Ali wiped her eyes on the back of her sleeve and sniffed loudly. 'No.'

'Is it time that you did?'

'I don't know. It's probably too late. The harm's done. He'd never understand.'

'I think he does understand, I've a feeling that he's come to terms with a lot more than you give him credit for. The question is, if he's forgiven you, can you do the same for him?'

When Ali didn't respond, Sarah said, 'Forgiving Elliot doesn't necessarily mean that you have to be involved with him again.'

'I'll think about it,' Ali said, getting up from her chair and indicating that she'd had enough of the conversation. 'It's late, we should go to bed now.'

Sarah woke to the sound of tapping on her bedroom door. She muttered a sleepy, 'Yes,' and Ali, still in her pyjamas, came into the room with a large tray. She placed it on top of the duvet and climbed into the double bed beside Sarah.

'It's ten thirty, time you were stirring,' she said brightly.

'Ten thirty. You're joking.' Sarah sat up, looked at her watch, and saw that Ali was telling the truth. 'But I never sleep this long,' she said.

Pouring their tea, Ali said, 'That's because the Donovan homestead is the coldest place on earth and if you stay put for too long you'll die of frostbite.'

'It's not that bad. Is it?'

Ali passed her a mug of Rose Pouchong and a plate of toast. 'Bloody freezing with knobs on,' she said.

They ate their breakfast in companionable silence and Sarah thought how glad she was to be here with Ali. Despite the nature of everything they'd discussed since she'd arrived, her usual inner calm seemed to have been fully restored. It was odd that for some weeks now she had begun to doubt her faith, but when yesterday it had come under attack from Ali, she had instinctively leaped to its defence. Which was encouraging. It meant, reassuringly, that it was still intact. After its rough handling of late by Trevor and the Slipper Gang, it was a wonder it hadn't packed its bags and left home in a sulk. She smiled at the thought of this improbable analogy and pictured the sight of Faith pouting and slamming doors and stomping off down the garden path in a state of high dudgeon – *And don't go thinking I'm ever coming back!*

'Something amusing you?' asked Ali.

'A private joke,' Sarah said, 'and one you wouldn't appreciate.'

'It's not Sarah the Impudent showing her face again is it?'

'Not quite.'

'You didn't tell me last night why she suddenly appeared on the scene again.'

'Just a case of needing some inner moral support, I guess.'

'God not enough, then?'

Sarah smiled. 'He was busy watching over you.'

'And having a damn good laugh, no doubt. Did you sleep okay? The bed all right?'

'Fine. How about you?'

'Badly. I kept going over everything we discussed. Or, rather, what you dragged out of me while putting me through open heart surgery without the aid of an anaesthetic.'

'I'm sorry. Am I forgiven?'

'I'll let you know.'

'Well, promise me one thing. Promise you'll talk to Elliot. It would help you both so much in coming to terms with what's happened.'

'Mm . . . Again, I'll let you know. One thing puzzles me, though. Why did you wait until now to push me against the wall and make me admit what I'd been doing?'

'I took a huge gamble last night and simply trusted in my belief that you were willing to listen to me. I wouldn't have dared to try it a year ago. You weren't ready then – you'd probably have ended our friendship.'

Ali thought about this and was forced to agree that Sarah was right. It also made her acknowledge that, without knowing it, she had very slowly been learning to cope with some of her anger at the injustice of losing Isaac. 'I'd like to think that you're wrong about me flying off the handle and ending our friendship, but I'm glad you didn't risk it. Now, enough about my problems, I want to carry on where I left off with you last night.'

Laughing at Ali's ceaseless desire to strip-search her marriage, she said, 'No surprises there, then.'

'And I don't want you slipping in any more of your clever diverting questions. Got that?'

'Standard procedure, Ali. I've learned it all from you.'

'Well, be prepared to be outwitted. First question. When you arrived yesterday afternoon and were hitting the wine like a woman who'd been in the desert for forty days, you said you wanted to be the Sarah you were meant to be. What was that about?'

Sarah proffered her empty mug for some more tea and said, 'I'm afraid I was being a touch melodramatic.'

'That's certainly one way of describing it, but it begs the question why you were being uncharacteristically melodramatic. Especially when I don't think it relates directly to Trevor's bout of madness. I've a strong feeling that whatever drove you to say what you did has less to do with Trevor and more to do with you.'

'You're right. It has. I drove here at screaming pitch realising that I was tired of being Sarah the peacemaker. Just for once I wanted to be Sarah the hell-raiser. I wanted a little drama of my own. I've had years and years of being an extra in the drama of other people's lives.'

Ali felt guilty. 'Oh dear,' she said, 'and within no time at all you were back to being Sarah the peacemaker and counselling me on my troubles.'

'But don't you see? That's what I always do. It's of my own

226

doing. I much prefer helping others sort out their troubles than dealing with my own. I'm nothing but a coward.'

'The hell you are! Living with Trevor is a supreme act of bravery.'

'That's not true. I've turned away from Trevor's problems rather than confront them.'

'Such as?'

Sarah hesitated. Her hand rose instinctively to her sleep-tousled hair and pulled at a lock. As ever, the bond of loyalty she felt for Trevor was hard to shrug off. Or was she just plain old-fashioned embarrassed? She took the plunge and said, 'Well, for instance, Trevor and I haven't had sex for nearly ten years.'

Ali goggled. 'Why not?'

'He's not interested. Not since he became worried Hannah might hear us.'

'Does it bother you?'

'It did in the beginning, yes. But not now. I've got used to it not being there. In fact, I'm not sure how I'd react if he suddenly showed a renewed interest.'

Ali knew what her reaction would be: to run in the opposite direction. 'Tricky question on the horizon,' she said, 'and I'm on my guard for any diverting techniques you might have up your sleeve. At Christmas you told me that you've always felt sorry for Trevor. Is that all you feel, or do you love him?'

Sarah dabbed at the toast crumbs on her plate and drew a line through them with her forefinger. She contemplated lying, but in view of the degree of honesty she'd forced out of Ali it didn't seem fair. 'No, I don't love him,' she said, matter-of-factly.

'Have you ever loved him?'

'Sort of, yes.' Again the same reasonable tone.

Ali considered this. 'Okay,' she said, after a bit. 'Let's summarise. You've never truly loved Trevor – not in the heart-aching way. You have no real marriage, i.e. there's no nookie on offer. You won't divorce him because of your Christian belief in the sanctity of marriage and, lastly, you know that you could be happier without him. How am I doing? Have I covered everything?'

Sarah frowned. 'It sounds worse when you put it as bluntly as that. There's no mention of the respect I once had for Trevor for being such a good father and for all the—'

'Yes, yes, yes,' Ali cut in impatiently, 'so let's give the man a couple of Brownie points if it makes you feel easier.'

'It's not a matter of awarding –'

Ali held up a hand. 'Sarah, if you're about to embark on some sneaky diverting tactic, stop it now. I've got a seriously important question and I want it answered. According to your absurdly strict and antiquated Christian ethics, is divorce *ever* permissible?'

Sarah sighed. 'Yes,' she said.

'Hallelujah! Finally we're getting somewhere. I knew there'd be some convenient loophole tucked into the depths of all that gobbledegook. So what is it?'

'Adultery.'

Ali stared at Sarah. 'And that makes it permissible in your view? As simple as that?'

'Hypothetically, yes.'

'So if Trevor was to have an affair it would change everything?'

'As I just said, hypothetically, yes.'

Ali threw back her head and laughed. 'So all we need to do is find someone daft enough to go to bed with Trevor and you'd be a free woman?'

Sarah rolled her eyes and tutted at Ali's madness of thought.

'How about that weird Shirley character?' Ali said, when she'd stopped laughing. 'Do you think she's a likely candidate?'

It was Sarah's turn to be amused now. 'About as likely as you!'

*

Later that day as Ali stood outside the mill in a light drizzle of rain waving Sarah goodbye and wondering what cold misery awaited her at Smithy Cottage, she reflected on what her friend had told her that morning. Adultery, then, so it seemed, was the answer to all Sarah's problems. As easy and as uncomplicated as that. Just one illicit feverish fumble on Trevor's part and it would all be over.

The thought stayed with Ali for the rest of the afternoon, niggling away at her annoyingly as she curled up on the sofa watching television for something to do. Restlessly channel-hopping through a programme selection of golf, football, rugby, a musical adventure and a re-run of *Are You Being Served?*, she kept thinking the craziest of ideas. What if . . . what if *she* slept with Trevor?

No.

No, no, *no*, NO!

It was madness. It was lunacy of the highest order. She loved Sarah to bits, but seducing the ghastly Trevor for the sake of freeing her from her pointless marriage was way beyond even her loyal devotion. Cringing at yet another indelicate reference to Mrs Slocombe's feline companion, she suddenly pictured the scene of a panting, heaving Trevor on top of her. She shuddered with heart-stopping revulsion. *Jeez*, she'd have to be smashed out of her brains on a keg or two of Jack Daniel's to pull off a stunt as selfless as that.

Chapter Twenty-Five

It was the end of June, and since the start of Hannah's A-level exams in the middle of May, the weather had been glorious. A baking sun had cruelly taunted Hannah and Emily to abandon their revision and go outside to lie on the parched grass in the seductively hot sunshine. They'd resisted the temptation with admirable determination. And as the temperature had steadily risen, so had the tension inside Smithy Cottage – though in fairness to Hannah, once her exams were under way, there had been only a couple of nail-bitingly fraught days to cope with. This was when she had been utterly convinced that she'd messed up her French literature paper and had taken out her frustration on her father. But now all the hard work was over and Smithy Cottage was a relatively stress-free zone again.

It was also on the verge of becoming a daughter-free zone. As Sarah watched Hannah checking her small black-leather rucksack, which contained her passport and a meagre supply of cash and travellers' cheques, which would hopefully see her through the summer, she tried not to feel too envious. What wouldn't she give to throw a few essentials into a bag and head for six wonderfully carefree weeks in the sun?

For the past fortnight, and since the exams had finished, Hannah had been unable to talk about anything other than her impending holiday. She and Emily were joining Jamie and his friend, Craig, on their trip to France. They were going in Jamie's new car and the plan was to explore Brittany and the Atlantic coast and slowly make their way down to Biarritz, stopping *en route* for a couple of nights with an aunt of

Craig's who lived somewhere near La Rochelle. During the last few days a fever pitch of anticipation had been rapidly brewing, with Hannah and Emily constantly making last-minute adjustments to what they would and would not take with them.

Were high-cut shorts in or out?

Did the short silky dress make Hannah's hips look smaller?

Would the bikini or the fluorescent all-in-one make more of Emily's spectacular cleavage?

The backpacks were packed and repacked.

And all the while, Trevor hung about muttering darkly of the potential dangers awaiting Hannah on the other side of the Channel.

'She'll be fine.' Sarah had had to placate him. 'It's not as if she's going to be on her own – there's Emily, Jamie and Craig. She'll be quite safe.'

'Emily's got the sense of a half-wit,' he'd retorted, 'and those boys, well, what do we *really* know about them?'

But Sarah had great faith in Jamie. He was everything she would want in a boyfriend for her daughter. He was polite, caring and mature for his years. As for being a distraction during Hannah's exams, as Trevor had predicted, he'd been the opposite: he'd helped her to revise as well as kick into touch her occasional moments of panic. And much as Trevor had been desperate to consign Jamie to life's overflowing dustbin of no-hopers, Sarah had been delighted when he'd reluctantly admitted that there was little to object to in him – other than that he was not a brother in Christ.

Jamie's friend, Craig, who had been at school with him and was also on a gap year, was 'wacky, but cool', according to Hannah. And this brief description was sufficient to explain his affinity with the dizzy Emily. And no sooner had the perfectly balanced foursome been formed than the suggestion was made that the girls should join Jamie and Craig on their holiday. When Hannah came home one evening and raised the subject, Trevor's response was, 'But what if something went wrong? How would you cope? What would you do? You could be attacked and we wouldn't even know you were in trouble. I really don't think this is a good idea, Hannah.'

'But that could happen to me here, Dad,' Hannah had argued. 'They do have telephones in France, you know.'

Sarah's concern for Hannah's safety was just as great as Trevor's, but she knew there was nothing else for it but to let their daughter go. It was only France, after all. It wasn't as though she wanted to go trekking solo round Bogotá. She's eighteen, she reminded herself, eighteen going on twenty-five. But these reassuring words didn't drive away the worst of Sarah's fears, that Hannah might return home pregnant. In the past, sex was an issue that she and her daughter had discussed quite openly, but that had been in pre-Jamie days. Sarah sensed that Hannah would be a little more guarded on the subject now.

Hannah had now finished checking her bag: a travel packet of tissues had been added, as had a pair of sunglasses, a paperback, some chewing-gum and a stick of strawberry-flavoured lip balm.

'You will be careful, won't you?' Sarah said.

Hannah sat on the bed beside her mother and said, 'Careful to clean my teeth every night or careful with my money?'

'Careful with your body,' Sarah replied.

Hannah gave Sarah one of her grown-up looks that of late had become her stock-in-trade. 'Are you asking me if I intend to have sex with Jamie during this holiday?'

'Something like that, yes.'

Hannah smiled. 'And who's to say we haven't been at it, already?'

'I think I'd know if you had.'

'All parents think that.'

'Am I wrong, then?'

Hannah smiled again. 'Why are we having this conversation, Mum?'

'Because I don't want you coming back from France with any extra luggage. It would spoil your holiday.'

'To say nothing of my future.'

'Exactly.'

'Did I spoil your future, Mum?'

Ouch! thought Sarah. I asked for that.

At an awkwardly precocious age, Hannah had figured out that her arrival in the world had precipitated an early marriage for her parents. 'So I'm a mistake, am I?' she'd said, when she had realised the implications of the date of her birthday coming only a few months after her parents' wedding anniversary. 'Not a mistake,' Sarah had been at pains to point out, 'a surprise, and a lovely one at that.'

Leaving Hannah's question unanswered, Sarah went to the window that overlooked the sun-drenched garden below. The borders were bright with colour: pinks, lavender, nemesia, phlox and petunias held the foreground of the beds, while behind, and standing tall and erect against the rickety old fence that wouldn't see another winter through, were fox-gloves, delphiniums and lupins. At the far end of the lawn there were bushes of lavatera, their branches weighed down with soft pink flowers. She had worked hard at creating a loose, natural feel to the garden, just as she'd tried to do for her marriage. With a weary sense of defeat she had to acknowledge that she'd been more successful with one than the other.

Hannah joined her at the window and, from the cluttered sill, picked up one of the many fluffy toys she hadn't yet parted with. 'The question wasn't meant to sound as nasty as it did,' she said, putting an arm around Sarah's shoulders, 'but you must have regretted having to leave Oxford before completing your degree.'

Sarah turned and looked at her – or, rather, looked up at her, for Hannah was a good five inches taller.

'There are always compensations to one's disappointments,' she said.

Hannah hugged her. 'You always say the right thing, Mum. I shall miss that while I'm away.'

'Oh, please, don't start talking like that or you'll have me crying and that would never do.'

Hannah stroked the fluffy toy in her hands, then settled it back amongst its brightly coloured comrades. 'You'll be okay, won't you?'

'In what way?'

'In the coping-with-Dad way.'

'Oh, you know me, I'll manage.'

'I wish you'd tell it to him straight, like I do.'

Sarah smiled, remembering the scene when she and Hannah had returned home after the diary incident. Hannah had certainly given it straight to her father when he'd greeted her with one of his typically graceless apologies. Rather than meet her fiercely defiant gaze he had kept his eyes lowered and practically skewered his bearded chin into the collar of his shirt, giving the impression that he was addressing his creased old Hush Puppies rather than Hannah. He appeared contrite enough and certainly seemed to be professing that he'd gone too far, blaming his behaviour on an excess of duty to parental care and guidance – but had his performance been sufficiently convincing for Hannah to forgive him? Sarah had waited with bated breath for their daughter's response. It came in the form of a long, bored sigh that contained a pitiful note of contempt. 'Dad,' she said, 'have you looked at me recently?' He raised his head and his puzzled expression indicated that she needed to expand on this question. 'Take a good look,' she continued. 'Do you notice anything different since you last cast your eyes over me? Because, just in case you hadn't realised, I'm now technically a woman. I don't ride about on a tricycle any more, neither do I play with Barbie dolls. So give it up, Dad. Don't keep going with this heavy-father routine.' She'd then gone to her bedroom where she'd taken out her flute and started to play one of her favourite pieces. The clear, silvery, mellifluous sound of

Poulenc's flute sonata had drifted down the stairs and had signalled that all was superficially well again. Trevor's relief was so great that he had even enquired after Ali.

'How was she?' he asked, as he watched Sarah getting the tea ready.

'She's fine and sends her best wishes,' she'd lied, then turning to face him she'd said, in a gentle but firm voice, 'Trevor, you must promise never to do anything as potentially harmful as that again to Hannah. You've been very lucky to get off so lightly. A lot of daughters in her place wouldn't have forgiven you.'

Grave-faced, he'd frowned and tugged at his beard. He looked wretched with shame and Sarah's heart went out to him. 'I really don't want to talk about it,' he said, getting up from the table and retreating to the sanctuary of his workshop.

He knows, she thought, that he came within an inch of losing her. She hoped it would be the saving of him.

From that day on, he certainly did his best to treat Hannah with more respect, especially in the weeks before her exams. He even held his tongue when one evening during supper, after the allegedly botched French literature paper, she attempted to goad him into a discussion on the evils of indoctrination. The scene was uncannily reminiscent of Ali arguing with him, except in this instance, Trevor let his opponent have her inflammatory say then muttered afterwards that he would pray for her.

Now, as Sarah considered her daughter's confident, forthright face before her, she thought, She's right, of course, I should tell it to him straight.

But I probably never will.

'Come on,' she said, glancing over to the bed. 'Is there anything you might have forgotten to pack? No, on second thoughts, forget I said that. I couldn't stand to see you riffle through the contents of that rucksack again.'

Hannah smirked. 'Just wait till I bring it home with six weeks' worth of dirty clothes festering in it.'

Sarah pulled a face. 'I'm counting the days already.'

'But you know I'm worth it, really.'

Sarah smiled indulgently. 'Oh, you're worth it, all right. Every little bit of you. And just for the record, you didn't spoil my future. Far from it, you gave it its focus.'

Hannah hugged her again. 'And for the same record, Jamie and I haven't been to bed with one another.'

When they pulled apart, Sarah said, 'But if or when the time comes, you will be careful, won't you?'

'Hey, wasn't this where we came in?'

'I just need the reassurance.'

'Okay, then, how's this? I've got a handy packet of condoms packed away in my wash-bag . . . just in case.'

Sarah's astonishment was undisguised. 'You have?'

'Wait till you hear how I came by them. It was Ali.'

'Ali!'

'Yes, she sent them as a kind of joke present. I wasn't supposed to let on to you, but she said that it was part of her duty as my godmother. She also sent me some money for the holiday, but I wasn't to tell you about that either.'

Sarah rolled her eyes heavenward. 'Well, whatever you do, don't tell your father. He'd kill Ali three times over!'

The thought of what Ali had done stayed with Sarah for the rest of the morning and through till the afternoon when Trevor, poker-faced and brooding, drove them the half-hour journey to Jamie's father's house where everybody was meeting for a farewell drink. She couldn't get over the interfering audacity of Ali's actions and couldn't decide whether she was cross with her or not.

She hadn't seen Ali since that revelatory weekend in March because the past few months had been devoted to Hannah and seeing her through this crucial period. But they had spoken regularly on the phone, and usually when Trevor was at a craft fair or visiting one of his specialist wood suppliers. Ali had made her promise that if Trevor started pulling any more pious party tricks on her, she was to call her at once. Mercifully, Trevor seemed happy to believe that he'd hauled his wife back into the fold and, not wanting to disabuse him of this thought, she had played her part. She had gone along with the Slipper Gang who all treated her with sickening solicititude, no doubt worried she might backslide into her old sinful ways. No direct reference had ever been made to that bizarre night when they had prayed for her, but doubtless she was constantly in their self-righteous thoughts. Some evenings when they were together, smugly rejoicing that their names were written in the Lamb's Book of Life, she longed to cause a flutter of God-fearing consternation. But it was too risky and she had no wish to jeopardise the peace that had descended on Smithy Cottage by arousing Trevor's suspicions that she wasn't as committed to the group as he was.

They met twice a week now, having cut themselves off from St Cuthbert's, and held their own service of worship, claiming that it was more meaningful than anything the Church of England had to offer. It was a step Sarah wasn't happy with: she sensed the group was dissociating itself from the real world, that they were beginning to advocate an alternative lifestyle and were putting themselves in a position of authority over others. There was very much an air of complacency to their meetings now, as though the faith anybody else experienced wasn't the real thing.

But more upsetting was that Sarah missed St Cuthbert's. She used to enjoy evensong; it had been a reliable source of solace. Now that was gone and all she had in its place was the inane blathering of the Slipper Gang. They now referred to themselves as a house church and this elevated status was leading them to consider expanding and reaching out to other needy souls. There was much talk of building a community of faith, which amused Sarah as she found it difficult to think of this inept bunch of people building anything more complicated and lasting than a bonfire. But, to be fair to them, the original men of faith of the Bible were always getting it wrong and bickering amongst themselves. Not that there was any bickering going on within the Slipper Gang: rather worryingly, they agreed all too readily with whatever Trevor said. His latest crusade was making them understand how important it was 'not to intellectualise the Lord, but to experience the Lord'. He was very much into 'experience' and was currently immersed in a book on the subject of 'special spiritual gifts'.

The thought of Trevor speaking in tongues was too much for Sarah and she hadn't dared tell Ali about it. She could predict the reaction she'd get: 'I thought he'd been doing that for years.' Signs and Wonders was another of his preoccupations, and just recently he had met a man at one of his craft fairs who had spoken at length to him about something called the Toronto Blessing. He'd told Trevor how the Holy Spirit, 'was wonderfully at work in his local church, spiritually slaying great numbers of the congregation'. Sarah had tried not to laugh when Trevor had told her earnestly that this was exactly what the group needed to fire it up. She could think of several members of the Slipper Gang she'd like to see slain, but knew that this wasn't quite what Trevor had in mind.

They arrived at Callum's a few minutes late and added their car to the line of parked vehicles on the driveway. Jamie greeted them at the front door, and took them through the elegant Victorian house and out to the impressively well-cared-for garden where his father was pouring drinks for Emily's parents – Craig's parents must have arrived first as they already had near-empty glasses in their hands. Trevor had never met Callum before so that was the first of the introductions to be made, followed by Mr and Mrs Jackson, Craig's parents, whom neither Sarah nor Trevor had met previously. When the handshaking came to an end, Trevor, who had the look of a man still considering a last-ditch attempt to sabotage his daughter's plans, said, 'I caught the forecast at lunch-time. It looks as though the Channel will be a little choppy tonight. Perhaps it wouldn't be a bad idea for them to wait until tomorrow before setting off.'

Callum let out an avuncular laugh. 'A spot of seasickness should set them up nicely,' he said amiably. 'We can't let them have it too easy.'

'Yes,' agreed Emily's father. 'By rights they should be roughing it on public transport, never mind all this luxury of travelling by car. When I was a student I crossed the States in a Greyhound bus. God, it was cramped. Cramped but cheap.'

After numerous ee-by-gum-they-don't-know-they're-born stories had been exchanged, Callum offered Sarah a drink. 'I've got red wine, white wine, beer or soft drinks in the house. Or perhaps you'd like a gin and tonic. What's it to be?'

'White wine would be lovely.'

He took a bottle of Jacob's Creek from a terracotta wine cooler on the wooden table behind him in the shade of a lilac tree, and poured her a large glass. 'By the way,' he said, as he handed it to her, 'Grace is here. She's in the kitchen putting the finishing touches to a surprise she's arranged for the "young people", as she so charmingly refers to them. If you want to go in and see her, feel free.'

'Thanks, I will.' After chatting for a while with Emily's mother, Sarah went in search of Grace. It was hot outside in the south-facing garden, and she was glad of the opportunity to cool off.

They'd seen a lot of each other recently and Sarah viewed Grace as more than just a neighbour: she was now a good friend with whom she had shared a number of confidences.

Mostly about Trevor.

Without letting Sarah know what he was doing, and much to her horror when she did find out, Trevor had called on Grace one afternoon with two objectives in mind: to research the young man who had designs on his daughter, and to learn if their new neighbour had opened her heart to the Lord, or was interested in doing so. Sarah had cringed when Grace told her about his visit.

'I'm so sorry,' she'd said, mortified that she would now be tarred with the same brush of fanaticism.

'No need to be,' Grace had said cheerfully. 'I've seen it all before.'

'You have?'

'Yes, in my last church. There was a man not dissimilar from your Trevor who never went anywhere without his faith on his sleeve. He was very sincere, very hot for Jesus. He had the Bible completely sewn up. There were no grey areas in it for him at all. Sin and retribution were meat and drink to him.'

Up until this point, the subject of religion had never been broached between the two women, and even though it was now out in the open, Sarah was wary of discussing it. But Grace had no problem. 'Trevor was trying to encourage me to come along to your house church,' she said, with a friendly smile. 'Do you think I should give up on St Cuthbert's and join you?'

'No. Definitely not,' Sarah had blurted out, not giving her answer a second thought.

Grace had broadened her smile. 'You don't think it would suit me, then?'

'I wouldn't have thought so.'

'And does it suit you, Sarah?'

That's when the first of the confidences had slipped out. Nothing too personal, nothing too disloyal, just little everyday vexations that occur when you live with a man who is intent on winning souls for Christ.

Compared to the heat outside, the interior of Callum's beautiful house was refreshingly cool, and as she wandered through the polish-fragrant dining room and paused in the hall to admire a pretty Victorian watercolour landscape above a tasteful serpentine-fronted sideboard, she heard the nerve-jarring thump-thump of loud music from above. The light fitting rattled and she wondered how Callum would feel living here all alone when Jamie had left home for college in the autumn. She was already dreading being deprived of Hannah's company permanently and couldn't bring herself to picture the cold emptiness of the days to come.

She found Grace in the Provençal-style kitchen. She was bent over an oval-shaped table, guiding an ancient, discoloured piping-bag across the surface of a large square cake on a silver board.

When she realised she wasn't alone she raised her eyes.

'Sarah,' she said, with obvious pleasure in her voice, 'how lovely to see you.' She straightened her back. 'What do you think of my handiwork? Be kind, though, I'm no expert when it comes to icing, and my fingers are too stiff these days anyway.'

Sarah drew near and inspected the cake and its decoration. A cocktail stick had been pushed into the sponge with a French flag glued to it and next to this was a toy car just like Jamie's red Nissan Micra. Written in spidery red icing all the way around the edge were the words '*Bonne Chance*' and '*Bon Voyage*'. 'It's absolutely perfect,' she said.

'Not too childish for the young people?'

'They'll love it.'

'I had wondered about a few of these. What do you think?' She showed Sarah a margarine pot of candles and waited for her verdict.

'No cake's complete without them,' Sarah said with a happy laugh. 'Here, let me help you.'

The cake was a great success, and after the candles had been blown out, Callum decided to embarrass his son by making a speech.

'There's nothing that needs to be said—' he began.

'Then shut up and sit down!' heckled Jamie good-humouredly.

Ignoring him with a grin, Callum carried on, '—other than to say that I wish you all a bloody fantastic time, and don't you dare come back as the same people you went away. I expect horizons to be widened, wills strengthened, perceptions deepened, and a bootload of duty-free booze for me!'

An hour later it was time to say goodbye. All the cars on the drive had to be shunted so that Jamie could reverse his out, and after backpacks had been squeezed into position and final instructions issued – Trevor gave Jamie a last-minute test on the Highway Code and reminded him which side of the road to drive on once they reached Cherbourg – they were off. Hands waved out of windows, and the tranquillity of the quiet, respectable road was blasted away by several seconds of ear-splitting noise as Jamie hit the horn, and Craig poked his head out of the sun-roof to yell, 'So long, suckers!'

Trevor's face curled itself into a tight knot of disdain, but everybody else laughed. 'Well,' said Callum, when the car had disappeared from sight and Sarah had taken her last look at Hannah for what seemed for ever, 'now we're rid of the rabble, why don't we have another glass of wine?'

There were general murmurs of consent. Sarah had never felt more in need of a drink; she was all set to fall in step with Grace and offer to help her tidy up, when Trevor produced his keys from his trouser pocket and said, 'Thanks, but we really ought to be getting off. Things to do,' and her heart plummeted. She wasn't ready yet to return to an empty Smithy Cottage. She had no inclination to confront what the dismal little house now symbolised without Hannah's presence. And as if sensing her hesitation, and having no truck with it, Trevor started to shake hands with everyone and sealed their departure.

Chapter Twenty-Six

A fortnight had passed since Hannah had taken her first real step into the unknown expanse of her future, and Trevor had spent most of it in an agony of anticipatory torment as he hovered conspicuously in the hall each morning waiting for the postman to make his usual seven forty-five delivery.

Today, as Sarah came down the stairs with a small bundle of washing under her arm, she hoped that he would be spared another day of disappointment. 'I think we should take no news as a good sign. It means she's having too good a time to be bothered with letter-writing,' she'd told him yesterday morning when the post had consisted of nothing but a piece of junk mail.

To give Hannah her credit, she had phoned when they'd arrived at Cherbourg, just to let them know that so far all was well: the ferry hadn't sunk; she hadn't been mugged; Craig hadn't got them arrested with his criminal sense of humour and Jamie wasn't driving while under the influence of anything more hallucinatory than a can of Pepsi. Sarah had told her not to worry about ringing again. 'It's much too expensive,' she'd said. 'Just send us a card when you have time.' But Trevor had wanted more and had extracted from Hannah a promise that she would keep them regularly posted as to her exact whereabouts. But his insistence had merely ensured that he was to suffer a daily dose of unease as he waited anxiously for the much-anticipated communication.

Leaving Trevor to stand guard over the letterbox, Sarah went through to the kitchen and pushed the dirty clothes into the washing-machine. She added the powder and turned the dial to the economy half-load sequence. It was extraordinary just how little washing there was without Hannah. She wondered with amusement how she and Emily were surviving on the few clothes they'd taken with them. Or were they already frittering away what little money they had on just-have-to-have skimpy tops to supplement their pared-to-the-bone wardrobes?

The sound of the letterbox scraping open had Sarah silently praying that today might be the day that Trevor was put out of his misery. Just a few scribbled lines on a card would suffice, she added, as a postscript.

Within seconds Trevor was standing in the kitchen, a smile on his face and an airmail letter in his hand. 'At last,' he said, waving it at her, 'she's written, at long last.' He looked as if all his birthdays and Christmas had been rolled into one. Then he sat at the table and picked carefully at the first sealed edge with his thumbnail. Desperate to seize it from him, rip it open and feed off Hannah's writing to satisfy her hunger for some comforting contact with her daughter, Sarah turned away and put the kettle on. She watched Trevor out of the corner of her eye, saw him smooth out the single sheet of paper, handling it as though it were a priceless scroll of papyrus. He started to read.

It didn't take him long.

Annoyingly, though, he went through it one more time. Sarah was itching to know what news it contained. 'Well?' she asked at length. 'How's she getting on?'

'Read it yourself,' he said gloomily. He rose from the table and went over to the bread bin.

Eagerly Sarah scanned her daughter's neat writing, looking for the vital clue that had caused Trevor's mood to change so suddenly.

Dear Mum and Dad,
Guess what, we got bored in Brittany and went to Paris instead. It's the coolest place. We went to Montmartre

and Emily nearly got her portrait painted, except it wasn't just her face the piss artist was interested in! We stayed in a campsite just north of Paris and it was the pits. Flies everywhere, especially in the bogs (or crap-holes as Craig calls them) – they stank to hell and back. The site was so rough we had to sleep in the car at night to stop it from being nicked. Emily's father would be proud of us.

Yesterday we went to Chartres. We're now heading for La Rochelle to see Craig's aunt. God, what I wouldn't give for a bath and a decent loo that I can actually park my bum on!

The others all say hi.

Love, Hannah

As Trevor had, Sarah also read the letter twice. She would have done so again had the toaster not decided to play up. While Trevor hoicked charred bread out of the decrepit appliance she threw open the window to get rid of the awful smell. 'It's time we bought a new one,' she remarked. When he didn't respond, she said, 'It's good to know that Hannah's okay and that she's enjoying herself, isn't it?'

He grunted, gave up on the idea of toast, put away his unused plate and helped himself to a bowl of bran flakes.

'What's wrong, Trevor?' she asked. 'She wrote, just as you wanted.'

He raised his eyes from his cereal, which he was eating as he stood with his back to the sink. 'It didn't sound like Hannah,' he said, with a sulky frown.

Oh, so that was it, thought Sarah. He'd been expecting a letter from the old Hannah; the little girl who used to go off on Christian-camp holidays, who within a day of being away would dutifully send them a tightly worded I-hope-you-are-well-I-am-having-a-good-time note with a cross at the bottom of the page against a beautifully coloured-in rainbow. The contrast from that to talk of crap-holes and disreputable

245

goings-on in Montmartre couldn't be greater. But surely not even Trevor could have expected a sugar-coated letter from Hannah saying that she was homesick and counting the days until she was back in Astley Hope. She glanced at his furrowed face as he returned his attention to his breakfast. He looked so unhappy. So downcast. Forgetting her own sadness at being parted from her daughter, Sarah considered Trevor's feelings. It was always so easy to disregard anything he said or thought, but couldn't it be the case that he was missing Hannah more than she was? It was generally thought that a child flying the nest affected the mother more than the father. But what if that father had spent the last eighteen years idealising his daughter? What if he had lovingly and selflessly invested every spare minute of his time into her upbringing? Wouldn't that give him just as much right to be lonely and devastated by her leaving as her mother? If not more?

With lightning speed, guilt overtook Sarah's feelings of compassion towards Trevor. While she had been missing Hannah and wallowing in her own trough of self-pity, where had been her support for Trevor? Then a worse thought occurred to her: was it possible that through her thoughtlessness she had driven him to seek understanding from elsewhere? Somebody in the Slipper Gang, perhaps.

But as fast as this thought had presented itself, she dismissed it as erroneous. There was no one to whom Trevor could turn within the group because as their leader he couldn't be seen to be in anything other than full control. That was the trouble with being held aloft as an infallible linchpin: you couldn't have earthly problems. You could wrestle day and night with a thorny spiritual issue – or even have a wife who was in danger of becoming an apostate – but you couldn't have emotional problems because that would mean you weren't in step with the Lord. What kind of example was that for the group? Had St Paul ever admitted to feeling a little wobbly? Had Christ ever said he was having a bad-hair day and that the Sermon on the Mount would have to wait until he'd got his act together? It was hard enough for any man to admit to being unhappy, but for a spiritual guru it was well nigh impossible. Again she glanced at Trevor's miserable face and wondered if he had the same feelings as she had, that having served their purpose with Hannah, their future now comprised nothing but a slow, lonely decline into old age.

Experiencing the familiar need to make everything right for Trevor, Sarah poured him some tea, and said brightly, 'What are you doing today? If you're not busy I could put a picnic lunch together and we could go for a walk. Peckforton perhaps. It's such a lovely –'

'I've got too much to do,' he interrupted. 'I've got three craft fairs on the trot and I've my notes to prepare for tonight.'

'Oh,' Sarah said flatly, her compassion for him instantly dispelled. She watched him take his mug of tea with him to his workshop and muttered under her breath, 'Trevor Donovan, you're a difficult man to help.' She didn't even care that it was such an uncharitable thought.

Later that morning, when Sarah had finished the bedroom curtains that she'd been making for Grace and was running the iron over the pretty blue and white fabric, she thought how well the material would look in Ali's bathroom with all those lovely Delft tiles. She had spoken to Ali the day after Hannah had set off for France, to thank her for the extra money she'd given Hannah, as well as refer to the other more dubious gift.

'You're not cross with me, are you?' Ali had asked.

'Now, why would you think that?'

'Oh, my God, you're furious. I can hear it in your voice. You sound as winsome as an avenging Margaret Thatcher.'

'And you sound as guilty as Bill Clinton.'

'My, my, you're sharp this afternoon. Does that mean I'm

not your friend any more? Are you going to write me out of your will?'

'I did that years ago.'

'Oh, shucks!'

'So tell me why you did it, Ali.'

'Why I did what?'

'Don't play the innocent with me. Tell me why you gave my daughter a packet of condoms to take on holiday with her.'

'Good heavens, you've got it all wrong. They weren't condoms. They're the latest thing in the world of camping. You use them at night to ward off unwanted insects.'

'*Ali!*'

'Okay, okay. I admit it. I was interfering under the guise of doing my fairy godmother bit. I knew you and Trevor would never be sensible enough to be so practical so I felt I should do it. I didn't want to see history repeating itself.'

'You mean you didn't want to see her ruining her life as I did?'

'Exactly.'

It was absolutely typical of Ali to be so brutally frank. But she'd been right to do what she did, Sarah knew that. Trevor, of course, would never agree with her. He would bang on about the Christian ideal of sex within the bounds of marriage, and that anything less was a sin. How easy it would be for her to throw at him their own flouting of this ideal. But she never would. Not ever.

When she'd finished ironing Grace's curtains she phoned her to see if it was convenient to call round with them.

'Goodness,' Grace said, 'you're a fast worker. I only gave you the fabric the other day.'

'They were very straightforward.'

'For you, maybe. I would have taken for ever fumbling around with my old Singer. Why don't you come now and have an early lunch with me? Or are you too busy to stop that long?'

'No, that's fine. I'll be along just as soon as I've put the washing out and made a sandwich for Trevor. Do you want me to bring anything?'

'Certainly not. I don't approve of people who invite friends for a meal then expect them to supply it.'

When she'd said goodbye, Sarah went out to the garden and pegged the washing on the line. The sun was directly above her head and was hot and bright. Feeling its scorching strength she hoped that Hannah was being careful to use the wickedly expensive high-factor sun cream she'd bought for her. Back inside the house she threw a sandwich together for Trevor, covered it with clingfilm and went to tell him where she was going.

He switched off his lathe, lifted off the white dust mask that covered his mouth and nose and stared at her through his bug-eyed safety goggles. Tapping his chisel on his workbench, he said, 'You're spending a lot of time with that woman, aren't you?'

'That woman?' Sarah repeated. 'That doesn't sound very polite. Her name's Grace.'

'Mm . . . I'm just not at all sure about her.'

'I'm not with you.' Though, sadly, she was. Trevor didn't approve of Grace, not since he had discovered at Callum's, when they'd been seeing Hannah off, that she was a retired psychotherapist. As Martin Wade of the Slipper Gang would be only too quick to inform anyone stupid enough to listen, psychotherapy was of the devil, along with yoga, aromatherapy and anything else he felt inclined to condemn.

'People like her have some pretty unorthodox views, in my opinion,' said Trevor, giving the workbench another little tap. 'I'm not at all sure she's our type.'

'What would be our type, Trevor?' she asked innocently.

'You know what I'm getting at, Sarah. She professes to know the Lord, but I'm not sure that she's actually saved.'

Sarah very nearly said, 'Well, in that case I'd have thought it was your Christian duty to get to know her better,' but wisely refrained. A challenge such as that might well stir Trevor to try once more to lure Grace along to the group.

Grace was delighted with the curtains. 'They're beautiful,' she enthused. 'You really are so clever. How much do I owe you?'

'Nothing. They took me next to no time to do.'

'Sarah, I shan't ask you again, how much?'

'I'll let you know later.'

An impasse reached, Grace said, 'Don't think I shall forget to remind you of that. Now, come along, your lunch awaits.' She took Sarah outside to the small garden, which in a strange way reflected the inside of the bungalow. It was very simple, very plain. There was an old, gnarled crabapple tree in the right-hand corner, a perimeter hedge of recently trimmed copper beech, and a tidy square of daisy-spotted lawn. That was all. There were no scent-filled borders, no rockery features, not even a solitary tub of summer bedding plants. Being such a keen gardener herself, it always struck Sarah as odd whenever she looked at Grace's garden that there was so little in it. She'd once asked Grace if she would like some help to brighten it up. Her elderly friend had obviously been amused by her offer. 'Why?' she'd asked. 'Is there something wrong with my garden as it is?'

'No, of course not,' she'd said, instantly worried that Grace would think she'd been poking her nose in where it wasn't wanted. 'I have so much in my garden I wondered if you'd like some cuttings.'

'How very thoughtful. But I'm not a fan of fuss and frills. I prefer everything to be understated. To be seen for what it is.'

And as Sarah took her seat at a small circular table in the dappled shade of the crabapple tree, she could see that Grace had set their lunch in her typically modest, straightforward fashion. This didn't mean she hadn't put any thought into it – Sarah could see that she had – but unlike a lunch table at Audrey's house, which would be decorated to death with silver plate, tiny vases of flowers, fiddly paper doilies, precision-folded napkins and silly little flags to distinguish one plate of food from another, Grace had kept her offering to an unassuming informality. A plain white cloth adorned the garden table and placed on this were two glasses of orange juice, two plates, each containing a slice of quiche, a helping of rice salad and a roll; and in the middle, two glass bowls of mouth-watering strawberries lightly dusted with icing sugar.

'I hope you approve,' Grace said, as she sat opposite Sarah.

'I do. It's much more than I expected. You've gone to such a lot of trouble.'

'Yes, I have, haven't I?'

Sarah caught the mocking tone in Grace's voice and met her eye. 'One of us isn't being sincere,' she said, with a smile.

Reaching for her knife and fork, Grace said, 'Well, eat up, then we'll decide which of us it is. So how are things at Smithy Cottage?'

'Dull is the word I'd use.'

'Oh dear. Missing Hannah?'

'Enormously. I can't begin to think what I shall be like in the autumn when she goes away to college.'

'Then don't think about it. Put it on hold until you have to face it.'

'Isn't that rather silly? I didn't have you down as an ostrich, Grace.'

'Ostrich I'm not. But realist I am. What possible advantage can you gain worrying now about something that won't take place for another four months? And, besides, don't you have enough worries on your mind as it is?'

Sarah stopped eating. 'Is that how you see me? Worried?'

Squinting in the dappled sunlight, Grace fixed her surprisingly strong gaze on Sarah and said, 'Yes. And, more than that, sometimes you give me the impression of being one of the unhappiest people I know.'

'Then I must learn to smile more often in your company,' Sarah said glibly.

'Or be more honest.'

Her glibness evaporated and Sarah was on her guard. 'Why do you say that?'

'Because I suspect it to be the truth.'

Sarah shifted uncomfortably in her seat, remembered that Grace was a qualified psychotherapist and wondered if she was treating her as she would a client. She resumed eating, but for a few minutes avoided looking in Grace's direction, which was no mean feat given that they were sitting so close to each other.

'Have I offended you with my honesty?' Grace asked, after a few minutes had passed. 'Because if so, I'm very sorry.'

Sarah's composure had now fully returned. 'Don't be silly, you haven't offended me in the slightest.'

'But I have unnerved you, haven't I?'

'Only because I'm beginning to think that every conversation I have with you is the equivalent of me lying on your professional couch. Plus the fact that you've just accused me of lying.'

Grace looked serious. 'I was very cross with Callum for telling you and Trevor what my line of work used to be. I knew that it would have this effect on you. If it helps, I really don't go in for analysing friends at the drop of a hat, it's far too exhausting. And as for accusing you of lying, I didn't say that.'

'You implied that I was –'

'No, Sarah, you took my words to mean that. I was suggesting that you're somewhat economical with your feelings and have been so for a long time.'

'If that isn't the sound of me being analysed I don't know what is.'

'I'm merely being honest and objective. If your friend Ali was here in my place, wouldn't she be saying much the same?'

Sarah smiled unexpectedly. 'Outside the work environment, Ali doesn't have an objective bone in her body. She reacts first and thinks later. She's very headstrong, which—'

'Which can preclude a rational conversation on a delicate and personal issue that's worrying you.'

'Exactly. I can never, for instance, discuss Trevor and my marriage with her without her totally overreacting. She always—' Sarah broke off as, too late, she saw how clever Grace had been. 'You did that deliberately, didn't you?' she said crossly. 'You tricked that out of me.'

Again, Grace looked serious. 'Sarah, I'm not some hocus-pocus hypnotherapist sitting here making you do things against your will. We're two friends enjoying lunch together and having what I would hope was a civilised conversation based on my concern for you.'

Sarah felt the severity of Grace's words and apologised immediately. 'I'm sorry. Truly I am. It's just that I've become . . . I've become so very defensive lately.'

'Dare I ask why?'

Sarah leaned back in her chair and considered the question. It required a simple yes or no. The consequences of no would mean that she would go on dodging Grace's well-meant questions. Whereas a yes . . . a yes might help her. Grace's clear, objective thinking might do for her what Ali could never do: she might help her to see her future with Trevor in a more positive light.

She made her decision and, winding her hair round her finger and keeping her eyes on a sparrow hopping through the dusty undergrowth of the copper-beech hedge, she said, 'I've spent the greater part of my life trying to love the unlovable and I don't know if I have the energy to go on doing it.'

If Grace was at all surprised by what Sarah had just told her, she gave no outward sign of being so. 'Trevor?' was all she said.

Sarah slowly turned her gaze back to Grace. 'Trevor,' she confirmed, with a slight nod.

'And you feel you have to go on trying, do you?'

'Oh, yes. I owe it to Trevor and Hannah. And everything I believe in.'

'But not you personally?'

'I don't think I come into it.'

Grace made no immediate response to this comment and they sat in silence, listening to the flutter of a wood-pigeon's wings as it flew overhead and a pair of doves cooing in the sun on the roof of the bungalow. All the antagonism Sarah had felt only moments ago was gone. She let go of her hair and waited patiently for Grace to speak, knowing that, when she did, whatever she said would be worth hearing. She was right.

'Of course,' Grace said slowly, reaching for her orange juice, 'as Christians we're supposed to be following a man whose chief commandment was to love the unlovable . . . even a difficult husband, and there's no denying that there's great virtue in working at a failing relationship. The rewards would be immensely satisfying if one was successful.'

'And if one failed?'

'Ah, well, then I suppose one would have to determine what counts as a failure.'

'I'm sure that deep down Ali thinks that I've been very weak staying with Trevor all these years when I don't love him. In her book that would be a classic example of failing to be true to oneself.'

'Whereas the truth is you've been amazingly strong to stay in a difficult marriage, which makes it a success. Relationships are never easy. My mother used to say that there were more challenges to overcome in a marriage than there ever were in the fiercest of battles. I know you're terrified of me putting on my professional hat, and I assure you I'm talking to you as a friend, but would you mind if I asked you a question?'

'Go on.'

'Just now you said that you thought you didn't come into the matter, as if you're not a part of the equation. Did you really mean that, or did you say those words because you think that's what scripture expects of you? St Paul was a great advocate of self-deprecation, but there's no getting away from it, he had quite an opinion of himself, although that was probably due to his upbringing and culture. Not that I'm suggesting that you have an overinflated opinion of yourself, Sarah, but you're as human as the next person and I would imagine that you harbour the odd hope and expectation for yourself.'

Sarah thought about this. It was hard to admit it, but the truth was she *did* hanker after a better life, and surely that was the root of the problem. Putting others continually before herself was becoming a mighty uphill struggle and she was tired of pushing that cartload of humility before her. She wanted desperately to let go of it. But she couldn't. The consequences were too frightening. 'Yes,' she said, realising that Grace was studying her face and waiting for her answer. 'Yes, I do have hopes for myself. I'm tired of understanding Trevor and constantly making allowances for him. I would love a life of my own.' She decided to tell Grace about her conversation with Ali back in March when she stayed with her at the windmill. 'I said then that I wanted to be the Sarah I was meant to be, not this pretend Sarah I've become.'

'But, Sarah, my dear, there's only one person who's allowed that to happen and that's you.'

'But—'

'One more thought for you to consider while I go inside for our dessertspoons, which I've stupidly left in the kitchen, just how big a sacrifice do you think you have to make?'

Chapter Twenty-Seven

There was the usual chaos that evening at Smithy Cottage of shoes being exchanged for slippers. There was also the usual exchange of chit-chat – 'Sorry, was that your foot? . . . Super weather . . . Well into the upper eighties I shouldn't wonder, maybe even the nineties . . . It doesn't suit me at all, I can't sleep at night . . . Me neither . . . No, no, you have that space, my shoes won't fit . . . Do you think we'll be in for a hosepipe ban?'

Sarah watched the Slipper Gang in quiet amusement. The scene reminded her of *Dad's Army* and Captain Mainwaring's many frustrated attempts to marshal his platoon into an effective fighting force: the intent was there, but the flesh was weak and much more interested in enjoying a few snippets of gossip rather than jumping smartly into line.

The first to sit down was Shirley, commandeering, as per the norm, the most comfortable armchair over by the window, which tonight was open in the vain hope that a cool breeze might manifest itself from the sultry evening air.

With Trevor still stationed at the door, the rest of them trickled in, and when the last of the group had been rounded up and brought to heel – typically Dave was last, apologising for Brenda's absence – it was eyes down for their quiet time.

Sarah took her seat and closed her eyes gratefully. She gave Holman Hunt's *Light of the World* a quick going-over, checking that the detailed painting had not been defaced by any new attacks of doubt. She held it firmly in her mind and found that all was well: the seven-sided lantern was glowing softly; the weeds were rampant and untidy; the apples were rolling around on the ground; and best of all, Christ was still there knocking on the door. She then switched her thoughts to that afternoon and her lunch with Grace.

While she had become adept at not answering some of Ali's more probing questions if she so chose, she had discovered that Grace, whose easy manner disguised how intuitive she was, was a far more disarming proposition. A few minutes of the older woman's carefully put questions had soon cut through the layers of self-preservation that Sarah had so skilfully applied to her persona. Grace was quite correct in saying that it was Sarah who was responsible for allowing her marriage to develop as it had. It was true, and she alone was responsible for bringing herself to where she was now. Grace had said, 'And why do you think you've done that?'

'I . . . I don't know,' she'd responded.

A kindly smile on Grace's face had told Sarah that she didn't believe her. Very persuasively she had said, 'You're an intelligent woman, Sarah. If you had wanted your husband to treat you better, you would have made it happen. Instead it seems that you have deliberately chosen to let Trevor behave in the manner of a spoilt child. And you've indulged him like a guilty parent, haven't you?'

'I suppose I have.'

'Why?' Again that same quiet, persuasive voice, which was as gentle as the cooing of the doves on the red-tiled roof of the bungalow, but as penetrating as the sun shining its hot rays through the leafy shade of the crabapple tree.

'Because I've always felt so guilty,' Sarah had confessed. She explained about Hannah and their subsequent hurried marriage. 'Trevor's parents never forgave him.'

'Despite him providing them with such a delightful grand-daughter?'

'They never saw her. They refused to have anything to do with us. They were very strict traditional Methodists. They didn't drink, they didn't dance and they certainly didn't approve of a child conceived out of wedlock.'

'How sad.'

'And cruel.'

'Yes. It was very cruel of them. And what of your parents? How did they greet their son-in-law?'

'They didn't approve of him. They didn't think he was good enough, and unfairly held him responsible for bringing my education at Oxford to an abrupt end.'

'Do you think Trevor has ever felt guilty about that?'

'I've never looked at it from that angle before.'

'No, I shouldn't think you have. You've been too preoccupied with blaming yourself for cutting Trevor off from his family, haven't you?'

'But that's exactly what I did. If it hadn't been for me—'

'No, Sarah. It wasn't your decision but theirs that removed their son from their blinkered vision. Blaming yourself for somebody else's actions is futile and ultimately harmful. Look where it's got you.'

'Now you're beginning to sound like Ali.'

'I'm sorry. Shall I make us some tea now?'

'Please, won't you let me do it? I feel so lazy sitting here doing nothing.'

'No, you stay where you are, but have a ponder on what I mentioned earlier about the sacrifice you think you have to make – because that's what you're doing by staying with Trevor, isn't it? By lying prostrate across the sacrificial altar of your faith I would imagine you see yourself as a permanent atonement for the past.'

Left alone with this uncomfortably razor-sharp observation, Sarah was seized with the desire to sneak away from Grace's quiet, orderly house and garden and go back to Smithy Cottage where, amongst the clutter and chaos, there would be no danger of anyone seeing through her so clearly.

When Grace returned with a tray of tea-things, she said, 'From the expression on your face I'd say you're cross with me again, aren't you?' Undeterred by Sarah's hostile silence, she said, 'Good. That means we're getting somewhere. What sort of answer have you prepared for me?'

Sounding distinctly peevish, Sarah said, 'I don't have one.'

Grace smiled. 'You know, Sarah, when our self-interest is at stake, we have the most astonishing ability to convince ourselves that all manner of falsehood is true.'

'Now you're being tiresome and far too esoteric for a sweltering summer's day in the garden.'

'Well, then, let's leave it there, shall we? Have you heard from Hannah? I had a postcard this morning from Jamie. They seem to be having a fabulous time. I'm so envious.'

Without so much as a backward glance at what they'd previously been discussing and at what had threatened Sarah with its unnerving directness, Grace steered the conversation through less rocky water and kept it there until Sarah went home.

'Ahem,' said Trevor's voice from across the room.

Sarah raised her head and saw that everyone was looking at her, including Trevor who must have brought their quiet time to an end a few moments ago. Embarrassed, she tried to appear as though she'd been fully absorbed in contemplative prayer.

Trevor cleared his throat and opened the file on his lap. 'Now I expect you all saw this in your Sunday newspapers at the weekend and will have had the same reaction to it as I did. But for the sake of clarity,' he cast a quick glance towards Dave, 'I thought we'd go through it together, just to be absolutely certain that we know exactly where we stand on the issue, which has repercussions—'

'Um . . . sorry, Trevor,' said Dave, 'sorry to interrupt, but we were with Brenda's mother at the weekend. She's having a hip-replacement operation soon. I don't suppose we could pray for her at the end, could we?'

'Of course, Dave, I'll make a note of that,' said Trevor, already scribbling a reminder on his notepad. 'Now, what I wanted to discuss is –'

'Sorry,' Dave interrupted again, 'but what I was trying to say is that Brenda and I didn't see the papers on Sunday, so I don't know what it is that we're all supposed to be reacting to.'

Trevor patiently held up a carefully cut-out half-page from the *Sunday Times*. Just as Dave hadn't seen the papers at the weekend, neither had Sarah: she'd been too busy working in the garden. She glanced at what was in Trevor's hands and took in the headline: 'Bishops Push for Divorcees to be Remarried in Church.' Well, there'd be no prizes for guessing which direction Trevor's comments would be going in.

He began reading aloud from the newspaper cutting: '"Centuries-old doctrine is to be thrown on the scrap heap of outmoded tradition and convention as senior bishops call for change within the Church of England."' He raised his scandalised eyes to them all. 'And there we have it. Once again the Church of England is bowing to secular pressures. By the time the right-on clergy with their woolly-minded views have had their way, there'll be nothing left of what the original Church was founded on.'

'Quite right,' agreed Audrey. 'Remarriage after divorce is adultery in the eyes of the Lord.'

'Absolutely,' nodded Maurice.

'It's the breaking of the seventh commandment, "Thou shall not commit adultery,"' Beryl chipped in.

Elaine was flicking through her Bible for a relevant passage, but Shirley was ahead of her. 'Luke states it quite clearly,' she said. 'Chapter sixteen, verse eighteen. "The man who marries a divorced woman commits adultery." '

'Well, I'm glad to see that we're all of one mind on the matter,' said Trevor.

But out of the corner of her eye, and much to her delight, Sarah saw Dave scratching his head. 'Um . . . not sure I'm entirely up to speed with you, Trevor.'

'Yes, Dave, what is it that you don't understand?'

'Well, it's Brenda's sister.'

'Yes.'

'She married a divorced man last summer. It was a lovely

wedding and his daughter was a bridesmaid, but is that the same as Shirley was just saying?'

'It makes no difference which sex does the divorcing or remarrying,' Trevor said.

But Dave still looked confused. 'So where does that leave Brenda's sister, Susan? If Russell is an adulterer, does that mean that when Susan and Russell first, well, you know, when they first had . . . um well, when they –'

'Are you referring to when they first had sexual intercourse, Dave?'

Dave visibly shrank beneath Shirley's forthright question. Even Stan and Valerie's puppy-dog slippers looked embarrassed: their noses were digging into the carpet and their ears had flopped over their eyes. 'Yes,' murmured Dave, and returning his gaze to Trevor, he said, 'So when they had, um . . . marital relations, does that mean that they both became adulterers, in that Russell has turned Susan into one?'

Sarah wanted to leap out of her seat and hug Dave. If she didn't know him as well as she did, she'd be tempted to think he was deliberately sending the group up, but as ever his genuine confusion was making a mockery of the Slipper Gang's self-righteous dogmatism. 'Adultery isn't a disease, Dave,' she said, when nobody answered him. 'It's not something you can catch.'

'If I may be so humble as to suggest it, Sarah, that's just where you're wrong,' said Martin, from his God-fearing, bottom-numbing kitchen chair. 'Sin is exactly like a disease. It can spread its micro-organisms without us realising it. We can be jogging along quite happily with not a single thought in our head for the sins of the flesh, then suddenly *wham!* we're up to our armpits in the mire of temptation. Make no mistake, we're in the devil's laboratory of disease at every minute of the day.'

'Sounds as if we need inoculating,' muttered Sarah, under her breath.

But Trevor heard her and said, 'We have inoculation

through God's Word, Sarah.' He gave his Bible an irritating little tap with his index finger.

'So back to Susan and Russell,' persisted Dave. 'Where do you suppose they stand in the eyes of the Lord?'

Sarah waited for somebody to answer Dave's question, but the room had gone unnaturally quiet. Cowards, she thought, as the continued silence and lowered glances condemned the likes of Susan and Russell to whatever hell it was that this crazy lot believed in. 'Dave,' she said, 'if what your sister-in-law and her husband have done is considered a sin, and I'm not convinced it is, then be assured that it's not a greater sin than most of the ones we all commit each and every day of our lives.' She then turned her attention to the rest of the group and said, 'Shall I make the coffee now? Or would you prefer something cold?'

Yes, something as cold as your compassion for your fellow human beings, she thought, when she was out in the kitchen waiting for the kettle to boil and tipping a packet of biscuits on to a plate. Through the open door she could hear Trevor in the sitting room trying to explain to Dave that what she had omitted to say was that Susan and Russell actively needed to seek God's forgiveness. And, though Sarah couldn't see him, she knew that Trevor would be putting on one of his specially earnest and oh-so-humble expressions – the sort that made her want to slap his face. She then heard Dave's concerned voice say, 'But, Trevor, how can they seek forgiveness when they don't even go to church? Or do you suppose it would work if I did it for them on their behalf?'

Oh dear, thought Sarah. How complicated it became when one's beliefs were thrashed to bits like this. Had any of this nonsense been a part of God's original plan? And why is it, she wondered, as she poured boiling water into the mugs of instant coffee, that she believed implacably in the act of redemption for the whole of mankind, but refused point-blank to consider herself worthy of it?

Chapter Twenty-Eight

That same evening, over in Little Linton, Ali put her key in the lock, hoping to find that the thick-walled windmill was cool inside as it had been since the heatwave began. The temperature wasn't too bad on the ground floor, but after she'd scooped up that morning's mail from the mat and had climbed the stairs to the next level, she was met by a stuffy, airless white heat that took her breath away. She dumped her bag, briefcase and post on the kitchen table then opened the fridge door. She stood in front of it, revelling in the cool blast against her flushed damp skin, and reached inside for a bottle of spring water. She pressed the icy glass to her forehead, rolling it over her face and down her neck. Then she twisted off the metal cap and gulped down the contents.

'You're turning into a slob,' she said, when she'd satisfied her thirst. 'Yeah, and what of it?' she answered herself, wiping her hand across her mouth and returning the bottle to the fridge. Next she kicked off her shoes and peeled away her tights. She stood for a few delicious moments letting her hot, sweaty feet absorb the relative coolness of the wooden floor. Then she crossed the room and unlocked the door to the galleried balcony outside. She attached the wrought-iron handle to the metal hook on the wall and left the door wide open while she went upstairs for a shower.

The drive home from Blackpool, where she'd spent the day with a client, had been the pits. As if it wasn't bad enough that several miles of roadworks had been added to the normal mayhem of the M6, an overheated car engine had brought the scarcely moving traffic to a standstill. The air-conditioning in

Ali's Saab had decided not to work and, with the soft top pushed back, she'd been stuck for nearly forty minutes in the vicious heat. She'd had nightmare visions of completing the rest of her journey with her tyres coated in recently laid, melting black tarmac. The thought of a cold shower was all that had kept her sane while she'd tried to ignore the unwelcome, leering glances of truck drivers in their sweaty Bruce Willis vests.

Stripping off her clothes, she stepped under the power-shower. An explosion of freezing cold needles pricked at her skin. Tilting her head, she jet-blasted her face under the force of the water. It was heavenly, wonderfully revitalising.

No two ways about it, it's the little things in life that bring the greatest pleasure, she thought, when an hour later she was sitting on the balcony enjoying the view of cornfields and distant hills to the south that stretched lazily across the heat-hazed horizon like the bumpy back of a sleeping dinosaur. Refreshed and dressed in a pair of old shorts and a Tommy Hilfiger T-shirt, a glass of chilled wine in her hand and a packet of crisps on her lap, she was a new woman.

It was pathetic that such an ordinary moment could be so blissful, but in the barren landscape of her day-to-day existence, it was as good as it got. It made her think of something she'd once read: that if there wasn't any misery in the world, we might be conceited enough to think we were in paradise and would consequently miss out on the best bits. Well, there was no danger of an excess of pleasure diluting what little enjoyment she was currently experiencing.

She popped another crisp into her mouth and savoured it. Mm . . . delicious. Was there ever a better combination than good old salt and vinegar for tickling the palate? The only improvement would be if it was a bag of chips on her lap rather than the footballer-endorsed crisps. Chips would be the ultimate perfection. Her mouth watered at the thought, which brought with it the memory of Sarah and her, windblown and bathed in warm sunshine, sharing a portion of fish and chips on the beach at Hayling. And what did they do when they'd finished eating and had licked their fingers clean? What they always did. They'd gone straight to the funfair and ridden the waltzer. How they had kept those chips down she didn't know. If they tried it now they'd be ill within seconds.

Illness wasn't something she associated with her holidays spent with Sarah at Hayling: not once could she remember either of them being sick. It never rained either, or so it seemed. Sun-warmed idyllic days simply drifted from one to the next as the pair roamed the island at will, carefree and happy.

But that was childhood memories for you. Recollections of seaside holidays were the favourite sweets in Nostalgia's tin – the tedium of school and endless hours spent doing home-work were the orange cremes that nobody relished.

From this evening on she was supposed to be enjoying a holiday. Officially she was off work, but unofficially she'd slip into the office for the odd day – if she didn't, she'd probably die of boredom. Last week Daniel had got into a regular old strop because she hadn't booked a proper vacation. Ever since he'd returned from a fortnight in a whitewashed villa in Andalucía where he and Richard had done little more than eat, drink and swim in their private pool, he'd been clicking his flamenco fingers at her to organise something for herself.

'Come on, Ali,' he'd said, after he'd told her yet again what a wonderful two weeks he'd had. 'When was the last time you packed a bag and headed out of town?'

Her muttered response of being too busy was rejected out of hand. 'Ali, just get your shit together and book something.'

'It's not as easy as that,' she'd moaned. 'You've got Richard to go away with, but I'd be on my own. I'd be miserable company for myself.'

'Why not try one of those specially arranged activity holidays for singles?'

'What? Abseiling in Aviemore or candlemaking in the Cotswolds? I don't think so, Daniel.'

'Not even bonking in Borneo?'

'Anything as good as that would be booked by now.'

'You don't know that.'

'Yeah, well, I'll tell you what I do know, those activity holidays are for single saddos, and I ain't joining in with them for anybody, not even you.'

'Saddos such as yourself, Babe?'

'Ho bloody ho, you're creasing me up with your humour, these days.'

'And I'm filling up with your self-pity.'

'Then leave me alone.'

She had noticed that for the past few months Daniel had been treating her differently. If she wasn't mistaken, she'd say that he was having a go at bullying her. It had started after that night in March when she'd cooked supper for Elliot. The following Monday, Daniel had come into the office and put her through her paces as to how the evening had gone.

'It was okay,' she'd said noncommittally, switching on her computer and hiding behind it when he'd hit her with the first question.

A lowering of his glasses had told her that he was expecting her to be a touch more revealing.

'All right,' she'd said, 'it was a whisker more than being okay. We didn't accuse, we didn't blame, and we didn't snipe. It was all very dull.'

'Dull?' he'd repeated, unconvinced. 'I doubt that, some-how. The two of you together were never that, not in the good times or the bad times.'

'I meant in the sense of there being no drama to report back to you.'

'Did you feel comfortable with him?'

'If you really want to know, being with Elliot was like wearing an ill-fitting shoe. It pinched now and again.'

He'd smiled at that. 'And when it wasn't pinching how did it feel?'

'Scary.'

'Was that because you realised how it could be between the two of you?'

She had refused to answer him and had made a show of getting on with her work. But Daniel being Daniel had started applying the Chinese water-torture trick of drip-dripping his I-know-better questions and comments to her whenever he could.

Meanwhile, the days and weeks slipped by, and she didn't hear from Elliot. Daniel had suggested she should ring him, but she couldn't bring herself to do it. Elliot had obviously regretted the evening and had thought better of any ideas he might have had for seeing her again.

Sarah had also tried her luck at making Ali ring Elliot. 'After all that open-heart surgery I carried out on you,' she complained, 'and you're not going to do anything about it. I'm disappointed in you. Just see him once more and tell him what you told me. It would help you both so much.'

'I'll think about it,' she'd told Sarah.

But they'd both known that she wouldn't. The impetus to act had been lost.

However, the effect of that conversation she'd had with Sarah, back in March, had not been lost. It was the nearest she'd got to being honest, not just with another person but with herself. It had been the hardest thing for her to do, to admit that she'd deliberately wanted to hurt Elliot. But there was another reason behind her actions; a reason that was so dark and threatening it clouded any thought she had for him. So potentially harmful was it that even now she couldn't own up to it. She wasn't sure that she would ever be able to.

Afraid of the gloomy mood descending upon her, especially in view of the significance of this particular weekend – the day after tomorrow would have been Isaac's fourth birthday – she rose from her chair and went inside to replenish her now empty wine-glass. She caught sight of the bundle of mail that she'd put on the table when she'd arrived home. She took it outside, along with her refilled glass, and flicked through it. It was mostly the tedious variety of correspondence that would take up residence beside the fruit bowl, but a flash of blue sky and surf-crested sea hinted at something a lot more interesting. It was a card from Hannah and her writing was microscopic with the amount she had to tell.

Dear Ali, I said I'd write, and so I am. Having a blast of a time. We're now in La Rochelle. We've got our own annexe to stay in – very posh with proper beds and an ace swimming-pool to use. Emily and I are dead brown – don't breathe a word to Dad but we're topless by day and legless by night! Thanks for the money by the way, I've used some of it to buy Mum a present. Love, Hannah

Ali smiled. Good for you, girl. You go for it, kid. Grasp every opportunity of happiness while you can. She took a sip of her wine and stared thoughtfully at the card. She turned it over and looked at the stretch of beach, the impossibly blue sky, the inviting water and the brilliance of the white sand. It made her think of Daniel and his bullying.

Maybe he was right.

Perhaps she shouldn't hang around here being bored out of her skull just for the sake of taking time off work. She put her glass down beside the leg of her chair, went back inside the mill and rooted through her bag for her diary. She studied the entries for the week after next, then reached decisively for her mobile. There was nothing like acting on the spur of the moment. Tapping in her parents' number, she wandered outside again. As she waited for the phone to be answered at Sanderling, she leaned against the wooden rail of the balcony and watched the glowing ball of evening sun slowly sink on the horizon. At last she heard her father's voice. 'Ali,' he said, 'how the devil are you? We were only just talking about you.'

'Kindly, I hope.'

'Of course, what else would I have to say about my best girl?'

'You been at the pop again, Dad?'

'Why? Can you smell the fumes at this distance?'

'Practically keeling over.'

'Cheeky as ever, Ali. But you'll never guess what, Alistair's just phoned to announce that he's officially engaged to Phoebe and is combining a working trip to London with a visit to his lowly parents to show off the bride-to-be.'

'Good God, I don't believe it.'

'Nor can we. We were wondering if we could pull off a right royal family get-together. What do you think? Can I tempt you to come and see us?'

'Don't be so daft, of course I'll be there.'

'That's marvellous. Shall I put the memsahib on so you can finalise the details with her? You know I daren't promote myself to the dizzy heights of social secretary.'

'Hi, Mum,' Ali said, when her mother came on the line. 'How about that, then? The aged bachelor boy has finally gone and done it.'

'I know, your father and I can hardly believe it. After all these years he's succumbed. She must be quite special to have made him change his mind.'

'I'll say. So when are they arriving?'

'Next Saturday, a week tomorrow. You will come, won't you? We'd love to see you.'

'Actually, that's why I rang. I was hoping to cadge a holiday with you. Any chance of there being a bed for a couple of weeks as from Monday?'

'Oh, Ali, that would be lovely. Only trouble is we're away in Dorset for a few days and we leave on Monday morning. But you're more than welcome to make yourself at home while we're not here.'

Ali thought about this. Being at Sanderling on her own would be the same as being here all alone. What would be the point? She'd be just as miserable.

Her mother must have sensed her disappointment. 'Isn't there anyone you could bring with you?'

'What? A nice, handy bit of beefcake to keep me company?'

'Don't be silly, darling, I was thinking of Sarah. Didn't you mention on the phone last week that Hannah was away in France and that Sarah was down in the dumps and missing her? A holiday would cheer her up no end. It would be just like old times for you both.'

'Mum, you're brilliant!'

'Well, if you say so.'

'I'll ring Sarah straight away and see what she thinks. I'll call you in the morning with a yes or a no, shall I?'

'That's fine. But not too early. Your father and I enjoy our lie-ins, these days.'

Sarah answered the phone at Smithy Cottage.

'Hello, Ali,' she said, in a hushed tone that gave a clear indication to Ali that she wasn't alone.

'Is it a bad time to talk?'

'Yes, the group's here.'

'Oh, well, in that case I'll make it short and sweet. How do you feel about coming down to Hayling with me for a holiday? Just the two of us,' she added hastily, keen to ensure that Sarah wouldn't make the mistake of thinking Trevor was invited as well.

'Goodness, I don't know, Ali. When did you have in mind? And for how long?'

'Starting from Monday and for two whole weeks.'

'*What?*'

'I know it sounds impulsive but it would be fun, wouldn't it? And if you're worried about work, bring your sewing-machine with you. I could even help you.'

'If that's supposed to encourage me, forget it. I'm not having you anywhere near my machine.'

'So what do you say?'

'More to the point, what do I say to Trevor?'

'Tell him the truth, that you're desperately missing Hannah and you need something to take your mind off her. Oh, please say yes. I really want you to come. Mum and Dad will be away for the first week and we'll be able to do exactly as we want.'

'Oh, okay, then. You've twisted my arm.'

'Great! I'll come for you on Monday, about ten. That way we'll miss the early-morning crush on the motorway. Now get back to the Slipper Gang before they wake up and realise that you've gone.'

Ali felt ridiculously happy at the prospect of going away with Sarah and decided to ring Daniel and tell him what she'd done, as well as see if he could cover the extra week she'd decided to take off.

'Nice one, Babe,' he said. 'I knew I'd get through to you in the end. But, hey, this doesn't mean you're dropping out of Richard's barbecue on Sunday, does it?'

'And miss the culinary highlight of the year? I wouldn't dream of it. Though I might be a little late as I'll need to go into the office to sort out a few things.'

'Well, if there's anything you want me to do while you're away, leave a pile of instructions on my desk.'

'Will do. See you Sunday.'

Ali switched off her mobile and leaned back in her chair, pleased with her evening's work.

It was almost dark now, and as she stared into the gathering blackness and listened to the silence all around her, she realised just how quietly inert the evening was. The air was warm and still with hundreds of tiny insects hovering in it as if trapped by the thick humidity of the night. Then, way off in the distance, across the windless fields, she heard barking, but it was a lazy half-hearted bark, and probably from a dog that was too hot to make a better job of it.

She found her eyelids drooping and to keep herself awake she began putting together a things-to-do list. First she'd make a start on the packing, then she'd call Lizzie and tell her not to bother coming in for the next fortnight, and when it was late enough she'd ring her parents to confirm the arrangements. Then she'd go shopping for a few essentials – some sun cream and a selection of books to help her while away the long hours she intended to spend on the beach or on a sun-lounger in her parents' garden. Food shopping she'd do when they arrived. Anyway, her mother's freezer was bound to be overflowing with goodies long overdue for consuming: the Bermuda Triangle, her father called it – stuff went in but never came out!

She reached for her glass to drink a toast to herself for having such a good idea and found that a long-legged insect had taken a nose-dive into the remains of her wine. She picked it out and hoped it wasn't an omen of the flies-and-ointment variety. She didn't want anything to spoil the next couple of weeks. For the first time in ages, she had something to look forward to.

It was nearly eleven o'clock when Elliot reached home. The Heathrow–Manchester shuttle had been delayed by nearly two hours and even when they'd been allowed to board the plane, they'd been stuck on the tarmac for a further forty minutes waiting for a slot, without the benefit of air-conditioning. It had been as hot as hell and he'd had the bad luck to be sitting next to a foul-mouthed man who thought he had the right to be as gratuitously unpleasant as he wanted to the young stewardesses.

The house was in darkness when he let himself in. He'd forgotten that Sam was over in Yorkshire with his card-playing cronies. He crossed the hall to his study, put his briefcase by the side of his desk, and slipped his suit jacket over the back of his chair, along with his tie. He gave a cursory glance to the post Sam had put there for him and quickly dismissed it as uninteresting. But an envelope at the bottom of the pile stood out from the rest: it was square and very white, with the address written in gold ink, not in a hand he recognised. He slit it open. It was an invitation from Daniel, inviting him to a lunch-time barbecue to celebrate Richard's fortieth birthday. He checked the date and saw that it was for this Sunday.

Now, why had Daniel done that? he wondered, fanning himself with the thick, expensive card. Not since he and Ali had separated, when Daniel had felt that his loyalty lay with Ali, had there been any invitations of this sort.

Puzzled, he left his study and went through to the kitchen where he poured himself a large glass of orange juice from the fridge. He added a couple of ice cubes, swirled it round, then drank it slowly, speculating all the while as to the motive behind Daniel's invitation.

Was it just a harmless gesture of letting bygones be bygones, or was there more to it?

Such as?

Such as Ali putting him up to it because she wanted to see him?

No, he told himself firmly. He was not to let his thoughts go off in that direction. He'd been there earlier in the year and had lived to regret it; he wasn't inclined to make that mistake again.

He decided to go for a swim.

The pool room was airless and stiflingly hot. He switched on the underwater lights, but not the main ones, went over to the three sets of patio doors and slid them open. It was marginally cooler outside and while the temperature inside might not be greatly affected, the strong smell of chlorine would at least be diluted. He flung off his clothes and dived into the cool, refreshing water. It was undoubtedly the best bit of his day. The meeting in London had been a classic example of watch-your-back-and-keep-your-guard-up, and while it was mentally stimulating keeping one step ahead of the game, he also saw it as rather tiresome. For the first time in his career he had wondered if any of it was important to him.

It was a dangerous thought when his work was all he had.

He swam on and blamed the hot weather for making him feel so jaded and cynical. What he needed was a relaxing weekend. He'd do nothing but laze about the house and garden and generally wind down.

But the thought occurred to him that as Sunday would have been Isaac's fourth birthday, it might be better to accept Daniel's invitation and have something to occupy him.

Question was, would Ali be there?

Of course she would.

He hadn't been in touch with her since that night in March when he'd had supper with her. Even now he flinched at the painfully humiliating memory of his attempt to kiss her goodnight and her reaction to it. He hadn't meant it to be anything other than a simple parting act of courtesy, but her response had told him in no uncertain terms that she found him totally repugnant and would no more entertain the idea of physical contact between them than she would with a rattled cobra.

So it would probably be for the best if he phoned Daniel in the morning and politely declined the invitation.

Chapter Twenty-Nine

It was Sunday, the day of Richard's party, and beneath a sweltering hot and humid sky, Daniel carried the last of the bowls of salad from the kitchen and added them to the shaded table of food that the caterers from the village had prepared. Running his eye over an adjoining trestle table laden with drink, and knowing how thirsty everyone would be, he hoped they would have enough. It really was the most incredible weather – nearly as hot as Spain had been. The forecast on the radio that morning had mentioned the possibility of thunderstorms in the north of England; hopefully, though, they would keep until tonight.

A sudden waft of thyme and rosemary met his nostrils and he looked over to the side of the house where the man in charge of the barbecue had just chucked a handful of herbs on to the coals. He helped himself to a glass of sangria and searched the crowd of guests checking for two faces in particular.

There was no sign of either so he widened his search to the garden, then to the shade of the orchard. Again he drew a blank. But his gaze fell on Richard who, like himself and most of the other male guests, was dressed casually in shorts and a polo shirt. His head was turned to one side and Daniel took a moment to admire the cheerfully smiling, dark-eyed countenance that was as familiar to him as his own. Amusing, charming and with a love of witty anecdotal repartee, Richard was lethally intelligent, and Daniel knew that when he was in court he became a dangerous man. He could cut through the most persuasive and carefully constructed cases with a skill envied by anyone who had seen him in action. Right now, though, he looked as benign as the ancient apple tree he was sitting beneath while talking to Julia, a fellow barrister from his chambers who was expecting her second child. Her first, four-year-old Toby, was sitting on what was left of her lap, dipping his fingers into her lemonade then sucking them dry.

A hand tapped his shoulder and Daniel turned round, thinking it might be Ali. It wasn't, it was the barbecue man. 'Everything's about done,' he said. 'Do you want to give folk a shout?' He pulled off his straw boater, which bore a wide ribbon with the words Smoky-Joe's Mobile BBQ printed on it. He mopped his glistening forehead with a paper napkin and stuffed it into the front pocket of his butcher's-style apron.

'That's great,' Daniel said. 'I'll get people moving.' To attract everybody's attention he went over to the house and rang the brass ship's bell beside the door. 'Lunch is served,' he shouted. 'Women and children from steerage class go first, no pushing or shoving.'

'My timing, as ever, is spot on,' came a voice from behind him.

This time it was Ali.

'At last. I'd almost given up on you.' He raised his sunglasses and bent his head to kiss her. Then tracing a finger over a shoe-string strap that was slipping off her bare shoulder, he said, 'Nice dress, Babe. You've buffed yourself up a treat for the occasion.'

'Which is more than I can say for you. That shirt might be Armani's finest, but there's a hole in it, just there.' She pointed to his chest and he lowered his eyes to see. She laughed and flicked him lightly on the nose with the back of her hand. 'Don't mess with me, Dan Divine. Now, where's the birthday boy?'

'Cooling off in the orchard.'

'Sensible man. I'll go and give this to him.'

Daniel eyed with interest the present she was carrying. 'What is it?'

'Never you mind. You see to your other guests and leave me to have a nice, malicious gossip with Richard. And no guesses for who we'll be tearing apart!'

Daniel smiled and watched her make her way through the crush of guests on the terrace, down the three steps that led to the garden and the orchard beyond. He saw Richard get to his feet when he caught sight of her. He hugged her warmly then pulled up another chair so that she could join him and Julia. Knowing that Ali never gave anyone a gift that she hadn't put a lot of thought into, Daniel was tempted to go over and see what she had brought for Richard.

But this wasn't the only reason he wanted to join them. He was losing his nerve. Sending that invitation to Elliot now seemed the dumbest of ideas and he felt as though he ought to come clean with Ali so that she could prepare herself. On the other hand, it was almost two o'clock and it was just possible Elliot might be a no-show. In which case, if he kept his mouth shut, Ali would be none the wiser.

It was late on Tuesday night when he and Richard were in bed that Daniel had thought of inviting Elliot to the party. 'What do you think?' he'd asked Richard. 'What would they do?'

Glancing up from the brief he was working on, Richard had said, 'Doubtless Elliot would behave impeccably, as he always does, but Ali would probably disembowel you on the spot, toss your tasty little sweetbreads on to the hot coals of the barbecue and then kebab the rest of you.'

'So you reckon I shouldn't do it?'

'I didn't say that.'

'What then?'

'I'm suggesting that you must be prepared for the consequences, should Ali decide that you've been scheming behind her back.'

'But only with her best interests at heart.'

'Naturally. What else could you possibly have in mind?'

'You're beginning to sound as though you're cross-examining me.'

'Just send Elliot the invitation. No real harm can come of it. Ali will always love you, she can't help herself. The worst that could happen is that she'll be cross for a while and then when she's calmed down you'll kiss and make up.'

'And the best that could come of it?'

Returning his attention to the papers on top of the duvet, Richard had said, 'I think we both know the outcome that you're hankering after, don't we? You're a sentimental old fool looking for a happy ending.'

The queue for food was now well established and after Daniel had chatted with some friends from the choral society and made sure that everybody was helping themselves to drinks, he went to check on the tennis court where the older children had congregated. He told them that if they didn't get going all the burgers and sausages would be gone. They threw down their rackets and raced out of the court. Amy, his thirteen-year-old niece, his sister's eldest child, gave him a smile and he flicked at her CK baseball cap as she rushed past. He wondered at their energy in all this sticky heat. I'm getting old, he reflected. And what a depressing thought that was. The noise of an approaching car made him turn and he knew at once who it was. Now, should he go and meet Elliot? Or should he sneak back to the house and hide anything that was long and sharp which Ali could use to disembowel him?

Elliot slowed his speed and parked behind Ali's Saab. He switched off the engine and reached for the bottle of vintage port he had brought for Richard. When he stepped out of the car, he saw Daniel coming towards him.

'Hi,' Daniel said, 'I thought perhaps you weren't going to make it.'

'I wasn't sure that I would,' Elliot said.

And wasn't that the truth? He'd changed his mind about coming so many times since Friday night that in the end, and only an hour ago, he had let the decision rest on the toss of a coin: tails, and he'd stay at home for the afternoon to read the Sunday papers; heads, and he'd put himself through another bit of hell. He inclined his head towards Ali's Saab and said, 'What sort of mood is she in?'

'Relaxed and happy, having a gossip about me with Richard.'

'Does she know I was invited?'

'Er . . . no.'

'A surprise, then?'

Daniel nodded guiltily.

'Well, let's hope it's not too horrible for her.'

Passing the long line of cars, they walked up to the house, and when they reached the terrace, Daniel offered Elliot a drink. 'Looks as if we're getting low on sangria,' he said, lifting a large Spanish pottery jug and peering inside it. 'How about some wine?'

'I'd prefer a beer, please.'

'I think I'll join you.' Bending down to one of the cool boxes under the table, Daniel picked out a couple of cans of Budweiser.

'Thanks,' said Elliot, snapping back the ring-pull. 'Cheers.' After they'd both taken a few mouthfuls, and as if it was clearly understood between them exactly why he was here, Elliot said, 'It was good of you to invite me. I appreciate it.'

Daniel responded with a casual shrug, which belied what he really felt. 'It seemed a good idea,' he said, wanting to add, 'at the time.' And doing his utmost not to visualise his entrails being slowly drawn out of him he vowed never, *ever*, to meddle again in Ali's private affairs.

With a hint of a smile, Elliot said, 'Let's hope you still think that later today. Shall we get it over and done with, then?'

Daniel's insides went into liquidised mode. 'Why not?' he muttered, thinking of a million good reasons why not. 'She was in the orchard the last time I saw her. I'll take you.'

They were half-way across the lawn when, above the noise of music and party chatter, Elliot heard the unmistakable sound of Ali's laughter. He squinted to find her in the shade of the apple trees. She appeared to be just as Daniel had described, relaxed and happy. She was sitting alone with Richard who was leaning in close, like an attentive lover, and feeding her something from his plate. Her head was tilted back and the pale slender line of her throat was alluringly exposed. Elliot couldn't remember the last time he'd seen her looking so at ease. Certainly not in his company. His body stiffened as a powerful surge of jealous love for her rose up within him and he knew that he'd made a terrible mistake in coming here. But it was too late to retreat. Richard had caught sight of him and, as they advanced further, Elliot noted the smallest of exchanges pass between him and Daniel.

'How amazingly good it is to see you, Elliot,' said Richard, on his feet now and smiling genially. 'I'm so pleased you accepted my invitation. Daniel, being the ultra-sensitive soul he is, was dead against it, but I insisted. It's my party, I told him, and I'll do as I please. Now, then, you don't have anything to eat. Daniel, why don't you see to that and I'll get Ali another drink? And is that a present I spy in your hands, as the Virgin Queen was heard to remark to Sir Francis Drake on his return to these fair shores of England?'

When they were alone, Elliot motioned towards the wooden chair Richard had vacated. 'May I?'

She nodded and he sat down. She said, 'I know barristers are known for their acting skills, but what, I wonder, am I supposed to make of that little charade?'

The vibrancy of her voice suggested irony rather than displeasure. He ventured a similar tone. 'That Richard was pleased to see me?'

She turned and stared at him suspiciously. 'Possibly. Which was more than Daniel looked. His face wore an expression of abject terror and I swear it had a label attached to it that said, in big black letters, "Shoot me now."'

As usual she was right, Daniel had indeed looked terrified, but not wanting to pursue the hows and whys of this, Elliot opted for the safety of a round or two of small-talk – if there was such a thing with Ali. 'How are you?' he asked, when she'd removed her sceptical gaze from him. 'You look well.'

She leaned back in her seat and adjusted the hem of her dress as well as the strap on her shoulder, which seemed to have a mind of its own. 'Thank you. It's probably the thought of going away on holiday tomorrow.'

'Somewhere nice?'

'Down to Sanderling. Sarah's coming with me.'

'A trip down Memory Lane for you both.'

'Indeed.'

'Sam's away this weekend. He's in Yorkshire with a gang of his poker cronies.'

'Leaving you at liberty to accept lunch-time barbecue invitations.'

'Something like that, yes.'

Their supply of small-talk now used up, Elliot stared straight ahead. His gaze came to rest on a small fair-haired boy in navy blue shorts and a blue and white striped T-shirt. He was sitting at his mother's feet pushing a toy car through the long grass, giving it his entire concentration, *brrming* his lips with noisy enjoyment. His mother, who was about six months pregnant, Elliot guessed, smiled down at him. She then spoke to the man at her side who kissed her while gently passing his hand over their child-to-be in a gesture of protective affection. It was an exquisite cameo of intimacy; a snapshot of a loving family. Elliot tore his eyes away from the scene. 'Look,' he said, his voice thick with emotion, 'if I'm spoiling your afternoon, tell me and I'll leave you alone.'

Ali had been observing the same touching tableau, and it struck at the heart of her: in another life she had been that woman, Elliot had been that man . . . and Isaac had been that son. The poignancy of it made her want the impossible, to turn the clock back, to experience that tender love all over again. The need to feel it once more was so great in her it hurt. But she knew it could never be.

But you could say sorry, she heard Sarah's soft voice whisper in her head.

You could make amends.

Do for Elliot what he can't do for himself.

Forgive him.

Just say the words and you could be nice to one another.

And suddenly Ali knew that the time had come. At last she realised that the pain and bitterness she had lived with for so long had to be eradicated once and for all. She took a deep breath and turned to Elliot. To her surprise, he was on his feet and already moving away from her. Puzzled, she looked at his retreating figure. Then she realised what was wrong. She'd taken too long to answer his question and he'd assumed that her silence meant that she didn't want him near her. Stunned by the discovery that she was now ready to put the past behind her, she watched him march out of the dim light of the orchard and step into the brightness of the garden. She decided to give him time to cool off before going after him.

Elliot had been all for going home, but Daniel had intercepted him with a plate of food and later challenged him to a game of tennis. It had seemed as good a way as any to beat the shit out of himself. He was two sets up and was now serving for the match. Facing into the sun, which was now partially eclipsed by a hazy canopy of thundery clouds, Elliot tossed the ball high into the air. He swung his borrowed racket behind him, then snatched it over his shoulder, throwing all his weight and frustration against it. The ball hurtled over the net and shot passed Daniel before he'd even had a chance to prepare for it.

'That's the last time I play tennis with you,' puffed Daniel, when they walked off the court.

'I was on a lucky roll,' Elliot said modestly, wiping the sweat off his face with his hands, then rubbing them on his linen trousers.

'The hell you were. You completely outclassed me.'

They strolled back to the house and helped themselves to two ice-cold beers. 'I don't know about you,' Daniel groaned, 'but I need to sit down. I'm knackered.'

There were no free seats in the orchard so they flopped on to the grass. The small boy Elliot had seen earlier with his parents came and joined them. He had a bowl of raspberries in his hands and set it carefully on his crossed legs as he sat down. 'You look very hot,' he remarked to Daniel.

'That's because I am, Toby. I've just been playing tennis. One of those nice juicy raspberries would make me feel a whole lot better, though.'

The little boy smiled, showing two rows of tiny white teeth, and offered him the bowl. Shyly, and despite there being only a few left, he then passed the dish to Elliot. Touched by the child's generosity, he said, 'No, thanks, it looks as if you're down to your last.'

'Well, we'll soon remedy that,' said Daniel. He rose to his feet and went over to the terrace and the tables of food.

'Is Daniel getting us some more?' asked the little boy.

'I think so.'

He popped the last of the raspberries into his mouth and looked thoughtfully at Elliot. 'Did you know that my mummy's having a baby?'

'I'd guessed that that might be the case.'

'Are you a daddy?'

Elliot said no, and wished that Daniel would hurry back. He didn't want to be alone with this child and his naturally inquisitive chatter. He knew the score only too well. It would be one question after another. Why? Why? Why? That's what children did.

'Don't you like children?'

Oh, here we go. 'I'm very fond of them,' he murmured

edgily. He looked across to the terrace for some sign of Daniel. He saw him laughing with a young girl in a baseball cap. Come on, Daniel, he urged silently. A rumble of thunder rolled overhead and he plucked distractedly at the grass between his feet. Without raising his eyes, he wondered how old the boy was. Odds on he was four . . . the very age Isaac would have been today. At this thought he felt his throat tighten. He passed a hand over his face and became aware of his heart beginning to thump in his chest. He blinked hard and let out his breath; he was hotter now than when he'd been playing tennis. It's the humidity, he told himself firmly, desperately groping for some reasonable, trivial explanation for what was happening to him. He'd do anything but accept the truth. All he could do was hope that the moment would pass. Then, with relief, he saw Daniel ambling slowly towards them.

The little boy saw him too and when Daniel had lowered himself on to the grass and had stretched out on his side, he said, 'Is your friend like you and Richard? Is that why he doesn't have any children?'

Daniel stared at Toby in amusement. Good God, trust Julia to be so bloody open with her son! But his expression soon changed when he saw Elliot's deathly pale face. Shit, he thought, what the hell's been going on here? He handed Toby the bowl of raspberries that he'd just fetched and said, 'Elliot isn't at all like Richard and me. Now eat up and don't ask any more nosy questions.'

Toby smiled and leaning into Daniel, he said, in a loud whisper, 'Why does he look so cross?'

'He's not cross,' Daniel whispered back.

'Is he sad, then?'

Other than putting a gag on Toby, there seemed no way of stopping the flow of innocent questions, and Daniel looked helplessly at Elliot. Then to his surprise he heard Elliot say, 'I'm not cross, Toby, but you're right about me being sad.'

'Why?'

'Because I had a little boy once. He was quite a bit younger than you and ... and he died.'

Both Elliot and Daniel expected this to be the conversation stopper it usually was, but all it did was provoke yet another question from Toby. 'Did he die in his sleep? Mummy says that's the best way to die.'

The conversation had now spiralled completely out of his control and, as another rumble of thunder rolled in the distance, a gut-wrenching pain propelled Elliot to his feet. He realised to his horror that his heart was pounding even faster than it had been a few minutes before and that every inch of his body was clammy with sweat. He stumbled away and out of the orchard. He knew with terrible certainty that he was going to be sick. He followed a small path that led down the gentle slope of the valley towards the wood on the edge of Daniel and Richard's land. His head was throbbing and his stomach pitching. He leaned over a crumbling drystone wall and vomited violently.

When at last it came to an end, he slipped his hand into his trouser pocket and pulled out his handkerchief. With shaking hands, he wiped his face and remained where he was, leaning heavily on the wall, his shoulders taut, his chest heaving. But though his eyes were focused on the flock of sheep sheltering in the shade of a tree in the nearby field, his thoughts were with Isaac on the night he died.

There had been nothing peaceful about Isaac's death, nothing of the fairy-tale slipping away to heaven in his sleep that Toby had probably been taught.

The day had started ordinarily enough; there hadn't been a single clue at breakfast that by the end of the day their lives would be so irredeemably smashed apart. The only difference in their routine was that their nanny, who had been with them since Isaac was four months old, had taken a day off and, with Ali flying to Frankfurt that afternoon, Elliot had said that he'd stay at home and take care of Isaac. They'd waved Ali goodbye as she'd left for work and everything had been fine until around five, when Isaac began to look unwell and refused to eat his tea. Thinking that perhaps he was coming down with a cold, Elliot had bathed him and put him to bed. He'd read him a story, kissed him goodnight and gone downstairs to answer the phone. It was Gervase from the office: the wretched man had drivelled on for more than an hour.

When he'd finished on the phone, Elliot had gone back upstairs to check on Isaac. The second he saw him, he knew that something was wrong. His breathing was noisy and painfully laboured; his face pale, his eyes wide and staring. Pulling back the tangle of bedclothes, Elliot touched his flushed skin and realised that his temperature was worryingly high. He unbuttoned his pyjama top and saw that his tiny chest was being sucked in with the struggle to breathe. He knew vaguely about young children suffering from croup, but this seemed far worse than anything he'd read or heard about. He'd gathered Isaac in his arms, rushed him downstairs and outside to the car. He drove as fast as he dared to the nearest hospital, glancing almost every other second in the rear-view mirror, but seeing only what he feared most – that his son was dying.

The noise of twigs crackling underfoot made Elliot spin round. 'What the hell do you want?' he said sharply, when he saw who it was.

Ali hesitated. 'Daniel suggested that I came to look for you,' she said. 'Are you okay?'

He twisted the handkerchief in his hands, screwing it tighter and tighter around his fingers until it hurt. 'No, I'm not okay and I'd rather you left me alone.'

Genuinely alarmed, especially in view of what Daniel had just told her, Ali took a few cautious steps towards him. She leaned against the drystone wall and when she saw what lay the other side of it, she knew that Daniel had been right to make her come and find him. 'Elliot,' she said gently, 'what's wrong?' He turned slowly and she saw an expression of such distilled misery in his face that instinctively she reached out to him and placed a hand on his arm. 'Please, tell me, what is it?'

His jaw tightened. 'Do you really need to ask that?'

'Was it that little boy, Toby?'

He pushed away her hand and squeezed his eyes shut. 'Leave me alone. Just go. You're good at doing that.'

The bitterness in his voice was hard to bear, but she remained where she was. 'Elliot,' she said softly, 'I left you alone once before and it didn't help either of us, did it?'

He opened his eyes and looked at her. 'So what are you saying?'

'I'm saying that we've hidden too much from one another. I think we should put a stop to it. Don't you?'

'What is it that I'm supposed to have hidden from you?'

'Many things. Such as how you feel about me. How you still feel about Isaac. Perhaps even how you feel about what happened that night.'

Her over-simplification of what he was suffering caused something to explode deep inside Elliot. The tortured anguish that had covered his face suddenly turned into an expression of raw anger. 'Okay, then,' he threw nastily at her, 'so you want me to be honest with you, do you? In that case I'll share with you exactly what happened that night. I'll tell you all the grisly details. I'll spare you nothing. You can have the unexpurgated version. Then every day, just as I do, you can live through the hell of it. Is that what you want?'

Ali had never seen or heard Elliot act so savagely and, frightened by the brutality in his voice, she could do nothing but nod in mute agreement.

'Then you're welcome to it.' He moved away from her and as the first soft drops of rain started to fall, he paced the stony path, backwards and forwards, as he pieced together the events of the worst night of his life. He told her how he had driven Isaac to hospital as soon as he'd known something was wrong. 'I don't know who was the more terrified,' he said, 'Isaac because he couldn't breathe or me because I didn't know if I was doing the right thing. We'd only been in the car a few minutes when he literally turned grey. Then he started to drool, and worse – oh, God, much worse – the terrible noise of his tiny lungs struggling for breath began to fade.' He paused, ran a hand through his hair then rounded on her. He grabbed her shoulders and almost shook her. 'Can you understand what that did to me? Do you have any idea what it feels like having to choose between driving on for help that might be too late anyway, or stopping so that a small, frightened child could at least die in his father's arms?'

Shocked, Ali trembled in his hands. 'What did you do?' Her question was little more than a faint whisper. This wasn't how she'd imagined it. Not at all. She'd needed to believe that there had been no pain for Isaac. That it had been quick – quick, but painless.

The rain was coming down more heavily now, wetting their clothes and faces. Ali's flimsy cotton dress was already drenched and clinging to her. She wasn't cold but she was shivering. Oblivious to the rain, Elliot let go of her and began pacing again. And although the vociferous, accusing fury that had led him to this point had subsided, the desperation was still in his immeasurably wretched face. 'I decided to drive on,' he said, his tone altogether softer. 'All I could think of was getting Isaac to somebody who would know what to do, somebody who would be able to save him. But then he turned blue and when the convulsions started I knew I had to stop. It was awful, his legs and arms were twitching and by the time I got round to the back of the car, he'd lost consciousness . . . He wasn't moving. He was so still. So bloody still and I knew I'd lost him. I tried to resuscitate him. I kept on trying – it seemed like for ever. But it was no good. Nothing I did was of any use. I then – I then –' But his voice cracked with the choking horror of reliving the ordeal. He fixed his gaze on the distant hills and from somewhere, he didn't know where, the strength came to him to carry on. 'I had to drive the rest of the journey to the hospital knowing that our son was dead. I carried him in and he was taken from me. A nurse came and sat with me and when I thought I was calm enough I phoned you.'

He fell silent, closed his eyes, and let out his breath in one long sigh. He stood perfectly still, listening to the rain as it pattered all around him, his anger now spent. The worst had passed. Thank God. He was back in control again.

He opened his eyes, turned to look at Ali, but then from nowhere, a sickening wave of agony swept over him as he recalled pressing his lips to Isaac's soft cheek for the last time, his limp body already cool to the touch as he carried him from the car. Unable to stop himself, he started to shake. He covered his face with his hands and wept. He thought that he'd already experienced every conceivable pain there was when he thought of his son, but he hadn't. What he was feeling now, after finally admitting to another person what he'd gone through that night, was the fusion of everything he'd ever suffered.

Then, gradually, he became conscious of Ali moving behind him. He felt her hands on his shoulders. At first he held back from her, rigid and unyielding, but when he realised that she was crying as much as he was, he gave in to her embrace, and in the deluge of rain that had now thoroughly soaked them, they did what they'd never tried to do since losing their son: they cried in one another's arms.

'Oh, Ali,' he sobbed into her neck, 'I swear I did everything I could to save him. It was a nightmare. A total fucking nightmare. It was all so quick and there wasn't anything I could do. You have to believe me.'

Chapter Thirty

It was Ali who spoke first. Lifting her head from Elliot's shoulder, she raised her eyes to his ravaged face and said, 'Elliot, we have to talk.'

They took a moment to compose themselves, then followed the path back up to the house, to where all the other guests had now fled for shelter. Without a word to anyone they left the party.

In silent concentration, Elliot drove them to Timbersbrook, the seriousness of his blue eyes and the hard line of his jaw determining that now was not the time to embark on what they had to discuss.

How adept he is at isolating himself, thought Ali, as she sat beside him, sensing that, as physically close as they were, he was far beyond her reach. And wasn't that exactly what he had done since Isaac's death? He'd shut himself off from everyone. Including her. It had been his way of coping with his grief; his naturally quiet, insular disposition had simply brought down the shutters and forced him to retreat into himself. It was obvious now, with the benefit of hindsight, that she should have tried harder to reach him, to infiltrate his defences and knock down that impenetrable shield with which he'd protected himself, but she'd barely had the strength to haul herself through her own misery, never mind sustain Elliott.

If only he had told her what he had really endured that night, how different it all might have been. But her own willingness to accept the original story he'd given – that Isaac's death had been so quick that he'd hardly suffered –

was surely partly to blame for that. She had wanted, *needed*, as any mother would, to believe that her son had experienced the minimum of pain. All this time she had believed that Isaac was conscious until Elliot got him to the hospital, that it was only then as he'd arrived that death had taken him. She had believed all too readily Elliot's claim that their child's death had not been precipitated by a gruelling struggle for survival. But now she knew differently. Now she knew that he'd struggled to live, every bit of his small terrified body fighting painfully to the last. To the very last.

She squeezed her eyelids shut as the horror of what Elliot had just revealed to her flashed through her mind. With new and hideously clear understanding, she pictured the chilling scene of Elliot, all alone, trying desperately to revive Isaac and the awful moment when he'd been forced to acknowledge that he'd failed. That there was nothing he could do. How would she have reacted if that had been her? To what depths would she have sunk had she been in his place?

But she had never put herself in Elliot's place. All she had thought about was Isaac. And, selfishly, herself. Her loss.

Not even at the hospital when she had been told what had happened did she pause to think of the ordeal Elliot had just lived through. She had been only half listening to the doctor as he had explained that her son's death was a scenario all medical staff dreaded: there had been so little warning that something was fatally wrong. She had been informed that Isaac had died from a rare case of bacterial croup, epiglottitis, which had resulted in his larynx swelling so much that he couldn't breathe. The doctor had gone on to say, just as he had earlier told Sam and Elliot, that there was nothing Elliot could have done. All that might have saved Isaac was an emergency tracheotomy.

But she had refused to believe the doctor. A child's life could not be snatched away so swiftly. It couldn't end like that. It just couldn't. Somebody had to be accountable.

Cruelly, she had wanted to hold Elliot accountable; he should have got Isaac to hospital in time.

Later, when Sam had driven them home from the hospital, he had insisted on staying the night with them. But no one had slept, and while she had cried alone on the bed upstairs, and Sam had made an endless succession of cups of coffee that nobody drank, Elliot had begun to withdraw into himself. At four in the morning, when it was still dark, she had looked out of the bedroom window and had seen his desolate figure in the shadows at the end of the garden. She had no idea how long he'd been out there, but he must have been frozen for she could see his breath hanging in the wintry air. She knew that he needed her, but her own grief was so great that it overwhelmed anything she felt for him, and with her forehead pressed against the icy pane of glass she had mouthed the words, *You could have saved him . . . You could have saved him.*

In one form or another she had been thinking those words ever since.

She had never once verbally blamed Elliot for failing Isaac, but she knew she had done the next best thing: she had punished him relentlessly by making him hate her.

This, then, was the final confession, the truth that not even Sarah had guessed: this was what had really destroyed her marriage. It hadn't just been Elliot's rejection that had fuelled her need to punish him: it had been her terrible, misguided need to make him pay for allowing their son to die. Initially she hadn't been aware of what she was doing, but when she realised the destruction she was causing, she had been beyond caring. It was entirely his fault; he had let their child die.

Consumed now by the heaviest weight of guilt and shame, she wrapped her arms around her wet shoulders and shivered. How could she have behaved so despicably? And to a man who she now knew had gone through a nightmare far worse than her own. Of course he had done everything he could to save Isaac. Why had she ever thought that he hadn't?

Elliot had loved Isaac with all his heart. He'd never been too busy or too tired to play with his son. Not once had he ever refused to take his share of the disturbed nights when Isaac was teething. He would hold him lovingly in his arms, gently rocking him back to sleep. One night she had heard him talking to Isaac in a low, soothing voice as he'd tried to settle him. He was sharing with Isaac some of the things they would do together when he was old enough. Slipping out of bed, she'd gone and listened at the door.

'I'll take you to Yorkshire,' Elliot was murmuring softly as he rested Isaac, hot and fractious, against his shoulder and stroked the wispy curls of damp blond hair in the nape of his neck. 'I'll show you where I grew up. We'll take a kite and go up on to the moors. Your grandfather used to do that with me. Perhaps we'll take him with us. Your mother too. And there's something you should know about your mother. I'm sure you've noticed it already, but she's the most beautiful woman in the world. She's also the smartest and you'd do well to watch her. One day you'll realise just how special she is. I'll warn you now, it'll come as a shock. It did to me. Of course, you won't love her as I do, but love her you will, because I promise you, you won't be able to help yourself. And when the time comes for you to fall madly and indescribably in love, I hope that you'll be as lucky as your father and marry the woman who means the world to you. But before all that happens, you've got your parents' love to make do with. And that, I might say, is considerable. There's nothing we wouldn't do for you. We'll always keep you safe. Nothing will ever harm you.'

With tears in her eyes she had wanted to let Elliot know that she was there, that she had heard what he'd said. She had wanted to tell him how touched she was, but knowing that this was the most effusive she'd ever known him, she had crept quietly back to bed and waited for him to join her.

Thinking now of all the love she had so wilfully destroyed, Ali hated herself. She felt physically ill. Worried that she was going to be sick, she opened her eyes and saw that Elliot was watching her. The concern in his face only added to her guilt.

It had stopped raining when Elliot brought the car to a halt and the sun was shining once more. He let them into the house and, without a word, took her through to the sitting room where he poured two enormous glasses of Jack Daniel's. Ali stood awkwardly in the large room watching him. Then, when he passed her drink to her, she caught sight of the group of framed photographs on the baby grand. For something to do, she went over to take a look and was surprised to see an old picture of herself included among the collection. Unnerved, she ran her hand over the lid of the piano and said, 'Do you still play?'

'Hardly ever,' he answered.

'Why's that?'

He took an unsteady gulp of his drink. 'I lost my most appreciative audience.' He didn't wait for her response, but turned on his heel and crossed the room to the french windows. They opened on to the garden, which was flooded with sunlight. He breathed in the freshness of the air, now that the storm had passed.

She came and stood next to him. 'Shall we sit outside?' she asked.

He took her to a wooden bench in a small shaded area of garden. The ground was flagged with moss-darkened Yorkshire stone and dotted with large pots of hostas and specimen lilies. Everything was washed clean and bright by the downpour of rain and jewel-like droplets of water hung in suspended animation from the drooping leaves and petals. It was very tranquil.

'You should never have kept the truth of that night to yourself,' Ali said, after Elliot had wiped the bench with his handkerchief and they were settled.

'I had to,' he said simply.

'But why?'

'I was trying to protect you . . . I didn't want you to have the kind of nightmare memories I have of Isaac.'

'Perhaps if you had told me the truth I wouldn't have added to your pain in the way I did. I might have understood better – been able to help you.'

'It wouldn't have done any good. I wouldn't have let you near me. I hated myself for letting Isaac die.' He lowered his head and stared with unseeing eyes into his glass. 'I still hate myself. For the rest of my life I have to live with the knowledge that if I had realised earlier that Isaac was ill, if I'd shut Gervase up sooner – if I'd got to a hospital quicker—'

She laid a hand on his forearm. 'Elliot, you have to stop thinking those thoughts.'

He raised his head and looked at her. 'I don't think I ever will. Every night when I sleep I'm haunted by his frightened face, I see how betrayed he felt, that his own father was letting him suffer, that I didn't stop it. I hear my voice shouting at him not to die. Again and again I relive that moment when I'm trying to revive him . . . Sometimes it works . . . but usually he just lies there limp and cold in my arms.' He took a gulp of his drink. 'Sometimes I dream it's you I'm trying to bring back to life.'

Her throat tightened. 'Does it ever work?' she asked.

'No,' he said bleakly. 'I'm always too late . . . just as I was with Isaac.'

'Oh, Elliot, why did you never try telling me these things?'

'I'd done too good a job of making you hate me, I guess.'

She frowned. 'No, it's the other way around, I deliberately *made* you hate me.'

'I pushed you away, Ali because I couldn't stand to have anyone near me, but I never hated you. Please, if nothing else, believe that to be true.'

'Then I got that wrong as well.' She sighed. 'I needed to think you did. It was a crazy way of punishing myself – and you. I wanted to spoil everything we had. By making you feel worse I convinced myself that I was feeling better.'

'Did it work?'

'What do you think?'

'I suppose not.'

She turned to him. 'If I said I was sorry a thousand times would you ever forgive me?'

He stared at her. 'But, Ali, I need *your* forgiveness. If I'd acted sooner Isaac would still be alive, if I'd—'

'No, Elliot, you did all you could. I can accept that, and so must you. You have to stop punishing yourself.'

He didn't say anything but, very gently, he put his arm round her and drew her close until her head was resting on his shoulder. She linked her fingers through his and they sat there silently holding one another, just letting the serenity of the garden wrap itself around them.

'I feel strangely at peace,' Ali said, when at last she moved.

'I know what you mean. I feel it too.'

'If there is such a thing as an afterlife, do you suppose Isaac is looking down on us and saying, "Thank goodness for that."'

'Probably. He was a smart lad.'

'Unlike his parents.'

'Unlike his parents,' agreed Elliot.

They fell silent again. Then Elliot said, 'You might think this inappropriate, but as we ought to get out of these wet clothes anyway, do you fancy a swim?'

She shifted her position and sat up. 'A swim?'

He pulled her to her feet decisively. 'Come on. It'll do us good. It'll help us relax.'

'But I don't have anything to wear,' she protested, when he led her back inside the house and into the pool room.

He pushed open the patio doors. 'I promise I won't look.'

'You mean skinny-dipping?'

He ignored her question and its tone of incredulous propriety. 'Changing rooms are down the other end. I'll get you a robe and a towel.' He opened one of the mirror-fronted cupboards behind him and handed her a bundle of neatly folded white towelling.

When she emerged from the changing room, coyly wrapped in the oversized robe, she saw that Elliot was already in the pool modestly attired in a pair of swimming shorts. True to his word, he didn't look at her until she was fully immersed. It was stupid that she should be embarrassed at the thought of him seeing her naked, but there was something wrong about one's ex-husband viewing the goods that had once been for his eyes only but which were now strictly out of bounds.

Keeping a suitably respectable distance between them, they swam to and fro. Neither spoke. But it wasn't long before she realised that Elliot had been right about feeling better for a swim. She already felt less raw from the painfully honest, vulnerable ordeal they'd just experienced. She hoped he felt better too. Every now and then she looked across the pool to check that he wasn't sneaking the odd glance her way. But as ever, when he wanted it to be, his face was unreadable. She found herself wondering what he was thinking. Were his thoughts running along the same lines as hers? That they had found the key to set themselves free?

What she had said in the garden about being at peace was true. She hadn't ever thought that there would come a time when she would be able to say those words. But it had happened. As if by magic the weight of the past two and a half years had been lifted from her. In real terms nothing had changed – Isaac was still dead and her grief for him was still there – but what had gone was the cruel need to punish herself. By feeling compassionate towards Elliot and knowing, deep in her heart, that she no longer blamed him, she felt almost restored to her former self. Perhaps even a better self.

She was tiring and, knowing that she couldn't keep pace with Elliot's strong arms and shoulders as he cut effortlessly through the water, she watched him swim on ahead of her. He was a difficult man not to admire and she found herself wondering whether there had been any women in his life since their divorce. She suspected the answer had to be yes. She couldn't imagine any woman not falling for his special brand of understated sexual magnetism. It must have been put to excellent use at some stage since their separation. She was smiling at this thought when she noticed that he'd stopped swimming and was waiting for her at the shallow end.

'It's been ages since I've seen you smile like that,' he said. 'What were you thinking?'

'Of you,' she said, as she came to a stop alongside him. 'And don't you dare lower your eyes from my face,' she added, remembering that she didn't have a stitch on, 'not even for a second.'

He was privately amused. 'So what was making you smile?'

'I was wondering whether there'd been many women in your bed since me.'

He raised an eyebrow. 'And do you think you have a right to know?'

'Not really. I gave up that right when I divorced you.'

He sharpened his gaze on her. 'Well, I'll tell you anyway, just to satisfy your curiosity. There hasn't been anyone.'

'Not one?'

He shook his head. 'You seem surprised at my hermetically sealed sex life?'

'Frankly, I'm amazed.' She was also amazed that she felt so irrationally relieved.

'What about you?'

'Hundreds,' she said, with a light-hearted smile.

He frowned. 'What does that mean exactly?'

She laughed and swam away from him. 'It means zippo, lover-boy.'

He went after her and caught her up in one long easy stroke. Matching her pace and swimming barely a few feet away from her, he forgot his earlier promise and allowed his eyes to linger over her sinuous body. In that moment, it seemed to him to be a fluid, shimmering vision of loveliness. Almost at once she saw what he was doing. She ducked and disappeared beneath the water, but not before he'd glimpsed a hint of a smile. He filled his lungs with a gulp of air and dived in after her. Taking her unawares he caught her by the waist and pulled her down to the floor of the pool. He covered her lips with his and gently filled her mouth with air as her surprised resistance gave way and she relaxed into his arms. He kissed her for as long as his breath held out and when eventually they floated to the surface they stared transfixed at each other. It was Ali who made the next move. She pulled him to her and kissed him, urgently and with passion, her body alive to the aching desire she felt for him. Pressing his body against hers and revelling in its familiarity – there wasn't a bit of it she didn't know – she alternated between kissing him and frantically whispering his name, over and over. There seemed no doubt in either of their minds what would happen now. It was more a matter of where. Ali wanted him so badly she would have splashed around in the water and risked drowning. But Elliot had other ideas. He helped her out of the pool, laid her on top of the towels and robes, and just as they always had, they made love with a passion that was tender and uninhibited.

'I was worried that after several years of celibacy I might have lost my touch,' he murmured, when they lay stunned and exhausted, and not a little self-consciously, in one another's arms.

'You have,' she said breathlessly, 'I was faking it.'

He lifted himself up on to one elbow and gazed into her contented face, her features so soft and loving, just as her hands had been a few moments ago. This was the Ali he loved. The Ali who, one minute, could be tough and wildly assertive but who, when they made love, trembled and moaned and became defenceless with desire. It had always knocked him out that he could have such an effect on her.

'Ali—?'

She opened her eyes. 'No,' she whispered, 'don't talk. Not now. Kiss me again and make me believe I'm not dreaming.'

'I can do better than that.' And wrapping themselves in the towelling robes, he took her back inside the house and through to the sitting room.

He sat her on the piano stool next to him and she laughed when she realised what he was doing.

'Well, you know what the outcome will be,' she said warningly.

He flashed her one of his cruise-missile smiles. 'That's exactly what I'm banking on.'

He played from memory and had hardly made it through to the end of the second movement of her favourite Beethoven sonata when she insisted that he take her upstairs. In the falling twilight, and as a warm breeze blew in at the open window, they made love again.

'I believe it,' she said afterwards. 'You've convinced me I'm not dreaming.'

They slept for a short while and when they woke they realised they were hungry. They went downstairs and inspected the fridge. 'How does a plate of cold chicken and a bottle of Chardonnay sound?' asked Elliot.

'Perfect.'

They put a tray together and went back up to his bedroom. He poured their wine and when he handed her a glass, his face grew solemn. 'What should we drink to?'

She knew, though, what he was really asking: was this a one-off or was it the start of a renewal of their relationship? 'I don't know,' she said, in a carefully measured tone. 'What do you think?'

'To the future would seem a safe bet,' he said, equally cautious.

'Do we need to define that?'

His eyes wavered slightly from her face, as though he wasn't sure how best to answer her question. Then setting down their glasses, he kissed her lightly, their lips scarcely touching. He slid a hand inside his shirt that she was wearing and traced the soft, warm curve of her breast. He could feel her heart thumping and pulled away from her so that he could gaze into the dark depths of her eyes. 'Ali, the future without you would be as empty and meaningless as the past two and a half years have been. I need to be with you. I need to have you in my life.'

Chapter Thirty-One

Elliot woke to the brightness of an early-morning sun streaming through his bedroom window. It took him less than a second to recall the events of yesterday and last night, and very carefully, so as not to disturb Ali, he rolled over on to his side and studied her peacefully sleeping face, taking in the smoothness of her cheek and the lovely line of her jaw and chin. His heart swelled with love and more than anything he wanted to linger in bed with her for the rest of that day, but a nine o'clock management meeting put paid to that temptation. He was conscious, as his eyes trailed the length of her body beneath the thin cotton sheet and he listened to the soft rise and fall of her breathing, that he had to treasure this moment in case, when she woke, she regretted what had taken place between them.

There was a very real danger of that, he knew. Through their vulnerability they had sought comfort from each other and maybe now, this morning, when they were feeling less raw and exposed, Ali might view things differently. She might even think that he had exploited her for his own gratification.

But he hadn't. Ali's response in the pool when he had kissed her had been all her own – though he was acutely aware that she had the perfect right to accuse him of classic caveman behaviour, using his strength to overpower her. Certainly there was a strong element of truth in that. In his defence, all he could say was that his desire for her had got the better of his normally restrained nature.

It had been in the way that she had answered him – *It means zippo, lover-boy* – that had made him throw restraint aside and give in to his true feelings. The challenging lightness in her voice had rung out in the echoey pool room with an air of suggestive flirtatiousness, just as it had when they'd first got to know each other. They had been working late one evening, just the two of them, and he had asked if he was keeping her from anything more worthwhile at home – a euphemistic query as to whether there was a boyfriend in tow. Her response had been a slight lifting of an eyebrow and the words, 'Now, what could be more worthwhile than an evening of number-crunching with my immediate boss?'

Other than what was written in her personnel records, all he'd known about Ali Edwards was that she lived with Daniel Delafield who, in those days, before his sexual orientation had become generally known, was attracting above-average interest from most of the women in the office. As a consequence Ali had been a focus of their envy. Unlike most of his colleagues, who were not averse to mixing pleasure with business, Elliot had always believed that it was better not to. He had witnessed all too often the sticky results of the office sexual honey-pot and had wanted none of it. An intensely private man, he had preferred to keep his relationships outside the firm. But despite this self-imposed restriction and Ali's tough reputation – she'd told a partner to bugger off and threatened to knee him in the groin for groping her – Elliot had been drawn to her.

When they'd finished what they were doing, he had plucked up courage to ask if she'd like to go for a drink with him. He had been quite prepared for a thinly disguised, 'Get lost, you're as bad as the rest of them,' but she'd readily agreed and they spent the next two hours in a nearby wine bar. Listening to her barbed but entertaining impressions of some of the senior partners, he had been captivated by her. He'd watched her closely, as if committing to memory the way she ran her hand through her short, wavy hair, the tilt of her head when she laughed and the flashing darkness of her intelligent eyes when she fastened them on his as she asked a question. There was a spirit of assured confidence about her that was immensely appealing, as well as a sparky sense of humour.

It wasn't long into the evening before he found himself wondering what she was like in bed and thinking how very much he'd like to find out. After he had walked her back to her car and was driving out of Manchester, heading for home, he'd known that he would be tireless in his pursuit of her. She was, he decided, the woman he would marry.

He was a steadfastly rational man so it came to him as an eye-opening shock to know that he was capable of such an unreasoned thought. This was not how he ran his life. He never made a judgement based on emotional whim. Clear-headed analytical deduction was what counted.

But red-blooded instinct seemed greater than any cerebral prudence he might have been inclined to exercise, and within a short time he was seeing Ali regularly outside work. The hardest part was keeping the strength of his love and desire for her firmly under control; he was terrified of her feeling trapped so he forced himself not to declare his heart too soon. Exactly a year after that first drink together, he took her on a surprise long weekend to New York and on the eighty-sixth floor of the Empire State Building he had steeled himself to ask her to marry him, having assiduously rehearsed himself throughout the seven-hour flight while she slept.

'I was wondering when you'd get around to proposing,' she'd said, as they stood on the crowded observation deck with Manhattan spread out before them.

'Does that imply you're not opposed to the idea?' he'd asked cautiously.

'You know what you'd be taking on, don't you?' she'd responded, without answering him. 'I'd be hell to live with.'

'It would be a worse hell without you.'

'So I'd be doing you a favour?'

'I'd be for ever in your debt.'

She'd smiled and, with a glint in her eye, had said, 'Did you ever consider the possibility that I might have wanted to propose to you?'

Her question had floored him. 'Er . . . no,' he'd faltered. He should have known that a proposal of marriage to Ali would never have provoked an outright yes or no.

'Did it never cross your mind that there's no one I'd rather spend my life with?' she'd asked. 'Did you never suspect that I think you're the most amazing man I know?'

'More amazing than Daniel?'

She'd laughed. 'Don't push it, Elliot. Daniel's in a class of his own.'

He'd laughed too and taken her in his arms. 'What's your answer?'

But before Ali had opened her mouth to reply, a small elderly American woman with a face as wizened as a Californian raisin had leaned over and said, 'Hey, hon, if she's dumb enough to say no, will you give me a trial run?'

But Ali hadn't said no, and they'd spent the afternoon choosing a ring.

Looking at Ali now, as she lay sleeping beside him, he wondered what she had done with the diamond ring they'd chosen that day. Had she sold it? Or had she thrown it away in a symbolic gesture of casting off a layer of her life of which she wanted no reminders? As for the gold wedding band that they had picked out for him, he had never thought of parting with it and since the divorce it had been stored in the antique wooden chest at the end of his bed where he kept his other bittersweet keepsakes – Isaac's New York Yankees baseball cap and a precious photograph album. Only in moments of real strength was he able to open the chest and look at the photographs of his son, or hold the cap in his hands and allow himself to remember Isaac wearing it. But maybe now it would be different, less painful.

Long into the early hours of the morning, he and Ali had talked about Isaac, as they never had before. They spoke of how much they missed him, what he had meant to them and what he still meant to them. And as intimate as their lovemaking had been, he sensed that in those heartfelt revealing words, as they admitted and shared the pain of losing their son, they had never been closer or more open with each other. Knowing that Ali no longer blamed him for not saving Isaac came as the most profound relief to him. It gave him cause to hope that one day he might fully accept that it wasn't his fault, that Isaac's death had been due to the wrecking ball of fate smashing their world apart rather than his negligence.

Even the memory of his reaction to that small boy at the party yesterday, and the innocent but wholly explosive line of chatter that had brought him to his knees, didn't disturb him as it might otherwise have done. He saw now that without it he would never have been pushed so low as to share with Ali the truth of that night two and a half years ago. Half of him still wished that he had kept her in ignorance of what had really happened to Isaac: he didn't want her menaced by the kind of nightmares he'd experienced all this time.

Glancing at his watch, he saw that it was nearly half past seven. He needed to get a move on. He lowered his head and gently brushed his lips against Ali's. She stirred and slowly opened her eyes.

He held his breath. This, then, was the moment of truth. In the cold light of day, would she regret that she was lying naked in his bed, or would she welcome the unexpected change of direction that their lives had taken?

Chapter Thirty-Two

With nearly an hour before Ali was due to arrive, Sarah went out to Trevor in his workshop to tell him that she needed to see Grace. He took off his dust mask and goggles and, above the noisy rumble and whine of the lathe, said, 'But what if Ali comes while you're out?'

'She shouldn't be here until ten but if she's early I'm sure you can talk to her for a short while.'

He looked at her doubtfully. 'You know Ali and I can never find any common ground.'

'That's because neither of you makes the effort.'

Trevor creased his sawdusty brow with a childishly obstinate frown. 'And what's so important that you have to see Grace?'

Without giving an answer she edged away from the workbench. 'I shan't be long. I'll be back before Ali gets here, don't worry.'

Minutes later she was hurrying the short distance to Grace's bungalow in the bright summer sunshine and knocking on her door. Ever since Friday afternoon and their conversation over lunch Sarah had wanted to apologise to Grace. Her churlish manner that day had been very much on her mind over the weekend and she didn't want to go away for the next two weeks leaving Grace thinking she had caused any real offence.

'Goodness, you're out and about early,' said Grace, when she opened the door.

'Is it inconvenient?'

'Of course it isn't. I was on the verge of having a cup of

coffee before starting on some jam-making. Would you like to join me?'

'I'd love to,' Sarah said, as she followed Grace through to the kitchen and saw the colander of strawberries waiting on the draining-board to be hulled and washed, 'but I really can't stop.' She explained about the unexpected invitation to go away with Ali.

'What fun. And what good timing.'

Sarah smiled. 'Why is it that when I talk to you I always have the feeling that you're one step ahead of my every move?'

Grace smiled too. 'But I'm right, aren't I? This little holiday with Ali will do you no end of good. How does Trevor feel about being abandoned?'

'Quietly put out, is the best description.'

'Playing the hurt boy?'

'A little.'

'He'll manage well enough. No doubt help will be on hand the minute you've departed.'

Sarah caught the playfulness in Grace's voice. 'Right again. Shirley and Audrey have already offered their services. They'll be falling over themselves in their eagerness to feed him and do his washing. Oh dear, do I sound very heartless?'

'Just shrewdly cynical.'

'I never used to be like this.'

'We're all forced to adapt to the changes around us. And it's not what we used to be that counts, it's where we see ourselves currently that matters.'

'But what if we don't like where we are?'

'Then we must pursue what exactly it is about the present that annoys and irritates us. Identify the root problem and deal with it.'

'And if we can't do that?'

Grace looked at her closely. 'Can't or won't, Sarah?'

Sarah went over to the draining-board and picked up a strawberry. She looked at its perfect ripe form and wondered if, as life itself, its flavour would disappoint. She put it back in the colander and, leaving Grace's question unanswered, said, 'I just wanted to come and apologise for Friday afternoon.'

'Why? What did you do?'

'I got cross with you.'

'I think you were more cross with yourself.'

'Probably, but I'm still sorry for my behaviour.'

'I would imagine that it was little more than a ripple on the surface of what you were really feeling, wasn't it?'

'If you were Ali I'd tell you to shut up.'

Ali knew that she was going to be late, but even so, she still took the time to double-check that she'd locked the door to the windmill – telling Owen that his precious home had been trashed due to her carelessness was something she was keen to avoid. Convinced that all was secure, she heaved her large bag into the boot of the car and set off down the lane. It was only twenty to ten, but already she felt as though she'd put in a full day's work. After Elliot had left her at Timbersbrook House, she'd had to get a taxi to Daniel's to collect her car then tear across half of Cheshire to the mill to change and sort out the last-minute holiday details she was supposed to have done last night.

When she had woken that morning to Elliot's kiss, she had been aroused instantly by the sight and touch of him. Ignoring the bits of her body that ached from their night of mattress antics – and Elliot's half-hearted protestations that they didn't have time – they had made love again. If he had been serious about losing his technique after a prolonged period of celibacy he needn't have worried. If anything, his bedroom skills were even more finely honed. They had showered, eaten a hurried breakfast, and when it was almost time for Elliot to leave for work he had said, 'Ali, we need to discuss what happens next. If there's the slightest chance that you'll go away to Sanderling and regret what we've done, I need to know. I don't think I could cope with the uncertainty.'

She'd kissed him and said, 'Stop worrying, I'm not going to regret it. When I come back we'll decide what we're going to do. But perhaps having a little distance between us at this stage is a good thing. It'll give us time to be absolutely sure what we feel about one another.'

He'd held her tightly against him. 'I've got to go to the States in a fortnight. Can't you shorten your holiday to just the one week?'

'No,' she'd said firmly, then pushed him away and added, 'Now go, or you'll be late and Gervase will score a smug point of office oneupmanship over you.'

'Will you ring me tonight?'

'Yes. I promise. Now *go*!'

She'd watched him drive away reluctantly, sensing that he was terrified that once his back was turned she'd revert to the person she'd been since Isaac's death. If she were honest, a tiny part of her was frightened of that happening too.

But she had to have time away from him to come to terms with the consequences of the past twenty-four hours, as extraordinary as they were, and what Elliot had told her. She doubted whether she would ever justify her son's death and put it down to being part of some greater and higher plan, but she was now able to accept that it was no one's fault he had died.

Least of all Elliot's.

Last night he had spoken at length of the torment of guilt that had plagued him at not being able to save Isaac. He'd also shared with her the pain of looking into her eyes and seeing his culpability reflected back at him.

It was this, more than anything, that she needed to come to terms with: the painful shame of having treated him so unfairly.

She pulled in behind Sarah and Trevor's old Sierra and

honked the horn loudly to announce her arrival. Within seconds Sarah was at the front door. 'I was beginning to think I'd dreamed your invitation. What happened? Did you oversleep?'

Much as Ali was bursting to share her incredible news with Sarah, she steeled herself to keep it for later when they were alone and when she could savour the expression on her friend's face. 'Long story,' she said guardedly, 'and one I'll save for the journey. Where's Trevor?'

'In the workshop. I'll give him a shout and let him know you're here.'

While Sarah was fetching him, Ali hurriedly put her friend's luggage into the boot of the car: she was determined to make a speedy getaway.

Trevor greeted Ali patronisingly, with what he thought was humour. 'How's the nefarious world of finance, then, Ali? Still able to sleep at night? Your conscience not keeping you awake?'

Did he have any idea how insulting he was? 'My, what a side-splitter you are this morning, Trevor,' she said, with a friendly smile – in her current mood of all's well in the world she was prepared to be magnanimous. 'No worries about my conscience, it's doing just fine. How about yours?'

'Mine?'

'Still shilly-shallying around in your workshop and wasting valuable resources?'

'I don't quite follow you.'

'Wood, Trevor. Rainforests. Scandinavian pineforests. Wildlife threatened in the name of ornamentation.'

He wagged a long, dirty finger at her. 'Now, you know perfectly well that I only use wood that has come from natural waste or from sustainable forests.'

'I think Ali is only teasing you, Trevor,' said Sarah, stepping between them. 'Now, you're sure you'll be okay? I've left plenty of food in the freezer and there's—'

'I'll manage,' he said testily. 'I'm not completely incapable.'

No, thought Ali, just completely incompetent.

At last they were off, and as the distance grew between them and Astley Hope, and the road ahead shimmered in the heat-haze from the hot sun, Sarah was looking forward to the next fourteen days. It was years since she'd had a holiday and she was determined to make the most of this one. Grace had been right when she had said the timing couldn't have been better.

Breaking into her thoughts, Ali said, 'Seeing as this is a bit of a wander down Memory Lane, I thought we could stop off in Oxford for lunch. What do you think?'

'Do we have to?'

'Such keenness, I'm overwhelmed.'

'I'm sorry.'

'You've never been back, have you?'

Sarah shook her head. It was true, she hadn't. Not once. Not even for Hannah's interview last December. Trevor had insisted on accompanying her and she had all too readily stayed at home, maintaining a low profile on the grounds of too many parents spoiling the candidate's broth.

'Is it because you regret not finishing your degree?'

'Hannah asked me that the day she left for France.'

'Well, do you?'

'Of course I do.'

'But you never talk about it.'

'What's to be gained? I can't change anything. I had my opportunity and I threw it away.'

Ali was surprised to hear Sarah speak so vehemently. 'But you could study now, couldn't you?' she said. 'In fact, with Hannah going away in the autumn it's the perfect opportunity. It would give you something to aim for, to focus on.'

'I couldn't afford to study full-time. Anyway, what would be the purpose? It would be a lot of effort just to prove to myself that I could do it.'

'To hell with that! It would improve your job prospects.'

'You don't see me making curtains till the day I drop?'

'If it would make you happy, yes. But I'm convinced that you want more than that.'

'It's funny how we always think we know what's best for another person.'

Ali laughed. 'Mrs Donovan, keep your snidey comments to yourself.'

'And, Mrs Anderson, stop trying to organise me.'

As usual Ali had her way and they stopped for lunch in Oxford. It was now that she planned to tell Sarah about her weekend. They came into the city on the Banbury Road, found a space in Broad Street – despite all expectations to the contrary – and headed in the direction of Turl Street. Cutting through the cool shade of Brasenose Lane, they stepped into Radcliffe Square where the sward of grass and honey-coloured stone buildings were picturesquely bathed in sunlight. A group of noisy foreign summer students were lying stretched out on the parched grass, and a party of Japanese tourists, listening to their fast-talking guide, were gazing intently up at the circular domed building of the Radcliffe Camera.

'It's just the same,' Sarah said, staring round at the scene. 'All these years on and it's just the same.'

'Is that good or bad?'

'I'm not sure.'

Taking her by the arm, Ali led Sarah towards their old college. She was surprised to feel the stiffness in her friend's body as they neared the main gate where an enormous camper van with a German numberplate was parked on the cobbles and an irate college porter was engaged in some pretty unfriendly badinage with the driver.

'Let's go and have lunch first,' Sarah said, holding back as she caught sight of the once familiar porter's lodge and the front quad with its perfectly kept lush green lawn.

'You really have a problem with this, don't you?' Ali said.

She nodded. 'Give me a glass of Dutch courage and I'll be okay.'

Ali looked at her sceptically. 'All right,' she conceded, 'if that's what you want. But we're not eating at Brown's like every other nostalgic idiot who makes the return journey here to relive their youth.'

They found an elegant but unpretentious French restaurant tucked away in a tiny side-street off the High – just the kind of place that as students they would never have been able to afford. They ordered a half-carafe of house red and two plates of melted goat's cheese on a herb salad from a fresh-faced young man in a heavily starched white apron. Only when the food and wine were on the table, accompanied by Annie Lennox doing her rendition of 'A Whiter Shade of Pale', did Ali tell Sarah about her and Elliot.

Sarah listened in silence, amazed and absorbed. She was visibly moved when Ali described Elliot's shock reaction to the small boy at Richard and Daniel's party. And, like Ali, she had to blink away the tears when her friend explained what Elliot had really gone through that night, when, alone and frightened, he had been faced with the certain knowledge that his son was dying and there was nothing he could do. How easily they had all accepted his story that Isaac had barely suffered, that he had slipped painlessly into uncon-sciousness before dying.

When Ali stopped talking and they had taken a few moments to compose themselves, Sarah said, 'How exactly do you feel about what's happened between you and Elliot?'

Ali looked at her over the top of her wine-glass. 'What? No "I told you so"?'

'I'm saving that for later.'

'I don't doubt it. But to answer your question, I feel a whole gamut of emotions: wretched that I abused Elliot in the way that I did, consumed with the most profound relief that we've stopped fighting, and,' she paused to smile, 'bloody exhausted after so much fantastic sex.'

Sarah smiled too. 'Anything else?'

Ali's expression became serious again. 'Yes. I feel extraordinarily at peace.'

'With Isaac?'

Ali nodded. 'Resolving matters with Elliot has somehow taken the edge off all that pain.'

'That's because you weren't only grieving for Isaac. When you lost him, you lost Elliot, your marriage, and the future the pair of you had planned for yourselves. It was a quadruple bereavement.'

'It needn't have been,' Ali said despondently. 'If I hadn't been such a bitch—'

'You've been many things, Ali, including pig-headed, stubborn, determined, arrogant, confused, but a bitch isn't one of them.'

'I disagree.'

'That's because you think it's *de rigueur* for you always to have the last word.'

'Nonsense.'

'There you go again.'

'Oh, eat your lunch and be quiet!'

They spent so long over their meal discussing what might or might not lie ahead for Ali and Elliot, that it was a mutually reached decision that they should forgo the delights of doing a *Brasenose Revisited* and carry on with the rest of their journey. 'We'll save it for the return trip if you want,' Sarah said, as they strapped themselves into their seats in the car.

'We'll see,' said Ali, reversing at speed out of the parking space. It was as clear as daylight to Ali that Sarah was enormously relieved not to be retracing their college days with too much exactitude, but it wasn't so clear why this issue had never been raised before. In the intervening years since Sarah had left Oxford, she had hardly ever referred to what she now saw as her lost opportunity. Was it possible that Hannah's hopeful following of her mother's footsteps had triggered this sense of regret in her?

Though it was hardly a new phenomenon when she thought about her friend, Ali felt an acrimonious surge of anger towards Trevor. Why hadn't the stupid idiot taken more care with Sarah all those years ago? If he hadn't got her pregnant, her life would have been infinitely different.

And so much better.

Joining the line of traffic at the lights alongside the Randolph, Ali vowed that at the top of her agenda this holiday was to make Sarah see sense. They would be together for the next fortnight and by the end of those two weeks if Ali hadn't convinced Sarah to take steps towards making a new future for herself then she'd – she'd bloody well sleep with the silly man so that she could give Sarah the necessary conscience-saving grounds for a legitimate divorce in the eyes of her precious God.

Recoiling from the loathsome thought of an all-out adulterous bonking session with Trevor, she turned away from Sarah so that her friend couldn't see her face. She stared at the Martyrs' Memorial on her right, then saw the irony in what she was looking at. Martyrdom and suffering for the cause were hardly her style but . . . but was it possible that just this once she could make an exception? And when you got right down to it, how bad would it really be? All she'd have to do was close her eyes, lie back with gritted teeth and think of England. It would be over and done with in a matter of minutes and it wasn't as though she'd have to repeat it. Suddenly she smiled and shook her head, realising how worryingly close she was to giving the idea serious considera-tion. I must be out of my mind, she thought. And cocky with it. How could she be so sure it would be that straightfor-ward? Could Trevor really be seduced so easily? She smiled again. Of course, he could. For crying out loud, here was a man who hadn't had a sexual encounter in the last decade, he'd be more than up for it. Question was: was she?

As perceptive as ever, Sarah said, 'Something funny, Ali?'

The lights turned to green and Ali slipped into first gear. 'You don't want to know,' she said.

Oh, you *so* don't want to know.

Chapter Thirty-Three

Early next morning, and as eager to get started on the day as she had been as a child whenever she was at Sanderling, Ali flung open her bedroom window. She knelt on the cushioned window-seat, rested her elbows on the sill, and breathed in the fresh sea air as she looked down on to the large, well-kept garden. It contained so many memories. And they were all good ones. Nothing bad had ever happened here at Sanderling. Or was that merely a childish perception she hadn't yet outgrown?

No. She was convinced it was true. Her grandmother's house, now her parents' home, was a place of true happiness, a haven from all life's travails. Her visits here as an adult – including when she'd brought Isaac – had been just as perfect and idyllic as when she'd been a young girl.

She smiled as she recalled bringing Elliot here for the first time to meet her parents. They'd made a long weekend of it and her mother and father had taken to him straight away, describing him as a step up from the usual wets she dragged behind her.

Without batting an eyelid they had allowed him to sleep with her and in this very room. She looked over her shoulder to the rumpled duvet, remembering how strange it had felt having Elliot in the bed in which she had slept as a child, and which occasionally she had shared with Sarah when there had been more guests at Sanderling than beds. She could also remember how much she had wanted to make love to Elliot that night and how amusingly hesitant he had been, muttering that he didn't want to push it with her parents. 'If you're worried about them hearing the squeaking of old mattress springs,' she'd teased, 'that's easily remedied.' She'd pulled the duvet and pillows on to the floor and proceeded to banish his reluctance.

'Just so long as you don't make your usual noise when the earth moves,' he'd said.

'Can't guarantee that,' she'd answered, with a gasp of pleasure as his lips and hands began working their magic on her.

'Then I'll have to keep you quiet myself.'

And he had. Just at the vital moment, when her body soared heavenward and exploded like a Disneyland firework display, he had covered her mouth with his and kept it there until she relaxed in his arms.

The following morning, when her mother had knocked on the door with a cup of tea, she had found them on the floor and had smiled at her daughter. 'Was there something wrong with the bed?' she had asked ingenuously over breakfast an hour later, with the kind of smile on her face that suggested she knew exactly what had been going on.

'We didn't want to disturb you,' Ali had said, with the kind of smile on *her* face that suggested she was quite prepared to give her mother all the juicy details if provoked. But at her side, deeply engrossed in his boiled egg, Elliot's normally composed face was steadily reddening. The following day he had confessed to Ali that he had expected that to be the last time he ever saw her parents.

'We're a very open family,' she'd told him in the car on the way home, as they headed north.

'So I see.'

For a man as buttoned-down as Elliot, her family's attitude must have come as something of a shock.

Shock was something they'd discussed last night on the phone. It was gone eleven when she called him on her mobile from her bed. He'd just got in from wining and dining a client, and had sounded pleased to hear her voice. She had asked him if, as she was, he was still reeling from the shock of what they'd done.

'Yes,' he'd admitted, 'and it's compounded by not being with you. You haven't changed . . . You're not having second thoughts, are you?'

The fear in his voice had touched her and she had been quick to reassure him. 'No,' she said, 'not at all. I told Sarah what happened. You don't mind, do you?'

'Of course not. What did she say?'

'Lots of things. She said that we've experienced a quadruple bereavement: Isaac, losing one another, the loss of our marriage, and the loss of all our dreams.'

'She's right.'

'It's a lot to work through, isn't it?'

'It is.'

She heard him sigh. 'Elliot, are you okay?'

'I miss you,' he said simply.

'I've only been gone a day.'

'In the circumstances that's a day too long.'

She laughed. 'I think it's just as well I'm here and not there with you. My body needs to recover from the onslaught of so much unexpected sex. I must be getting old.'

'I know what you mean. But it was good, wasn't it?'

'Better than good.'

There was a pause.

'Ali?'

'Yes.'

'Ali, I just . . . Will you ring me tomorrow night?'

She hesitated. 'Elliot, was that what you really wanted to say?'

Another pause.

'No, but it'll keep.'

'No, that's not fair, you can't do that to me. I'll lie awake all night wondering what it was. Tell me.'

'I – I just wanted to tell you that I love you.'

It was her turn to pause.

'Ali?'

'Say it again – please.'

'I love you.'

'Again.'

'I love – Ali, are you crying?'

'Well, of course I am.'

'I'm sorry. I knew I shouldn't have said anything.'

'Don't be so stupid. It's me. I'd forgotten how wonderful those three words could sound.'

Still sitting in front of the open window and staring into the infinite blue of the sky, Ali drew her knee up under her chin and longed to hear the sound of Elliot's voice. She looked at her watch and thought of ringing him before he set off for the office.

No, she told herself firmly.

If she did that she'd start ringing him up on the hour every hour, and that would never do. A persistent nuisance caller was not what Elliot needed. Tonight would be soon enough. She'd ring him then, just as she'd promised she would.

But there was one phone call she did need to make, and soon. It was to Daniel. He and Richard deserved an explanation for the abrupt manner in which she and Elliot had left their party, and for her leaving her car on their drive overnight. Though presumably the pair of them had not been slow in putting two and two together.

When the taxi had dropped her off at their house yesterday morning both Richard and Daniel had already left for work, but an envelope was tucked under one of the windscreen wipers. The note inside had said, 'Are you still talking to me? If so, fill me in with the details when you've got a moment. Love, Daniel.'

Poor old Daniel, he was probably busting a gut to know what had transpired as a result of his skulduggery. If he hadn't meant so well, and if things hadn't turned out as they had, she might have decided to keep him in the dark for the duration of her holiday. But she loved Daniel too much to torment him so she would ring him later in the day, when he was at the office, and put him out of his misery.

She turned her attention to the garden once more. As the hot weather had been going on so long and there was a hosepipe ban in place, Ali suspected that her mother must have been watering the garden sneakily in the dead of night. The impressive borders that her grandmother had so carefully designed and nurtured were a delight, full of colour, and the lawn was lush and green – there were no dusty dry patches as there were in her garden back in Cheshire. She wouldn't be at all surprised if later that day her mother phoned to give her instructions on the subversive methods Ali would be expected to take on in her parents' absence.

She heard the sound of the letterbox being thrust open with what appeared to be above-average paperboy strength, wondered if it was the postman trying to deliver a parcel and went to investigate. Her parents had either forgotten to cancel the papers or had decided to let her and Sarah have the benefit of them. Lying in a heap on the mat was her father's *FT* – the only paper fit for a gentleman, these days, he claimed; the *Daily Mail* for her mother – otherwise known at Sanderling as the *Daily Sniff and Tell* – and a glossy but slightly damaged edition of *Country Life*. Ali carried the bundle through to the kitchen where she was met with the unappetising pong of last night's fish-and-chip supper. She and Sarah had been too lazy to put the plates into the dishwasher and had left them to extend their greasy, vinegary charm to their surroundings. Ali tidied up hastily and closed the dishwasher door on the offending plates and cutlery. She opened a couple of windows and the back door, then filled the kettle. She made herself a pot of tea and, with the papers tucked under her arm, took the tray to the bit of garden that caught the early-morning sun where her parents usually started the day in fine weather. Years ago, and in pre-Alan Titchmarsh and Charlie Dimmock days, before the nation had become obsessed with mirror-backed water features and purple garden fences, Ali's grandmother had had a gazebo built; she'd had it kitted out with comfortably padded seats and a small stow-away table. The cushions had been replaced many times, but it still made the perfect bolthole, especially now that it was covered in a fragrant tumble of honeysuckle.

Ali settled herself in for the next hour or so while she waited for Sarah to surface, poured her tea and set to with the *FT*. She began with a piece about the recently proposed legislation for unapproved share options exercised by non-UK residents, but didn't get beyond the second paragraph before she turned to the *Sniff and Tell*. Though even the shenanigans of some dolly-bird game-show hostess and her aged Viagra-enhanced rock-star boyfriend failed to hold her attention.

Was it any wonder when she had her own shenanigans to dwell on? She lowered the paper and stared up at the house with its pebble-dashed walls, which were almost entirely covered with Virginia creeper.

I love you, Elliot.

She had said it. In response to his declaration on the phone last night she had actually said, '*I love you, Elliot.*'

How was it possible? How was it remotely conceivable that she could have uttered such words?

Because you've always loved him, she imagined Sarah whispering in her ear.

Because you've never stopped loving him, echoed Daniel.

And it was true. That's why the past two and half years had been so awful, so perversely destructive. She had torn herself apart by denying that most essential truth, that she loved Elliot.

She lowered the newspaper to her lap, pushed back her sunglasses and closed her eyes, letting the warmth of the sun wash over her. Then, very slowly, she pictured Elliot that evening at the mill when he had fired that cruise-missile smile at her. She'd known only too well in that moment the effect he could still have on her, and yet she had subsequently talked herself out of it. Which goes to show, she told herself ruefully, that there was no one to touch her when it came to the fatal art of self-delusion.

Just then, a shadow crossed her face and for a wild, fantastical, fleeting second she thought it was Elliot – that he'd put work on hold, had leaped into his car at daybreak and driven all the way down to see her.

But it wasn't Elliot. It was Sarah.

'How long have you been up?' she asked, moving the discarded *FT* and sitting in the seat next to Ali.

'Ages and ages. I've been for an early-morning swim, jogged down to the newsagent's for the papers, and prepared a light brunch.'

'I wish that were true. I'm starving and can't think why.'

'It's the sea air. Don't you remember it does peculiar things to your stomach?'

After a leisurely breakfast in the garden of croissants and locally made blackcurrant jam – all courtesy of Ali's mother's thoughtfulness in stocking up for them – they decided it was time to head for the beach. They didn't have far to go, just a ten-minute walk along the tree-lined road that was home to Sanderling, out into the sunshine, across the main road that joined the east and west of the island, then through the sand dunes and prickly gorse and blackberry bushes that bordered the golf course.

It was all just as Sarah remembered it: the sheltered warmth provided by the dense windbreak of overgrown bushes; the clusters of yellow flowers nestling amongst the purple thistles; the feathery grasses dried by the sun. Even the tyre tracks made by countless bikes on the much-used path looked the same.

Leaving the shelter of the dunes behind them, they came to the open stretch of pebbly beach, already littered with scores of families surrounded by the trappings of a day at the seaside: there were territorial windbreaks pushed into the stones, brightly coloured towels laid out like mosaic tiles, cold boxes, plastic buckets and spades and inflatable beach balls. Down by the shoreline, tiny bare-bottomed toddlers were cautiously dipping their toes into the rushing waves, while older, more adventurous children were splashing about in the deeper water, their shrieks of delight muffled by the breeze that blew in off the sea.

Sarah took in the scene. Apart from the extensive construction of beach defences further along the seashore to keep the threat of erosion to a minimum, there was little evidence of anything different from nearly two decades ago. She felt pleased that the essence of Hayling, like Oxford, had successfully withstood the pressure to change for change's sake.

Last night she had lain awake in bed thinking of how Oxford and its quintessential finery had remained resolutely the same. Conversely, this immutable status quo had reminded her just how much she had conceded to the fickle winds of change.

Getting pregnant had thrown her completely off course; it had meant that overnight she'd had to restructure her life.

Before becoming pregnant she had had a comprehensive plan for her future: she was to graduate from Brasenose with a law degree, follow it up with a stint at law college, then be articled to a provincial firm with a reputation for fair play – the aggressive big-city establishments she would leave to the thrusting types hungry for fame and distinction. She had seen herself working for several years before marrying and having children, then taking some time out while the children were young and, when it seemed right, she would have picked up where she had left off. Her marriage, of course, would have been happy. Her husband would have been loving and supportive, and between them they would have produced two or even three well-behaved, adorable children. They would have been a contented, untroubled, close-knit family. In short she had wanted a duplicate of Ali's family.

Rather naïvely she had hoped that, despite getting the order of events out of sequence – namely the conception of the first, and what proved to be the only, well-behaved, adorable child – the rest of her plan might still follow suit.

The night she had told Trevor she was pregnant was not a night she was ever likely to forget. It had taken her days to summon the courage to put it to him. She knew that he was extremely fond of her and would, as he had told her one evening over a bowl of spaghetti Bolognese in a run-down café on the Iffley Road, do anything for her. 'You know how much I admire and respect you,' he had said. 'There's nothing I wouldn't do for you.' But she couldn't be sure that 'anything' would encompass the commitment of marriage because she was pregnant. Fondness and respect were perfectly valid forms of affection, but were they sufficient to form the basis of a lifelong commitment? Surely it had to be love. But not once had love ever crossed the threshold of their strange rather lopsided relationship.

At their age, lots of men would have suggested that she abort the child on the grounds that they were too young for the responsibility, that it would ruin everything, that it would hamper them. But Trevor's views were not those of the average twenty-one-year-old, and in the time she had got to know him through the prayer group they both attended, he had voiced his opinions on the murdering of innocent foetuses in the strongest terms. Her fear was that he might suggest the child be given up for adoption. And though it was something she didn't want to consider, she could see how tempting it might be for him: it would conveniently leave them to get on with the rest of their lives with clear consciences.

It was Trevor's conscience and his sense of honour and goodness that she was relying on when he came to her room in college that evening for what he thought would be a cosy couple of hours together. As she waited for him to arrive, she had frantically brushed her teeth several times in the hope of disguising the fact that she'd just knocked back two glasses of vodka from a bottle she had sneaked out of Ali's wardrobe.

Ali had been fussing over her appearance in readiness for yet another date with some hapless young man and wouldn't have noticed if there'd been an earthquake, so preoccupied was she with the colour of her eye-shadow.

When Trevor arrived she let him in, made them some coffee, and told him that she was pregnant. The rest she left up to him. His initial reaction had been one of pure astonishment.

'But – but how? I don't understand.'

He was right to wonder how. They had, after all, been to bed together only once.

He started to blame himself. 'This is all my fault,' he said, pacing the small room and running his hand through his collar-length hair, 'I knew it was wrong at the time, but I let my better judgement be ruled by my heart.'

They were strange words coming from a twenty-one-year-old man in the late seventies, but not so strange when one knew his background: he was as he was because through all his formative years he'd been constrained by a strict religious upbringing that would have stunted the most wilful of young men.

Compassion for him made her reach out to him and say, 'It's not your fault, Trevor. You must never say that.'

He looked at her, his eyes glazed with bewilderment. She manoeuvred him into a chair and forced his untouched mug of coffee into his hand. 'I'm not expecting anything from you,' she'd said, a sentence that had taken all her courage to utter. What she really wanted to say was, 'You have to agree to marry me. This baby has to have a father. He or she is entitled to a proper mother and father. This child deserves more than I can give it alone. A loving family is what counts. Right now we might not love each other, but it will come, I know it will.'

He set the mug – still untouched – on the desk beside him and stared out of the window at the view of the front quad where a group of first-year physicists were larking around with a bottle of cheap champagne. He returned his gaze to her. 'Sarah,' he said, 'it strikes me that there's only one option open to us. If you agree, I think we should marry.'

It was not the hearts-and-roses proposal she had dreamed of as a romantically inclined teenager, but it would suffice.

They then discussed what plans they needed to make – Trevor was hoping to take up a teaching post in Sheffield that autumn and he would now have to review the accommodation he had found for himself. When he had finally left her to cycle back to his digs at Headington, she was violently sick.

She wanted to blame it on the stolen vodka, or even late-in-the-day morning sickness, but she knew that the real cause of her nausea was feeling consumed by both relief and regret.

The next morning she told Ali that she and Trevor were to be married in the summer. She would not be returning to college in the Michaelmas term as she would be with Trevor in Sheffield where he was due to start work as a teacher.

She had never before seen Ali lost for words and the sight of her friend's horrified expression appalled her. She had burst into tears.

'But you can't,' Ali said, also now in tears, her arms wrapped around her. 'I won't let you marry him. I won't allow it.'

'But I have to,' she had whispered in shame, 'I'm pregnant.'

Ali had pulled away from her. 'Pregnant?' Her expression of horror now dramatically intensified. 'I don't believe it.'

'Nor did I at first.'

'But, Sarah, this needn't be the disaster you're turning it into.'

'What do you mean?'

'I mean, you don't have to marry Trevor.'

'And how would I manage?'

'I'd help you – so would your parents.'

'You know they wouldn't.'

'Once they'd got over the shock they would. Nobody their age can resist the urge to play grandparent.'

Ali proved to be right, her parents indeed got over their shock – about two years after the wedding took place – and in their undemonstrative way proved more than adequate grandparents to Hannah. Ironically, it seemed they were better suited to this role than the one of parent to Sarah.

But they never took to Trevor. Their disappointment in their daughter's chosen husband was as real as Ali's, and remained so until they died.

After they had risked the cold water for a swim and had sunbathed for a while, they gathered their things together and went in search of something to eat. Beyond the row of brightly painted beach huts was the old kiosk where, as teenagers, they had spent a couple of summers serving beefburgers, hot dogs, questionable meat pies, cans of drink, ice creams and chocolate bars to hungry day-trippers. Ali's grandmother had known the woman who ran it and had inveigled her into taking the girls on while they were staying at Sanderling. The money was good and the perks weren't bad either – they were chatted up by a regular stream of good-looking and not so good-looking boys and, even better, they were allowed to eat the broken ice-lollies that couldn't be sold.

As they approached the kiosk Sarah found that nothing much had changed here either. The pies looked just as questionable and a group of spotty, sunburnt lads were doing a bad job of chatting up the two young girls behind the counter. Sarah smiled at Ali and said, 'Can you believe that used to be us?'

'Away with you! We were much more efficient.'

'Rubbish, you were hopeless with the money, you were always giving out the wrong change.'

'So why do you think I became an accountant?'

They ordered their hot dogs and cans of Fanta and strolled slowly back to the beach.

'You've gone all quiet on me,' Ali said, when they were

stretched out on their towels on the pebbles again. 'Are you overdosing on nostalgia?'

'Yes. It's making me feel decidedly old and decrepit.'

'Give over,' laughed Ali, 'there's not a mark on you.'

'We're thirty-eight, Ali, and heading fast for forty.'

'Well, as somebody once said, it ain't over till the fat lady sings. Anyway, what you should be doing instead of dwelling on the past is looking to the future.'

But Sarah knew there wasn't any point in doing that: her future would always be eclipsed by the past.

Chapter Thirty-Four

That evening, Ali poured herself a glass of her father's excellent Islay malt and, leaving Sarah in the kitchen working at her sewing-machine, went upstairs for a bath and to ring Elliot. She lay back in the Crabtree and Evelyn scented water and tapped his number into her mobile. While she waited for him to pick up the phone at Timbersbrook, she sipped her drink, savouring its smooth peaty flavour.

'Hang on a minute,' he said, when he realised it was her.

'Is it a bad moment?' she asked, when he spoke again.

'No, I just wanted to close the door.'

'Why? Have you got people there?'

'Only Sam.'

'Aha, so when did the old hustler get back?'

'This morning.'

'And is he richer or poorer?'

'This is my father we're talking about, Ali. Of course he's up on the deal. God knows how many hundreds of pounds he's robbed his friends of.'

Ali laughed. 'Have you told him about us?' She heard him hesitate. 'Elliot?'

'No, I haven't.'

'Why not?'

'I thought it might be tempting fate. Besides, he'd want to know what happens next and I don't have the answer for that.'

'Sarah asked me the same question.'

'What did you tell her?'

'That we need to take things slowly.'

'Not too slowly, I hope.'

'Slow enough to be sure of what it is we both want.'

There was a long pause. Then Elliot said, 'I know exactly what I want, Ali. It's what I've always wanted.'

It was Ali's turn to hesitate and not by choice: her throat was constricted with a mixture of happiness and nervousness. 'Are you saying what I think you're saying?' she asked.

'I'm saying that I want to spend the rest of my life with you.'

Although he had merely voiced what was in her own mind, it still came as a shock to hear him stating the case so boldly. She hadn't imagined either of them taking that step so soon. Not when they had so much to talk through.

When she didn't respond, he said, 'Ali, I'm sorry. I suppose that's going too fast, isn't it? Have I blown it?'

'It could be a terrible risk, Elliot,' she murmured.

'But one worth taking.' His voice was as low as hers.

'You sound so sure,' she said.

'And you sound so unsure.'

'That's because I'm frightened.'

'Of what?'

'Of hurting you again.'

'I'm not prepared to let that happen a second time.'

'You mean you had any control over it the first time?'

'In a way, yes. If I had blamed myself less, hated myself less, I might have worked harder at saving our marriage.'

'Oh, Elliot, it wasn't just you. It was me as well. We both made an appalling mess of it all.'

'In our defence I guess we knew no better.'

'And we do now?'

'Yes, I think we do.'

'I'm still scared, though . . . of myself mostly. I'm not convinced that you, or anyone else for that matter, would ever have much control over my actions, least of all me. You know what Daniel's always said – that I'm a loose cannon on deck.'

'That may well be true, but the issue of control should never be a part of a committed relationship, not one that's based on love.'

She laughed suddenly. 'You know, that's exactly what my parents hoped you'd be able to do. That first weekend I brought you down here, my mother was so impressed with you that she said, 'Good choice at last, Ali. He's so much better than the boys you've pushed around to date. This one will actually stand up to you.'

'As fond as I've always been of your mother, she must have been mad to think that I could have any control over you.'

Glad that the tone of their conversation had lightened, Ali went on to tell him how she had been reminiscing about their first night together at Sanderling.

'I remember it well,' he said, 'especially the next morning.'

'Hah! So a boiled egg sticks in your mind more than the brilliant sex we had.'

'Please, don't mention sex. It's not fair when you're so far away and I can't touch you.'

'Did I mention that I'm talking to you while I'm lying in the bath?' she teased.

He groaned. 'I could be there in four hours.'

'I'd be in bed by then.'

'Even better.'

'I'd be asleep.'

'Better still. I'd wake you with a kiss.'

'Is that all?'

'I didn't say where I'd kiss you.'

She laughed again. 'This is turning into one of those sex lines.' Then, in a more subdued voice, 'Elliot, what are you doing at the weekend?'

'I haven't thought that far ahead yet. Why?'

'Why don't you come down here? Mum and Dad will be back by then and, given the circumstances, they'd love to see you again.'

'What shall I tell Sam?'

'The truth.'

'Which is?'

'That you're spending the weekend with your ex-wife with a view to planning a new future together.'

A short while later Elliot put down the phone and shook his head in disbelief. One of the many things about Ali that he'd always loved was her unpredictability. Just as he'd resigned himself to having wrecked everything by revealing his hand too soon and listened with a sinking heart to her less-than-encouraging response, she had floored him.

He got to his feet, left his study and sought out his father. He found him in the kitchen flicking through a magazine on classic cars and singing along to one of his favourite musicals that was being belted out on the CD player next to the wine rack. It was *Mack and Mabel* and the song was 'I promise You a Happy Ending'.

With a wry smile, Elliot crossed the kitchen and lowered the volume on the hi-fi. 'Dad,' he said, 'I've got something to tell you.'

Sam looked up at him. 'Oh, aye, lad, what's that, then?'

Chapter Thirty-Five

Friday was soon upon them and, exerting more energy than they'd used so far during their holiday – the most energetic they'd been in the previous twenty-four hours was to paint their toenails – Ali and Sarah spent the best part of the day tidying the house, making beds, and doing the shopping that Ali's mother had asked them to do on the phone last night, as well as going strawberry picking, which had always been a highlight of a summer stay at Sanderling. As children Ali and Sarah had invariably made an afternoon of it: they would cycle up West Lane and spend hours crouched on their hands and knees gathering the sun-ripened fruit and listening to the gossiping women around them who thought the girls were too young to understand what they were talking about. No matter how many baskets they filled, Grandma Hayling would question them on the ones that got away. How many did you eat this time?' she'd ask, when they returned with juice-stained hands and sweetly reddened lips.

Now, stretched out on sun-loungers, they were enjoying what the weather forecasters had predicted as the tail end of the hot dry spell. From tomorrow there would be a drop in temperature and a brisk north-westerly wind to spoil everybody's fun.

Ali put down that morning's copy of the *Daily Sniff and Tell* and glanced across at Sarah. She hadn't said a word for the past half-hour and, though her eyes were closed, Ali knew she wasn't asleep because one of her hands was tapping listlessly at the armrest of her wooden chair. If she didn't know better, Sarah, who was inner calm personified, was restless. 'You okay?' Ali asked.

Sarah's fingers came to an abrupt stop. She opened her eyes. 'I'm fine. What made you ask?' Her voice rang with defensiveness.

'You seem on edge.'

After a few moments Sarah said, 'It's called guilt.'

'What on earth have you done to give you an attack of that?'

Sarah leaned forward and swung her legs round so that her bare feet were on the grass between her and Ali. 'It doesn't feel right me being here. I should be at home with Trevor.'

'Aha,' said Ali, 'I was wondering when you'd start beating yourself up. It's a miracle it's taken you this long.'

'That's not kind.'

'No, it isn't. But it's true. Don't spoil it for yourself, Sarah, there's nothing wrong in a wife taking a holiday with a friend. Even the rosiest of marriages can benefit from a bit of time-out space.'

But Sarah looked far from convinced. 'I should never have allowed you to talk me into this,' she muttered.

Ali smiled. 'I don't recall having to twist your arm too far to make you come.'

Sarah frowned and stood up. 'Do you want another drink?'

'No thanks.' Concerned, Ali watched her cross the lawn and go inside the house. She wondered what had provoked Sarah's change of mood. Was she worried that she would be playing gooseberry when Elliot joined them that evening? Or was she uneasy about Alastair and his bride-to-be arriving tomorrow? But that was nonsense! Sarah had no reason to feel like an outsider – she had always fitted in just as if she were a member of the family. Perhaps it wasn't anything as complicated as that. Maybe Sarah *was* feeling guilty about abandoning Trevor for so long. And just as Ali was wishing that Trevor could do the decent thing and drop dead, Sarah reappeared in the garden. 'Ali,' she called, 'your parents have arrived.'

Like most parents, Maggie and Lawrence Edwards were unable to view their offspring as anything but children, Sarah included. Short of patting her head and saying, 'My word, haven't you grown!' they were lavishing upon her every form of parental delight and affection. 'Heavens,' cried Maggie, after she'd hugged her and insisted on an update on life in Astley Hope, especially Hannah, 'how long is it since you stayed here with us?'

'I know when it was,' said Lawrence, moving his wife aside so that he could have his share of Sarah. 'It was the year you got married.'

'So it was,' Maggie agreed. 'It was Easter.'

'No, it couldn't have been then,' asserted Lawrence, 'it must have been earlier. I remember it snowed. It was February.'

'Goodness,' said Sarah, feeling a little overwhelmed but loving it anyway, 'what an incredible memory you both have.'

'It's their age,' smirked Ali. 'We'll be the same one day. We'll recall everything fifty years back in the tiniest detail but won't be able to remember where we put our slippers and glasses.'

Lawrence laughed, and before Ali had a chance to slip away from him he'd taken her in his arms. 'A little respect,' he said, lifting her a clear twelve inches off the ground, 'that's all I've ever asked of you.'

'Never!' she shouted, as she struggled to get free.

He squeezed harder and tickled her ribs as if she were a small child. 'Can't hear you,' he said. 'I must be going deaf.'

'Well, Sarah,' said Maggie, with a happy smile, 'I think we'll leave them to it, shall we? Let's go inside, I'm gasping for a cup of tea.'

'And that's another sign of old age,' Ali shouted, over her

father's shoulder as Maggie and Sarah disappeared, 'dodderers spend all their time having nice cups of tea.'

'Whereas you, young lady,' Lawrence said, finally lowering his daughter to the ground, 'have probably been hitting my stash of single malt.'

'Only the cheap stuff.'

'Cheap stuff?' he roared. 'I don't have anything of the kind! For your insubordination you can help me in with the luggage. There's loads of it – you know how fond your mother is of packing for every eventuality.'

By the time Ali had helped her father unload the car and taken the cases upstairs, Sarah and Maggie had put together a tea-tray along with a chocolate cake that Sarah had made especially for the occasion.

'Ali never makes me cakes,' Maggie said, with mock hurt as they sat in the gazebo and she poured their tea.

Ali rolled her eyes and said, 'Oh, here we go, suddenly I'm the daughter from hell.'

'No "suddenly" about it,' said Lawrence, munching his cake appreciatively and fighting off a wasp, 'trouble from the moment you were born.'

'Love you too, Dad.'

He blew her a kiss. 'I'd love you even more if you made delicious cakes like Sarah does.'

Sarah drank her tea quietly and observed the closeness between Ali and her parents, listening wistfully to the warm exchange of affection. It wasn't difficult to see where Ali's sense of humour came from.

The first time Sarah had met her friend's parents was when Ali had taken her home for tea one day after school; the invitation had been made a week after their initial encounter. 'I should warn you that they're completely mad,' Ali had said matter-of-factly, as they waited for her mother to pick them up at the school's main entrance. 'Nutty as two bars of Fruit and Nut. Dad makes the most awful jokes and Mum's silly enough to encourage him.' From this brief description of Mr and Mrs Edwards, Sarah had expected there to be a coolness between her new friend and her parents. According to the girls at school, it was a foregone conclusion that you had to act as if you were superior to your aged and past-it parents. But Sarah quickly realised that Ali's description of her mother and father had been a smokescreen: she clearly adored them as much as they did her, and when she'd used the word 'nutty', she had meant it in the nicest way, because as far as Sarah could see, Ali was as barmy as they were. Mrs Edwards turned out to be exactly the mother Sarah would have chosen, warm-hearted and generous with a subtle skill for putting her at her ease. Ali had never spoken about the kind of house she lived in – unlike so many of the others at their rather pretentious prep school who tried to outdo one another – so Sarah had concluded that, as she herself did, Ali came from a humble background. She couldn't have been more wrong. Ali lived in a vast house that could have consumed Sarah's for breakfast several times over and still had room for a couple of bungalows for elevenses. Sarah had never seen anything so enormous. Or so beautiful. It was light and airy, and full of space. It was the type of house she'd only ever seen on television, or in magazines. The rooms were all large and decorated with pretty patterned wallpaper – she was later to realise that Mrs Edwards was a bit of a chameleon when it came to home décor, and had been going through her Early Laura Ashley Phase before moving on to her Sanderson Days, as Ali described her mother's faddish taste.

Ali's father had come home unexpectedly early that afternoon so they had all eaten together. At first Sarah was a little frightened of him – he seemed so loud and so big, not at all the small, stiff-lipped man her own father was. 'Lawrence, darling, keep your voice down. Can't you see that you're frightening our guest?' Ali's mother had said, when she must have noticed Sarah shrinking away from this larger-than-life man who had burst into the kitchen with all the force of a tornado. 'Don't worry, Sarah,' she had added, 'he's nothing but a six-foot-five giant who wants everybody to play with him.'

Sitting in the prettily decorated kitchen where everything was co-ordinated with red and white polka dots – even the tea-towels matched the curtains and wallpaper – Sarah had tried hard not to appear gauche and unused to such style and lively conversation, which ricocheted around the table at head-spinning speed. But as she'd eaten the lovely meal Ali's mother had served them she had fought back the rising sense of disappointment within her. She had thought that she had made a friend in Ali, but even so young, Sarah knew how the world worked: the differences between them were so great that the first time Ali had tea at her house would be the last. Ali would drop her the minute she realised they came from opposite worlds.

But Ali hadn't dropped her and here they were, almost thirty years on, still the closest of friends. It would have been nice to say that they were older and wiser, but Sarah didn't believe that.

Older, yes, but certainly not wiser.

Between them they had an impressive hoard of academic achievements, but what real good had any of it done them? Had it stopped either of them making some awful mistakes? Had a first-class honours degree taught Ali how to handle bereavement? Had it taught her how to hold her marriage together? And had a failed attempt at getting a degree helped Sarah to be a better wife? Had it helped her come anywhere near accepting the consequences of the selfish, needless risk she'd taken all those years ago?

The answer was a resounding no.

Elliot arrived a little after eight o'clock.

Ali had been watching anxiously from the sitting-room window for his car. When at last she saw the now familiar XK8 sweeping through the brick pillars at the end of the driveway, she jumped off the window-seat and raced out of the room. She would have liked to bundle him into the house unseen, drag him up the stairs and relive a moment of history on her bedroom floor, but her mother appeared in the hall drying her hands on a tea-towel. With her head tilted playfully, she said, 'Was that a car I heard?'

'You know perfectly well it was, Mum.'

Lawrence and Sarah joined them in the hall. They were grinning at her.

'You'd better let him in then,' said Lawrence, with a wink.

'I will when you've all backed off. I don't want you scaring him away.'

Nobody moved.

'Oh, I give up! You're hopeless the lot of you.'

She opened the door and went to Elliot. He was reaching for a small bag in his car but let go of it the second he saw her. He took her in his arms and kissed her. It was no brush of lips on cheek, no polite nice-to-see-you kiss. This was a real passionate show-stopper, and tilting her back against the side of his car, he said, 'Any chance of having my way with you right now?'

She laughed out loud. 'Yes,' she said, 'if you don't mind an audience.'

He straightened up and glanced at the house. Three smiling faces greeted him.

That night in bed, after much concentrated thought, and while applying her special anti-ageing cream to the skin just below her eyes, Maggie asked her husband if he thought there was a chance of Ali and Elliot remarrying.

Lawrence, who had been staring up at the ceiling rose and contemplating much the same line of thought, said, 'If they have any sense they will.'

Maggie turned and looked at him. 'They're like us, aren't they? So right for each another.'

He smiled, took her hand and raised it to his lips. 'You say the mushiest things.'

'But it's true. I just wish we'd tried harder to stop them divorcing in the first place.'

He shook his head firmly. 'Come on, now, there was nothing we could have done. As parents we had no choice but to stand back and let them sort things out.'

'But they've wasted so much precious time.'

'Well, from what we saw of Elliot's arrival this evening, I'm damned sure they'll make up for it one way or another. And before you even suggest it, I don't think they need any help from us in determining the future.'

'You wouldn't be accusing me of interfering, would you?'

He smiled and kissed her. 'Goodnight, Mistress Cupid.'

They switched off their bedside lamps and snuggled comfortably into one another's arms. But Maggie couldn't sleep. She hadn't been able to sleep last night either. She'd been too elated. When Ali had told her on the phone yesterday evening that there would be an extra visitor for the weekend, not in her wildest dreams had she thought it would be Elliot. 'But why didn't you say you were back together again?' she'd demanded, when Ali had explained who the mystery guest would be.

'Because it's all been so sudden, and after everything we've been through I need to be very sure what it is I feel for him.'

'And what do you *think* you feel for him?'

Ali had laughed and said, 'It begins with L and ends with E.'

'Oh, darling, I'm so pleased for you both. Let me tell your father – he'll want to talk to you, don't go away.'

Now, as the moon shone through the gap in the curtains at the open window and streaked across the faded Oriental rug that had belonged to her parents, Maggie smiled to herself as she thought of the happiness in Lawrence's face when she'd told him the news. He'd always been such a big softie when it came to Ali. Many a time in the aftermath of Isaac's death he had wanted to take his daughter in his arms and comfort her. He'd tried it once, on the day of the funeral, but she'd pushed him away tearfully.

'Lawrence?'

'Mm – ?'

'I can't sleep.'

'It's easy. Nothing to it. You just close your eyes.'

'Lawrence?'

'Yes.'

'Do you think Sarah's happy?'

He turned over and faced her in the darkness. 'What's brought this on, then?'

'It was seeing Ali so bright and cheerful this evening that made me realise how sad Sarah looks in comparison.'

'I know what you mean. She gives the impression of not being as happy as she could be.'

'I've always thought that.'

'So have I. And, seeing as we're in perfect accord, may I go to sleep now?' He kissed her cheek and resumed his earlier position.

After a couple of minutes, Maggie said, 'I wish I could wave a magic wand.'

'Believe me,' Lawrence grunted from the depths of his goosedown pillow, 'so do I. You'd be the first to catch the benefit of it.'

'I'm being serious.'

'So am I.'

'But don't you feel the same? Don't you want to make life better for everybody?'

'I'd settle for making my own better right now.'

'In an ideal world I'd give Sarah the courage to leave that idiot Trevor.'

'In an ideal world I'd never have allowed her to marry him.'

'You've always had a special place in your heart for Sarah, haven't you?'

Lawrence gave up on the idea of sleep and turned on to his back. 'Yes,' he said simply. 'Those parents of hers didn't deserve her. They gave her nothing. No love. No real guidance. And certainly no support.'

'In their defence, they did give her an education they could ill afford.'

'Very big of them, I'm sure. Don't forget she had a sizeable scholarship. They didn't have to dig their cold, unloving hands too deeply into their pockets.'

'I remember when Ali told us about her being pregnant and that she was leaving Oxford to marry Trevor, you were all for driving up there and talking some sense into her. And for taking Trevor by the scruff of his neck.'

He smiled. 'All that stopped me was that I knew it would do no good. In her own quiet way Sarah is, and always has been, as headstrong and tenacious as Ali. How else could she have stuck being married to that drip?'

'Perhaps there's more to him than meets the eye.'

'Oh, yes. Can you name just one finer point you think Trevor might be in possession of?'

'Well, in his own way he's very sincere. Dependable too.'

Lawrence groaned. 'And so very dull.'

Maggie smiled. 'I didn't tell you this, but a few months ago Ali told me that it's all down to Sarah's religious convictions that she stays with him.'

'Well, thank God I'm an atheist, then. Now, are you going to let me go to sleep or shall I go downstairs and make us a drink?'

'I'd rather you made love to me.'

He laughed loudly. 'Good grief, woman, you're as bad as your daughter, sex, sex and more sex.'

'Once would be sufficient.'

'In that case, lie back and prepare yourself to be amazed.'

Chapter Thirty-Six

The next morning, when Ali and Elliot finally showed their faces downstairs, long after breakfast had been cleared away, Maggie, with her customary tact and intuition, suggested that they should go for a walk.

'What about the preparations for the return of the ghastly old prodigal?' said Ali.

'All under control,' Lawrence replied from the kitchen sink, where he and Sarah were on new-potato-scrubbing duty. 'We're going out to the fields to kill the fatted calf when we've finished here.'

'Are you sure we can't help? I'd hate to miss out on all the fun.'

Maggie looked up from the onions she was chopping, her eyes brimming with tears. 'Take her away, Elliot,' she sniffed, 'and don't come back until you've exhausted her.'

The weather, as predicted, had indeed taken a turn for the worse. Yesterday's seamless blue sky was now patched with ragged white clouds being hustled by a strong, bullying wind.

They headed towards the beach, cutting through the sand dunes and golf course, then on towards the wooden beach huts before braving the blustery open expanse of the beach. It was high tide and the only people about were a group of hardy wind-surfers in wetsuits, preparing to take on the crashing waves, and a lone woman walking a frisky black Labrador. She raised her hand in greeting at Ali and Elliot and the dog came to inspect their legs, bouncing around them as if expecting them to throw a ball for him. When his owner called him to heel he bounded away.

'So what's it to be?' asked Ali. 'Which way do you want to walk? To the funfair or the Ferry Boat?'

Elliot pushed his hands into the pockets of his jeans and looked left, then right. 'Mm . . . a ride on the dodgems or a drink. It's a difficult choice. No, second thoughts, it's easy. You were always a devil in a dodgem. We'll go to the pub, at least that way I shan't end the day with my neck in a brace.'

'Chicken!'

Without warning, he snatched her hands and dragged her down to the shoreline. 'What did you call me?'

'Chicken!' She laughed.

He picked her up and held her threateningly near the water. 'I don't suppose you'd care to review your opinion of me, would you?'

'No!' she screamed, clutching his arms. 'You're still a great big chicken!'

He made as if to drop her and, to the amusement of the wind-surfers, she screamed again. 'Okay, okay,' she cried, 'I give in. For a mere man you're incredibly smart and very brave.'

He carried her to safety, then when she was back on her feet, he slid his hands around her waist and kissed her.

'Resorting to brute strength is a sure sign of weakness,' she said, with a smile, when he stopped.

'That's an interesting paradox. And one we'll discuss over a drink. Come on.'

They walked hand in hand along the pebbly beach, to the sound of gulls screeching overhead and their shoes crunching noisily on the shelving stones.

'I can't remember when I last felt this happy,' Ali said, then added, 'It takes some getting used to, doesn't it?'

He put his arm around her. 'You're right, it does.'

'I just wish Isaac was here to share it . . . It doesn't feel right to be so happy when he . . .' Her unfinished sentence drifted away on a gust of wind. She came to a standstill and turned to look at the sea, swelling and rolling beneath the

346

grey sky, ominously dark and menacing. She watched a pair of seagulls circle an area of heaving water, their broad, curved wings working against the wind. 'He should be here with us,' she said, in a sad, faraway voice. Then, turning to Elliot, 'If I could just feel him. Just to know, for sure, that there was more to his short life than the eighteen months he was with us. It might make sense to me then.'

A moment passed. 'You never did believe in heaven, did you?' said Elliot.

Surprised at his question, she said, 'Not Trevor's kind of celestial happy-ever-after nonsense.'

'What about Sarah's version?'

'I'm not sure that hers is much different from Trevor's. At the end of the day it all comes down to a lot of allegorical tomfoolery.'

'You don't think religion is a way of making sense of the incomprehensible, of making order of chaos, of making the unattainable – ?'

'No. It merely confuses the issue. It conquers and divides.'

'It doesn't strengthen and restore, then?'

She resumed walking. 'It misguides and offers nothing but a bitter drop of false hope.'

He squeezed her shoulder and changed the subject. 'Your parents are looking well.'

'Aren't they just? And all the better for seeing you again.'

'When did you tell them about us?'

'On the phone the night before they came home. I tossed it casually into the conversation, "Oh, by the way, do you mind if we have an extra guest over the weekend?"'

'Were they very surprised?'

'Completely and utterly. Mum was fine to begin with, then she went all gooey and burst into tears and couldn't speak and Dad had to take the helm – except whenever he tried to say anything Mum kept chipping in, wanting to know all the details.'

'I told Sam.'

'And?'

'He wants to know when he can rush out and buy a hat.'

Ali laughed. 'Not just yet, but when the time comes our Sam can have the biggest and most ostentatious hat going – feathers, flowers, veils, the whole shebang. Carmen Miranda or bust.'

Elliot slowed his pace, then stopped. He held Ali firmly in his arms and stared into her face.

'What's wrong?' she asked.

His expression was solemn. 'We are doing the right thing, aren't we, trying again?'

'Cold feet, Elliot?'

He frowned. 'I'm worried that I've rushed you into this.'

'You of all people should know me better than that. Nobody's ever made me do anything against my will.'

'But I need to know that I haven't forced you into something you might later regret.'

'Are you suggesting I don't know my own mind?'

He didn't answer her. Instead his eyes gazed into the depths of hers as if searching for the truth.

'You are, aren't you?' she said.

He stroked her windblown hair out of her face. 'It's just that it's happened so quickly. One minute we can hardly cope with talking to each other and the next we're—'

'—lying exhausted in bed and planning to be together. Bizarre, isn't it?'

'That's one way of describing it.'

'Well, you know what they say, love and hate are two sides of the same coin. We hated one another, now we love each other.'

He flinched. 'I never hated you.'

'And deep down I didn't hate you, but you know what I mean.'

'Supposing the coin flips over again?'

'Then we let it go.'

'As simple as that?'

'Yes.' She stooped to pick up a large flat stone, contemplated it, then threw it into the sea. 'Then we'd just have to resign ourselves to another lifetime of pure hell.'

He, too, chose a stone and skimmed it across the water. 'So we make the most of what we can, when we can. Is that what you're saying?'

'I guess so.'

'It sounds a bit hit-and-miss.'

'Relationships are. Life is. One minute it's there, the next it's not . . . as we both know only too well.'

They stood in silence for a bit. Then Elliot said, 'Ali, what made you abandon the idea of taking things slowly?'

'I suddenly realised there was no point. Playing at courtship after what we've been through seemed the most colossal and futile waste of time.'

'So you're sure, then? You really want us to get back together?'

'Elliot, what is this? Do you need it in writing?'

'You know how thorough I am.'

'Yes,' she smiled, 'and I'm beginning to find it a pain.'

He reached for her hands, drew her near, and lost himself in her soft, dark, loving eyes. 'I'm sorry,' he said. 'Sam told me not to go and ruin things by being too serious.'

'You should listen to Sam more often. Now, come on, let's get going or we'll never get that drink.'

When they reached the Ferry Boat Inn, the clouds had parted sufficiently to let the sun shine through. They paid for their drinks, took them outside and sat on a wooden bench to watch the activity in the harbour. A couple of young flash types on jet-skis were showing off, sending up plumes of spray in their wake, while a group of shouting men and women over on the concrete ramp were launching a powerful speedboat from the back of a Land Cruiser. Away in the distance was the small ferry that crossed the busy stretch of water between Hayling and Portsmouth – a mode of transport Ali and Sarah had used frequently as teenagers whenever they fancied more action than the island could offer.

'Where shall we live?' asked Elliot, breaking into Ali's thoughts.

She sipped her cider. This was something she had thought of in bed last night while lying next to him and luxuriating in the feel of his body wrapped around her own. Given that she was only renting the windmill from Owen and his secondment to Brussels couldn't go on for ever, the most obvious answer was for her to move in with Elliot. But where would that leave Sam? In fact, wherever they chose to live, where would that leave Sam?

As if reading her mind, Elliot said, 'Dad and I were hoping that you would move in with us at Timbersbrook.'

'But what about—?'

'Sam?'

'Yes. Won't he feel like the proverbial gooseberry?'

'When I bought Timbersbrook the plan was that we would convert one of the outbuildings into a house for him. We were both keen to preserve a degree of privacy between us.'

'So why didn't you?'

'I'm not sure, really. Sam suddenly lost interest in the project.'

'Until now?'

He nodded. 'Yes.'

Ali knew that Elliot's proposition made perfect sense, but she also knew that Sam would do anything for his son when his happiness was at stake. 'I don't know,' she said. 'I'd feel that I'd pushed him out.'

Elliot reached across the table and laid his hand on top of hers. 'He said you'd say that. He also said that you were to talk to him about it so that he could put you right.'

She laughed. 'You mean so that he could sweet-talk me round to his way of thinking.'

'Something like that.' Taking a long swig on his beer, Elliot thought that if anyone could persuade Ali to do something it was Sam. It was, after all, the ideal solution all round.

When Elliot had told his father about him and Ali, Sam had initially, and predictably, made noises about finding himself somewhere else to live, but Elliot had refused to listen to him. 'Timbersbrook won't be the same without you,' he'd said, 'and apart from anything else, it's your home as much as mine.'

What he hadn't said was that there was the future to consider. As improbable as it seemed, given that Sam had the apparent constitution of an ox, there might come a day when he would need a watchful eye kept on him. With everything his father had done for him, this was exactly what Elliot intended on doing.

Chapter Thirty-Seven

On their return to Sanderling, Ali and Elliot saw an extra car on the driveway.

'Alastair and Phoebe, one supposes,' remarked Ali, as they went round to the back of the house and let themselves in. There was a pile of expensive leather luggage in the hall and voices coming from the sitting room. Maggie and Lawrence must have put Alastair in the picture about Elliot for when they entered the room Ali's brother greeted him as if the past two and a half years had never happened. He then advanced on Ali and, towering over her, gave her a crushing hug. 'And how's my little sis? Still not grown, I see.'

She pushed him away affectionately. 'Get off, you horrid beast, and introduce me to the poor girl who must be crazy to have agreed to marry you. Five minutes with me and I'll soon have her reviewing the situation.'

'Only because she'll worry that there's madness in the family.'

Phoebe was a picture of enviable streamlined looks and youth, and was, Ali decided, as near as damn it, probably a whole decade younger than her and Sarah. With the aid of a pair of cripplingly high strappy black sandals she was almost as tall as Alastair, but where he was fair like Ali and their mother, Phoebe was dark and sultry. Her skin had a smooth, Mediterranean quality, and her hair, scraped back from her face and tied into a chic knot at the nape of her neck, gave her an air of refined beauty. She was stunning, and as she stepped forward to be introduced to her sister-in-law-to-be, Ali wondered how on earth her boring old brother had attracted somebody so gorgeous. It must be all his money, she thought, as she shook hands and noted the chunk of dazzling diamond speared by the long, elegant third finger. She was suddenly conscious of her own appearance and wished that her hair wasn't quite so messed up from their walk on the beach. She wished, too, that she wasn't dressed in her seen-better-days T-shirt and battered trainers, or that she didn't reek quite so obviously of the draught cider that she'd spilled down her jeans at the pub. She caught Sarah's eye across the room and when the introductions were over, she joined her friend on the window-seat. 'Quite a babe, isn't she?' she whispered, sure that nobody could hear them as Alastair was now well into his voluble stride, telling Maggie and Lawrence how he and Phoebe had met at a charity ball in Singapore.

'Looks *and* brains,' Sarah whispered back. 'She's an investment banker, like Alastair.'

'Heaven knows how my ugly pain-in-the-butt brother hit the jackpot with her. She's so sophisticated.'

'Come off it, Ali, he's far from ugly. He's really quite handsome.'

'Get away. He's totally gruesome. He's got all the charm of Freddy Krueger.'

Sarah smiled. 'That's because you see him through the eyes of a younger sister.'

'And how do you view him?'

'Slightly more objectively.'

Ali shook her head in disbelief. 'Diplomatic to the end, that's my Sarah.'

Elliot joined them and, in a lowered voice, said, 'All you need are a couple of fans and you'd be dead ringers for those two women from *Dangerous Liaisons*. I can't begin to think what you two are gossiping about.'

Ali moved along the seat and made room for him.

'She is rather lovely, though, isn't she?' Sarah said wistfully.

'Careful how you answer that, Elliot,' warned Ali. 'I can

turn very nasty when I'm made to feel jealous. You know how chronically insecure I am.'

Elliot stared across the room to where Phoebe was sitting on the sofa next to Alastair, her long legs elegantly crossed in a pair of tight black leather trousers. She was, as Sarah had just said, a very attractive woman. But for him she was too cool, too poised. There was an unreal quality about her that reminded him of the scores of trophy wives he'd seen at office parties over the years. 'I prefer blondes any day,' he said, taking Ali's hand in his, 'especially the small, ruffled variety.'

'God, but you're smooth,' Ali said, with a happy laugh.

Maggie insisted that everybody dressed for dinner that evening. 'Go on, you two girls,' she said to Ali and Sarah. 'Up those stairs and dollify yourselves.' Ali's protestations that she and Sarah hadn't brought anything remotely glitzy with them, were met with a firm, 'We've a lot to celebrate tonight, your brother's engagement and you and Elliot getting back together, so do as you're told and make an effort. I know you probably both pride yourselves in being slimmer than me, but have a rummage through my things and see what you can find.'

Ali took Sarah upstairs to investigate the contents of her mother's fleet of wardrobes, and while Sarah sat on the bed, she threw open the cupboard doors. 'Imelda Marcos or what?' she said, as she stood back and took in the rails of clothes and neatly stored shoeboxes.

'Imelda Marcos, but with a great deal more taste.'

Ali was riffling through the colour-ordered clothes. 'What do you fancy?' she asked. 'Something in emerald or fuchsia, or both?'

'Something a little quieter, please.'

Ali moved along the rails and pulled out a simple shift dress in a warm shade of caramel. It was made of silk and shimmered luxuriously in the light. 'You'd look great in this,' she said.

'Do you think so?' asked Sarah doubtfully, slipping off the bed and taking the dress from Ali. 'It looks terribly expensive.'

Ali tutted. '*Ergo*, unless it costs less than a tenner it won't suit you?'

Sarah ignored her friend's salvo of sarcasm, held the dress against her and went to inspect her reflection in the cheval glass in the bay window. But the sight of Alastair and Phoebe sitting in the gazebo in the garden below deflected her gaze. They were staring up at the house as though Alastair was recounting some part of his childhood that had been spent here. They looked completely at ease with one another. From nowhere Sarah felt a stab of jealousy. All around her people were caught up in the rapture of a happy, loving relationship.

There was Maggie and Lawrence, still as devoted to each other as they'd ever been; there was Ali and Elliot, who had beaten the terrible odds stacked against them and realised that they'd never stopped loving one another; and now there was Alastair, that one time committed bachelor, who had finally found a woman with whom he was prepared to share his life.

And what of her? Oh, dear God, what of her? What real happiness did she have? Or was ever likely to have?

Maggie was delighted with the way the evening was going. Staring round at her family in the flickering candlelight, she felt a rush of matriarchal pride. At the other end of the table, beyond the swathes of damask, cut-glass and best silver, was Lawrence, his face slightly flushed from an excess of good food and wine. He was chatting amiably to Phoebe, who was sitting on his right wearing a glamorous, low-slung number that revealed more than just the string of pearls around her neck.

On Lawrence's left, where he insisted she sat whenever she was at home, was Ali. She was wearing a strapless dress of black velvet, which, had she worn it a year ago when she'd been so gaunt and pale, would have looked dreadful on her. Tonight, though, there was nothing wan or haggard about Ali: she was bright-eyed, and glowing with a radiance Maggie hadn't seen in her for a long while. With an elbow on the table she was resting her chin on her hand, leaning in towards Elliot and listening to him intently, watching his face as closely as if she needed to lip-read him. Maggie almost felt sorry for the pair that they had to join in with a family get-together – they'd probably prefer to be alone upstairs.

From the first time she had seen Ali and Elliot together she had known that they were right for each other: there was such an obvious compatibility between them. Before Elliot had made his appearance in her daughter's life, Maggie had been concerned that Ali would make a disastrous match with a man who would be threatened by her forthright, head-strong nature and would either feel compelled to change her or slink off to find a more compliant companion. From the cross-section of young men with whom Ali had dallied, the latter situation had invariably taken place – though frequently it was she who told them to sling their hook. But Elliot had stayed the course. She could remember when, out of the blue, Ali had phoned to say that she'd met somebody 'special' at work. 'He's something else, Mum,' she'd said. 'He never smiles and he hardly speaks, he just stands there and does this amazing thing.'

'And what amazing *thing* would that be?'

'He gives out this spellbinding aura of sexiness. Bucket-loads of it. I think I'm in love.'

Their subsequent conversations had run along similar lines and had left Maggie in no doubt that her daughter was indeed in love. She had cherished the fact that she had the sort of relationship with her daughter that enabled them to talk in a way that was usually the reserve of close friends.

And, thinking of close friends, there was Sarah on Elliot's left, talking to Alastair across the table. The silk dress she'd picked out looked particularly well on her and was one

Maggie hadn't worn in ages; she wondered whether she dared offer it to Sarah to take home with her. She noticed the pretty gold chain around Sarah's neck and remembered Ali telling her last year that she had bought a necklace for Sarah for Christmas but was worried she might refuse it seeing it as too extravagant. Poor Sarah, thought Maggie, continually having to fend off a best friend's well-meant generosity, not to mention the good intentions of that best friend's family.

She listened to what Sarah and Alastair were discussing and was astonished to hear her son showing an interest in something other than himself – much as she loved him, Maggie had no qualms in admitting that her eldest offspring had a tendency, at times, to behave as an exasperating self-congratulatory big-head. He was asking after Hannah, and Sarah was telling him about her being in France with a group of friends before taking up her place at Oxford.

'Which college has she applied to?'

'Brasenose.'

'Aha. A touch of the old *alma mater*. What do you think her chances are?'

'She needs three straight As.'

'And is that a tall order?'

'Yes and no.'

'You don't sound very sure she'll make it.'

'I don't doubt her academic ability, it's just that one can never be certain how things will turn out.'

Maggie knew that to have been a comment on Sarah's own life. She admired Sarah immensely. So many women in her position would have made a victim of themselves. But not Sarah. Well, she had no need to, did she? In a sense, and not intentionally, the Edwards family had done that for her. When she'd been a child they had taken it upon themselves to improve her lot and had tried to do much the same thing for her as an adult when they'd privately denounced her marriage as little more than a state of prolonged purgatory. Some might say they'd been arrogant to make such a sweeping

357

assumption, but Maggie liked to think it was because they cared for Sarah, as if she were one of their own.

Leaving Sarah and Alastair to their conversation, Maggie turned her attention once more to Phoebe. When Alastair had called to tell them he was engaged, nothing could have surprised Maggie more. She had resigned herself to having a son who lacked the inclination to pursue a meaningful relationship to its logical conclusion. His problem, she suspected, was that he was that infuriatingly restless type of man who couldn't keep still for more than two minutes. It would have to be an exceptional woman to hold his attention long enough to avoid being shown the door. In his late teens, he'd been the same and had annoyed Ali no end: she'd hoped that the presence of a permanent girlfriend would mean he'd spend less time hanging around her and Sarah. On more than one occasion, Ali had been furious when he had overplayed his big-brother role. 'No, you can't come and play tennis with us,' she had shouted at him, when he had tried to follow them on his bike down to the park and the tennis courts. 'We're going to play singles, not triples.' Sarah had been more patient and tolerant, and had suggested he could join them another day. There was no doubt in Maggie's mind that Ali had resented Alastair pitching in on what she clearly saw as her territory, but she had also wondered whether he had been keen on Sarah. Maggie had once hinted as much to Ali, who had fallen about laughing. 'The only person Alastair's keen on is himself,' she'd said. 'That, and getting on, is all that matters to him.' Certainly ever since leaving college 'getting on' had been important to Alastair and had been the focus of all his energy. But looking at the beautiful girl at the far end of the table who was soon to become a member of their family, Maggie could only conclude that her son must have changed – miraculously he had found the time and reason to fall in love. Maybe in the not too distant future there was even a chance of him becoming a father. Now, that would be a real turn-up for the books.

But it would also be a sad reminder of little Isaac.

How delighted she and Lawrence had been when Elliot had phoned to say that Ali had given birth to a baby boy. 'He's perfect in every way,' Elliot had said ecstatically, 'just as his mother is.' Maggie had never forgotten the rare rush of emotion in his voice as he'd gone on to describe the fairness of their grandson's hair, the smoothness of his skin, the blueness of his eyes and the impossible smallness of his hands and feet. 'His fingers,' he'd burbled on, 'they're so tiny, you wouldn't believe it. So tiny.' It had been particularly touching to hear their laconic son-in-law being so effusive.

How different had been the phone call eighteen months later when he had called to tell them that Isaac was dead. She didn't think she would ever lose the memory of his voice cracking up as he'd tried to break the news. Unable to finish what he was saying, Sam, who was at the hospital with him, had taken over and explained what had happened. She and Lawrence had both wept and lain awake in bed until they could stand it no longer. They had dressed, packed a couple of bags, got into the car, and driven up to Cheshire, never once suspecting the extent of the nightmare that lay ahead for Ali and Elliot.

She turned her attention back to them at the dinner table and saw that they were still deeply and exclusively engrossed in one another. It struck her how two people who loved with the intensity that they did could inspire in each other either a blissful happiness, or a crushing sadness.

Oh, let them know only happiness from now on, thought Maggie, as she raised her glass and silently wished her family well.

Chapter Thirty-Eight

After lunch the following day, Elliot set off for Cheshire.

'I wish you weren't going,' Ali said, when everyone else had wished him a safe journey and discreetly left them alone to say their goodbyes. 'Couldn't you cancel, postpone or delegate whatever it is you have to do?'

He pulled her closer to him. 'If you were in my shoes, would you consider doing any of that with Gervase on the scene?'

'Mm . . . maybe not. Will you ring me when you get back?'

'Of course.'

'Give my love to Sam and tell him he's on for a lunch-date when I'm home. Warn him there's a lot we need to discuss.'

'Am I included in this little *tête-à-tête*?'

'No. I want Sam all to myself.'

The traffic was surprisingly light, given that it was a Sunday in the height of summer, and not even the sprawl of cone-lined roadworks on the M6 and endless cavalcades of caravans did much to slow Elliot's progress. He reached Timbersbrook shortly after six o'clock and found a note from his father in the kitchen informing him that he'd gone to the Morris Minor Specialist garage in Flint to fetch Tilly after her paint job and should be home around eight. He poured himself a glass of orange juice, wandered over to the table and looked at the large pieces of paper that Sam must have been studying in his absence: they were the plans he'd drawn up for the Lurve Nest. For some inexplicable reason he hoped that Sam wasn't jumping the gun. Though he had no cause to doubt Ali's love for him, or what he felt for her, there was deep within him an anxiety that something might go wrong between them.

He wanted to put it down to his naturally cautious nature, but he knew that his concern stemmed from that most basic of instincts: fear. He was frightened of being so vulnerable again. Loving Ali as he did put him in a position of excruciating defencelessness.

He had loved Isaac and lost him.

He had loved Ali and truly believed that he had lost her.

The thought of losing her again was too much. What if she had a fatal accident? What if she developed cancer as his mother had when he was at Oxford? How would he cope with watching the vibrant and vital woman he dearly loved slowly die before him? He had held his own son in his arms as he died. Did the same awful fate await him with Ali?

Appalled at the mawkish trajectory of his thoughts, he carefully folded Sam's plans for the future and went through to his study to ring Ali, needing the sound of her voice to dispel the disturbing image of her being taken away from him.

At nine thirty-five the following morning, Elliot was waiting for that week's partners' meeting to get off the ground. Everyone was there around the large oval table in his office – everyone except for Gervase who, annoyingly, was ten minutes late. It was Gervase to whom Elliot needed to speak. The question was, should Elliot talk to him in front of the others, or wait until the meeting was over? A public flogging was an appealing prospect, given the dislike Elliot had of the man, but a private word one-to-one was undoubtedly the more professional approach.

Lying in a file in his desk drawer was a letter of complaint from Paul Davidson, the managing director of Hayes and Clarke, one of their key clients. He had written to Elliot that he was far from happy with the service he had received on an important acquisition project, and that if matters weren't resolved to his satisfaction he would have no choice but to move his firm's business elsewhere.

In Elliot's opinion, to let down a client, especially a well-established, lucrative client, was not only sloppy and unprofessional, it was unforgivable.

And who had been in charge of that particular account? None other than Gervase Merchant-Taylor.

Elliot was furious that the reputation of the firm had been compromised and he was determined that Gervase would be found accountable and make amends. Right on cue, the door opened and in he strolled. The man's smug face and lack of apology for keeping everybody waiting made Elliot want to confront him on the spot, but he allowed Gervase a few seconds to settle into his chair and arrange his papers. Then, as was Elliot's habit, he opened the file in front of him, removed the lid from his fountain pen and suggested that they get on with the big crunchy issues of work in progress and the accounts still to be billed – he was conscious that Howard's department had a more than average amount of audit work that had time running up on it and it wasn't unreasonable to expect an explanation, or better still an assurance that matters would improve.

Two hours later and they were done. He rose to his feet and was about to ask Gervase if he'd spare him a moment, when Gervase announced that he and his wife were having an impromptu do at the weekend. 'Nothing special,' he said, in his annoyingly pompous voice, 'but you're all invited. Eight for eight thirty.' General murmurs of acceptance were made, some marginally more enthusiastic than others.

Poor devils, thought Elliot, moving away from the table and going over to his desk at the far end of the room. None of them had the guts not to be present at one of Gervase's ghastly gin-and-tonic parties for fear of not being there to defend themselves.

'How about you, Elliot?' Gervase said. 'You'll come, won't

you? You know what they say, all work and no play makes Elliot Anderson a thoroughly tedious boy.'

In view of their impending conversation, Elliot responded with a noncommittal, 'Thanks, but I'll have to check my diary.' Then he said, 'Have you got a minute? There's something I need to discuss with you.'

'It'll have to be quick and to the point, old chap. I'm expecting—'

'It'll be quick and to the point, I promise you.'

When they were alone, Gervase sat in front of Elliot's desk and said, 'I suppose it's Howard you want to discuss, isn't it? Frankly I'm surprised it's taken this long for the shambles of his department to come to your notice. What do you propose to do about the situation?'

Elliot leaned back in his chair and steepled his fingers together. He considered staying quiet for a bit longer, thereby giving Gervase the opportunity to carry on digging himself a bigger and deeper hole. It would, after all, serve the obnoxious bastard right. But instead he reached for the confidential file in his drawer, opened it, and pushed Paul Davidson's letter across the desk.

'What's this, then?' asked Gervase.

'You tell me,' he remarked casually.

Shrewd enough to be on his guard now, Gervase raised the letter and began reading it. Elliot watched his face closely, noting the change in colour as well as the thought process that was going on behind the piggy eyes that were darting from side to side as they scanned the piece of paper. Elliot's money was on Gervase blustering about some kind of misunderstanding that had occurred and that it was little more than a storm in a tea-cup that Paul Davidson was overreacting to. But when Gervase passed the letter back to him and said, 'I was hoping against all odds that this wouldn't happen,' he was momentarily wrong-footed.

'I think you'd better explain what's been going on,' he said. 'Just what's been the problem?'

Gervase held up his hands in a gesture of resigned weariness. 'Rachel Vincent is the problem. Or, rather, she was.'

Once again Elliot leaned back in his chair and contemplated the man before him, narrowing his eyes imperceptibly. So that was the way he was going to play it – deny all responsibility and shove it on the shoulders of a senior manager who had, much to Elliot's surprise, left the firm unexpectedly a couple of weeks ago. He had viewed Rachel as professional and highly competent. Now Gervase was implying otherwise. 'Rachel always struck me as being one of our most meticulous managers,' Elliot said slowly.

'I thought so too.'

Far from convinced that this was Gervase's true opinion, Elliot said, 'Perhaps you ought to share some of your reservations with me.' He hoped that by giving the man enough rope he would eventually hang himself.

Gervase picked at a minuscule bit of fluff on his pinstripe trouser leg and said, 'Of course, if she were here, she'd deny everything, but the sad truth is she made the classic mistake of not knowing what the left hand was doing from the right. She presented the client with a bill that was well over the agreed fee.'

'If she made such an obvious mistake, why would she deny it?'

'You know how it is with women.'

Instinctively sensing trouble, Elliot said, 'No, Gervase, I don't. How is it with women?'

Gervase laughed one of his infuriating self-important laughs. 'No head for business is the polite way of putting it.'

Elliot thought how Ali would react if she were here. Very probably she would have pushed Gervase's genitals through the shredder by now. 'I'd like to see the billing file,' he said. His words had the satisfying effect of instantly slamming the door on Gervase's pompous men's-locker-room laughter.

'Good Lord, there's no need for that, surely?'

'Sorry?'

'What I mean is, just leave it to me. I'll speak to Paul Davidson and see if we can put matters right by agreeing to write off the excess fee.'

'If anyone is going to speak to Paul it will be me. And until I've seen the billing file I won't do that.' Suddenly he snapped forward in his seat, rested his elbows on his desk, and fixed Gervase with a cold, piercing stare. 'Now, as Rachel was reporting directly to you, I assume you knew exactly what was going on and can tell me the precise figures involved.'

Gervase shifted uncomfortably in his seat. He scratched the back of his neck then fiddled with the knot of his tie. 'I'll get somebody to dig out the file,' he muttered testily.

'Good. I'd like to see it first thing tomorrow morning.'

'Tomorrow morning?'

'Got a problem with that?'

'I'm out for the rest of the day and I've a lot on.'

'So have I. I'm in the States next week and I want this awkward and embarrassing mess cleared up by then.'

When he was alone, Elliot sat back in his chair, considered what Gervase had told him, and knew it to be a monumental work of fiction. The man was lying through his tonsils never mind his back teeth. He wondered whether he ought to make a pre-emptive strike and go in search of the file himself. He wouldn't put it past Gervase to come back to him and say, in his poncy voice, that it was the strangest thing but he couldn't find the file. Elliot was in no doubt that Gervase had caused the problem and that it was his fault, not Rachel's, that the correct fee hadn't been agreed. Even if Rachel had got it wrong, what Gervase had failed to acknowledge was that as a senior partner the buck stopped with him as regards the actions of one of his managers.

But what rattled Elliot most was that no matter how incompetent the Gervases of this world were, with their moneyed backgrounds and inbred patronising attitudes, they always surfaced from the pit of shit smelling sickly sweet.

Well, not this time. Not if Elliot had anything to do with it. He was determined to expose Gervase for the posturing fraud he was.

To achieve that he needed to do two things: first he had to get his hands on that billing file before anyone else did, and second, he had to speak to Rachel Vincent and find out the real reason behind her sudden departure. At no stage had she given him cause to think she wasn't happy in her work. As far as he was aware, she had had a healthy interest in pursuing what, by all accounts, was a promising career with the firm.

Elliot had a strong suspicion that Gervase had been using his secretary as an extra pair of eyes and ears, so didn't given a moment's thought to enlisting Dawn's help in obtaining Rachel's home address or the information he needed on Hayes and Clarke. He told her he would be unavailable for the next hour and left his office. He took the lift down to the second floor and hoped that he wouldn't bump into Gervase with the same task in mind. He found Rachel's old office, but instead of starting his enquiries there with her replacement, he tapped on the shoulder-high partition next door.

Two graduate trainees looked up at him. They immediately stopped what they were doing and scrambled to their feet as if they were a pair of fifth-formers caught smoking in the loos by the headmaster. This was definitely an aspect of his job that Elliot hated: no matter how hard he'd tried to cast himself as an approachable my-door's-open-any-time-of-the-day boss, his position in the firm made the junior members wary of him. These two girls were no exception. They stared at him nervously, clearly fearing the worst.

He stepped into their small office and, glad that he had the capacity never to forget a name, he said, 'Claire and Louise, could you spare me a few minutes, please?'

With an unconcealed display of edgy distrust, they offered him a seat and the tallest of them, Claire, said, 'Of course, Mr Anderson. There's nothing wrong, is there?'

He refused the chair, preferring to try to put them at ease

by leaning against the block of filing cabinets. 'Not at all. I just wondered whether you could help me. Do you know what Rachel's up to now?'

The question took them by surprise. They looked at each other guardedly, then back at him. 'I think she was taking a few weeks' holiday before starting a new job next month,' Louise said.

'Do you know if she was going away on holiday or just staying at home?'

Again the two girls exchanged reticent glances. Neither seemed inclined to answer him. He suddenly realised what was going on. They had him down as another Gervase who wouldn't think twice of using his sex and position to get exactly what he wanted. This, then, was the reality of working in a male-dominated office such as theirs, where an excess of testosterone reigned supreme and where female employees were automatically marginalised and expected to toe the line accordingly. Annoyed and disgusted that he hadn't taken steps sooner to change such a deeply ingrained culture, Elliot decided to be straight with the two young women. 'Look,' he said, 'do you have any idea why Rachel left so unexpectedly? Was she, for instance, recently made to feel unhappy working here?'

From the expression of scorn on both their faces his worst fears were confirmed. He tried an even more direct line and lowered his voice. 'You don't have to go into details if you don't want to, but, please, just tell me, was it, in your view, a case of sexual harassment?'

After the briefest of sideways glances, they both nodded.

Half an hour later, Elliot left the second floor and returned to his office. He now had the file he needed, as well as Rachel Vincent's home phone number. He locked both vital pieces of information in his desk to deal with that evening and got on with what he should have been doing instead of playing amateur detective.

Chapter Thirty-Nine

When Elliot had told Gervase that he was busy, he had not been exaggerating, and though he had had time at home to go through the Hayes and Clarke billing file – and discover that crucial bits of information were missing – he had not had time to do anything about it. Neither had he been able to make contact with Rachel Vincent: she hadn't responded to any of the messages he'd left on her answerphone, and until he had spoken to her he couldn't make a further move on Gervase. With his trip to the States scheduled for the day after tomorrow, he had no choice but to be patient and hope that the reason Rachel had not contacted him was that she was still away on holiday.

In the meantime he had replaced the billing file and spoken to Paul Davidson to reassure him that the matter was being looked into. He'd also told Gervase that until his return from New York the situation would be on hold. The man's relief had shown itself in the form of a flamboyant wave of a hand. 'I expect we'll just have to treat it as one of those things, old chap,' he'd said airily, 'a damn nuisance, but nothing that can't be smoothed out by exercising a little judicious writing off of the excess fee.'

Elliot would have liked to exercise a little judicious knuckle-flexing into the side of Gervase's arrogant, overfed jaw, but instead, and to lull him into a greater sense of false security, he said, 'Oh, and by the way, I shall be able to make it on Saturday night, after all.'

When he'd told Ali on the phone what he was doing and why, having confided in her his suspicions about Gervase, she had wished him luck. 'I can't think of anything worse,' she'd said, 'than an evening with Gervase and that ghastly wife of his, the Bitch Queen of Prada Accessories.'

'I'm hardly thrilled at the prospect myself.'

She'd laughed. 'A perverse part of me wishes I could be there with you.'

'If you were here, I wouldn't even consider going. I'd have a much better evening planned.'

'Pining for me, are you?'

'What do you think?'

'I think you're running up a terrible phone bill. We've been talking for nearly an hour and mostly about Gervase.'

'I'm sorry, it's just that you and Sam are the only ones I'm prepared to confide in at this stage.'

'Don't worry, it doesn't bother me. But do you really believe Gervase would be dumb enough to think he could get away with it? Most of us girls in the office knew that he and others like him considered us fair game for a bit of slap-and-tickle, though I have to say he never once tried it on with me. This is shaping up into quite a different ball-game, though.'

'Oh, I think he's more than stupid enough. And don't forget, he counted on Rachel being too scared to give her side of the story for fear of jeopardising her career, and so far it's worked beautifully.'

'Well, Elliot, for the sake of the sisterhood, nail the so-and-so!'

Elliot parked his car and, with Ali's words echoing in his ears, approached Gervase's prestigiously large house. It was a centuries-old pile that had been in the Merchant-Taylor family since one of Gervase's ancestors had made an obscene amount of wealth from exploiting men, women and children in his cotton mills. It overlooked the greens and fairways of the nearby golf and country club in one of Cheshire's classiest areas.

He rang the bell and cringed as he heard it clang

ostentatiously on the other side of the studded oak door. He planned to stay just long enough to make Gervase think that all was well in the office – an unprepared Gervase was what Elliot wanted when he made his strike.

It was Fiona who answered the door. She was the second Mrs Merchant-Taylor, having replaced the former some seven years previously. Fifteen years Gervase's junior, she had, once upon a time, been little more to him than his secretary – but that was before they embarked on a standard workplace affair. It had been going on in a semi-clandestine manner for several months when one day, Barbara, Gervase's wife, under the influence of whatever alcohol she'd earlier consumed, stormed into the office and dramatically announced to anyone who would listen that she knew exactly what her vile, womanising husband was up to. A messy divorce followed, as did a precipitous marriage between Fiona and Gervase. And according to what Ali had told him from ground-level gossip, Fiona had at once adopted the air of a county-set wife and overnight had become an expensive liability. No longer was she prepared to do anything as menial as sit in an office typing letters or answering the phone. Her new occupation was as a lady who lunched, who filled her days consulting interior designers to be rid of all evidence of her predecessor's taste in her newly acquired home. And when she wasn't agonising over lunch menus or choosing between samples of thirty-pounds-a-roll wallpaper, she was pampering herself at the local country club, tanning on sunbeds and having her gold-digging nails manicured. According to the office gossip, she also spent a staggering amount of money on clothes to ensure that she could play to the hilt the part of glamorous young wife married to older man. Elliot had always thought it a shame that the previous generations of Merchant-Taylors had not taken better care of their wealth; if they had, he would have been spared having to work with a git like Gervase. But gambling debts and reckless investments had ensured that Gervase's generation would be denied the privilege of sitting on their fat backsides living off old money.

'Elliot,' drawled Fiona, as she extended a languid hand that was all varnished nails, emeralds and diamonds, 'Gervase said you'd be coming. We'll all have to be on our best behaviour now, won't we?'

'Not on my account, please.'

She took him through to what she pointedly called the drawing room, and which was high-ceilinged and swagged and draped with the kind of rich, heavy fabric more commonly seen as theatre curtains.

A large number of what Elliot called the Blazer Crowd had already arrived and were standing about in small noisy groups. They were being waited on by a couple of girls in short black skirts, white blouses, thick black tights and huge platform shoes. They looked thoroughly bored as they passed round trays of smoked-salmon canapés, and Elliot hoped they were being well paid to prop up Fiona's status-conscious ego.

Clicking her fingers to attract one of the young girls, Fiona said, 'We had hoped to be outside in the garden, but one can never rely on the weather in England. I've told Gervase that, come the autumn, we shall have to get away for some real sun. I feel so dreadfully pale.'

There wasn't anything Elliot could say in response to this vacuous remark. She was clearly more stupid than he thought.

'What would you like to drink?' she asked, when the summoned waitress was by their side. 'Everyone else is having Pimms or G and T.'

'I'll have orange juice, please.'

'You wouldn't like a splash of something with it? Gin? Vodka?'

'Just ice.'

'How very boring. Hardly worth you coming.'

When the girl returned with his glass of orange, Fiona said, 'Now, then, I've got somebody special for you to meet.'

He nearly choked on his drink. 'Fiona, there's really no need—'

'Nonsense. You'll love her. Look, she's over there, talking to Dawn. Isn't she stunning? It was Gervase's idea. He thought the pair of you would really hit it off. We both think you've been on your own for far too long. It's time to put your silly old divorce behind you and find yourself a new wife.'

Elliot was horrified, and furious, to hear his private life referred to so glibly. He stared across the room and saw the woman to whom Fiona was referring. When she realised he was looking in her direction, she waved coyly at him.

'Her name's Miriam,' Fiona said, 'but everyone calls her Mitzi. Come on, I'll introduce you. I've told her all about you.'

Elliot held his ground, determined not to be ambushed into the arms of a woman who went by the name of a miniature poodle. 'Fiona, you had no right to do this.'

But she threw back her head and laughed. 'You're so set in your ways, Elliot. You really should lighten up.'

He knew that the easiest thing to do was to tell Fiona about him and Ali, but he had no desire to do that: it was absolutely none of her business. Then, to his annoyance, he saw that it was too late to protest further. Mitzi was advancing and he was trapped. As soon as the introductions had been made Fiona made herself scarce, claiming that she had to keep an eye on the hired help. 'You have to watch them the whole time,' she said, with an exaggerated roll of her eyes, 'or they'll knock back all the drink and make off with the silver.'

'Fiona tells me you're divorced,' Mitzi began unimaginatively.

He nodded reluctantly.

'Me too. It was a horrible time, lots of nasty solicitor's letters and no end of rows about money. You wouldn't believe how petty my ex was – we very nearly had a custody battle over Twinkle.'

'Twinkle?'

'My Siamese cat.' Smiling meaningfully at him, she went on, 'But it hasn't put me off men entirely, I'm quite prepared to give marriage a second chance with Mr Right. How about you?'

Elliot inwardly groaned and considered telling her that he was gay. He decided not to and said, in his politest voice, 'I'm sure that's the healthiest and most positive attitude to adopt, but I doubt you'll find him here tonight.' Seeing Howard Jenkins standing on his own, he added, 'Now, if you'll excuse me, there's somebody I need to speak to.'

'Bloody awful party,' Howard said morosely, when Elliot approached. 'I don't know why I bother. Same crowd, same crap being said, and the same traps being set. I watched you being set up with the rent-a-bimbo. A lesser man would have gone for it. But not you, eh, Elliot? Coolest man on the block is what the trainee conscripts say about you, did you know that? Mr Cool. Better than what they probably call me.'

Elliot was surprised to hear Howard speaking so vociferously. He wondered if he'd had too much to drink. 'Everything okay?' he asked.

'Oh, everything's hunky-dory. Hunky-bloody-dory.'

'Annabelle not here with you?'

Howard turned his empty glass around in his hand, then raised his dim watery eyes to Elliot's. 'You might as well know,' he said. 'She's left me – for a man who understands her apparently. God, I thought that was supposed to be our line, "My wife doesn't understand me," and all that rubbish.' He sounded the bitterest of men.

'Howard, I'm sorry. When did this happen?'

He shrugged. 'Been going on for a while. Well, it does, doesn't it? There are always the warning signs, one just chooses not to act on them. But, then, you probably know all about that, don't you?' He frowned. 'Sorry,' he mumbled awkwardly, 'shouldn't have said that. Not my place to pry into why your marriage sank without trace. But do you know what the worst bit is?'

'Go on.'

'It's not seeing the children.' He shook his head and frowned again. 'Sorry, shouldn't have said that either. Keep putting my foot in it, don't I, what with your little Isaac?'

'It's okay, don't worry.'

'I don't know how you coped. Must have been the most bloody awful time for you.'

'It was,' Elliot said simply. 'Is there really no hope of saving your marriage?'

'Don't think I haven't tried – God knows I have – but she's not interested. In a way, I don't blame her. I've not been the best of husbands. I've always put work first, so I guess it serves me right. Now, if you don't mind, I want another drink. An extremely large one. I'm going to get embarrassingly drunk and then vomit messily all over Gervase's expensive carpet. Something I shall enjoy doing. I only hope I can remember it in the morning.'

Elliot watched Howard weave his way through the crowd of guests in search of a waitress. It distressed him to see yet another marriage ruined through work. If it wasn't the stress of the job and the long hours that did it, it was a consequence of the environment: too many middle-aged insecure men with something to prove and usually with the younger women in the office.

But Howard's broken marriage at least explained why he hadn't been running his department with his usual efficiency, and now that he knew what the problem was, Elliot could do something about it. He would ensure that Howard was given the support he needed while he was going through what he knew from his own experience, was a pretty bleak period.

It was odd, but the conversation he'd just had with Howard was the nearest he'd ever got to sharing with a work colleague what he had gone through during the past two and half years. Immediately after Isaac's death he had shunned the merest hint of sympathy from anyone in the office, and very soon he had trained himself to appear – according to accepted male conventions – as though he was fully in control of his grief. No one would have guessed at the extent of his misery. He supposed that this was one of the aspects of his character that had helped perpetuate the office myth that he was Mr Cool. It struck him also that his controlled demeanour worked the other way: nobody here tonight would have the faintest notion that he and Ali were back together and that he was what Sam would call top-dollar happy.

An hour later, when Elliot thought he'd shown his face for long enough, he went in search of Gervase. Unable to find him, he asked Fiona where he was.

'You'll find him in his study,' she said, 'second door on the left. It's the only place I allow him to smoke those disgusting cigars of his.'

Elliot followed her directions and indeed found Gervase.

But he wasn't smoking one of his disgusting cigars.

He was sitting behind his desk, his head tilted back, his eyes closed, his mouth open, with Dawn the Porn astride his lap.

Very quietly, Elliot edged out of the room.

He drove home wondering how much more rope Gervase would need to make a proper job of hanging himself.

Chapter Forty

Their holiday was over and Ali and Sarah were heading north. Although they'd enjoyed themselves immensely at Sanderling, they were both looking forward to getting home – Ali because she would be seeing Elliot that evening, and Sarah because it wouldn't be long before Hannah returned from France.

Sarah had spoken to Trevor on the phone last night and he had said he'd received a postcard from Hannah that morning to say that they were planning to catch a ferry on 18 August – two days before the dreaded A-level results would be out.

For most of the fortnight Sarah's conscience had been doing its best to make her feel guilty for leaving Trevor on his own. She had called him frequently but he hadn't once asked how she was or what she and Ali were doing. From their conversations it was evident that he was surviving pretty well without her. Audrey and Shirley were keeping him in wholesome casseroles and iceberg-lettuce salads and, not to be outdone, Elaine had washed and ironed a few shirts. Most of his news revolved around the Slipper Gang. 'Brenda's mother is recovering well from her hip operation,' he told her one evening, 'which comes as no surprise as we've been praying very hard for her.'

His unshakeable belief in the power of prayer had caused Sarah, rather unworthily, to enquire after Shirley's back. 'Is it any better?' she'd asked, knowing perfectly well that it wouldn't be.

'No,' Trevor had answered blithely, 'but then Shirley's

come to the conclusion that her sciatic nerve is a special gift from the Lord and that she must use it as a witness to others.'

This last comment had had Sarah quietly sniggering in bed that night as she imagined a bent-double Shirley hobbling through the streets with a placard strapped to her shoulders with the words 'The Lord heals!' As marketing campaigns went, it would not be the most convincing or direct route for establishing God's kingdom here on earth.

She smiled now as she imagined the scene.

'You've been doing a lot of that lately,' Ali remarked, taking her eyes off the motorway for a couple of seconds and flicking her gaze over Sarah.

'A lot of what?'

'Smiling.'

Sarah tutted. 'Oh, why not go straight for the subtext, Ali?'

'Do I need to?'

Ignoring her friend's question, Sarah turned away to look at the stream of traffic they were overtaking. Just as she lived her life, Ali drove at lightning speed in the outside lane and treated anyone who wasn't quick-witted enough to notice her in their rear-view mirror to a battle-cry flash of her head-lamps. In contrast, Sarah lived her life meandering along in the inside lane doing her utmost to keep out of harm's way. She knew perfectly well what Ali had been getting at in saying that she had done a lot more smiling of late: it was the effect of Sanderling. As a child she had believed there was something magical in the brickwork of the large, rambling house, which charmed and captivated its many visitors. As an adult she knew better: the magic was all down to its hospitable owners – Ali's grandmother, in those far-off childhood days, and now Maggie and Lawrence. Even the beautiful but cool Phoebe had been warmed by the infectious bonhomie of Maggie and Lawrence and had lost some of her sophisticated aloofness. Alastair had actually got her into a pair of shorts and on a bike and had taken her on a tour of the island, sharing with her his old haunts: the disused railway line, which was now an official leisure trail, the sailing club, and the park with its tennis courts and pitch and putt.

The following day, Alastair and Phoebe had left Sanderling to drive to Bath so that he could meet his future in-laws, and start to plan the wedding. 'It's to be a real old medals-and-swords affair,' Alastair had told them over breakfast on their last morning, 'so, Dad, you'd better start trimming yourself down for that morning suit.'

Lawrence had grinned and said, 'Don't you worry about me. With or without the extra pounds I'll cut a fine old dash in a top hat. Isn't that right, Ali?'

'Only if we can find one big enough, Dad.'

It had been strange seeing Alastair again after all these years. Gone was the thin, gangly, rather intense youth she remembered and in his place was a tall, thickset man with a head of fair hair heavily peppered with grey. His manner was confident and relaxed, and he seemed totally at ease with himself. She wondered if he had found her much changed: she had not gained weight and had only a few strands of grey hair – which she dyed at regular intervals – but to somebody who hadn't laid eyes on her for nearly two decades did she seem an altogether different person? Had the passing of years taken a greater toll on her than she was aware of?

Chiding herself for her vanity – what did it matter what Alastair had thought of her anyway? Compared to the Phoebes of this world she was just a drab little housewife – she said to Ali, 'Thank you for inviting me to come on holiday with you. It's been wonderful.'

'Good. We'll do it again.'

It was a nice idea, but Sarah knew it wouldn't happen. Now that Ali and Elliot were reconciled, there wouldn't be room for an old friend muscling in on their precious leisure time.

'I know what's going through your mind, Sarah Donovan, but I meant what I just said.'

'Ali Anderson, keep your telepathic nose out of my thoughts.'

'I wish I could, but you're so damned easy to read. You might just as well write what you're thinking on your forehead. If I'm offering you a holiday with my parents, that's exactly what I mean, Elliot or no Elliot. Empty gestures are not my forte. Got that?'

'If you say so.'

'And while I'm having my say, what are you going to do about Trevor?'

Sarah laughed at the absurdity of the question. 'What do you suggest?'

'Lots of things, all of which you wouldn't approve.'

'Oh, Ali, you just don't give up, do you?'

'I always get my way in the end, you should know that.'

'But not on this occasion.'

Ali heard the firmness in her friend's voice and chose to ignore it. She hadn't forgotten the promise she'd made when they'd been driving out of Oxford two weeks earlier, and was still committed to making Sarah see the sense of planning a new future for herself. Something told her that this might be their last opportunity in a long while to have a real heart-to-heart. 'Sarah,' she said, 'don't be angry with me, but please, just hear me out.'

Sarah took a sideways glance at her but didn't say anything.

Ali plunged in. 'Everything I'm about to say I know will have passed through your head at some stage or other, so don't accuse me of speaking rubbish. When you're with Trevor, you know as well as I do that you're only half alive. His presence literally snuffs you out. Without him I know you could do anything you wanted. So, please, why don't you throw away this partial existence and live? Think how happy you've been these past two weeks. I can't remember the last time I saw you looking so well. Or so relaxed.'

Sarah returned her eyes to the slower moving cars on her

left. 'You make it sound as if it's the easiest thing in the world to throw a whole life away then start again from scratch.'

'I'm not saying it would be easy. But it is possible. It really is.'

'What of my commitment to Trevor?'

Ali pursed her lips. 'A commitment that's slowly suffocating you.'

'Don't over-dramatise it, Ali.'

'I don't think I am. And I don't think you were over-dramatising the situation in March when you said you could imagine a better life without Trevor.'

'What we want isn't necessarily what we get . . . or what we deserve.'

'No!' shouted Ali, giving the steering-wheel a thump and making Sarah start, especially as they were cruising at a cool ninety-five miles an hour. 'No, no, *no*! I simply won't allow you to hide behind that worthless disreputable theory. We live in an age when, as women, we don't have to make do with second best. We're entitled to make better and more informed choices these days. It's our right.'

'It's exercising that right that usually leads to there being so much misery in the world.'

Ali's face darkened with exasperation. 'Why do you always have to think of other people? Couldn't you, just for once, put yourself at the top of the list and say to hell with everybody else?'

'Trevor would say that I've done exactly that by coming on holiday with you.'

'Then you should do it more often.'

When Sarah didn't respond, Ali said, 'Nothing to say?'

Suddenly Sarah smiled. 'I was letting you have the last word.'

Ali smiled too. 'You really are the most tiresome friend a girl could have. But I haven't finished with you yet. I'm going to pull off at the next service station for the loos and while we're having a cup of tea you can tell me one more time why you stay with Trevor. As you're talking, try listening to yourself and hear how crazy you sound.'

By the end of their journey, and despite everything Ali had thrown at her, Sarah knew that none of it had changed the resolve she had made during the last few days at Sanderling. Time away from Trevor had given her the space to realise that she had the strength to turn her marriage round. In the days before quick-fix divorces this was exactly what dissatisfied wives had to do. They rolled up their sleeves, straightened the antimacassars and forgave their husbands for their failings and inadequacies.

And, as she'd frequently told Ali, who was she to say that Trevor's failings and inadequacies were any greater than her own?

Revitalised by Maggie and Lawrence's high spirits and affectionate generosity, as well as feeling the benefit of long walks in warm sunshine, she felt better equipped to cope with Trevor than she ever had. There was also the rather amusing idea tucked away at the back of her mind of one day proving Ali wrong. 'There!' Sarah would say. 'We came through the tricky patch and here we are with a happy and enduring marriage. What do you think of that, then?'

They reached Smithy Cottage just as Trevor was locking the front door to go out. He had a large Bible tucked under his arm, and on his face the kind of expression that only a man intent on saving the world would dare to wear.

'Can't stop,' he said, as he hurried to his car. 'Brenda's mother's hip has taken a turn for the worse.'

Off he went without so much as a welcome-home kiss for Sarah or a patronising comment for Ali.

Ali was stunned by his behaviour. But she was more appalled by the look on Sarah's face. She could see in her friend's dejected expression that, in one fell swoop, the happy afterglow of their holiday had been doused.

That's it, thought Ali. That's absolutely it. Nobody hurts my friend and gets away with it.

Trevor bloody Donovan, you insensitive, pig-ignorant fool, you're in for the shock of your life.

Chapter Forty-One

Ali was met by a loud wolf-whistle from Daniel when she arrived at work the following morning.

'Take a look at you, Babe,' he said, getting up from his desk and coming to greet her. 'I bet you're sun-kissed in places I don't even know exist. You look fabulous.'

Smiling, she put down her briefcase and gave him a hug.

'Mm . . .' he said, breathing in deeply. 'Is that the smell of an old sea-dog, or is it the whiff of a woman in love?'

She laughed, pushed him away, then handed him a package. 'I saw this and immediately thought of you,' she said.

He tore off the paper and held up a china mug that had on it a rear-view shot of a broad-shouldered, tiny-waisted man wearing only a pair of boxer shorts.

'When you pour boiling water into the cup he loses his pants and shows his bum.'

Daniel laughed. 'The cheeky boy. As tacky seaside novelties go, it's perfectly hideous. I love it. And to be sure you weren't conned, I'll make us a drink right now. While the kettle boils you can tell me what it's like to be in touch with your joy button again.'

After spending time away from the office, Ali never found it a problem to get back into the swing of work, but that morning she was unusually distracted and making slow progress on the correspondence Margaret and Daniel had laid on her desk for her return. It wasn't just that Daniel kept bombarding her with questions about her and Elliot, or that she was thinking of Elliot now on his way to New York: she felt as if she was standing on the edge of a precipice.

After she had driven Elliot to the airport at the crack of dawn, she had gone home, sat on the balcony with a cup of tea, listened to the lively chorus of birds, and experienced the remarkable sensation that everything was right with the world.

In particular, her own world. She was filled with a marvellous sense of well-being. It didn't seem possible that the fragments of her life could have been pieced together again, and to such great effect. It had made her think of the occasion at Sanderling when she had accidentally broken one of the Wedgwood vases. Grandma Hayling had carefully picked up the pieces and said, 'Not to worry, a properly mended vase is often stronger than its flawless counterpart.' It was only now that Ali understood what the old lady had meant: her splintered heart had been reassembled and indeed she felt stronger. In fact, she felt invincible, as if there wasn't anything she couldn't do or overcome.

It was then that her thoughts turned to Sarah.

Or, more accurately, to Trevor.

If she had to believe in any kind of mystical mumbo-jumbo she would plump for voodooism. In her current mood, she'd gladly fashion a nice little wax effigy of Trevor and systematically torture him for all the miserable years he'd inflicted on Sarah.

The unthinking brutality of the man when he didn't notice Sarah's hurt yesterday afternoon had incensed Ali to the extent that she'd vowed silently to put an end to the mockery of her friend's marriage.

It wasn't fair that Sarah should have to live that way.

It wasn't right that Sarah believed in a set of unsound rules that precluded her from living the life to which she was entitled.

It was so, *so* wrong that Sarah had shipwrecked herself on the rocks of her faith.

With this in mind, Ali had decided it was time for action. If Sarah's freedom hung on a technicality of faith, as she had admitted to Ali back in March, Ali would provide the means to liberate her. She would lure Trevor into bed with her, then tell Sarah what she'd done.

Except that appearances were going to be highly and convincingly deceptive. If she could pull it off, it would be the illusion of illusions.

It was while she had been driving into work chugging slowly behind a heavily laden brewery wagon that she had hit upon the perfect plan: a plan that was so beautifully simple yet such a masterstroke of cunning she didn't know why she hadn't thought of it before. What's more she wouldn't have to endure anything more sexually explicit than the removal of Trevor's clothes. All she had to do was get him so drunk that when he regained consciousness the following morning he'd believe any story she cared to feed him. If he was convinced he'd just experienced a night of passion, then Sarah wouldn't doubt it. And that was the crux of the whole plan. Sarah had to believe that Trevor had done the dirty on her. It didn't matter how or why, just that he had.

It was the sight of all those metal beer barrels on the wagon in front of her that had given her the idea. Initially she had thought that she would have to be the one who got drunk to go through with the plan, but then a thunderbolt of pure logic told her otherwise. If Trevor was out of it, then there would be no need for her to do what, in all honesty, she knew was beyond her. She was no coward but she had her squeamish no-go areas – and sex with a man she so thoroughly despised was at the top of the list.

Even with her track record of impetuous rushing in where angels feared to tread, Ali knew that what she intended to do was daring and shocking. But she so badly wanted Sarah to be happy that she was prepared to be as devious and audacious as it took. She knew, though, with unerring confidence, that once Sarah had recovered from her amazement at what Ali had done for her, she would be relieved and able to look to the future with an enthusiasm she probably hadn't felt in years.

Meanwhile Ali's number-one priority was to do the deed while Elliot was out of the country, which gave her only the next eight days.

It was not long.

It meant that the route to Trevor's supposed seduction was going to have to be simple and direct: it would be via his innate sense of misguided superiority and would appeal to what she'd always called his saviour complex. She would trick him into believing that she was offering herself up for conversion. She could just imagine the evangelical zeal with which he would treat her. He would be so blinded by his own self-importance at saving her and bringing her to Christ – 'Hey, Lord, I've caught you a big one' – that he wouldn't realise what was happening.

It was after lunch that Ali made her opening move. She waited for Daniel to leave the office for a meeting with one of his clients and, having sent Margaret on a spurious errand, she called Smithy Cottage. She was counting on Sarah being out at the shops or catching up on the weeds in the garden, and that Trevor would answer the phone. She was in luck. Hearing Trevor's pompous voice she clamped down her usual reaction of wanting to take him by the throat; instead she asked how he was and then enquired after Brenda's hip.

'It wasn't Brenda's hip, it was her mother's,' he corrected her, 'and she's gone back into hospital.'

'Oh, how awful.'

'Not if it's the best place for her.'

'You're so right, and of course, it could be . . .'

'Could be what?'

Come on! Don't bottle out now! Just start spouting the rubbish he does. 'I was going to say that it could be the will of God.'

Her words must have made him suspect that she was about to make one of her usual off-the-cuff asides, for he said standoffishly, 'I'll tell Sarah you called.'

Quick, you're losing him. Be nice to him. Keep him talking. 'Actually, Trevor, it was you I wanted to talk to.'

'Me?'

Well, who else is there in this conversation, you idiot? 'Yes. Um . . . I don't know how to put this but – and I'd rather you didn't mention this to Sarah – but . . . Well, it's just that in the past few days I've been thinking a lot about some of the conversations we've had over the years.'

'Which conversations would they be, Ali?' His tone was stalagmite hard with suspicion.

She gripped the receiver in her hot, sweating hand, clenched the other on her lap, and curled her toes over till her feet were arching painfully in her shoes. 'It's this whole business of God, Trevor,' she said. 'I've begun to think that there might be something in it, after all.'

There was a pause and then an oleaginous laugh trickled down the line. 'Well, well, well, Ali, I knew it would happen one day. You've finally stopped being cynical long enough to feel the Lord tapping you on the shoulder. Congratulations!'

His unctuous, patronising manner had her wanting to work methodically through the alphabet and hurl every known obscenity at him. Arrogant Arsehole would be first, followed by Banal Bastard. But with strained politeness, and a little stomach-churning meekness and humility thrown in, she said, 'I was wondering, Trevor, and I know that we've not always seen eye to eye, but I was hoping that you might be able to help me make the next step.'

'Ali, the next step is vital and I'd be failing in my duty as a mature, experienced Christian if I didn't offer you the benefit of my relationship with the Lord. Why don't you join us here on Friday when we have our next discipleship meeting?'

'*No!*' she blurted out. 'I mean, that's a nice idea, but I'm not ready yet to join in with a group.'

'I quite understand. Then the ideal solution is for you to come and talk things over one evening with Sarah and me.'

'I'd rather it was just the two of us. Call me a silly, sentimental girl' – *don't you dare!* – 'but I thought I'd surprise Sarah with a *fait accompli*. You know how she's always been so tolerant of my views on religion, well, I feel that I'd like to make amends for some of the things I've said in the past and present myself, with your help, with a clean slate, so to speak.'

'The only person who can clean your slate, Ali, is the Lord, not me.'

Oh, do us both a favour, Trevor, and save the sales pitch for your precious Slipper Gang. 'But you can show me where God puts the Brillo pad and the Mr Muscle, can't you?'

'Indeed I can.'

'So when can you come over to see me?'

'You want me to come to *you*?'

Well, of course I do, you stupid moron. 'Yes, if that's possible.'

'When were you thinking of?'

'This evening?'

'That's a bit short notice, Ali. I have various commitments and you don't exactly live next door.'

'Oh, please.'

A weighty pause followed. 'All right, then.' He capitulated. 'I suppose I'd never forgive myself if I said no and the devil slipped in and claimed you back.'

The man is completely barking she thought when, minutes later, she put down the phone.

Madness was something Ali accused herself of several times throughout the rest of the day, right up until that evening when she heard a car approaching the mill. It was dusk and she noticed that only one of the Ford Sierra's headlamps was working. She let out a groan of heartfelt torment at the prospect of spending an evening alone with Trevor. Not only was she going to have to survive a one-to-one with him, but she was going to have to be nice and put him at his ease so that he would be relaxed and comfortable with her. She was almost tempted to back out now. But no. She was committed 100 per cent to saving Sarah from throwing away the rest of her life. Nothing would stop her now.

Not even the thought that had occurred to her in the car on the way home from work; a thought that had made her break into a sweat. What if the unthinkable happened and she had to explain the situation to Elliot?

Her hope – and it was a solid, unequivocal hope – was that Elliot would never find out what she'd done or, more to the point, what it would appear that she had done. It was a dangerous game of double-bluff she was playing but logic dictated that the episode would become a secret that would be safely contained within the consciences of the three parties involved. She couldn't conceive of Trevor wanting his sin of sins to be made general knowledge; he, of all people, would want it kept firmly under wraps. And, of course, Sarah wouldn't breathe a word of it – she would have no cause to anyway.

But if the worst came to the worst and Elliot discovered that she'd apparently gone to bed with Trevor – a lie she would need to keep up for Sarah's sake – she would have to make him see that her actions had been justified. More importantly, she would have to convince him that she hadn't betrayed his love.

When Elliot had arrived at the mill last night and after she'd taken him upstairs to bed, he'd held her in his arms and said that he'd always love her.

'But what if I did something dreadful?' she'd asked guiltily, her face turned away from him as they lay in the dark.

He'd stroked her bare shoulder and said, 'Such as?'

'Oh, I don't know. What if I robbed a bank?'

'I'd still love you.'

'What if I defrauded all my clients of their hard-earned money?'

'I'd still love you.'

'And if I had an affair?'

'Anyone in mind?'

'Um . . . how about Trevor?'

He'd raised her face to his, kissed her on the mouth and said, 'I'd know you'd gone clean round the bend and have you certified.'

'But would you still love me?'

'I imagine I would.'

'No matter what?'

'I wouldn't be able to help myself.'

Oh, Elliot, she thought, with a heavy heart, as she heard Trevor hammering on the door downstairs, please don't go back on your word. What I'm about to do has nothing to do with you and me . . . You must believe that.

Chapter Forty-Two

Trevor seemed to have brought an extraordinary amount of stuff with him – two Bibles, several A4 notebooks, a bundle of pamphlets and a clutch of biros, one of which he dropped.

'How about a drink?' Ali asked, once she'd shown him up to the sitting room and he'd cast his eyes over his surroundings, commenting on the whimsy of such an unusual home.

'No, thanks, I had a cup of coffee before I came out.'

'I was thinking of something a little stronger, just to kick things off.'

He dismissed this with a further shake of his head, then parked his sawdusty bottom on the sofa and arranged his collection of soul-saving equipment on the low table in front of him. 'I think it would be appropriate if we began with a prayer,' he said, in a distinctly prudish voice, when he'd finished making himself at home.

Putting the fortifying thought of a large whisky on hold and realising that getting Trevor drunk wasn't going to be as easy as she'd thought, Ali moved towards the armchair furthest from him. Then she remembered that she was supposed to be acting the part of repentant simpleton with a bit of fawning coquette thrown in, and sat uneasily on the sofa next to him.

This is by far the scariest moment of my life, she thought, as beside her, and smelling vaguely of wood and linseed oil, Trevor grabbed one of her hands, closed his eyes and began to pray. 'O Father,' he intoned, his voice sepulchral, 'I bring before you Ali who has for so long hidden her shame in the darkness but whose eyes are now being opened to your shining light. I humbly pray, Lord, that through my guidance she will very soon be kneeling in your awesome grace. Amen.'

There we have it, thought Ali, slipping her hand out of Trevor's hot, damp grasp – *through* **my** *guidance*.

None of this God malarkey had anything to do with serving a higher divine being. It was, as she'd always suspected, nothing but a prop on which Trevor could hang his overstretched ego. How many lost souls did he need to believe he was responsible for saving? And what a monumental kick he must get out of it. No wonder he wasn't interested in having sex with Sarah – he was too busy getting off on the potent combination of self-aggrandisement and narcissistic ambition.

'Now then,' he said, leaning forward and fixing her with what she supposed was an I'm-here-to-help-you stare, 'first things first. We need to discuss eternal life, redemption and the remission of sin. How are you doing on confessing your sins, Ali?'

Hah! Never mind mine, what about yours! 'How do you mean?'

He smiled one of his overly smily smiles that made his eyes disappear into their crinkly crevices, which in turn caused a loose bit of something to come away from his straggly beard. She watched whatever it was drift down on to the rug between his battered Hush Puppies. 'To be saved, Ali,' he said, bringing her attention back to his face, 'you have to open your heart to the Lord. You have to jettison the clutter that you've hoarded and lived your life by and make room for the Holy Spirit to move in and do His work.'

She did her best to appear interested in what he was saying, but her mind was elsewhere – out in the kitchen pouring itself a huge shot of life-saving sanity. 'Um . . . this saved business,' she said, 'I'm not sure I really understand it. Perhaps you could explain it to me over a drink?' And before he could say anything to stop her, she leaped up from the sofa and disappeared to the kitchen where she unscrewed the top of the Jack Daniel's bottle and sloshed the dark amber liquid into two large glasses before raising one to her lips and taking a swig. Instantly she felt strengthened by the warm, glowing effect it had on her as it hit the back of her throat. Joining Trevor in the sitting room, she handed him his drink and forced herself to perch girlishly on the arm of the sofa next to him. 'Cheers,' she said.

He looked hard at the cut-glass tumbler, turned it round in his bony hands, and sniffed it. 'I don't normally drink spirits,' he said, 'I'm more of a *vin de* plonk man.' He gave a little chuckle as though he'd just said something terribly amusing. Any other time Ali would have treated him to a look of disdain, but knowing that if she were to get Trevor into a more relaxed state – and therefore oblivious to how much booze he was knocking back – she had to start serenading him with songs of saccharine-sweetness. She mustered an indulgent smile and laughed too. 'You know, you can be very entertaining when you want to be,' she said. 'A *vin de* plonk man, indeed.'

He took a tiny, cautious sip of his drink and, for an unnerving moment, fastened his beady gaze on her. 'I don't think you've always held that opinion of me, have you, Ali?'

It was the most astute comment she'd ever heard him utter, and sliding down on to the sofa she said, in a low, humble, slightly tremulous voice, 'I'm seeing everything and everyone in a different light these days – and I've come to realise I've misjudged you in the past.' *Oh, yuk! Any minute and she'd be giggling and fluttering her eyelashes.*

'That's what happens when you come to know the Lord.'

'I think you must be right, Trevor.'

'I know I am. I know what it is to be blessed by the Spirit.'

'But have you never doubted—?'

He shook his head adamantly and tugged at his beard.

Ali averted her eyes from the shower of dead skin that would surely cascade on to the rug and the polished floor.

'Not even a speck of – I mean an ounce of doubt?' She wondered if he'd notice her running the vacuum over him.

'No. Since the age of sixteen I've always known that I was saved and that God had designated a truly special task for me to perform.'

'Really? And what would that be?' *It wouldn't by any chance have anything to do with annoying the hell out of other people?*

'Like Billy Graham, I've always believed that I was called to bring people to Christ.'

'I thought that it was Christ Himself who knocked on the spiritual door, as it were.'

'Yes, but it's the foot-soldiers here on earth who help that person to open the door.'

'Oh, I get you. So you could say that our lively exchange of banter over the years has been you rattling the doorknob waiting for me to turn it?' *And there was me thinking you were just being a sanctimonious pain in the butt.*

He smiled. 'Exactly. Didn't I tell you last Christmas that I'd always seen you as my greatest challenge? I hoped I'd get you in the end.'

'Gosh, Trevor, you must be so pleased with yourself.'

He misread the sarcasm in her voice, put down his barely touched glass and said, 'Just doing my job. Though I don't mind admitting to you now, Ali, that there was a time, just recently, when I suspected your heart was hardened beyond even my power to bring you to the Lord. But to work! I thought we could go through some of the passages in the New Testament that I think are of paramount importance, cross-referencing them with Old Testament quotes and going over anything you're not sure of. When I've gone, I want you to read through my notes carefully then answer the questions I've prepared for you. I'm going to keep a close eye on you, Ali, and return on Friday evening so that I can check your answers, but more importantly to make sure that our old enemy the devil hasn't slipped in while my back was turned.'

Holy Moses, homework!

He saw the look on her face. 'Studying scripture is the backbone of our faith, Ali. Without it we're rootless, broken reeds swaying in the breeze, noiseless –'

'Yes, I'm getting the picture.' She was also getting the picture that she wasn't going to get anywhere with Trevor tonight: he was too fired up with the crazy zeal of a man intent on pursuing his own agenda. But Friday night would be different. She was sure of it. Confident, because she'd just come up with Plan B.

The week passed slowly. Each day seemed an eternity. She could hardly sleep and when she did she had nightmares of Trevor's hairy face leering at her in the most unlikely situations: when she was with a client in the office; when she was in the bath; and, scariest and most vivid, when she was lying in bed. The verisimilitude of the dreams had her waking in a hot sweat. Once she had to get out of bed and search the room to convince herself that she really was alone.

He arrived exactly on time and appeared to be revelling in their newly defined roles – he the wise teacher, she the simple child supposedly hanging on his every sagacious word. She noticed after he'd made himself at home on the sofa and set out his books and pens as before that he must have gone to some considerable effort to spruce himself up. The rumpled checked shirt of Monday night had been replaced with a freshly laundered blue and white one, and his dusty patched old jeans exchanged for a pair of clean brown corduroys. He'd also washed his hair and trimmed his whiskers, and in place of the nose-curling smell of sawdust and linseed oil was a suspiciously strong aroma of eau-de-Cologne. It wasn't at all the sackcloth-and-ashes image she was used to. Well, well, well, she thought, picturing the ascetic Trevor back at Smithy Cottage tarting himself up for his evening with her, 'vanity of vanities; all is vanity'.

'You're looking extremely smart this evening, Trevor,' she

said, unable to resist the temptation of seeing how he would respond to her flattery. 'Nice shirt. Suits you.'

Bingo! The hairless bits of his face flushed an incriminating crimson. But then, and with alarm, Ali remembered Elliot's theory that she and Trevor had never got on because subconsciously Trevor was threatened by her strong sexuality. Now – supposing Elliot was right, and let's face it, he usually was – where the hell did that leave her? Playing catch with live dynamite suddenly seemed a safer bet than schmoozing a sexually repressed Trevor.

Shunting this dangerous thought into the sidings of her brain where it could be dealt with at a later stage, she offered him a drink. 'I've got you a nice bottle of red *vin de* plonk. Is that okay?'

'Some red wine would be most agreeable. Thank you.'

She went out to the kitchen, picked up the bottle she'd already opened and poured Trevor a large glass. She then poured herself a tumbler of Jack Daniel's.

'How did you get on with those questions I gave you?' he asked, when she joined him on the sofa and handed him his glass from the tray she'd just settled on the table. 'I kept them as simple and straightforward as I could.'

She feigned a pathetic little shrug of her shoulders, a gesture that she hoped would appeal to his need to feel superior. 'Well, I did my best, Trevor,' she simpered, 'but no doubt you'll be able to put me right with anything I didn't understand.' She passed him the notepad on which she'd written her answers. He read aloud from it. '"Question: After reading Romans 7:15–25 what do you think St Paul was getting at in terms of the law of sin and death?

'"Answer: We want to do good but can't. We know what is right and what is wrong, but can't stop ourselves from doing wrong. Given the choice between right and wrong, we inevitably do what is wrong. We need help. That help comes in the form of Christ."'

Trevor lowered the notepad and stared at Ali. 'That's very

good,' he said, 'very spiritually sound. I'm impressed. You were really listening to me the other night.'

'It must be your excellent teaching,' she said, keeping to herself that after he had left her on Monday night she'd logged on to the Internet and got talking to a theology student in a chat room.

'I must say it makes a change to have such a keen student, to have somebody on the same wavelength. Between you and me, one or two members of the Disciples just haven't grasped the hallowed nettle. I spend most of my time covering the same things over and over again.' He sighed. 'I just have to keep having to remind myself that we're not all on the same intellectual footing.'

She clicked her tongue in sympathy and topped up his wine. 'That must be very frustrating for you,' she said soothingly.

'It is. And Sarah doesn't help. To be honest, I don't think much of her faith. It's not solid, not at all sound. It's affecting her judgement and the way she treats Hannah.'

Ali stiffened. She wasn't prepared to listen to a single word of criticism against her friend. 'Shall we move on to the second question you set me?' she said.

He smiled approvingly. 'Such eagerness, Ali, it does you credit.'

He checked through the rest of her work, and each time he flicked through his Bible searching for a relevant passage to emphasise his point, Ali surreptitiously refilled his glass. In a state of nervous anxiety, she watched him closely, which he naturally took to be attentiveness.

An interminable hour of Bible-bashing passed but, apart from the odd yawn, Trevor wasn't showing any real sign of succumbing. With a bitter sense of disappointment creeping over her, Ali began to lose confidence in Plan B. But then, suddenly, he swayed to his feet and excused himself to go to the bathroom. She gave him directions and waited anxiously for him to return.

And waited.

After fifteen minutes had passed and there was still no sign of him, she went to investigate. She discovered him lying on the floor, gazing glassy-eyed up at the ceiling. And, Hallelujah, praise the Lord with bells on, he was a multiplicity of sheets to the wind. He looked as happy as a pig in mud. Noticing that he was no longer alone, he grinned inanely at her as she stood over him. 'Ali,' he giggled, 'I can't move.'

She got down to his level and knelt on the floor. This wasn't quite the effect she had been expecting. But it would do. 'Are you okay, Trevor?'

He giggled again, then yawned hugely. 'I'm fine. I've never felt better. I think I'm experiencing something called the Toronto Blessing. I'll explain it to you one day.'

'The Toronto what?'

'It's the work of the Holy Spirit. I'm full of it, Ali, and I'm rejoicing in all its glory. It's what I've been waiting for.'

You're full of something, Trevor, but it ain't holy, that's for sure. 'Do you think you can stand?'

He laughed. 'No, the Lord has put me here on the floor and here I shall stay. Ooh, Ali, when I close my eyes I feel as if I'm flying. Are you sure you can't feel it too?'

'Sorry, but no. You don't think that God might want you nice and comfortable in bed?'

He shook his head from side to side like a small child refusing a dose of nasty medicine, but then very quickly he changed his mind. 'Oh,' he groaned, clutching his forehead, 'I'm feeling a bit dizzy now. Perhaps you're right.'

She hauled him to his feet and, staggering under the weight of him as he leaned against her, she shuffled him through to her bedroom. She pushed him backwards on to the bed and hoped that her punishment for what she'd done, and was going to do, wouldn't be him vomiting all over her duvet.

'Lali,' he said, not noticing that his speech was deteriorating, or that she was slipping off his shoes and tossing them over her shoulder, 'schpeaking as your new-found bluther in

Chris', I want to shtell you something. You may blot realise this, but hive always schbeen scared of you. You're sdifferent to other women.'

Too right I am, thought Ali, yanking off his socks and throwing them after his shoes. I'm not one of your sycophantic groupies who's had her brain removed.

'Lali,' he went on, yawning again, 'do you know why you're sdifferent?'

'Surprise me.'

'You've bot galls.'

She laughed out loud.

'Have I schlocked you?'

But before she could answer him, he yawned once more, closed his eyes and fell into the deepest sleep of his life.

Unhindered by his babbling, Ali carried on undressing him. When she finished she went downstairs and phoned Sarah.

'Hello, Ali,' said Sarah. 'I thought perhaps it might be Trevor ringing. He went out several hours ago after acting quite mysteriously. I've no idea where he was going, he –'

'He's here with me,' Ali interrupted.

'With you at the mill?'

'It's a long story but he's stopping the night. He's had some kind of weird experience.'

'Ali, are you winding me up?'

'For once, no, I'm not. Sarah, have you heard of something called the Tornado Blessing?'

'Do you mean the Toronto Blessing?'

'Yes, that's the fella.'

'But what's that got to do with – ?'

'It's gripped Trevor by the spirituals and he's crashed out on my bed.'

'Oh, good Lord, Ali, what's he been up to now? Do you want me to come over? I could get a taxi.'

'No. Leave it to me, I'll take good care of him. Come the morning, everything will be all right. Trust me.'

These glibly spoken words stayed with Ali as she climbed

the narrow staircase. As she surveyed her bedroom and the comatose, snoring Trevor, the first seeds of doubt began to germinate.

What if her plan went wrong?

Chapter Forty-Three

If there was going to be any credence to the story, Ali knew that when Trevor woke up she had to be by his side in bed. To achieve this, and as appalling as it was to her, she had made herself pass the night balancing on the edge of the mattress as far away from him as she could manage.

But she hadn't slept.

Through the dark, lonely hours as she'd lain awake listening to Trevor while he snorted and muttered, she had watched the luminous hands of the clock on the bedside table move slowly but inexorably towards dawn. It was now a quarter to seven and, through the gap in the curtains that she'd drawn so hastily last night, she could see that it was a bright, sunny day.

It was a brightness that was disquietingly at odds with how she felt.

An apocalyptic, eerie, shadowy darkness covering the land would have been more appropriate. It would match the inauspicious, bleak chill that was clutching at her heart.

She looked again at the clock. Thirteen minutes to seven. Would Trevor never stir? Would he never open his eyes to what she had in store for him?

Unable to lie there a minute longer, she feigned her own awakening: yawning, stretching and gently nudging him with her elbow.

But still he didn't wake.

She pushed her pillow towards him, then decided her only real course of action was a sharp, well-deserved kick.

He responded instantly, snorting himself out of his heavy

torpor and turning over. His eyes cracked open and slowly focused on her face, just a few inches away from his. Suddenly, and as dramatically as a rocket being fired, he launched himself into a sitting position. Then, realising that his chest was bare, he looked under the duvet and found that the rest of him was naked too. His mouth dropped open, his eyes popped, and he made a grab for the duvet. He pulled it chastely right up to his chin.

His eyes swivelling round the room, he tried to speak, but the only sound that came out was a stammering, 'Wh-wh-what's going on?'

Ali had had all night to consider what her first response would be when Trevor asked this question. 'Hey, big boy, you need me to tell you?' had originally struck her as comically appropriate, but as the clock had softly ticked away the darkness, she had grown subdued. Now she was rendered speechless. All she could do was look abashed and lower her eyes.

It prompted him to peer under the bedclothes again, as if he hoped to find something lurking at the bottom of the bed to allay his fears. He finally returned his horror-stricken face to hers and said, 'What happened, Ali?'

It was time to speak. It was time to lift the curtain on her performance. 'Don't you remember?' she said softly. Demurely. Eyes lowered.

He screwed up his eyes, ran his hands through his hair, then tugged at his beard. In a final gesture of confused frustration he shook his head. From the pained expression on his face, this had clearly been a mistake. 'Ali,' he groaned, 'we didn't, did we? Tell me we didn't.'

Again she lowered her eyes – she felt like one of those classic Hollywood movie actresses who did all their acting with their eyelashes while puffing curls of smoke into the air. 'It was the wine and whisky, Trevor,' she said. 'We both drank too much. I'm not proud of what I've done.' Realising that she was actually speaking the truth, she slipped out of bed and draped her dressing-gown over her shoulders, which were already covered with an old T-shirt that doubled as a nightdress in the winter. 'I don't know how I'm ever going to face Sarah again.' She forced a little wobble to her voice and added, 'She's my best friend and this is how I treat her.' She looked back at Trevor and saw that his face was bone white, his eyes wide and horrified.

'Oh, my God, Ali, you're not trying to tell me that we –' His voice broke off.

She looked straight at him and nodded. 'Yes, Trevor, that's exactly what I am saying.'

His eyes followed her as she went and stood at the end of the bed. 'But we can't have,' he muttered. 'I would have remembered. I would remember something like that.'

'You did knock back a hell of a lot of booze.'

'But, Ali, I don't get drunk. I'm not that sort of a man. In fact, I've never been drunk. Not ever.' His tone had taken on a more pleading and reasoned edge and, frightened that he might piece together the correct sequence of events, Ali knew it was imperative that she kept the upper hand.

'Well, you did last night,' she said waspishly. 'Now, tell me, does your head ache? Do you feel sluggish? Does your mouth feel as if it's been dried out with a blowtorch then scarified with a garden rake? And does everything feel a strange blur?'

'Yes,' he admitted, with a small, pitiful nod.

'Congratulations. You're suffering from your first hang-over. And to fill in the blanks for you, I'll tell you what happened. I found you smashed out of your brains on the bathroom floor, wittering on about something called the Toronto Blessing.' She could see that she'd fed him the right line. Recall was slowly dawning on his face.

'I remember being in the sitting room,' he said, in a vague, distant voice, 'and then I went upstairs to the toilet.'

'That's right,' she said, 'and I came to look for you.'

'Why?'

'Because you'd been gone so long.'

'But why? Why was I gone so long?' He sounded like a small child pestering his mother.

'Because you were drunk, Trevor,' she said firmly.

'But I don't remember drinking enough to make me drunk.'

She was losing her patience. It was so bloody typical of the man to lose sight of the big picture and nitpick over the tiniest details. 'I'll show you the empty bottles if you want,' she snapped. Steering him back to the point of it all, she went on, 'When I found you, you were babbling on about feeling so fantastic that you could fly and then you said that I was wonderful and that as my brother in Christ you wanted to make love to me and that it would all be okay because it was what the Holy Spirit wanted. While you lay on the bed you told me how you thought I was different from other women. Afterwards you passed out, which is probably why you don't remember anything.'

He'd been listening open-mouthed to her carefully worded reconstruction of what had happened, no doubt recognising enough bits to make him accept the rest, and now he hung his head.

Overcome with shame, Ali gathered up her clothes – which she'd strewn over the floor for that authentic air of frantic undressing for sex – and left Trevor to his misery.

She couldn't face the thought of breakfast and didn't offer any to Trevor when, at length, he appeared in the kitchen. He was fully dressed now but was as awkward and self-conscious as if he were still naked. Clearing his throat several times, he said, 'Ali, we don't have to tell Sarah, do we? I mean . . . we could just . . .' but he didn't get any further.

Ali looked straight at him. 'Yes, we do, Trevor,' she said grimly. 'I couldn't ever lie to Sarah.' Hell, she hadn't gone to all this trouble only to have him sweep it under the rug of his conscience. He swallowed nervously and she could see the direction in which his cowardly thoughts were tunnelling: say nothing and nobody gets hurt, especially Trevor. She was incensed by his hypocritical cowardice. 'Surely the Christian response to what we've done is to confess and repent,' she said, hitting him smack on the head of his religious doctrine, while taking pleasure in the knowledge that, when pious push came to sinful shove, Trevor was as committed to his religion as she was.

'But you don't understand the consequences,' he bleated.

Oh, believe me, I do. 'Trevor, if you don't tell her the truth it will haunt you for the rest of your days. Besides, even if you don't feel the need to confess your sins, *I do*.'

This startled him sufficiently to set him pacing the kitchen; the soles of his Hush Puppies filled the silence as they squeaked loudly on the wooden floor. He suddenly turned on her. 'But do you think she would forgive me?'

'Only Sarah knows the answer to that.'

He considered this for a few seconds. 'I suppose it would be her duty, wouldn't it?' he said reflectively. 'As my wife, it would be her Christian duty to forgive me.'

Given what Trevor had done – or what he thought he had done – Ali was outraged that he could talk about Sarah owing him duty. 'Sarah is one of the most forgiving people I know,' she said, 'I'm sure that she'll give you all the redemption you need.' Yeah, and a clean-break divorce.

He nodded decisively. 'You're right,' he said, and as he ran his hand over his beard, Ali was further appalled to see what she could only describe as a tidal wave of relief wash over him. My God, she thought. He really thinks that he can be let off the hook as easily as that. She was about to bring him back down to planet Earth with a crashing bump when he said, 'It's most important that we work this out between the three of us, Ali. The fewer people who know about this, the better. At all costs, I don't want the Disciples to get wind of it. The damage this would do to the group is incalculable. I am their leader, after all.'

Ali was stunned. His marriage was on the line and here he was blatantly more concerned with his standing in the Slipper

Gang! Any niggling doubts about her manipulation of him were gone. He deserved everything, and more, that would shortly be coming his way.

They drove the forty-five-minute journey to Astley Hope, Ali following impatiently behind Trevor having insisted that they make a joint confession to Sarah; she wanted to be sure that Trevor owned up exactly to what he thought they'd done.

Driving along the quiet, early-morning sun-filled country lanes, Ali began to think about Sarah and how she would react to the revelation that was about to be sprung on her. Stupefied amazement would come first, perhaps, followed swiftly by understanding and an acknowledgement at what Ali had given her: her freedom. Thank goodness Ali didn't have to worry about Sarah being hurt by Trevor's apparent betrayal, though, of course, Sarah being Sarah she might feel inclined to spare his feelings by playing the aggrieved wife – How could you do this to me? – while secretly relishing the thought of hotfooting it to the nearest solicitor.

On reaching Smithy Cottage, Ali parked her car alongside Trevor's and followed him inside. She had agreed with him that she would stay in the background and let him do most of the talking, but she was determined that if he chose to be selective with his confession, she would jump in smartly and make sure that Sarah was fully aware of the facts – that it wasn't a bit of sofa grappling that he was owning up to but a full-blown case of commandment-breaking adultery.

Sarah greeted them anxiously. She looked first at Ali, then at Trevor's pallid face. 'Are you all right?' she asked him.

He nodded dumbly and went through to the sitting room. Sarah and Ali followed. 'You look as if you could do with a drink,' Sarah said. 'In fact, you both do. What's wrong, Ali?'

Ali saw Trevor's involuntary shudder at the mention of the word 'drink' and said, 'Sarah, I think you'd better sit down. Trevor's got something to tell you.'

Sarah remained where she was but Trevor flopped into the

nearest armchair. He rubbed the palms of his hands together then pushed them the length of his corduroy-covered thighs. He let out his breath and, without glancing either at Sarah or Ali, he began his confession. It didn't take long and when he'd finished he raised tormented eyes to Sarah and waited for her to speak.

Ali waited too. The chill that had clutched at her heart earlier that morning returned. This was it, then, she thought, with sickening dread. They were on the brink of a defining moment. From here on, it was all down to Sarah.

Sarah went over to Trevor. She touched his shoulder and, without a trace of bitterness in her voice, said, 'I'd be grateful if you would leave us alone, Trevor. I need to talk to Ali.'

He got clumsily to his feet. 'Are you throwing me out?'

She closed her eyes for a couple of seconds as though overcome with tiredness. 'Just go, Trevor. Come back later. Much later.'

'You will be here when I get back, won't you? You're not leaving me?'

'Trevor, for once in your life will you please just do as I ask?'

He left the room and quietly shut the front door after him. His car wasn't so sensitive to the moment, though, and the engine backfired irreverently as he reversed down the drive and drove off in a cloud of smoke.

Alone now with Sarah, and aware of a terrible silence between them, Ali's heart slipped into another gear and began to beat faster. Always the one with the smartarse response, the one who could outwit any opponent, the one who could sidestep with all the speed and agility of a featherweight boxer, she now felt extraordinarily feeble-minded. It seemed an age before Sarah spoke. When she did, she said, 'Ali, would you care to explain what you've done?'

Ali swallowed nervously. 'I think you know exactly what I've done.'

'But I want you to explain it to me.' Sarah's words resonated in the stillness of the room with chilling restraint.

Ali tried to meet her friend's gaze but found she couldn't. It had all seemed so reasonable in her head when she'd plotted and schemed to rescue Sarah. Even in the car a few moments ago it had seemed perfectly plausible and acceptable, but now . . . but now, hearing the coldness in Sarah's voice, she wasn't so sure. She went over to the open window and stared out at the beautiful garden her friend had brought to life, every inch of it cared for and loved. 'I did it for you,' she said softly.

'At least have the courage to look at me.'

Ali turned.

'Tell me exactly what you did, Ali. Spell it out for me. And, to quote you from only the other day, "Perhaps you'd take the trouble to listen to yourself and hear how crazy you sound."'

'That's not fair.'

'And it's fair what you've done?'

'Yes,' said Ali defiantly, her voice rising. 'Trevor's treated you abominably all your marriage. He worships a god made in his own self-deluded image and has gone around acting like one, keeping you under his thumb like some subjugated acolyte.'

The colour rushed to Sarah's face and her icy calm now gave way to an altogether different emotion: raw anger. 'How dare you accuse Trevor of acting like God,' she threw at Ali, 'when that's exactly what you've done?'

'I have not!'

'Oh, yes, you have. You've played God with my marriage, and that's unforgivable!' To Ali's horror, tears ran down Sarah's flushed cheeks. 'You've no idea what you've done!' she wailed. 'Why, oh, why, did you have to interfere?'

'But I don't understand,' Ali said, genuinely baffled. 'You told me . . . you said that if Trevor had an affair it would leave you free to leave him.'

'But I never said I *would* leave him,' shouted Sarah.

'Why not? Why not leave the stupid man? You don't love him. Or are you going to deny you ever said that?'

'Shut up! Shut up!'

'No, I won't. I've gone to a lot of trouble to provide you with the means to end your marriage with your Christian ethics still intact, so you can bloody well give me a damn good reason why you can't do it.'

'Okay, then.' Sarah rounded on Ali, her eyes flashing white-hot rage, her hands tightly balled at her sides. 'How's this for a reason? It's guilt that's kept me in this marriage and it's guilt that will keep me in it.'

'Guilt? You, the paragon of selfless love and honesty, what the hell have you got to be guilty about?'

Years of self-control, years of suffocating anger and years of bitter disappointment burst the strained banks of Sarah's carefully constructed façade, and in one explosive and irrevocable outpouring the damage was done. 'Trevor isn't Hannah's father,' she bawled, her eyes blazing, her face twisted with anger and fear, 'and I only married him because I was pregnant and desperate. How's that for a paragon of selfless love and honesty?'

Chapter Forty-Four

'Oh, that's complete nonsense,' retaliated Ali, without thinking. 'Of course Trevor's Hannah's father! You told me
yourself that –' But her words fell away as, all at once, she felt
the full force of Sarah's dark, hollow-eyed expression bearing
down on her. Its severity made her gasp. And in that moment
the world seemed to rock on its axis. She reached out to the
window-sill, needing its support. 'But – but it can't be true,'
she stammered. 'You would have told me. You were my best
friend. You *are* my best friend. Why didn't you ever tell me?'

Light-headed with shock at what she'd just blurted out,
Sarah couldn't speak. She hadn't meant to reveal her
shameful secret. She hadn't ever intended another living soul
to know the truth. She had kept it to herself these past
eighteen years and had sworn to keep it that way for ever.

But now somebody knew.

She felt a faint tremor building in the pit of her stomach
and, fearing that she was going to be sick, she breathed
deeply and slowly.

'Why didn't you share it with me?' persisted Ali.

Another few breaths and the wave of nausea passed, but in
its place came a further and more dangerous surge of fury for
what Ali had done. She stared at Ali and said, 'It's always
about you, isn't it?' She heard the poisonous hostility in her
voice, not recognising it as her own, but then she saw Ali's
hurt. With vengeful satisfaction, she knew that she wanted
Ali to suffer for her wilful interference. She wanted her to
know that her headstrong impetuosity had ruined everything.

Including their friendship.

Oh, yes, that was gone. Destroyed at a single stroke by Ali's arrogant belief that she always knew best.

She crossed the small room purposefully and stood by the open door. 'I want you out of my house,' she said, with ruthless detachment.

Ali remained where she was. 'Look, Sarah—'

'I said, get out of my house. I never want to see you again.'

Close to tears, Ali didn't know what to do. Whatever reaction she had expected from Sarah, it was not the wild, hysterical response of a few minutes ago, nor this cruel, dispassionate dismissal. 'Sarah,' she said, fighting back the lump of fear in her throat, 'please, just talk to me. Let me apologise properly. If I'd known about Trevor not being Hannah's father—'

'Be quiet! I don't want to listen to you. Don't you understand? I don't want anything more to do with you. You've done nothing but try to control me. Poor old Sarah, you've always thought. Well, I'm tired of your pity. And your charity. I don't want it any more.'

'I've never pitied you and I've certainly never tried to control you.'

'Yes, you have. You're always telling me what to do. Well, this time you've gone too far. You've wrecked everything that I've striven to create and preserve.'

'You mean I've forced you to stop flogging the dead horse of a marriage that was unworkable from the start.'

'It was *my* marriage, Ali, and it would have worked just fine if you hadn't been continually poking your nose into it. And while you were plotting to seduce my husband did you never think of what the consequences would be for Hannah?'

Ali swallowed and chewed on her lower lip. The awful truth was, she hadn't. She had thought only of her friend's welfare . . . and the future she thought Sarah secretly craved.

'And what about Elliot in all of this?' Sarah continued. 'What will he make of your betrayal when he hears of it?'

The lump of fear in Ali's throat grew bigger. 'He won't ever know – I shan't tell him.'

Sarah's small, pensive face took on a hardness that Ali would never have imagined possible. 'But I'll tell him,' Sarah said, slowly and menacingly. 'I'll make very sure he knows what a callous bitch you are. Maybe he'll end up hating you as much as I do. Now, please, get out and leave me alone. And don't try contacting me again. Our friendship is over. Do you understand that? I don't want you coming near me ever again. *Not ever!*'

'But, Sarah – please, please don't do this!'

'No, Ali, it's over. This is one act of impetuosity that you're going to regret for the rest of your life.'

As the sound of Ali's car faded into the distance, Sarah's composure went with it. She threw herself on to the sofa and sobbed. She cried so violently that once again she feared she would be sick. With tears blinding her, her breath coming in shallow gasps, she stumbled out of the sitting room and up the stairs, steadying herself with a trembling hand on the rickety banister. She stood over the toilet in the bathroom and retched painfully. Again and again. Finally, when her breathing slowed, she turned on the cold tap and filled the plastic tooth-mug from the shelf above the basin; she managed a few small sips.

She looked at her reflection in the mirror, forcing herself to see beyond the tear-stained miserable mess to the depths of the manipulative woman who had used and abused an innocent man. The irredeemable black despair of her guilt and shame stared back at her. She tore her eyes away and set about tidying herself up. She scrubbed at her face with a steaming flannel, then rubbed a towel roughly over her tingling skin. All the while she cursed herself for her selfishness so many years ago. Rehanging the towel on the rail, she heard knocking. Furious that Ali was refusing to do as she'd asked, she went downstairs and threw open the door.

It was Grace. So profound was her relief that it wasn't Ali, Sarah started to cry again. 'I'm so sorry,' she said, through choked sobs as Grace closed the door behind her and took her in her arms, 'I'm so sorry, so very sorry.'

For the next ten minutes Grace didn't say a word. She listened as Sarah told her what Ali had done and her reasons, and how Sarah had told her that she never wanted to see her again – she didn't refer to Trevor not being Hannah's father. When she'd finished, Grace made no comment on the drama that she'd walked into inadvertently, but said, 'Let's get you away from here.' She took the front-door key out of the lock, shut the door behind them and walked Sarah along the lane in the bright sunshine to her own neat little bungalow. 'There, now,' she said, when she had installed Sarah on the sofa and had fetched a bottle of Bristol Cream and two small glasses. 'Slightly early to be hitting the sherry, I agree, but on this occasion quite permissible. Something sweet for the shock.'

'This is very kind of you,' Sarah murmured, her face partially hidden behind a tissue as she took the proffered glass with a shaking hand.

'Yes, it is kind of me, isn't it?'

Hearing the light touch of irony in Grace's words, Sarah looked up at her and saw that Grace was smiling one of her knowing smiles. 'Shall we dispense with the polite comments, Sarah,' she said, 'and get to the nub of things? Or would you rather we ventured further into the field of evasion and discussed the weather?'

'Evasion. Why do you say that?'

'Well, I'd hazard a guess that evasion has been at the heart of all your problems. If it hadn't been there, I suspect your friend Ali wouldn't have needed to go to such mind-blowing lengths to help you. Moreover, her actions wouldn't have had the devastating effect that they've had on you.'

Sarah plucked at another tissue from the box Grace had placed on the rosewood table in front of them. She blew her

413

nose and fought back the instinctive desire to go on hiding the truth. She sipped her sherry and felt its sweet, sticky warmth trickle down to her empty stomach. 'Grace,' she said softly, 'I'm not at all the person you think I am.'

'Ah,' said the older woman, with a slight tilt of her head, 'and who exactly are you, then?'

Sarah sighed. 'A long time ago I did a very wicked thing.'

'And presumably have been paying for it ever since.'

Sarah frowned. 'Please don't patronise me.'

Grace put down her glass and laid a reassuring hand over Sarah's. 'I'm not, truly I'm not. Now, why don't you finally tell someone the truth? The whole truth. It must have been awful for you all these years keeping such a dead weight of a secret to yourself.'

Sarah raised her eyes and stared into Grace's intuitive gaze. She felt the warmth and love of her personality reach out to her. 'You know, don't you?'

Grace nodded. 'Yes, I believe I do.'

'But how?'

'To an objective eye, most children share a fairly balanced proportion of their parents' looks and mannerisms, but Hannah doesn't. There's not a bit of Trevor in her. I can see plenty of you, but nothing of Trevor.'

'But surely that's not enough to make you suspect that he isn't her father?'

'You're right, it isn't. The real clue was that I could find no logical reason, other than a guilty secret or – more accurately – a guilty conscience, that would let such an intelligent woman as you submit your will to Trevor in the way that you do.'

Sarah turned away in shame and instinctively reached for a lock of hair. It was a few minutes before she could speak. 'Oh, Grace, I've used him so badly.'

'Nonsense. You've given him the finest daughter he could have wished for. Some might say that that's better than he deserves.'

'But all the lies—'

Grace dismissed Sarah's unfinished words with a wave of her hand. 'What of Hannah's real father? Was he an older, married man, or a regretted one-night stand you never saw again? Was that why you couldn't turn to him?'

Sarah shook her head sadly. 'No. It wasn't like that. We knew one another and a situation developed – a situation that I should have prevented, but didn't. It was curiosity that made me do it. It was my first time. I was very naïve.'

'And, later, did you tell him you were pregnant?'

'I couldn't. He wasn't around any more. I didn't know what to do. I panicked. I couldn't bear the thought of my child not being part of a happy family. I wanted everything for my baby that my parents hadn't given me – a mother and a father who genuinely loved their child.'

'A perfect replica of Ali's family?'

'Yes. Stupid, wasn't I?'

'Not at all. You were very young. So when did you think of Trevor?'

'Almost straight away. I already knew him from the prayer group we both attended and we'd had meals out together as well as enjoyed a few evenings at the theatre. I knew that he was keen on me and, believe it or not, I was fond of him. He was different in those days, kind and generous, somehow freer. He stood up for what he believed in and I respected him for it. He wasn't like the students I was supposed to be hanging around with, the over-privileged élite who were hell-bent on milking life for all it was worth. Trevor and I had a lot in common, similar backgrounds and similar views. I knew he'd make a good father and that he'd do anything for me, so I . . .'

'So you seduced him?'

A flicker of anguish crossed Sarah's pale face and, wet-eyed, she said, 'Yes, I seduced him. I knew I had to trick him as soon as possible so that he would always believe that he was the father of the child I was already carrying. Call it madness, but I had convinced myself that as long as I stuck to the same story of when I'd conceived, I'd be able to pass off the baby's birth as premature. Very conveniently Hannah's arrival was two weeks later than expected and nobody was any the wiser. Though I did wonder at the time about the midwife. She made some comment about Hannah being a big bonny baby considering she hadn't gone full-term.' She fell silent, then said, 'Do you want to know how I seduced Trevor?'

Grace sipped her sherry thoughtfully. 'Only if you want to tell me. If it would help.'

Sarah sighed again and, with a resigned shrug of her shoulders, said, 'I've come this far, I might just as well. I invited him to my room in college and, over a bottle of wine, I practically threw myself at him. I knew it was a huge risk. Even then he was a deep-boned fundamentalist and didn't believe in sex outside marriage. The ironic thing was, neither did I. But having done it once, I told myself that one more sin couldn't make my situation any worse. Incredibly, he was a pushover. I hated myself afterwards. I'd compromised not just my own faith but his as well. The next day he came to see me and apologised for what had happened. He blamed himself for his loss of control and promised it would never occur again. Six weeks later, when I was actually twelve weeks gone, I told him I was pregnant and he nobly asked me to marry him. You see now how awful I am?'

'Oh, Sarah, you're not awful – of course you're not. But what is is that ever since then you've punished yourself so severely. Why could you never allow yourself to be forgiven?'

Sarah pursed her lips until they were almost colourless. 'I never felt I deserved it,' she said, in a tightly controlled voice.

'Yet I'm sure you would have been the first to point somebody else in the direction of their own personal redemption.'

'Oh, yes. I do it all the time. I told Ali to stop punishing herself over Isaac's death, to forgive herself and Elliot. Ironic, isn't it?'

'Not really. Given the amount of agony you've put yourself through, I would imagine there's no better qualified person to dissuade another from taking that particular route to hell. Now that you've had a chance to calm down, how do you really feel about what Ali's done? Do you still feel you hate her?'

'Yes. No. Oh, I don't know what I think. I still can't believe she did it. How could she willingly go to bed with a man she feels nothing for?'

Grace gave her a long, hard stare. 'She could ask the same of you.'

'Oh, that's cruel.'

'I'm sorry. But, from what you've told me, Ali saw it as a means to free you. As misguided as she was, you have to acknowledge that that was quite a sacrifice she made. She clearly has a very strong sense of commitment towards her closest friend.'

'No,' Sarah said angrily. 'It's just another example of her wanting to control me. I didn't need rescuing.'

'So what are you going to do now?'

Sarah let out her breath in a long sigh of despondency. 'I don't know.'

'Do you want to leave Trevor?'

'I can't.'

'Why not?'

'It would destroy him.'

'Staying together might destroy you both.'

'But what Ali did was unforgivable. She tricked him and I can't let him take the blame for that.'

'I hate to point out the obvious, but it seems that Trevor has rather an unfortunate weakness for being tricked by women.'

'That's an exaggeration. Twice is hardly a weakness.'

Grace levelled her gaze on Sarah. 'Still protecting him, Sarah?'

'I don't have any choice. I feel sorry for him. Just as I always have.'

'And now Ali's made you feel even sorrier for him, I suppose?'

'Yes.'

'Which means you'll forgive him and everything will go back to how things were before Ali tried to take charge.'

'I have to hope so.'

'Oh, come on, Sarah, you're deluding yourself. I guarantee that after today nothing is ever going to be the same again. You can't isolate the consequences of what Ali has done. Wasn't it Tennyson who wrote "Our echoes roll from soul to soul"?'

'"And grow for ever and for ever,"' Sarah finished for her, in a low whisper, praying desperately that her elderly friend was wrong.

Chapter Forty-Five

Ali had been driving aimlessly for the past half-hour. She didn't know what to do. Or where to go. She didn't want to go home – the thought of being alone terrified her. In her wretchedness the windmill, with its solitary structure and secluded situation, would only emphasise the heart-aching sense of isolation that was consuming her. Even in her confused, desperate state she couldn't fail to realise how ironic it was that she should now be shunning something that, only a short time ago, she had viewed as a symbol of her fierce independence.

I never want to see you again ...

This is one act of impetuosity that you're going to regret for the rest of your life.

I'll make sure he knows what a callous bitch you are ... he'll end up hating you as much as I do.

The bitterness with which Sarah had uttered those dreadful words terrified Ali. What if she had meant what she'd said? What if, when all the furore had fizzled out, Sarah still refused to see her? Ali couldn't imagine life without Sarah. It was inconceivable that they could be separated: they'd been together for ever. She suddenly thought of the Forever Friends Christmas mug she'd given Sarah and burst into tears.

She slowed the car, pulled off the road into a litter-strewn lay-by, slumped over the steering-wheel and howled like a baby.

What had she done?

Why had she been so determined to meddle?

She thumped repeatedly at the wheel then, frightened she

might activate the airbag, she stopped. But her frustration was still there, and for the first time in her life she wished that she believed in this God of Sarah's: at least then she'd be able to berate him. 'It's all your bloody fault!' she'd shout at him. 'If it weren't for you, none of this would have happened. Sarah wouldn't have tied herself up in a lot of religious hocus-pocus that's done nothing but made her feel guilty for the last eighteen years. Eighteen bloody years in some misguided act of atonement!'

Having expressed a tiny fragment of her shock and anger, she wiped her eyes and decided what to do next. She drove towards Nantwich, picked up the A534, skirted round Congleton then joined the A536 for Macclesfield and headed for Daniel.

'Please let him be there,' she murmured, over and over to herself as she was bumping along the dusty track towards the farmhouse that looked picture-book perfect in the bright sunshine. The sight of both his and Richard's cars gave her hope that her long drive had not been in vain. Leaving the Saab, she hurried across the terrace and rang the brass ship's bell beside the door.

There was no answer.

She tried again.

Still no answer. A knot of panic gripped her insides. Where, oh, where was Daniel when she needed him? Her lips trembled and the abject misery she had successfully controlled while driving threatened to overwhelm her: it made her want to throw herself at the door until somebody – anybody – came to her rescue.

Suddenly, above her head, a window opened and Daniel stared down at her bleary-eyed, his hair tousled, his chest bare. 'Ali? What on earth are you doing here?'

She gulped back her relief. 'Please, Daniel, I need to talk to you.'

Sitting at the kitchen table with a sedative mug of Earl Grey in her hands and surrounded by the ordinary and common-place – Richard making toast on the Aga and Daniel ferrying pots of jam, honey and marmalade from the pantry – Ali's composure slowly returned. Everything would be all right, she told herself. Daniel and Richard would know how to help. They'd tell her how to straighten out the mess she'd caused. 'I'm sorry I got you out of bed,' she said.

'That's the third time you've apologised,' Daniel said gently, as he put the last of the breakfast things on the table and slipped into the chair opposite her, 'but I think it's time now to tell us what's wrong. It's not Elliot, is it?'

She willed a stray tear to stay where it was and not breach her defences. 'Elliot's not my immediate problem,' she murmured morosely, 'but he soon will be.'

Richard came over with a rack of toast. 'Would you rather I made myself scarce?' he asked.

Ali was touched by his thoughtfulness. 'It's okay,' she said, 'you can stay, but I don't think you're going to like what you hear.'

Her eyes on the mug of tea in front of her, she told them everything, all the details, and all the reasons why she'd undertaken such a scheme. 'My original plan,' she explained, 'was to get Trevor so inebriated that he'd crash out and come to the following morning with only the sketchiest of memories. But I realised on Monday evening that I couldn't rely on getting him drunk so . . . so I decided when he came to see me for a second time to spike his wine with a couple of tranquillisers and a sleeping pill – stuff I'd been prescribed after Isaac's death but had never used. It worked perfectly. And although I had a few misgivings, I really believed I'd done the right thing by Sarah. Except now I find out that she's stuck fast to Trevor by her guilt. You see, he isn't Hannah's father. She tricked him into marrying her when she discovered she was pregnant. And now she won't speak to me. She says she never wants to see me again – that she hates me for what I've done. Even worse, she says she'll tell Elliot.'

Both men stared at her in deathly silence, their hands poised over their plates of untouched toast, their eyes wide and incredulous. It was Daniel who spoke first. He rose from the table, walked over to the other side of the kitchen, and leaned back against the dishwasher. He ran his hands through his uncombed hair. 'I don't believe I'm hearing this. What in hell were you thinking of, spiking the man's drink with potentially lethal drugs? You could have killed him!'

'I was very careful. I—'

'Oh, good call, Ali. You were careful, were you? *Bullshit!* My God, I've heard of date rape, but this is something else!' He turned from her and stared out through the window. Then he whipped round. 'And what possessed you to think that you had a right to take hold of somebody else's relationship and stamp the viable life out of it? If you could do that to a friend, what the hell would you do to an enemy?'

Ali covered her face. 'I did it with the best of intentions,' she whimpered. 'It was an act of faith in our friendship, it was—'

'An act of faith!' exploded Daniel. 'You have to be joking. It was a malicious act of devious hatred. You've always hated Trevor and you saw this as a way to have Sarah all to yourself and make like a bloody heroic saint into the bargain.'

'That's not true!' cried Ali, springing to her feet and scraping her chair noisily on the tiled floor. 'It wasn't about hating Trevor, it was about loving Sarah and wanting the best for her.'

'Well, no argument there, then. She'll be a darned sight better off without you around.'

Ali glared at him. 'If that's how you feel, then perhaps it would be better if I left. I'm sorry to have disturbed your Saturday morning. Thanks for the tea and sympathy.'

His arms folded across his chest, Daniel stayed where he was. He watched Ali move towards the door, but Richard intervened. He went after Ali, placed both his hands on her

422

shoulders and drew her back into the kitchen. 'Don't go,' he said softly. 'Daniel didn't mean half of what he just said.'

Unconvinced, Ali glanced over to him, but his dark, brooding gaze was fixed on a spot on the floor at his feet. In all the years she had known and loved him, she had never seen such an expression on his face. She realised then what it was. It was disappointment. He was disappointed in her. 'I think Daniel meant exactly what he said,' she murmured sadly, 'and he's probably right.'

'Daniel,' urged Richard, 'Ali needs our help and support, not our animosity.'

Slowly, Daniel raised his eyes from the floor and met Ali's tear-filled gaze. Gradually the darkness cleared from his face, he unfolded his arms and held them out for her. 'I'm sorry, Babe,' he said.

She went to him and held him tightly, desperate for his forgiveness: to be rejected by Daniel was as unthinkable as it was to lose Sarah's friendship. 'I'm sorry too,' she said, 'sorry for what I've done and sorry for letting you down.'

'You haven't let me down.'

She released herself from his arms and looked up into his face. 'I have, I know I have.' She began to cry again, her breath catching in long, choking sobs. 'I've ruined everything. Sarah won't talk to me and God knows what Elliot will do when he finds out. I never intended to hurt so many people. Oh, please help me. Tell what to do.' Her crying grew louder and she shook violently. Daniel took her in his arms again and held her protectively to his chest.

'Let's get her upstairs to bed,' Richard suggested. 'She needs to rest.'

Between them they helped her into their bed, which was still warm from where they'd been sleeping. She lay in the middle, Richard on one side of her with a box of tissues at the ready and Daniel on the other stroking her cheek and holding her hand.

Shortly afterwards she fell asleep, and when Daniel

423

checked on her five hours later, she opened her eyes and asked him what time it was.

'Half past four, Babe.' He came and lay down with her. 'Feeling any better?'

'I think so.' She sat up and shifted the pillows behind her into a more comfortable position. 'I'm sorry I lost it downstairs.'

He put an arm around her and kissed her forehead. 'Nothing like a bit of drama to nourish the soul.'

Her face broke into a small smile. 'Oh, Daniel, whatever am I going to do?'

'I've no idea, but for now, explain to me one more time what, in the name of all that's wonderful, you thought you were doing.'

'Do I have to?'

'Yes. I want to try and understand what you did.'

As painful as it was, she went through the story again, labouring the point about Sarah's religious convictions. 'She told me she could never leave Trevor because of her beliefs, but that if he was to have an affair it would change everything.'

'So you took her at her word, literally?'

'Yes. I swear I thought she meant it. If I'd doubted her I'd never have dreamed of interfering. I truly believed that my actions would leave her free to be happy and fulfilled. I just wanted her to be happy. Do you understand that?'

'Mm . . . I'm getting there. But carry on. Tell me the rest.'

Ali did, and when she'd finished, she said, 'And to make matters a thousand times worse I know I have to tell Elliot.'

Daniel looked at her doubtfully. 'Don't do it, Babe. If you've got any sense you'll leave him well out of this.'

'But I can't. I have to tell him before Sarah does. And I know she'll do it. Oh, Daniel, if you'd seen her face, heard the terrible hardness in her voice. Believe me, she meant every word of what she threatened. Even if she doesn't, Elliot will want to know why the pair of us aren't speaking to one another and the lies will just hang over me. I don't think I could live with the dread of him discovering accidentally that I'd been to bed with Trevor.'

'But, Ali, you didn't go to bed with Trevor. In real terms, you've done absolutely nothing to betray Elliot.'

Ali chewed on her lip. 'But I've got to pretend that I did, for Sarah's sake.'

'Now you're losing me.'

'Look, if I share with Elliot what I really did, he'd make me tell Sarah and Trevor. Elliot is a man of true honour. He's loaded to the gunwales in scruples. He wouldn't let me get away with deceiving them over something as serious as this.'

'Then tell Sarah the truth.'

'If I do that she won't have what she thinks is adultery as a reason to leave Trevor with a free conscience.'

Daniel sighed. 'So, let me get this straight. If you stick with the lie about you and Trevor bonking the night away, you might lose Elliot, and I hate to say it but I think there's a high risk of that happening. But if you tell Elliot what really went on, you get to keep him but have to tell Sarah that Trevor's honour is still intact and she loses her legitimate bid for freedom. How am I doing?'

'On the nail.'

'So, what's the problem? You have to take the second course of action.'

Ali shook her head. 'No, I won't. If I do that Sarah will never leave Trevor and all this would have been for nothing.'

'From what you say it sounds as though she never will. If she's stayed with him this long because of her guilt, she's hardly going to jump ship now.'

'But the point is, she could if I keep quiet. She'd always believe that, at the end of the day, she could take a hike if she really needed to. The get-out clause would still be there for her.'

'If you go for that option, you realise that you're in danger of sacrificing your love for Elliot in favour of your friendship for Sarah?'

She nodded gloomily.

Daniel stared into Ali's miserable face and found himself remembering the radiant smile with which she had greeted him on Monday morning when she'd returned to the office after her holiday. How clearly her happiness had flowed out of her, and equally clear had been the cause of it: her reconciliation with Elliot. And now she was prepared to risk all that for the sake of a friend. He took one of her hands in his and squeezed it between his own. 'Ali, I won't let you do this. After what you and Elliot have been through, I won't let you risk a single moment's happiness with him.'

She slowly withdrew her hand. 'I have to do it, Daniel. I've known Sarah practically all my life and she's always been there for me. I owe her this.'

'And Elliot? What do you owe him?'

'Please,' she whispered, 'don't make it any more difficult for me.'

But Daniel wasn't prepared to be so easily swayed. 'Look,' he said, 'I'll do you a deal. I'll go along with this madness, but only for so long.'

'What kind of a deal?'

'You can tell Elliot all the lies you want in the vain hope that Sarah will kick Trevor into touch, but I'm putting a time limit on your deception with him. If Elliot hasn't forgiven you by the end of next month, you tell him what you really did.'

Ali frowned. 'I don't know, Daniel. That's not long. He'll need time to calm down. He'll need to let—'

'It's that or nothing, Ali. That's the deal. Take it or leave it.'

'If I don't agree?'

'Then I'll speak to him myself.'

She paused. 'Give me until the end of October.'

'Okay,' he said reluctantly, 'but no longer.'

They sat in silence, each with their own thoughts. Then,

raising her tearful eyes to his, Ali said, 'So have you forgiven me?'

He smiled. 'Of course I have. I've never been able to stay cross with you for more than two minutes.'

'That's because he worships the ground you walk on, Ali.'

They both turned to see Richard standing in the doorway. He came in with three mugs of tea and a packet of chocolate digestives tucked under his arm.

'How's the patient?' he asked.

'Much better, and I really don't deserve to be spoiled like this.'

'Ulterior motive, my little cuddle-muffin,' laughed Richard, settling himself beside her and offering her a biscuit, 'I'm sweetening you up for a three-in-a-bed romp later tonight.'

Ali laughed, but Daniel rolled his eyes and tutted. 'Barristers,' he said, 'they're full of shite. It comes of spending too much time in a horsehair wig.'

'Language, Danny boy. Now tell me where we're up to, *vis-à-vis* our very own Greek tragedy.'

Recognising that Richard was deliberately lightening the mood for Ali, Daniel filled him in on the details.

When he'd brought him up to date, Ali said, 'Do you think Elliot will forgive me?'

'Well, we have,' Richard said, 'so I don't see why he won't be able to.'

'Yes, but you both know the truth,' said Ali, 'which is—'

'Which is,' cut in Daniel, 'that our reckless Ali didn't actually sleep with the cerebrally challenged Trevor.'

'"Aye, and there's the rub," to quote that greatly troubled prince of Denmark.'

'The rub indeed,' echoed Daniel reaching out for Ali's hand again. He loved Ali dearly, but he couldn't pretend he wasn't appalled by what she'd done. Or perhaps it was the measure of his love for her that dictated the level of his shock. She'd always been one of the most headstrong, gutsy people he knew, but this was taking daredevil hotheadedness to unimaginably risky heights. This ill-conceived plot of hers was one hell of a quantum leap even for the most foolhardy of desperadoes. 'When's Elliot back from the States?' he asked.

Ali swallowed hard and stared out at the view to which Daniel and Richard woke up each morning. It was lovely, so throat-catchingly beautiful with the sun shining down on the green hills, picking out the ribbons of drystone walls and dots of recently shorn sheep. 'Tomorrow, early lunch-time,' she said, returning her gaze to Daniel. 'I'm meeting him at the airport.'

'Then you'd better stay the night with us,' said Richard, 'and no arguments.'

The following morning Ali said goodbye to Richard and Daniel and drove the half-hour journey to the airport. She would have liked to have their company but she knew that she had to get through the next few hours on her own. She paced the arrivals hall nervously, glancing up at the row of monitors, waiting for one to show that Elliot's plane had landed. So far his flight was twenty minutes late. She wondered whether he would be so jet-lagged that all he'd want to do would be sleep for the rest of the day.

No. That would never happen. She had never seen Elliot suffer from jet-lag. He could get off a twelve-hour flight, go straight into the office, work a high-pressure day, then go home and catch up with the backlog of his correspondence before going to bed at the normal time. It was so typical of him, always able to make time work for him.

It had been the same while he was in New York attending the world-wide partners' conference and meeting several key clients: he had still found space in his busy schedule to call her. Mostly it had been around midday when he phoned – breakfast time for him. He'd said how much he was missing her and that he had been thinking a lot about their future.

What future? she thought now, wretchedly.

An influx of weary-faced travellers pushing trolleys with luggage piled skyscraper high made her study the monitors again. Her stomach churned as she saw that Elliot's plane was on approach. A sudden desire to run seized her. She didn't want to confront Elliot. She didn't want to reveal her shame to him. She wanted only to run away and hide.

She hadn't expected to feel so ashamed – she might as well have had a fully fledged affair with Trevor – but what surprised her most was that she felt sorry for Trevor. Now, that was a blow.

What a hornet's nest she had unwittingly disturbed. Trevor wasn't Hannah's father. Why, oh, why hadn't Sarah told her? If only she had shared it with her at Oxford, the last eighteen years might have been so different. And who the hell was the real father? Would Sarah feel compelled to tell Trevor the truth? And what of Hannah? How would she react to being told that Trevor wasn't her biological father?

She looked again at the monitor, and her heart missed a beat. Elliot's plane had landed. He was probably a mere twenty minutes from coming through those doors expecting to see her smiling face.

As self-pitying as it sounded, she doubted that she'd ever smile again after today. On top of losing her dearest friend, Sarah, she was now in danger of losing Elliot.

For the second time.

Oh, if only she could turn back the clock. If only she hadn't been so sure of herself or so confident that she knew how Sarah would react. How arrogant she had been to think that Sarah would accept what she'd done in her customary undemonstrative way, and be gratefully relieved, seeing Ali as her liberator.

But Sarah hadn't acted as usual so she hadn't set in motion the pattern of events Ali had foreseen and relied upon. It was only to be expected that, if she could so wildly miscalculate Sarah's response, she was hoping for too much understanding from Elliot – after all, he would see only that she had slept with another man while his back was turned.

Another posse of travellers came through the automatic doors. Mostly they were casually dressed holidaymakers with expanded waistlines and depleted wallets after enjoying the excesses of a trip to the States. But then, amongst the jostle of brightly coloured shirts, baseball caps, shorts and carrier-bags of duty-free purchases, there was Elliot, impeccably dressed in a lightweight pale grey suit, his white shirt open at the neck. Her throat went dry and her stomach lurched as he caught sight of her. She watched him square his shoulders and move impatiently through the crowd of people in his way. When, at last, he was standing next to her, he lowered his suit-carrier and two other bags to the floor, and took her in his arms. He kissed her long and deeply and she responded willingly, thinking, as she gave herself up to the tenderness of his embrace, that this might be the last time he would ever want to kiss her.

'You look tired,' he remarked, when they were driving away from the airport complex.

'I've not been myself these past few days,' she said cryptically. *Oh, and wasn't that the truth!*

'You're okay, though, aren't you?'

She heard the loving concern in his voice and could have wept.

When they reached the windmill and drew up alongside Elliot's car, Ali knew that she could put off her confession no longer. She had to do it now. Each minute that passed was a cruel reminder that she was waiting powerlessly for when Sarah carried out her threat. She, Ali, had to be the one who told Elliot. She owed him that much.

She let them in, and while Elliot was upstairs in the bathroom, she poured them both a drink. When he returned, she suggested he sit down and handed him his glass. 'You're going to need it,' she said flatly. 'There's something I have to tell you.' She saw at once that his senses were keenly on the alert and already piecing together a worst-case scenario.

'It's not Sam, is it?' he asked.

'No, it's not Sam,' she said and, giving him no time to question her further, she blundered on. 'It's me. You won't like what I've got to say and . . . and I've a pretty good idea what the consequences will be.' She sounded so much calmer than she felt.

He sat motionless on the sofa, his watchful gaze following her as she prowled the sitting room and told him what had gone on in his absence. Not once did she look at him – she didn't dare risk seeing the shock in his eyes. Or the anger. Her unworthy tale of guilt and deceit complete, she went and stood outside on the balcony, needing to breathe in the warm afternoon air as though it might purify her. She waited for him to join her and have his say, but then she heard him moving inside. Scared that he might leave with nothing said, she turned to stop him, but then saw that he was coming towards her.

He rested his hands on the balcony rail and leaned against it. 'I don't understand you, Ali.' His voice was scarcely audible. He looked vulnerably tired, his face etched with lines of sadness, his eyes clouded and distant. 'We had it all resolved between us and then you do this. What am I supposed to think? That you could make love to another man and it wouldn't matter? That it wouldn't hurt me?'

'I told you, it meant nothing,' she said lamely. 'It was purely a means to an end.'

He banged his fist down on the rail, sending a shockwave of restrained rage along the wooden bar. His vulnerability was gone and in its place was full-frontal anger. 'And that's supposed to make me feel better? Shit, Ali, I've heard bastards like Gervase come out with comments as low and vile as that and despised them with every ounce of my being.'

'Do you despise me?'

He stared at her, his whole body strained and tense. 'Yes,' he said coldly.

She flinched beneath the candour of his reply. 'But could you forgive me?'

Again he stared at her. Oh, God, she thought, he's trying to make up his mind. She held her breath and waited for his reply.

Finally he spoke. 'No,' he said, with grim resolution. 'No, Ali, I don't think I can find it in my heart to forgive you.'

He turned and went back inside the mill. She went after him. 'But you said the night before you went to New York that you'd always love me. You said that.'

He collected his things together. 'Oh, I'll always love you, Ali. To my cost, I doubt that I'll ever stop loving you.'

'Then why are you leaving?'

'Because I have to. What you did was beneath contempt, and I can't stand to be near you.'

Ali didn't argue with him. There wasn't any point. Everything he'd said was true. She'd lost the will to fight, anyway. The old Ali would have battled on tenaciously to prove that she was right, that the end did indeed justify the means. But this shamed and self-loathing Ali knew she was beaten, that she had made her biggest ever mistake and would pay for it dearly.

She went back outside on to the balcony and waited for Elliot to go. She heard him clatter down the wooden staircase with clumsy urgency, then the sound of the front door shutting behind him. She watched him get into his car and, though he must have known that she was looking down at him, he didn't so much as glance up at her. With more speed than care, he shot off down the lane.

Never had she felt more alone.

Or more unworthy.

She thought of the bargain she had struck with Daniel and suddenly doubted that she was strong enough to stay the course.

Wiping the tears from her cheeks, she closed her eyes and willed both Sarah and Elliot to find a way to forgive her.

Chapter Forty-Six

Sarah was working on some hand-sewing at a trestle table in the shade of her favourite spot in the garden. It was behind the previous owners' ugly old pigeon-loft, which was where she kept her gardening tools and which she had cunningly disguised by training honeysuckle over it. After years of selective pruning and encouragement, it was a mass of sweet-scented flowers. In the bright afternoon sunshine it was humming with bumble-bees going about their business. From here she could sit unseen from the house but, more importantly, out of view from Trevor who was in his workshop.

She had stayed with Grace for most of yesterday, leaving her reluctantly in the evening when she knew that avoiding Trevor was no solution to the problem. He was waiting for her when she reached home, his face pinched with fear, his manner edgy and smothering. 'I thought you'd left me,' he said, trying clumsily to embrace her.

'No, Trevor,' she responded, pushing him away, and searching her memory for the last time he'd so much as touched her. 'I haven't left you.'

'Where've you been?'

The question had annoyed her. What did it matter where she'd spent the day? 'I was at Grace's,' she said.

'Why her?' he asked, following her closely as she went into the kitchen.

Again annoyance had flared within her. He'd been to bed with her oldest and dearest friend and he was querying the company *she* kept. 'Grace has become a good friend to me,' she said.

For a man in his current position, his next utterance was outrageous: it was the most blatant piece of blame-shifting she'd ever heard. 'Which is more than we can say of Ali,' he observed, with weighty malevolence.

'What are you trying to tell me, Trevor?'

Shoving his hands into the back pockets of his corduroys, he said, 'I know what I did was wrong, and I have to take my share of the responsibility, but . . . but it wasn't just . . .' His words petered out.

'Go on,' she said, knowing exactly what he was building up to and despising him for it.

'Ali has to take more responsibility for this than me,' he said, in a voice that suggested he was all but abdicating his own part in the sordid affair. 'It was she who got me drunk.'

Of course, in a sense Sarah knew that he was right. Ali would have planned the whole thing with such consummate skill that Trevor would have been little more than a stooge in the scene she had devised. He wouldn't have stood a chance. She let his comment go and asked him the question she'd been puzzling over since that morning: how had Ali enticed him to the mill? What possible pretext had she come up with?

His manner became more strident and assured. 'She duped me, Sarah. I can see that so clearly now. She phoned on Monday afternoon when you were out and said she wanted my help. I went to see her that evening as well. She told me that she wanted guidance in coming to know the Lord.'

'And you believed her?' she asked, her tone openly ridiculing him.

'Yes,' he'd answered stoically. 'She was very convincing.'

Sarah had wanted to laugh at Ali's brazenness. She'd done a perfect number on Trevor. She had known his weakness and gone for it. No other ruse would have worked so effectively. By appealing to his pick-up-thy-cross-and-follow-me stance she had ensnared him with his own naïve conceit. She could picture the scene, Ali throwing him all the right lines and him thinking of all the heavenly kudos and glory in store for him. Dear God, if this was somebody else's crisis, it would be hilarious.

But it was her crisis and it was far from funny.

As furious as she was with Ali, she was now equally cross with Trevor for having fallen prey to such an obvious ploy. Couldn't he have seen what was coming? He'd told her that Ali must have plied him with drink. Well, fair enough. But did she pinch his nose, hold his mouth open and force in the bottle? Of course not. He had allowed himself to get drunk. He wasn't a child who didn't know the consequences of over-indulging. He was a grown man who knew exactly what he was doing. Perhaps he'd played his part more willingly than he was prepared to admit. How flattered he must have been when Ali turned to him for help – him of all people! And he'd certainly dressed up for the occasion, hadn't he? Clean clothes, trimmed beard, the rarely touched bottle of eau-de-Cologne. Oh, yes, they were all signs that the silly man had gone to Ali's that night like a lamb to the slaughter. What a fool he'd been. What an idiot not even to consider why she would be interested in going to bed with him when she had Elliot. Did he not wonder why she would go for a spin in a Robin Reliant when she had a Ferrari in the garage?

Not that she was defending Ali, but it was scandalous that he should be attempting to heap all the blame on her. He should have been more of a man and seen what she was doing. And if he was so drunk, how on earth had he managed to perform? Or was he going to claim next that Ali had slipped him some Viagra?

Oh, yes, when it really came down to it, she was just as angry with Trevor as she was with Ali. But whereas she had been able to launch a verbal attack on Ali, she couldn't do the same with Trevor. Her own shameless, unprincipled behaviour prevented her from displaying so much as a flicker of what she really felt.

At her suggestion they'd slept in separate bedrooms last night.

'That's quite understandable,' he'd said, in deference to her moving her things into the spare room. 'We each need a period of private cleansing.'

She'd lain awake for hours going over so many of the things she and Grace had discussed during that exhausting, seemingly endless day. 'Sarah,' Grace had said, 'please listen very carefully to what I'm about to say and don't disregard it out of hand. Not only do I think that you've hidden behind your faith, but I believe very strongly that you've used it as a stick to beat yourself. Would I be right?'

She'd denied it at first, but Grace had said, 'If you hadn't used it as a weapon against yourself, you would have forgiven yourself a long time ago, and who knows what that might have led to? You know, there are too many people in this world who won't allow themselves to be happy or loved, and you're one of them, Sarah. You said earlier that you felt you didn't deserve to be forgiven, which means that you've stuck with Trevor as a penitence for your deception. There was no surer way to punish yourself, was there? Now that really is some stick.'

'You're wrong,' she'd replied, still afraid to admit the truth, even though she knew Grace would see right through her. 'I've stayed with Trevor because he was a good father to Hannah.'

'Yes, I'll grant you that that was always important to you. But what about now? Hannah's an adult, she's flying the nest, she's leaving you both. She doesn't need her mother and father in the same way she used to. How much longer do you think you have to go on paying the price?'

'Beneath all his silliness, Trevor is a good man. He doesn't deserve to have his marriage taken away from him.'

'I applaud your selflessness but wonder where it will take you.'

It was on that thought that she had fallen asleep, and for the first time that day her battered psyche was given a much-needed rest.

Now as she sat in the garden, with a much clearer head, Sarah knew what she had to do. Despite what Grace had said, she owed Trevor so much that she had no choice but to forgive him his part in Ali's madness and carry on as normal. The irony was that the door that Ali had thought she had opened she had actually locked and barred: she had added another ton of guilt to the load Sarah was already carrying.

And what of Trevor's guilt?

Rather cynically she suspected that he wouldn't find too much trouble in coming to terms with it – if he hadn't already by blaming Ali for the whole seedy episode. She imagined that he would have high expectations of their lives returning to normal soon. He might even think their relationship would be strengthened by the crisis.

But one relationship would not have the chance to recover so easily: her friendship with Ali.

When Ali had said, 'I did it for you,' it had seemed to Sarah the most monstrous invasion of her free will. If she wanted to be married to Trevor, it was her choice. What right did Ali think she had to rearrange the furniture of somebody else's marriage?

In her anger, she had accused Ali of pitying her and of wanting to control her, but what she hadn't expressed was the sudden realisation that she was jealous of Ali. She was jealous that she was the kind of person who could do anything she chose. No challenge was too great for her. In their second term at Oxford she had vowed to leave with a first, and she had done exactly that. She'd then gone on to be the career woman Sarah had dreamed of being, and had topped it by marrying a man who was as passionate about her as she was about him.

One only had to scratch the surface of their friendship to realise that, beneath the genuine love she had felt for Ali, she had always been a little envious of her success and happiness. Even when Isaac had died and her marriage had self-combusted, Ali had somehow found the courage and energy to battle on and start up her own business. She was an impressive, enterprising woman, however one viewed her.

When Sarah had first met Ali at school she had seen her as an equal and, in their different and complementing ways, they were a good match, Ali all argumentative debate and Sarah thoughtful and reserved. Although Ali was never bothered by the disparity in their backgrounds, Sarah was constantly aware that there was an element of poor relative about her when she was absorbed into the welcoming bosom of Ali's family. By the time they were at Oxford it bothered her less, but then she had ruined everything by getting pregnant. From then on she had never felt Ali's equal. From her unsatisfactory marriage, Sarah watched Ali go from strength to strength and secretly envied her. And, all the while, Ali told her what a mistake she'd made in marrying Trevor.

As though she needed telling!

Each time Ali made some negative comment Sarah defended Trevor. She had to. She had to convince herself, if not Ali, that she'd done the right thing, that she lived as fulfilling a life as her friend.

So when yesterday Ali had announced that she'd saved Sarah, she was as good as saying that Sarah was a fool and couldn't be trusted to make a right decision for herself. The implication had incensed Sarah, and had led to the appalling outburst in which she'd revealed that Trevor was not Hannah's natural father. She wondered now if she hadn't thrown the confession at Ali to show her that there was more to her than met the eye – 'Hey,' she was subconsciously boasting, 'I'm not the saint you've always made me out to be!'

For more than eighteen years she had kept that secret tucked away deep inside her. In those first few weeks of her pregnancy she had nearly confided in Ali but, knowing that her friend would overreact, she had held her tongue. Then, as the months and years had passed, the secret had been easier to keep. And Trevor was so kind and loving towards Hannah that, to all intents and purposes, he *was* her father.

Sarah put down her sewing and rubbed at her fingers, which were stiff and sore. She leaned back in her chair and saw that her little red-breasted friend Gomez was looking at her from the garden fence. She stared at his cocked head and thought how pleasant it would be to swap lives with him. Dodging predatory cats and surviving the cold months of winter would surely be easier than the chaos she had to cope with.

The sun had moved round now and, feeling the strength of its rays on her neck, she picked up her wide-brimmed straw hat from under her chair and set it on her head. She resumed her sewing, badly wanting to get it finished: Hannah was coming home tomorrow and there was a lot she wanted to get done between now and then. At the top of her list was a talk with Trevor.

She worked for a further hour, and when she'd applied the last of the tassels to the Cluny-style cushion covers she'd been making, she took them inside the house and up to the spare bedroom. She then went to find Trevor, to tell him that, as far as she was concerned, what he and Ali had done was in the past and that it was now a closed book. She was also going to tell him that, for the sake of their marriage, she had decided not to see Ali again.

By getting rid of such a dangerously divisive element, Sarah hoped her marriage would stand a better chance of surviving.

Chapter Forty-Seven

It was late October and the weather was damp and cold. Beneath a drab iron-grey sky, the village of Astley Hope looked even drearier than it usually did. A thin, vaporous mist of drizzle hung in the windless air and the trees along the lanes looked black now that they were almost leafless. It was a comfortless, gloomy scene.

Upstairs in the spare bedroom of Smithy Cottage, cold and tired, Sarah was bent over her sewing-machine. She'd been up since six working on this particular pair of curtains – the fabric was a heavy chenille and had been a devil to handle but with a bit of luck she'd be finished by tea-time and could make a start on the next order. She was busier than she'd ever been, but that was of her own choosing: like many other mothers in her situation, she had made the decision, since Hannah had gone away to college, to keep herself fully occupied. The extra money was coming in handy and she was putting regular amounts into a building-society account for Hannah's inevitable rainy days – being a student was costly and Sarah didn't want her daughter to go without.

While Sarah's 'little enterprise', as Trevor referred to it, was flourishing, his was not. He was spending less time in the workshop these days and more hours at the kitchen table applying himself to the Bible. He'd started a home-study course, which took up the majority of his mornings as he laboured over the finer points of the Apocalyptic Age.

Since the summer, life at Smithy Cottage had more or less resumed its normal rhythm, and, as Sarah had predicted,

Trevor had turned what might have been a personal humilia-
tion into a blessing. Though what she hadn't bargained on
was an all-encompassing attentiveness towards her, which she
hadn't encountered from him in years. It reminded her of the
brief spell at Oxford when he'd openly held her in such high
esteem. But, instead of reassuring her, it stifled her, set her
nerves jangling and made her want to withdraw further from
him.

In the immediate aftermath of his fall from grace – his own
coy euphemism for the act he'd committed – his principal
concern had been to keep it from Hannah and the group. He
wasn't easy in the knowledge that Sarah had confided in
Grace and, despite all her assurances that her elderly friend
would never betray a confidence, he saw her as a weak link in
the chain of concealment. 'But what if she mentioned it to
Callum and he let it slip to Jamie?' he said in bed one night.
'Jamie would be sure to tell Hannah.'

'Grace wouldn't do that.'

'But how can you be so certain?'

'Because I am.'

His desire to screw down the lid on what he'd done was the
only tangible sign that the episode held any repercussions for
him. Otherwise he acted as if he'd just had the luckiest of
escapes. Which he had. How he had squared matters so easily
with his own conscience, never mind with God, was a
mystery to Sarah, especially when she thought of all the years
she had scrubbed at the dirty tidemark of her own guilt.
'Repentance is the watchword,' he'd said to her, when he'd
been helping her with the washing-up. In a crazy way, she
almost admired him for having faith so strong that he had
allowed himself to be forgiven just like that.

On the other hand Grace had said, 'I don't believe a word
of it. Classic case of self-deception. He's blamed Ali and
washed his hands of the whole affair. When he's least
expecting it, the reality will come crashing down on him.'

It seemed a probable and credible interpretation of his

behaviour but Sarah was not inclined to suggest it to Trevor and warn him of the potential crisis hanging over him. Not when he was so full of the wonder of the Lord, and how their faith had held them together through the crisis. 'Imagine how Ali must be feeling,' he'd said. 'She has no one to turn to when the chips are down.' His smugness had maddened Sarah.

Though she had stuck fast to her resolution not to see or speak to Ali again, Ali had made one attempt to communicate with her. She had written Sarah a letter. It was short and to the point.

> *I'm so very sorry for what I have done. If it makes you feel any better I've lost everything that I held precious. I've lost your friendship – which is bad enough – and I've lost Elliot as well. How careless can a person be?*
> *With all my love, Ali*
> P.S. *I will respect your wishes and steer well clear of you . . . but if you change your mind, you know where I am.*
> P.P.S *Love to Hannah – please don't ever tell her what I did, I couldn't take the shame.*

She hadn't shown it to Trevor. She'd known that it had come from Ali's heart and didn't want it tainted by one of his derisive comments. She still had it, hidden in one of the drawers in her workroom where she stored her offcuts. It was also where she kept the gold chain Ali had given her.

Her anger had now subsided sufficiently for Sarah to feel how badly she missed her friend. It made her ineffably sad to know that Ali had lost her second chance of happiness with Elliot. She felt guilty too, convinced that it was as a result of her threat to tell Elliot what Ali had done that had caused their break-up. Again, it was a classic example of Ali's feisty and courageous personality to own up. Anybody else would have kept quiet, but not Ali. Sarah wished now that she had never made such a vindictive threat, especially as, within hours of having made it, she'd calmed down enough to know that she had no intention of carrying it out. But Ali hadn't known that and must have forced herself to tell Elliot before Sarah had a chance to.

There were times in the dead of night, with Trevor asleep at her side, when Sarah longed to ring Ali. But she couldn't bring herself to do it. Seeing Ali again would take them all back to square one and she wasn't prepared to do that. As long as Ali wasn't around to pass judgement on her marriage, it would tick over as well as any other half-hearted union. She had tried to explain this to Grace, but Grace had said, 'It won't work, Sarah. That's as helpful as a surgeon putting a sticking-plaster over a burst appendix.'

Ineffectual or not, it was the decision she had made, and it was the one by which she would stand firm.

The lack of Ali in their lives had come as a relief to Trevor, but not so to Hannah. 'I don't understand,' she'd said, a couple of weeks after she'd returned from France, with her ears pierced, her hair cut spiky short, and looking vastly more sophisticated than when she'd gone away – she was also revelling in the news that her run of straight As had got her into Oxford. 'If you've had a bust-up with Ali just apologise to one another and it'll be cool again.'

'It's not as simple as that,' Sarah had said, hoping that Hannah would drop the subject. But she hadn't.

'Well, no matter what's gone on between you two,' she asserted, 'she's still my godmother. Are you going to ban me from speaking to her?'

'When did I ever ban you from doing anything?' had been Sarah's reply.

Whether or not Hannah did get in touch with Ali, Sarah never knew, but on the day she and Trevor were due to take Hannah to Oxford for the start of the Michaelmas term, and whether it was a coincidence or not, a good-luck card arrived in the post for Hannah. It was from Ali and contained a cheque. Hannah didn't let on how much it was for, but the smile on her face indicated that it was a hefty and welcome amount.

With Trevor at the wheel of their recently serviced car, the journey to Oxford took them considerably longer than when Ali had driven Sarah there in the summer. It was a trip of mixed emotions. While Sarah was delighted that Hannah's A-level results had secured her place at Brasenose, the sadness of letting her go was too much for her, and at times she'd had to hide her face in her hanky. Worse was to come when they'd arrived at the college and had lugged all Hannah's worldly possessions up the twisting wooden staircase to her room and prepared to leave her to settle in on her own.

'Oh, Mum,' Hannah had said, when the hanky made its appearance again, 'I'll be fine, no worries. I'll ring you every week.'

'I'm not crying for you,' Sarah had mumbled. 'I'm crying for me.'

This had made Hannah laugh, which had made Sarah cry even more, knowing how much she would miss the sound of her daughter's happy, unaffected laughter.

But Hannah had been true to her word and had made her weekly phone calls. There'd been much talk of all the things she had thrown herself into. She'd joined the college rowing team, though she didn't know if she'd last the course as she wasn't as fit as some of the others; she'd gone along to the Oxford Union and added her voice to the debate on euthanasia; she'd been for a picnic in Christ Church Meadow; she'd had a visit from Jamie; and she'd busked in Cornmarket with another flute player who lived on the same staircase as her. 'It was brilliant, Mum,' she'd crowed. 'We made over twenty pounds in two hours. The tourists are such mugs.' There was even talk of the odd tutorial and lecture.

To all this reported activity, Trevor's only comment was, 'What about the Christian Union? Have you joined that?'

He hadn't liked her answer. 'No, but I've been along to a Buddhist meeting.'

That night, with his worst fears confirmed, Trevor had asked the Slipper Gang to pray for Hannah. 'Pray that she's not put on the path to temptation,' he'd told them.

Sarah's prayers were of a wholly more basic nature: 'Don't let her throw her opportunity away as I did.'

Being back in Brasenose for those few hours while they'd helped Hannah unpack had not been as awful as Sarah had dreaded. When she'd been there in the summer with Ali, she had balked at entering the college because it held so many poignant memories for her, mostly of deep regret. Being there with Hannah had been different: there had been no time to dwell on her self-reproach by wandering the immaculate quads, reliving long-ago days and reminding herself of blighted chances. No, there had been no time for such maudlin retrospection: she had been too preoccupied with letting go of her daughter.

It had seemed the bravest, most difficult thing she'd ever done.

Letting go was something Elliot was sorely tempted to do. Gervase was due to meet him in his office in ten minutes, and the way Elliot was feeling he would give anything to be able to take out his frustration on the man. He closed his eyes and, for a few unprofessional moments, saw himself giving the over-privileged bastard the pasting of his life. He was shoving him up against the wall and punching that supercilious expression right off his face. Then he was kicking him to the ground and –

His eyes snapped open, and he leaned back in his chair, let out his breath and unclenched his fists. No. That was going too far. It was all very well using Gervase as a mental punch-bag to chase away the maelstrom of his anger and frustration, but the scenes of blood and chipped bones were signs that things were getting out of hand. Perhaps it was time to put a stop to the supposedly therapeutic imagery.

He lowered his gaze to the file on his otherwise clear desk

and read through the points he'd made last night at home. When he'd finished, he checked his watch and saw that it was five past six. As usual Gervase was late. He drummed his fingers impatiently, swivelled restlessly in his chair, then got to his feet. He went and stood at the panoramic window that looked out across the city, where offices all over Manchester glimmered in the fading light. Rivulets of water sluiced down the glass and above him the lacklustre sky was throwing a literal wet blanket over the remains of the day. Nine floors down, neighbouring office workers, some with umbrellas but most without, were hurrying to escape the heavy downpour. It was a murderously depressing view. Not what he needed at all. He turned away and went back to his desk.

After weeks of not hearing from Rachel Vincent he'd received a wary call from her. They'd arranged to meet in Altrincham last Monday evening at the Cresta Court Hotel and, after some gentle persuasion, she had told him the real reasons why she had left so suddenly. None of what she said came as a surprise, but Elliot had needed to hear from her what he had thus far suspected. He'd tried to encourage her to put in writing what she'd just shared with him, but at first she'd refused, claiming that if word got out her career would hit the skids faster than a runaway train. She was now working for a rival firm of accountants where the same prehistoric breed of male ruled supreme. 'Let's face it, Elliot,' she'd said, 'we all know that the Gervases of this world get away with it because they think sexual harassment is a big joke.'

In the end he had convinced her that, if that attitude was ever to be eradicated, women like her had to speak out. 'I'll make you an offer,' he'd said. 'Help me get rid of Gervase and there'll be a job for you.'

'My old job?' she'd asked doubtfully.

'No, with Gervase gone there'll be some shuffling to do. I think it's time there was a female partner, don't you?'

Elliot returned his attention to the file on his desk and

looked at the letter Rachel had written for him, a copy of which was now on file in London with their senior personnel officer. It was two pages of carefully worded condemnatory evidence cataloguing Gervase's repeated harassment of some of the younger women in the office. According to Rachel's testimony, Gervase picked his victims with care, choosing those who were unmarried and, in particular, those who valued their career prospects highly enough that they wouldn't report him for fear of reprisals. He had approached Rachel several times, and on one occasion had turned up at her house late one evening with a bottle of wine suggesting that they cement their professional relationship in the time-honoured manner. When she'd refused and had sent him packing, he had begun to make things difficult in the office, culminating in the fiasco with Hayes and Clarke and the under-budgeted fee. It looked as if Gervase had deliberately agreed an unrealistically low fee with the client over the phone and had then let Rachel bill for the correct amount, which was a cool hundred thousand pounds over the apparent budget. He'd then informed her of what he'd done, saying that if she didn't resign he would claim that it was she who had miscalculated the incorrect fee. What's more, he would argue that it had been a deliberate act of sabotage after she'd made improper advances towards him – which, naturally, he had turned down – and of course, as everybody knows, hell has no fury like a woman scorned. As an act of petty revenge for not having had his way with her it stank, and given the clear account of events with which Rachel had provided him, Elliot was sure that Gervase would now have to own up to his appalling underhandedness.

Except there was always the worry that a slimy piece of work like Gervase could smooth-talk his way out of the deepest hole.

If all else failed, Elliot did have another trick up his sleeve for showing Gervase the door. He didn't want to have to resort to such tactics but, if need be, he would. As partner-in-charge it was down to him to safeguard those who worked for the firm, and with the likes of Gervase roaming the building it seemed that no woman was safe.

Fifteen minutes late, Gervase finally breezed in. He didn't even acknowledge that he'd kept Elliot waiting.

'So, what can I do for you?' he asked, when he had made himself at home in the chair opposite Elliot and automatically tried to take a surreptitious look at the file a few feet away from him. 'Some problem you need help with, is it?'

Biding his time, Elliot regarded him for a few seconds. 'Problem is the right word,' he said, his mask of indifference set firmly in place, 'and it would appear that you're *it*.'

'Not with you, old chap. Is it National Riddle Day or something?'

'Sexual harassment mean anything to you?'

Gervase laughed and crossed one of his fat thighs over the other. 'Sexual harassment,' he said loftily. 'I'll tell you what that is. It's a lot of frigid women making a song and dance about something that comes quite naturally to chaps like us.'

'In what way?'

'Sorry, don't quite understand you.'

'Perhaps you'd explain what it is that comes quite naturally to you.' Elliot's tone was neutral and deceptively mild, betraying nothing of the trap he had waiting for Gervase.

Gervase studied his face warily. 'Would you mind awfully getting to the point?'

'Very well. The point is, I've received an extremely serious complaint about your behaviour in the office towards some of our female personnel. Anything to say?'

'Sounds like a lot of cock and bull.'

'I should warn you that a copy of the letter of complaint is with Personnel in London and they'll be sending somebody up here next week to investigate the allegations. Anything to say now?'

Gervase uncrossed his legs and tossed his head defiantly. 'You're one hell of a piece of work, Anderson. How you must

449

be loving this. This hasn't got anything to do with sexual harassment, this is about *us*. This is nothing but a class issue.'

'I don't think that's what Rachel Vincent would call it.' Elliot shifted his gaze from Gervase's insolent face to the file at his fingertips.

Gervase's eyes narrowed malevolently and also came to rest on the file. 'And what's that bitch been saying?'

'Bitch,' repeated Elliot drily. 'That's an emotive word.'

'Then try this one. Bastard. Because that's what you are.'

'Thank you, I appreciate your directness.' Elliot's voice was as icy cool as the look in his eyes.

'I'll fight you over this,' Gervase lashed out, his arrogant swaggering now turning to bullying threats. 'You won't get rid of me that easily. It'll be her word against mine. You'll end up with egg on your face and an early-retirement package.'

'I doubt that very much. Divorce, as you well know, is an expensive occupation.'

Gervase stopped in his tracks. 'Divorce? What the hell are you driving at?'

'I wonder how Fiona will react when she realises that you'll be facing a charge of sexual harassment. It will hardly go with the image she's cultivated for herself down at the *Club*.' He drew out this last word contemptuously.

But Gervase laughed nastily. 'I think you'll find you're clutching at straws there. Fiona will be right behind me if she knows what's good for her.'

'But not, I suspect, if she hears about you and Dawn. Presumably a second divorce settlement would stretch even your *old* money.'

With a rush of fury, Gervase leaped to his feet. He rested his hands on the desk and leaned in towards Elliot, his breath betraying the extended lunch he'd enjoyed earlier, a lunch that had been topped off by several brandies and a cigar. 'You're nothing but a slippery bastard,' he snarled menacingly, 'a slippery bastard who can't hack it with anyone not from the same shitty working-class background that you crawled out of.'

Elliot didn't even flinch. He stared impassively into Gervase's odious face and said, 'At least I'm an honest slippery bastard.'

Gervase backed off. He went and stood by the window. 'So what's your problem exactly, Elliot? Jealous of somebody having more fun than you? Is that it? Are you so sexually tight-arsed since Ali dumped and divorced you that you can't stand the thought of anyone else getting lucky?'

At the reference to his private life, all Elliot could think was that this was the man responsible for keeping him on the phone the night Isaac had died. If Gervase hadn't made that call, Isaac might still be alive. The desire to smash his fist into the other man's slack jaw was so powerful that Elliot nearly allowed himself the pleasure of doing exactly that. He saw himself punch Gervase so hard that his flabby body flew back against the window and crashed through the glass to his certain death on the cold, wet pavement below.

This wildness of thought lasted no more than a second but it was long enough for Elliot to pull himself together and meet Gervase's words with composed authority. 'You can fight the allegations and make things extremely messy for all parties concerned, and I mean *all* parties, or you can own up to what you've done and resign.'

'That's a load of crap and you know it. Either way I lose.'

'Yes, I suppose you do. Now, if you don't mind, I have things to do.'

'Bugger you to hell and back, Anderson.' And giving Elliot the finger, Gervase stormed out of the office.

It was dark and raining even harder when Elliot, weary and dispirited, reached Timbersbrook. He parked his car and made a dash for the door. Sam was in the kitchen doing battle with a piece of pork tenderloin that he was knocking seven bells out of with a rolling-pin. 'I'm trying to show it exactly who's boss,' he said, with a grin, taking another well-aimed blow.

Without removing his raincoat, Elliot reached for the bottle of red wine that Sam had opened. He poured himself a glass and said, 'Not dissimilar from what I've been doing this afternoon.'

'Oh, aye? Been flexing those big honcho muscles of yours, have you?'

'Something like that.'

'Want to talk about it?'

'Not really.'

'Suit yourself. Supper won't be ready for at least another hour so if you want to be unsociable you've plenty of time for a swim.'

'Is that a subtle way of saying, "Get your miserable face out of here"?'

'Hey, back up, pal, I only meant that maybe you could do with a bit of unwinding, that's all.'

They stood staring at one another, for a few hostile seconds, until Elliot said, 'I'm sorry, Dad. You're right, a swim would probably do me good.'

Sam watched his son leave the kitchen and, once again, cursed the way things had turned out. Elliot and Ali had been so close to getting back together again when she had gone and pulled off the most unbelievably dumb stunt. When Elliot had come home that day after his trip to the States and explained what Ali had just told him, Sam hadn't known what to think of her. In the days that followed, he had found himself hating her for what she was putting Elliot through, but then gradually he calmed down and suggested to Elliot that maybe he'd been a bit hasty.

'Forget it,' Elliot had said. 'I never want to see her again. And please don't go behind my back and talk to her as if on my behalf. If nothing else, promise me that.'

Sam had so far stuck to his promise, but now he was

wondering if it wouldn't be okay for him to see Ali, at least to let her know that not all the Andersons had abandoned her. Though he knew that his son was suffering, he didn't want Ali miserable either.

Over supper in the kitchen that evening he decided to test the water with Elliot.

Resignedly, Elliot said, 'You must do what you think is right.'

'You wouldn't consider talking to her yourself, then?'

'Don't push it, Dad.'

'Look, son, she made a huge error of judgement—'

'Is that what you call it?'

'Hey, don't get clever with me. But have you tried looking at it from another angle?'

'Any suggestions?'

'Well, how about this? She betrayed you physically but not mentally . . . not in her heart?'

'Sorry, but that almost makes it worse. What she did was so calculating, so premeditated.'

'We both know what she did was wrong,' Sam said sadly, 'and by now she knows that herself, so what harm a tiny act of forgiveness, eh?'

Elliot pushed away his unfinished meal. 'I wouldn't describe it as a tiny act of forgiveness.'

'So she made a mistake and you're too big and grand these days to forgive her, is that it?'

'Of course I'm not.'

'Seems that way to me.'

'Well, good for you.'

In bed that night, Elliot lay in the darkness thinking about what his father had said. He knew that it made sense, but he just couldn't bring himself to forgive Ali. Perhaps he was being stubborn, but he couldn't get it out of his mind that while professing to love him she had taken Trevor to her bed. Hadn't she realised how he would feel? Hadn't it occurred to her that he loved her so all-consumingly, so possessively, that he would be crazy with jealousy and that it would make him question what she really felt for him?

But, as angry as he was, he knew he was still deeply in love with Ali. She was an integral part of his being and always would be. She was everything he wasn't. She was his spontaneity, his sense of fun. In short, she made him feel complete. Like a perfectly balanced piano concerto, she was the colourful, triumphant cadenza to his more lyrically haunting melody.

And haunted was what he felt.

Since that fateful day in August at the mill, he had been grieving again for what might have been. The nightmares about Isaac had returned, and his every waking moment when he couldn't focus his thoughts on work was filled with a dreadful desire to take out his mood on the first person who got in his way.

He'd always seen himself as a fair man, but he wondered now if he hadn't let his personal life interfere with his professional one. Certainly Gervase was doing the firm no favours by harassing the women at the office, but had it been right for Elliot to use his knowledge about him and Dawn as a lever to oust him?

More importantly, had he let his grief over Isaac get the better of him? Had he allowed it to cloud his judgement?

He turned over in a futile attempt to sleep, and as he listened to the rain beating against the window, Gervase's last words echoed inside his head: *Bugger you to hell and back, Anderson.*

Oh, no worries, Gervase, I'm already there.

'Airports,' grumbled Ali, as she crossed one leg over the other and tapped the air impatiently with her foot. 'I can't stand them. Little more than air-conditioned palaces of the damned.'

Daniel smiled and offered her a small glass dish of cashew

nuts. 'It could be worse,' he said. 'We could be travelling economy.'

She took a handful and gave the executive lounge of Brussels airport a withering glance. 'Well, praise and thanks to our lustrous and most generous clients for treating us to business class, then. A shame they couldn't have laid on a Lear jet for our own personal use.' She recrossed her legs and looked at her watch. 'How much longer are we going to be kept hanging around?'

'It won't be long now. Do you fancy another drink?'

She nodded and got quickly to her feet. 'I'll get them. It'll give me something to do.'

Daniel watched her go over to the hospitality bar, and couldn't help noticing how thin she was. Her appearance wasn't helped either by the severity of the black suit she was wearing: it drained her of all colour and drew attention to the unmistakable fact that she was washed out with tiredness. Dog-tired himself and knowing how little sleep Ali was surviving on, he had no idea how she was managing to stay upright, never mind work the hours she was currently putting in. When he was knackered, he invariably adopted what Richard described as his manner of a man past caring, but Ali was the opposite: she became edgy and uptight and even more restless and impatient than she normally was. And these past few months, since August, he had never known her so restless. She was always at the office before and after him – long after him mostly: some nights, as late as ten o'clock, he phoned the office to see if she was still there. But she'd grown wise to him tracking her movements and had stopped answering the phone. He'd tried other tactics to tear her away from her desk, inviting her for dinner with him and Richard or asking her to join them for an evening at the theatre. She was no fool, though, and had seen straight through him. 'I know what you're up to, Daniel, and as grateful as I am, there's no need, I'm fine. Really I am.'

But Daniel knew that she was far from fine. It was all very

well claiming that the long hours she was working were doing wonders for their business – she was acquiring dozens of new clients, some of them quite prestigious – but it couldn't go on. 'It keeps me from thinking of Elliot,' she told him, when he'd literally taken her by the shoulders one morning at the office and told her to slow down.

Covering his mouth with a hand, Daniel gave in to a jaw-stretching yawn; it really had been a long, exhausting day. They'd been on the early flight out to Brussels, sat through countless meetings, then when they'd arrived back at the airport they'd been told that a small fire on the runway earlier that afternoon had delayed all incoming and outgoing flights by at least three hours. They'd toyed with the idea of checking into a hotel for the night, but had decided against it, both preferring the thought of half a night's sleep in their own beds to a disturbed one in a hotel room. Though it was debatable how much sleep Ali would get wherever she was. Sleep, he guessed, was something of a luxury to her, these days.

He saw her turn away from the bar and start walking towards him. She looked so fragile and young, and yet . . . and yet she was far from fragile. Without doubt she was made of tougher stuff than he was. He couldn't begin to understand how he would have reacted if he had gone through half of what she had. For one thing he couldn't have deliberately denied himself Richard's love – not even for a friend like Ali. But, then, maybe that just proved the old gender theory that essentially men were selfish, that by ensuring they always put themselves first their survival was guaranteed. It was generally accepted that the female of the species was the one who always went the extra mile and made the greatest sacrifices – and in this instance, Ali was making one hell of a sacrifice.

She handed him his drink and sat down beside him. 'You look tired,' she remarked.

'That's rich coming from you.'

She stared at him over the rim of her glass. 'Meaning?'

He shrugged. 'Nothing you don't already know.'

She sat back in her chair. 'Don't start, Daniel. Not another lecture about me working too hard. It's not what I need to hear.'

He sipped his wine thoughtfully. 'You realise, don't you, that your time limit's nearly up?'

She looked away and rested her gaze on one of the flight information monitors.

'Ali, you've got a week and then I talk to Elliot. That was the agreement.'

'A few more weeks wouldn't hurt you,' she said softly, still not looking at him.

'Oh, yes, it would. It hurts me every day when I think of what you're doing to yourself.'

'Then don't think about it.'

He put down his glass and turned to face her. 'Look at me, Babe. Look me straight in the eye and tell me what you see.'

She scowled and pursed her lips. 'Stop being so melodramatic, Daniel. People are watching.'

She was right: a few yards away, a large, heavy-set man with a distinctive set of Belgian whiskers was staring at them over his copy of *Le Soir*. But Daniel didn't care, he took hold of Ali's chin and forced her to look at him. 'Tell me what you see.'

'I see *you*, Daniel. What else am I supposed to say?'

'So you don't see a friend who loves and cares for you? A friend who wants only the best for you.'

She turned her head away. 'And what you're blind to is that's exactly what I want for Sarah.'

Daniel ran a hand through his hair in frustration. 'Ali, you've given both Sarah and Elliot plenty of time to reconsider how they feel about you. If they were going to change their opinion of what you did, they would have done so by now.'

'But a few more weeks might make all the difference. Oh,

come on, Daniel, give me more time. I know Sarah, she never does anything without putting a lot of thought into it. Coming to terms with what I did is not something she's going to rush in to. Once she's accepted why I did what I did, she'll get in touch. I know she will.'

'Ali, you're stringing me along. Face it, this is never going to work. We're not just talking about Sarah making the decision to leave Trevor, are we? She's actually got to divorce him while still under the impression that adultery took place, isn't that right? And even if she went through with it, you'd never be able to tell her the truth because it would make a mockery of everything she believes in.'

'But none of that would matter if she realised why I did it and could forgive me.'

'And if she never could?'

For the first time in their conversation, Ali hesitated. Tears sprang into her dark eyes and she gulped down the rest of her drink. 'I can't let myself think that,' she said, 'any more than I can allow myself to think that Elliot won't forgive me.'

And that was the cornerstone of her hope, thought Daniel. Ali had to keep faith with the belief that Elliot loved her so much that, no matter what, he would forgive her. If that happened, Daniel suspected that Ali would have the strength to wait however long it took for Sarah also to absolve her. But he doubted it would happen. As long as Elliot believed Ali had been unfaithful to him he would continue to think the worst of her and consign her to this everlasting misery. He put his arm round her shoulder and drew her to him. 'False hope is a soul-destroying business, Babe,' he said gently. 'I know you want to believe that Elliot will do the decent thing, but wouldn't it be better to tell him the truth and hope that you can convince him that it's in Sarah's interests to keep her in ignorance of what really happened that night?'

'No, it's too big a risk,' she said vehemently. Then, in a more conciliatory tone, 'Please, Daniel, instead of making it worse for me, why don't you help me? Elliot holds the key to this mess. Time's a great healer and the more of it that passes, the greater chance there is of him eventually forgiving me, and of Sarah getting the future she deserves.'

'Would you like me to speak to Elliot?'

Ali lifted her head from Daniel's shoulder. Fleetingly she considered saying yes, but then thought better of it. What if Daniel found himself unable to keep from Elliot the true course of events that night at the mill?

Sensing her hesitation and the reason behind it, Daniel said, 'If I'd wanted to go behind your back, I would have done so before now – and don't think there haven't been days when I wasn't tempted. Of course, if you don't trust me—'

'It's not a matter of not trusting you,' she cut in, 'it's . . . Oh, it's no good, you just have to accept that this is between Elliot and me. Only the two of us can resolve it.'

'You mean you have to get through this on your own, don't you?'

'Yes. Yes I do.'

He reached for his drink and took a long swallow. 'You know, Babe, sometimes I wish you didn't feel the need to be so bloody strong.'

'I can't help it, it's the way I am.'

'It's not a crime admitting that you need help. Millions of us do it every day of our lives.'

'But I have asked you for help.'

He looked up into her face. 'No, you haven't. You've asked me to stand back and leave you to it.'

'But it's what I want. Why can't you see that?'

He let out a weary sigh of defeat. 'All right, I'll do as you say. But I'm striking another deal with you. You have to ease off work. You're practically killing yourself with the hours you're putting in. I want to see some colour in that sad little face of yours and a decent bit of weight on you. And, what's more, we'll review matters in December. Is that clear?'

Much later that night, when at last Ali reached home, she

pulled off her clothes and crawled into bed. She felt overwhelmingly exhausted and suddenly wished that she didn't feel the need, as Daniel had put it, always to be so bloody strong. She held Mr Squeezy against her chest and eventually fell asleep dreaming that it was Isaac in her arms.

Chapter Forty-Eight

October had given way to November, and the short wintry days of December had brought forth the annual feeding frenzy of retail madness. Sarah had taken a day off from sewing and had brought Grace to Chester to do her Christmas shopping, but she wasn't enjoying the outing as much as she had thought she would. Unusually for her she was exhausted and finding it difficult not to lose her temper when yet another pushchair rammed her from behind or a flailing elbow dug into her side.

A little after four o'clock, when the crowds were showing signs of thinning, Grace suggested that they stopped for a cup of tea and a mince-pie. 'My treat,' she said, as they found themselves a table in the nearest café in Bridge Street. The tinsel-decorated windows were steamed up and the waitresses were as short on politeness as they were on spare tables and festive pastries. With only a couple of cherry scones left in the display cabinet, Grace and Sarah's choice was soon made and despatched to them with a singular lack of care and attention.

'Christmas,' said Grace, as she mopped up the milk the waitress had slopped when the small inelegant metal jug had been thumped on to the table. 'That special time of goodwill to all men.'

'Poor woman, I bet she wishes she was at home, as I do.'

Grace stopped what she was doing. She put the milk-soaked napkin into the overflowing ashtray and said, 'I'm sorry, Sarah, I didn't realise this was proving such a trial for you. Would you rather we finished and went back to the car?'

Sarah immediately regretted what she'd said. 'Oh, Grace, I'm sorry, I could have put that better.'

'Indeed not. If that's how you feel then that's exactly what you should say. I'd much rather have the truth from you than a polite white lie. Do you want to tell me what's wrong, or shall I mind my own business?'

Sarah stirred her tea with a buckled spoon. 'You're giving me the choice?'

Grace smiled. 'Don't I always?'

'No. No, you don't. With your sweet-tongued questions you always get right to the heart of the matter and make me confront things that are best left untouched.'

'You know, Sarah, I've never had you down as a coward, but now I'm beginning to think that you are.'

'Are you trying to bait me?'

'A fish only rises to the bait when it's hungry.'

'Or if it's curious.'

Grace cut her scone in half and slowly buttered both pieces. When she'd finished, she said, 'And, of course, you're neither of those things, are you, Sarah?'

Sarah drank some tea and wished that Grace would keep quiet. She was tired of her questions. She was especially tired of fielding them.

Hungry.

Curious.

They were both obvious metaphors for something else. She found herself wishing that the seat opposite her was filled by Ali. At least Ali wouldn't mess around with stupid metaphors. She'd be straight in there with a direct question: 'So what's bugging you today?' she'd say. 'A touch of the holier-than-thou Trevors?'

'I'm annoying you, aren't I, Sarah?'

In response to Grace's perceptive question, Sarah put down her cup. 'Yes, I'm afraid you are.'

'Well, then, there's an honest answer if ever I heard one. But am I the cause of your annoyance or merely a symptom?'

Before Sarah could reply, the people at the table next to them gathered together their bags of shopping and made a noisy exit. After they'd gone, she said, 'I feel that you're the cause, but very probably you're not. I think I'm annoyed with everybody.'

'But I would imagine there's one person who's annoying you more than most.'

'Are you referring to Trevor?'

'Oh, no, Sarah, not Trevor. I was thinking of you.'

'Me?'

'When we start accusing everybody else of irritating us, it's often because we're the person with whom we're most irritated. How's that sticking-plaster going, by the way? Still missing Ali?'

'Yes. And if you want to know the truth I was just wishing that you were her.'

'So what would you give to have her friendship reinstated?'

'That's an unfair question.'

'Only because you consider it so.'

'But you know why I can't see her. I'm protecting my marriage . . . preserving it.'

Grace chewed thoughtfully on the last mouthful of her scone. She dusted the crumbs off her fingers and checked to see if there was any more tea in the pot. There wasn't. She replaced the lid and said, 'And is it working? Is your marriage in a better state than it was before you got rid of Ali's threat to it?'

'We're still together.'

'You mean you're still bound by guilt.'

'It's got us this far.'

For the first time in their friendship, Sarah heard Grace's normally gentle voice become heated with exasperation. 'Sarah,' she said, 'are you really prepared to make such an extreme sacrifice? Can you really go on living with somebody you don't love? And, quite apart from it not being fair to you, what about being fair to Trevor? Where, might I ask, is your integrity in all of this?'

'It's integrity that's keeping me with Trevor.'

'Nonsense. It's fear. You're wrapped in fearful thinking, terrified of making the decision you know you should have made a long time ago. You need to strip away the layers with which you've protected yourself and rediscover the real you, the genuine Sarah complete with all her self-esteem.'

Sarah picked up the buckled spoon from her saucer and tried to straighten it. Despite her efforts, it remained twisted. She dropped it back into the saucer. 'But I'm too afraid,' she said, in a low voice. 'Can't you see that?'

Grace's expression softened. 'I know,' she said gently, 'and I also know that once you've made that important decision you'll be able to start forgiving yourself, because until you do you're never going to be truly at peace.'

'That's all very well, but when I've added yet another sin to the pile I've already accumulated, where will that leave me?'

'Oh, Sarah, there you go again being so hard on yourself. Why can't you accept that you've done your best? Stop hanging your guilty conscience on the peg of your faith, which you've turned into nothing more valid than a lucky talisman. And moreover, you—'

Sarah opened her mouth to speak, but Grace was having none of it. She quelled Sarah's protestations with a raised hand and said, 'Please, let me finish. I'm well aware that for somebody such as yourself forgiveness seems well out of your grasp, but some day you'll see that you were mistaken.'

'Perhaps some transgressions are irredeemable.'

Grace smiled suddenly. 'Trying to do God's job for him, are you, Sarah? Deciding what He can and cannot take on?'

Sarah didn't respond. Nor did she return Grace's smile.

'You know,' said Grace kindly, 'sometimes in our lives we have to admit defeat and hand over the burden of what we're not able to resolve. Maybe this is one of those occasions.'

Still Sarah didn't say anything.

When Grace had paid their bill, they left the warm, fuggy atmosphere of the café and stepped into the biting cold wind of early evening. It was dark as they made their way to the multi-storey car park, and as they plodded along with their heavy bags, Sarah felt even more weighed down than she had earlier. She knew that everything Grace had just said she had said with the right motive. She knew also that it made sense. But knowing the right thing to do and actually carrying it out was another matter. She wasn't brave enough to tell Trevor the truth. How could she tell him that their marriage had been a sham? How could she turn on him so brutally? Especially since the summer when he'd been trying so hard to please her. So intense had been his displays of loyalty and devotion that she had grown worried he might regain an interest in sex. To her relief, and shame, her fears on this score remained unfounded.

Keeping herself busy through the autumn and winter had seemed the best way to stop her thoughts wandering beyond the boundaries of her situation, that and writing long, chatty letters to Hannah, as if by concocting a happy fairy-tale version of the daily goings-on at Smithy Cottage it might magically become a reality. But nothing she did could disguise the one terrible, inescapable truth: she was desperately lonely. With no Hannah around and no Ali at the other end of a phone, there was no one to take the edge off her misery. Grace had tried to cheer her, she knew, but Grace wasn't Hannah, and she certainly wasn't Ali. But, then, nobody could ever replace Ali. Any feelings of rancorous envy that Sarah had thought she harboured towards Ali had vanished, along with her anger. She knew now that, more than anything, she wanted Ali's friendship back. But it was impossible. It was either Ali or her marriage. The two just weren't compatible.

All multi-storey car parks are the same and the one in which Sarah had left her car was no exception: it was dark and smelly, and now that it was night, it felt intimidating.

They took the lift up to the third floor and when they stepped out, they were met by a loud shriek. It was the cry of a girl. They couldn't see anybody, but as they moved away from the lift and towards the car they heard a further scream, followed by the ominous sound of male laughter. It was coming from beyond the pay-and-display ticket machine. 'Stay here,' Sarah instructed Grace. She dumped her shopping and went to investigate. She found a group of scuffling lads, one of whom – the largest and indisputably the ugliest – had a gruesome selection of nuts and bolts skewered through the fleshier, more protruding of his features. He was holding a girl by the hair and had her on the ground with one of his huge booted feet resting on her stomach. Among the onlookers was another girl, standing by with a helpless look on her face. Without a thought for her own safety, Sarah waded in. 'What the hell do you think you're doing?' she shouted at the youth. 'What kind of pathetic bully are you? Let go of her. Didn't you hear me? I said let go.' Her voice echoed, shrill and fierce, in the cavernous dimly lit car park.

Amazingly he did as she said, but then, stepping over the girl, he came towards Sarah challengingly. He towered over her and pushed his face down into hers. His stale breath smelt as bad as he looked. 'Just a bit of fun.' He smirked. 'What's it to you?'

'Fun?' she repeated with disgust. 'You call that fun?' She turned her attention to the girl, who was now on her feet, standing next to the other girl. They made an identical pair with their shaggy permed hair, leather jackets and tiny skirts. Giggling nervously, they were exchanging glances with the lads, whom they obviously knew. They looked old enough to know better but young enough to have been at home enjoying an episode of *Grange Hill*. Sensing that the situation wasn't as menacing as she had thought at first, and that it was probably a case of horseplay that had got out of hand, Sarah let rip at the girl who'd been on the ground. 'And what were you thinking of, letting him treat you like that? Don't you have any self-respect? Don't you understand anything about being a woman? Now clear off and go home.'

Not waiting for a reply from the stunned group, she stalked away to where she'd left Grace.

'Goodness,' said Grace, when they were climbing into the car. 'What a tough little thing you are beneath that marshmallow exterior.'

Sarah drove towards the exit and didn't speak until they were out on the streets, heading for the Nantwich road. 'I hope I didn't embarrass you back there,' she said.

'Embarrass me? I'm immensely proud of you. Not everyone would have had the courage to take on such a grotesque-looking Goliath.'

'I couldn't help myself. I can't stand people who take advantage of others.'

'Or girls who get themselves into a situation they don't know how to get out of?'

'Them too. Just what did she think she was doing? Didn't either of those girls realise the danger they were putting themselves in?'

'They looked very young.'

'That's hardly an excuse to behave so irresponsibly.'

They drove the rest of the journey in silence. Sarah dropped Grace off, then continued the hundred yards or so to Smithy Cottage. The lights were on in the house and she carried the bags of shopping up to the spare bedroom then dumped them on the bed. When she came downstairs Trevor was waiting for her. There wasn't a trace of sawdust in his hair or on his clothes so she assumed that he'd been hard at the Apocalyptic Age again. Angry, she thought of yet another day's potential earnings lost in the name of God.

'Sarah,' he said, 'I've invited the group round tonight. Any chance of you rustling up a cake or something?'

'Why?'

'Because everyone enjoys your cakes.'

She frowned. 'I didn't mean that. I meant why have you

467

invited the group round? It's not the usual night to get together.'

'Ah,' he said awkwardly. Was it her imagination or did he look shifty? 'Um ... it's a special evening,' he went on, 'something I feel called to do. It might set the ball rolling for other evenings like it. I truly think it will be a good thing for the group. Very liberating.'

Uninterested in this latest hare-brained scheme that Trevor felt 'called' to pursue, she sighed a weary sigh of resignation and went to the freezer for some mince-pies she'd made at the weekend. Well, whatever he had planned, it really didn't matter. Nothing he ever did had any direct bearing on her.

An hour and a half later, she found she couldn't have been more wrong.

They'd messed about in the hall with their shoes and slippers, they'd had their quiet time, and now they were chomping their mince-pies and sipping their coffee, waiting patiently for their very own oracle to speak to them.

Sarah was waiting too. There was something different about Trevor this evening, an air of mystery in which he was clearly revelling. He'd put himself centre-stage and was loving every minute of it. 'Why are we here, Trevor?' Dave had asked earlier, to which Trevor had replied enigmatically, 'All shall shortly be revealed.'

Shirley had been just as curious as Dave, but had tried to conceal it with a reference to her back. 'It won't take long, will it, Trevor? Only my back isn't good tonight and won't cope with sitting in the same position for too long.'

'Right, then,' said Trevor, putting his empty plate under his chair. 'I know you're probably all wondering why I've arranged this meeting, and I thank you for turning out in the cold, but by the time you leave here I sincerely hope that you'll be warmed by, and armed with, the essence of what fired those early Christians – the spirit of true faith, which is to love and to forgive.'

Suddenly he got to his feet, for what Sarah could only think was extra effect – and it might have worked had not a piece of pastry been stuck in his beard – and said, 'I want to tell you a true story of a husband and a wife, a husband who committed an act of adultery and a godly wife who committed an act of faith and forgiveness.'

Sarah froze.

He wouldn't dare.

Surely not.

But Trevor did dare, and he held the room spellbound for the next twenty minutes as he told them of his personal encounter with the devil. 'It was my appointed time of temptation,' he told them, 'and, being the poor wretch I am, I failed the test. I was offered sin on a platter and I feasted on it. But the point I want to make is that if a mature Christian such as myself can succumb to the charm of the devil then what hope for others not so secure in their walk with Christ?' He gave them no opportunity to respond, ignored Sarah's pleas for him to stop, but blundered on enthusiastically with his testimony, aligning himself with Old Testament heroes such as Samson, Gideon, Barak and Moses, at the same time dressing the whole thing up in childish Sunday-school language: Ali was Satan's messenger, he the innocent lamb, Sarah the water of forgiveness.

Sarah closed her eyes, realising that this was the future. Now that Trevor had revealed his sin of sins to a real audience there would be no stopping him. He would become a poor man's version of one of those cringe-making American TV evangelists spurting tears at the drop of a confession. She could even imagine him being a guest speaker at Christian men's breakfast meetings up and down the country baring his testimonial all.

He would be insufferable.

And he would make her life insufferable. He would hold her up as a model Christian wife – when she was anything but.

469

Her blood ran cold and, with a chilling calm, she knew that she had to stop him. She had to make him see that this madness could not go on. But, more importantly, she knew that she could not carry on living the lie.

She no longer felt sorry for Trevor. She no longer wanted to protect him from the truth. In fact, it was time he faced the truth. She hoped his faith was real enough to carry him through the days ahead. 'Trevor,' she said, just as he was drawing breath to continue his tale of good versus bad, 'I think you should sit down.'

'In a minute, Sarah, I haven't finished. I was just –'

'Trevor, sit down!' She spoke with the same anger that had earlier compelled her to take on the thug in the car park.

He did as she said and everyone looked at her expectantly, their amazed curiosity shining in their eyes. 'Trevor,' she began, 'I really can't allow you to cast me in the role of sainted wife who finds it in her heart to forgive her husband his momentary loss of control.'

'But that's just your natural Christian modesty preventing you from –'

'Be quiet, and don't open your mouth until I've finished. And, for goodness sake, get the crumbs out of your beard!'

He goggled at her, as did everybody else.

'There's something very important that you should know, Trevor,' she began again. 'In a sense I do forgive you for what happened with Ali because . . . because you were set up. You were used. Without my knowledge, Ali planned the whole thing. She lured you into her bed so that on the basis of you committing an act of adultery it would give me the necessary grounds, and courage I might say, to leave you. A pity, really, that she went to all that trouble, because when it comes down to it, I'm leaving you of my own accord. I'm very sorry, Trevor, but I've never been the wife you deserved. I only hope that one day you can forgive me.'

The silence that followed couldn't have been greater. Sarah got to her feet and swept out of the room. All she was conscious of, as she headed for the hall and the unknown world beyond, was Trevor's open-mouthed expression of horrified disbelief and the rustle of paper as somebody – probably Elaine – flicked through their Bible for a helpful piece of scripture.

My God, I've done it, she thought, grabbing her coat and bag and shutting the door after her. I've finally done it.

The cold night air stung her cheeks as she pulled on her coat and considered what to do next. Grand exits were all very well, but they only worked if you had somewhere to go.

Grace was her answer.

She hurried along the lane in the light of the glowing street-lamps, hoping that Grace would be in.

She was. Callum was there too.

Seeing the look of agitation on Sarah's face, Grace said, 'Callum, would you mind giving me a few minutes alone with Sarah? Perhaps you'd like to pour us a drink.'

When he'd disappeared, Sarah told Grace what she'd just done.

'And how do you feel?' asked Grace, when she had told her everything, including Trevor's ghastly testimony.

'Slightly euphoric.'

'Enjoy it while you can, it'll soon pass. If I know you, you'll be wallowing in guilt within the hour.'

'I'm not sure that I will. But, oh, my goodness, Grace, what do you suppose made Trevor do such a daft thing? And after weeks of insisting on absolute secrecy.'

'For some the need to confess outweighs the consequences. In Trevor's case, it's possible that the need to be absolved had to be on a grand scale. Given his rather self-seeking personality, what better way to shake off his guilt than to make a public confession and receive a public act of forgiveness?'

'But supposing the group doesn't forgive him?'

Grace smiled. 'After the treatment you've just dished out?'

Sarah allowed herself a small smile. 'Was it very brutal of me, do you think?'

'A little. But don't go fretting over it. I presume you didn't tell him about Hannah.'

Sarah shook her head vehemently. 'No. And I never will. He should be allowed to keep that much of our marriage.'

'Only time will tell on that score. Now, is it all right if Callum brings us those drinks?'

'Oh, please, I feel I could do with one. By the way, I don't mind him knowing. I'm sure he would be discreet.'

Grace laughed. 'If there's one thing you can rely upon with my son the solicitor it's discretion.' She went out to the kitchen where Callum had gone, to return with him and a tray of glasses.

'Sherry,' said Callum, passing a glass to Sarah. 'My mother's answer to any emergency. I'm sorry about you and Trevor. Speaking as one who's been there, done it and got the battle scars, are you sure that what you're doing is the answer?'

'It's not a spur-of-the-moment decision,' Sarah said, realising that she'd taken the best part of two decades to reach it.

'Sorry,' he said, 'none of my business, I'll keep quiet and let you two do all the talking.'

'That would be a first,' said Grace, good-humouredly. She smiled at her son, then returned her attention to Sarah. 'I'd offer you a bed for the night, Sarah, but I really think you should put a little more distance between you and Trevor. Why don't you go and see Ali?'

'Do you think she'd have me?'

'Now, what do you really think? Go into the hall and ring her. Go on, do it now. Before the rush of adrenalin fades.'

A few minutes later Sarah came back into the sitting room.

'That was quick,' Grace said. 'Wasn't she in?'

'Oh, she was there all right, I just didn't tell her why I was coming to see her. Do you mind if I ring for a taxi?'

'I mind very much, given that Callum has just offered to drive you.'

Sarah turned to Callum. 'I couldn't possibly expect you to do that. It's so far and completely out of your way.'

'Sarah, there's no point in arguing with my mother. Or me, for that matter. Have your drink and then we'll go.'

Once again Sarah found herself standing on a cold doorstep. She kissed Grace's soft cheek and said, 'Thank you for all your help, and I'm sorry I was such terrible company earlier today.'

'I'll forgive you. Now remember, when the euphoria wears off, think of what an empowering day you've had. Not only did you stand up to a bully twice your size but you took the first all-important step towards creating a new life for yourself.'

'Come on, ladies,' said Callum, his breath freezing in the cold night air. 'It's too bloody nippy out here for protracted farewells.' He kissed his mother goodbye, then opened the passenger door of his Mercedes estate for Sarah. A hard frost had settled on the windscreen but, within seconds of switching on the engine, the thin layer of sparkling crystals began to melt.

For the first few minutes of the journey neither of them spoke, until Callum said, 'Has my mother ever mentioned my divorce to you?'

Surprised, Sarah said, 'No. Should she have?'

'No. But usually people who don't know the circumstances wonder why I ended up with custody of Jamie when it's more usual for the mother to keep the children.'

Sarah admitted that this had crossed her mind.

'I fought to the death for Jamie and I'd do it again, if the need arose.'

'Was she such a terrible wife and mother?'

'Yes,' he said simply. 'She had a major problem with monogamy and when Jamie was six years old she wanted to take him to live in Acapulco with her then current lover. I came home from work one day to find the house empty and a note saying what she was doing. I intercepted her at the airport and literally snatched Jamie out of her arms. The bloodiest of custody battles then ensued. I was scared to leave him for a moment in case she took him.'

'How awful. Where is she now?'

'No idea. The trail went cold years ago. Do you intend to divorce Trevor?'

Again his question took her by surprise, as did his abrupt tone. 'I don't know, I haven't thought that far. I just know I can't live with him any more.'

'Think very hard about it, Sarah. Divorce can be a hellish business.'

'So can marriage.'

He smiled. 'Okay, we've covered the divorce issue. Tell me who this bully was that you stood up to today. Or was that a thinly veiled reference on my mother's part to Trevor?'

'Trevor may be many things but he's not an out-and-out bully.' She told him about the incident in the car park.

'No wonder my mother wanted you to remind yourself of your hidden depths. What made you wade in like that?'

'It's a long story. We need to turn right here, by the way. Look, there's Ali's windmill, you can see its lights.'

If ever Sarah needed a symbol of light at the end of the tunnel, this was it.

Chapter Forty-Nine

Sarah insisted that Callum drop her off at the top of the lane to the mill, saying that she wanted to walk the remaining few hundred yards.

'Are you sure?' he asked. 'It's very dark, and it's probably icy. My mother would never forgive me if we heard on the news about a frozen body that was found in a ditch and it turned out to be you.'

'I'll be fine. And thank you for the lift, it was very kind of you.'

'No problem. Take care, won't you? And if you need a solicitor, you know where to find me.' He handed her a business card from his wallet. 'No doubt I'll see you sometime when Hannah and Jamie are back from college for Christmas. Good luck.'

Sarah watched him drive away. Then, with the freezing night air cutting through her overcoat, she began the short walk. She soon realised that Callum had been right. She could hardly see where she was going and in places the ground was treacherous with patches of ice. Once or twice she slipped and nearly went over, but undaunted she pressed on. Just as she'd reached the safety of the illuminated area of the mill and was able to walk more steadily, the door opened and a burst of light spilled out in front of her. In the centre of it was Ali.

Suddenly doubt gripped Sarah. Supposing Ali was distant? What if she had hurt her friend irrevocably by refusing to see her?

'Is that you, Sarah?'

'Yes,' she called, 'it's me.' She hastened her step and came face to face with Ali. They looked at one another, then everything was a mad blur of tears, hugs and incoherent apologies.

When they finally drew apart, Ali said, 'Come on in, you're about frozen to death.' She pulled Sarah inside, banged the door shut, took her coat and hung it up. 'Let's get you upstairs and into the warm.'

They sat on the rug in front of the fire, their faces flushed from the heat of the burning logs as well as from their tears.

'I couldn't believe it when I heard your voice on the phone,' said Ali. 'You don't know how much I've missed you.'

'Oh, yes, I do,' Sarah said. 'It's been the same for me. Not a day's gone by when I haven't wanted to talk to you and find out how you were. I'm sorry for hurting you in the way I did. I said some terrible things to you.'

Never had Ali felt so humbled. She had thought she'd never see Sarah again, that she had lost her friend for ever. Losing Sarah's friendship had been almost as bad as losing Isaac. Never had she felt so isolated. Although she was quite used to living alone, the solitariness she'd experienced of late had become a painful ordeal: each evening when she came home from the office she was stifled by it. The mill had felt much too large for her, and in bed at night the wind kept her awake as it murmured a mournful lament. It was only when she was at work with Daniel that the monotony of her sadness was broken. She didn't know what she would have done without him to lift her spirits. When she could no longer keep it from them, her parents had tried to help too, but because she'd lied about the true nature of her split from Elliot – she'd said that they had had a row – she'd found their love and support only added to her shame. Even Alastair had called her from Singapore. 'Hey, little sis, what the hell's going on? Mum and Dad have just spoken to me. Is there really no hope?' So touched was she by her brother's unexpected sympathy that she'd disintegrated into a flood of tears – unprecedented in their relationship, which was bonded with super-strength, I'm-tougher-than-you sibling rivalry. He'd even offered to speak to Elliot: 'Do you think he'd listen to me?' She'd mumbled something about it being hopeless and that he wasn't to flaunt his huge wealth on another overseas call.

And, irony of ironies, she hadn't been able to get out of her head that wretched piece of homework on Romans 7:15–25 that Trevor had set her, about the choice between right and wrong and how we always get it wrong. Well, she'd certainly done that.

But for all the harm Ali had caused, here was Sarah, the injured party, offering her the olive branch of peace. She chewed her thumbnail and said, 'You had every right to say what you did. It's me who has to apologise.'

Sarah smiled. 'I can't condone what you did, Ali, and I know you thought you were helping me, but I've come here tonight to tell you that I've left Trevor, not because of anything you did but because I finally found the courage to face the consequences of my own actions.'

Ali was stunned. 'You've really left him? Left him – as in *left* him?'

'Yes, a couple of hours ago.'

'But you seem so calm.'

'That's the weird thing, I am calm.'

'I always knew there was more to you than met the eye. How on earth did Trevor take it?'

'I'm not sure. I didn't give him much chance to respond.'

Ali frowned. 'What – you've written him a letter?'

Sarah told her about Trevor baring his soul to the group and her reaction to it. 'Do you think it was very unfair of me to finish our marriage in so humiliating a fashion for him?'

'I don't know whether unfair is the right word, but it would have certainly got the message home to him. I take my hat off to you, girl. When you come out fighting, you don't take any hostages, do you?'

'I didn't stop to think. I was acting on an impulse far

stronger than anything I've ever experienced before. I just knew I had to put a stop to the madness.'

'Well, I'll tell you who'd be proud of you, Sarah the Impudent.'

They both laughed.

'But you realise you've turned Trevor into the biggest martyr this side of Joan of Arc, don't you?' said Ali. 'The Slipper Gang will be all over him, ready to have him canonised. You'll have done yourself no favours in their eyes either and you'll be the talk of Astley Hope for years to come.'

'I know and it's awful of me but I don't care.'

Ali gave her a hug. 'I want to say how proud I am of you and that I know you've done the right thing, but somehow it doesn't seem appropriate. From my own experience the end of a marriage is nothing to celebrate.'

'But we could celebrate the renewal of our friendship, couldn't we?'

'Good idea. No, don't move, stay here and throw another log on the fire while I do the honours.' She came back shortly with a bottle of red wine and two glasses. She filled them both and passed one to Sarah. 'To us,' she said, clinking her glass against Sarah's.

'And to the future, whatever it may be,' added Sarah.

'As to your immediate future,' Ali said, after she'd taken a reflective sip of her wine, 'you'll stay here with me, won't you?'

Sarah smiled. 'I was rather banking on that.'

Ali smiled too. 'So was I. I could do with the company.'

Sarah contemplated her friend. She was saddened at the change in Ali's appearance. She was pale and drawn, with dark smudgy shadows beneath her eyes. She was also much too thin. 'Is this the bit when I ask after Elliot?' she enquired gently.

Ali turned away and stared into the flickering flames of the fire, the soft light accentuating the shadows in her face. 'I haven't seen him since August,' she said. 'Losing him a second time feels immeasurably worse than before. It's reopened all the wounds that had begun to heal. For that brief spell in the summer the edge was taken off my grief for Isaac. It was as though we each had a part of Isaac within us, and when we were together we created a more complete memory of him. It made his death more bearable. But all that's gone now.'

'Oh, Ali, I'm so sorry.'

'Don't be, it was entirely of my own making. I made the same mistake with Elliot as I did with you. I took his forgiveness for granted. I thought that because he loved me he'd forgive me. So far I've been proved wrong.'

'Perhaps in time he will, when he –' But Sarah's words were cut short as Ali whipped round to face her. 'What is it, Ali?' she asked, alarmed.

'I've just realised something. But before I say anything, explain to me, hand on heart, and be prepared to swear on whatever is most precious to you, the bottom-line reason why you've left Trevor.'

Sarah looked confused. 'I don't understand.'

'Please, Sarah, it's important. Was it anything to do with my going to bed with him?'

Seeing the wild look of agitation in Ali's fiercely determined eyes, Sarah said, 'No, it wasn't. But I told you that a few minutes ago.'

'So what did it, then? What made you see reason at last?'

'I finally confronted the past, I suppose. Not only that, I realised that nothing I did was ever going to make my marriage right. I also knew I no longer felt sorry for Trevor, that I didn't feel beholden to him. Or beholden to a faith that I'd hidden behind – but that's another story, which I shan't bore you –'

'So adultery doesn't come into it?'

Sarah shook her head.

479

'You're positive? Absolutely positive? One hundred per cent sure?'

'Ali, what are you getting at?'

Ali took a gulp of her wine. 'There's something you have to know. I didn't do the unthinkable with Trevor. Trevor and I never had sex. It didn't happen.'

'But you said you did. And Trevor said that he and you—'

'I lied.'

'You lied?'

'Yes! Oh, heaven help me, but I lied. I'm not proud of what I did, you have to believe me, but I didn't seduce him as he thinks I did. It's worse than that. Much worse. I spiked his drink so that he'd crash out and wake up with only patchy recollections of the night before. That way I could make him believe anything I wanted. I undressed him and put him in my bed and the rest . . . the rest was pure fabrication on my part. Oh, Sarah, I'm so sorry. I should never have done it.'

Sarah took a few minutes to digest this dramatic turn-around in Ali's story. Her first and rather uncharitable thought was for Trevor and where it left him with his testimonial tale of the platter of temptation on which he thought he'd feasted. Her second thought was to be given more information.

'But, Ali, why didn't you tell me the truth sooner?'

'Because I wanted to keep the door open for you. If I'd withdrawn the lie it would have all been for nothing.'

'But why didn't you tell Elliot the truth? You could have told him what you'd really done.'

'No, I couldn't. He would have made me admit to you that Trevor was no guiltier of adultery than I was. You know what a straight, honest soul he is.'

Sarah was horrified at the sacrifice her friend had made for her. 'But, Ali, you lost Elliot in the process.'

'I very nearly lost you both.'

'Oh, Ali, you've got to speak to Elliot. You have to tell him you didn't go to bed with Trevor.'

But suddenly all Ali's earlier relief at knowing that the agony of her deception was over was replaced with doubt and melancholy. She returned her gaze to the flames. 'Perhaps it would do no good,' she said. 'He might think I was lying in the hope of winning him back.'

'Then I'll talk to him.'

'Maybe that wouldn't work either. He'd say I'd put you up to it.'

'But there has to be a way.'

'I'm not sure there is. If Elliot wanted to think well of me, he would have by now. I have to be realistic, I've turned myself into a classic wolf-crier. I'm a convicted liar whom no one will believe. It's probably only what I deserve.'

Seeing that Ali was close to tears again, Sarah put her arm round her. 'Hey there, you're not the only one who's a liar. What about my monumental piece of deceit with Trevor over Hannah? You can't steal my thunder on that.'

'Have you told him about it?'

'No.'

Ali sniffed and took another sip of wine. 'You know, I've given a lot of thought to Hannah's father, and I think I've figured out who he is.'

'You have?'

'Yes. It's my brother Alastair, isn't it?'

Sarah smiled and then she laughed. 'How did you reach that conclusion?'

'Quite easily, really. He was always trailing after you whenever you came down to Sanderling and I know you had a soft spot for him because you were always defending him. What's more, he came to see us in Oxford occasionally. But what I can't get my head round is why you didn't tell him you were pregnant. He would have married you, I know he would.'

'He wouldn't have had any choice, would he? You'd have been there with your shotgun.'

Ali smiled. 'So why didn't you tell him you were carrying his child?'

'For the simple fact that I wasn't. He isn't Hannah's father.'

'But he must be.'

'Ali, I think I know who I have and have not slept with.'

'But if it wasn't Alastair, who was it? I don't recall there being any other men on the scene at Oxford.'

Sarah took a hesitant sip on her wine. She lowered the glass and said, 'He was a tutor and I should have known better.'

'A tutor! Which one? Oh, my God, not Mr Creepy-I'm-so-Sleazy, the one in cowboy boots who chain-smoked, wore his jeans too tight and tried it on with all the first-years? Sarah, it wasn't?'

'Not even close.'

'Thank goodness for that. Who, then?'

'His name was John and he was on a sabbatical from Yale.'

Ali stared at her open-mouthed. 'Not John-John-Show-Us-Your—'

'The very one.'

'But he was a serial womaniser, Sarah. How on earth did you fall for him?'

'I didn't.'

'You just went with him for the sex?'

Sarah's face coloured. 'No!'

'What then?'

'He – he took advantage of me?'

Ali looked horrified. 'You're not saying he raped you, are you?'

Sarah thought of the two girls in the car park that afternoon and of what they'd got themselves into. 'I got myself into a situation with him. Then, when I changed my mind, he . . .'

'He wouldn't let you, is that it?'

'He was very persuasive and I was very naïve.'

'Sarah, the man was a complete bastard. Why didn't you tell me?'

'I was ashamed of myself for being so stupid and gullible, and I knew that you'd kick up a huge fuss and have the college authorities baying for his blood.'

'Too right I would have. It was lucky for him I never found out. Didn't he leave suddenly that year?'

'Yes. Shortly after I'd slept with him he had to go back to the States – his father was dying and he was needed at home. So, you see, there wasn't any point in telling him I was pregnant.'

'Oh, Sarah, what a dreadful mess. Will you ever tell Hannah?'

'I don't know. But if I do, that day's a long way off.'

'And what if she wanted to track down her real father? How would you feel about that?'

'A bridge to be crossed, if and when. But for now I think I have enough to contend with, don't you?'

At work the following morning, Ali received an unexpected phone call from Sam. She was just telling Daniel about last night when Margaret put the call through.

'How are you fixed for lunch?' he asked, without preamble.

'When were you thinking?' answered Ali. It was the first contact she'd had with Sam since the summer and, knowing what he must be thinking of her, she felt horribly embarrassed to be talking to him.

'Today,' he said.

She checked her diary. 'Okay,' she agreed. 'What time?'

'One o'clock at Franco's. And, Ali, no worries on my account, I'll be unarmed.'

'Thanks, Sam, I'll see you then.'

She put the phone down and saw that Daniel was staring at her over the top of his glasses.

'Do I detect Elliot's father at work again?' he asked.

483

'If only it were that easy.'

'Sounds to me as if it could be. Now that you've told Sarah the truth, you go right ahead and spill the real coffee-beans to Sam, then wait for the brew to filter back to Elliot. What do you reckon to him being on the phone the minute you get home tonight?'

'I'd rather put money on Elliot thinking that Sam and I have concocted this latest version of events as a last-ditch attempt to get us back together.'

Daniel regarded Ali as she switched her attention from him to the agreement she was preparing for a new client. She'd lost even more weight since October – weight that she could ill-afford to lose – and it didn't suit her. She looked as though she was wasting away. He hadn't seen her this bad since Isaac died. And it was coming up for that time of the year again. A week tomorrow was the anniversary of Isaac's death and he knew that over the coming days she would put herself through the same torture she'd gone through in previous years. He had made up his mind at home last night that at the end of this week he'd pull the plug on Ali's madness. But now it looked as if he wouldn't need to.

Ali reached Franco's five minutes late, but was disappointed to find that she was there before Sam. She was shown to the table he had booked for them and the waiter took her coat. 'Anything to drink while you're waiting for your companion?' he asked. Something in the way he used the word 'companion' made her wonder – hope – that maybe this was a clever ploy on Sam's part to bring her and Elliot together. She sat down and ordered a glass of mineral water. She would have preferred something stronger to steady her nerves, but thought that the combination of booze and her current agitation would not be a good mix.

Restlessly she scanned the menu on the holly-festooned chalkboard to the right of her, more out of the need to do something than to choose what to eat. She couldn't remember the last time she'd enjoyed a meal. When she'd tired of studying the menu, she glanced round at the other diners and listened to the record being piped through the restaurant. It was Whitney Houston singing 'I Will Always Love You'. Snatches of the lyrics struck home – 'bittersweet memories, that is all I'm taking with me, so goodbye, please don't cry, we both know I'm not what you need . . .'

Ali willed herself to stay calm. It's nothing but a sentimental song, she told herself. So what if it's a little close for comfort and reflects just how you should feel towards Elliot? Too right you're not what he needs. He needs the love of a good, sensible wife who won't give him any trouble. One who will love him and bring him only joy. He needs a headcase like you like he needs both his arms chopped off. But as stern as she was with herself, her emotions got the better of her and tears rolled down her cheeks. She fumbled in her bag for a tissue, but was out of luck. With nothing else for it, she grabbed the carefully folded linen napkin from the table and wiped her eyes with it. Bang goes my mascara, she thought, burying her face in the starchy fabric and blowing her nose noisily. She was mid-blow when she heard a familiar voice. 'So how's my favourite ex-daughter-in-law?'

She peered up from the napkin and saw Sam. She was so pleased to see his cheery face, yet disappointed that it wasn't Elliot, that she started to cry again.

'Oh, love,' he said, bending down to her, 'am I such a sight for sore eyes?'

'Yes, you are. Oh, Sam, I'm sorry, I don't seem able to stop blubbing, these days. The slightest thing sets me off.'

'Well, you go right ahead and while you're doing that I'll get us both a decent drink.' He attracted the attention of a waiter, who was doing a poor job at pretending not to notice what was going on and ordered two glasses of Scotch. 'No ice,' he said, 'this is strictly medicinal. There now,' he said, when the drinks were brought to their table, 'down the hatch in one and you'll feel a lot better.'

She tossed the drink back and wiped her eyes. 'How am I looking?' she asked.

'Like a very tired, unhappy panda.'

She groaned. 'I'm sorry.'

'And I'm sorry too. I wish now that I'd got in touch with you sooner, but the Boy Wonder wouldn't hear of it. Divided loyalty is a bloody awful thing.'

'How is Elliot?'

'A pain to live with. Perpetually snappy. Perpetually brooding. And perpetually miserable.'

She groaned again. 'And it's all my fault. I'm sorry.'

'Now quit apologising and help me decide what to eat.'

'Nothing for me. I'm in no fit state to keep anything down.'

'You'll have something to eat, my girl, or there'll be trouble. I'll order you an omelette and a small green salad. And for me, a nice big peppered steak should just about do it.'

When the waiter had taken their order and left them alone, Ali said, 'Why aren't you cross with me, Sam?'

He shook out his napkin and placed it on his lap. 'I was at first. I was bloody furious with you. You know what I am where Elliot's concerned and I could have said some pretty ungentlemanly things to you that day when he came home and told me what you'd done with Trevor. But then, as is generally the way with these matters, I cooled off and wanted to try to see it from where you were standing.'

'Was the view any clearer?'

'Not really.'

'Has Elliot calmed down at all?'

Sam sucked in his lips and shook his head. ''Fraid not, love. He's adamant that he doesn't want to see you again.'

'But, Sam, I didn't do it.'

'Come again?'

'I didn't sleep with Trevor. It was all a lie to make Sarah leave him.'

'Whoa there, you've lost me. Start at the beginning and tell me exactly what you did.'

Sick as she was of the story, Ali went through it again, just as she had last night with Sarah. Then she told Sam about Sarah leaving Trevor. 'She's forgiven me, Sam. Do you think Elliot could ever do the same?'

Sam sat back in his chair and let out his breath. 'Wow, Ali. They sure as hell broke the mould when they made you.'

'Are you being rude or paying me a compliment?'

'I'm saying you're a one-off.'

'Yeah,' she said miserably, 'and it's just as well, or imagine the mess the world would be in.'

Their meal arrived, and for a few minutes provided them with a distraction. Ali pushed her food round the plate until Sam said, 'Ali, eat your lunch. You're nowt but a waif and at your age it doesn't hang well on you.'

She burst out laughing. 'Give it to me straight, Sam, why don't you?'

He smiled and his dark eyes twinkled. 'That's better. Now, tell me what you're doing for Christmas.'

Ali tackled a tiny mouthful of omelette. 'I can't believe it's as good as a whole year since you were last asking me that.'

'And are you hedging as you did this time last year?'

'No,' she said, 'I'm not. I had thought of going to my parents, but now that Sarah's moved in with me a change of plan might be on the cards. We haven't got as far as discussing any of it and, of course, there's Hannah to consider, but I guess there's a chance that we'll have a quiet Christmas at the mill. How about you and Elliot? Going away again?'

'No. Elliot hasn't had time to think about a holiday. He's been too busy chasing his arse over some flash git at work.'

'Don't tell me, Gervase Merchant-Taylor?'

'Yeah, that's the man. He's been had for sexual harassment. It's raised a rare old stink, I can tell you. People up and down from London all the time. And from what I can make of all the phone calls the Boy Wonder's been making late at night, there's been more drama going on in that one office block than in all the soaps on telly put together.'

'Has he got rid of Gervase?'

'Oh, aye.'

'Bet that pleased him.'

'Not that you'd notice. You know what an inscrutable bugger he can be. Now, come on, love, I've nearly finished my steak and you've hardly made an impression on that omelette of yours.'

In the cold, sleety rain, Sam walked Ali back to her office, just as he had last year. This time, though, they were spared any poignant reminders of Isaac, and sheltering under their umbrellas, Sam kissed her goodbye. 'I'll do my best with Elliot, Ali,' he said. 'I'll tell him exactly what you've told me. And if my oh-so-cultured son has got a penn'orth of sense, he'll get in touch with you. Now take the greatest of care, won't you?'

Ali waited by the phone all that evening.

She pounced on it every time it rang at the weekend.

She did the same at work the following week.

But there was no call from Elliot.

Nothing.

His silence told her all she needed to know.

Chapter Fifty

It was a week now since Sarah had moved in with Ali. Most of her thoughts were wrapped up in disentangling herself from the fallout of leaving Trevor, but each day she became increasingly concerned for her friend's welfare.

Lying in bed, Sarah listened to what had just woken her – Ali's soft footsteps on the wooden floor beneath her. She raised her head from the pillow, reached for her alarm clock, and strained her eyes in the darkness to make out the time. A quarter past five. She sighed and lowered her head back on to the pillow. This was the fourth morning in a row that Ali had been unable to sleep beyond five o'clock. Then Sarah realised what day it was: the anniversary of Isaac's death. Poor Ali. She wondered whether she ought to offer to go with her when she made her visit to the church in Great Budworth. But instinct told her that Ali would reject such an offer. Sharing her grief had never been easy for her, and there was little hope that this had changed. All Sarah could do was be there for Ali when she came home that evening.

Just as Ali had been there for her this week, when Sarah had begun the task of coming to terms with the last eighteen years. Grace had been right when she'd said that she had to strip away the layers and rediscover the real Sarah. Nearly two decades of fearful thinking had enslaved her will – to use yet another of Grace's phrases. Ali's interpretation of her state of mind was less eloquent: 'Sarah,' she'd said over breakfast, the morning after she'd left Trevor, 'you're totally screwed up.'

'That's good coming from you,' Sarah had retaliated.

'Okay, so we're both screwed to hell and back. Any chance of this God of yours putting in an appearance and straightening us out?'

'Oh, so suddenly there is a God?'

'I didn't say that.'

'You're not wavering, are you, Ali?'

'God forbid.'

When Ali had left for work, Sarah had considered how best to let Hannah know what she had done. She had no idea how her daughter would react and her greatest fear was that she would condemn her and want to dissociate herself. Telling her over the telephone seemed inappropriate, so she had tried to write a letter. But the torn-up pieces of paper on the floor at her feet, as she had sat hunched over the kitchen table, bore witness to the difficulty she was having in expressing herself.

In the end the dilemma was taken out of her hands. Hannah phoned her, just as she was despairing of ever finding the right words.

'Mum, I've just had the weirdest conversation with Dad. He says you've had some sort of breakdown and that I'm not to worry because he'll sort everything. What the hell's he going on about?'

Steeling her courage, she had told Hannah the truth. 'Oh, Hannah, I wish I had had a breakdown. That would be so much easier for your father to cope with.'

'Bloody hell, Mum! You mean you've left him?'

'Hannah, please don't –' But Sarah couldn't carry on. She wanted to say, 'Please don't judge me,' but what right did she have to tell Hannah how to regard her?

'Please don't what, Mum?'

'Don't think too badly of me.'

There was a suspenseful pause.

'Hannah?'

'So what's brought this on? Okay, he can be a cent short of

a dollar, but you've stuck with him this long. Why the sudden need to change things?'

'Because I have to. And . . . because I don't love him.'

'Is there somebody else?'

'No. Absolutely not.'

'You don't sound very upset. It seems as if you've been planning this for some time.'

Her question had sounded too much as if it were an accusation and Sarah had countered with, 'You don't sound very upset either. You sound angry, but not upset.'

'I'm in shock.'

'Well, so am I.'

There was another pause.

'Look, Mum, I've got to go. I've got a lecture. I'll speak to you sometime.'

The word 'sometime' had resonated down the line with angry hurt and had stung Sarah into saying, 'Hannah, I love you, please try not to worry.' She had wanted to add, 'And please don't hate me for what I've done,' but hadn't wanted to risk putting that thought into her daughter's head.

'I'm bound to worry, Mum. I'd be a strange person if I didn't. Now, I really have to go, my money's running out.'

There were a million questions Sarah wanted to ask. A million things she wanted to say, just to keep the reassuring sound of Hannah's voice in her ear. But all she said was, 'One more thing, Hannah. How did you know where to find me?'

'Where else would you be?'

After she'd put down the phone and before she gave in to a burst of self-pitying tears, she wrote a short letter to Hannah in which she threw herself on her precious daughter's mercy. She sealed the envelope at once, stuck a stamp on it and, before she lost her nerve, walked in the icy rain to the nearest postbox. She was dripping wet and chilled to the bone when she returned to the mill. She lit the fire in the sitting room, made herself a cup of hot chocolate and, while warming her shivering body in front of the fire, she wrote a plan of action.

It was time to start taking a firm line with herself. There was to be no more wallowing in self-pity. She had made a decision to leave her husband and she was going to get on with it as best she could. Ironically, it was a case of for better or for worse.

At the top of the page she wrote, 'Speak to Trevor'.

Is that it? she asked herself, when ten minutes later that was all she'd written on the lined page of foolscap. It wasn't much of a campaign of action.

She spoke to him that night. An hour after Ali returned from work, she drove Sarah over to Astley Hope. Sarah had insisted that Ali stayed in the car while she went inside to talk to Trevor. She hadn't phoned ahead to make sure he would be there, but instead had left it to chance.

Chance presented her with Trevor in a mood of hopeful reconciliation. He offered cups of tea and a promise that he'd never refer to the previous evening again, if that's what she wanted. Without once looking at her, he said, 'I know you've been under a lot of stress, what with Hannah going away to college, but there's nothing we can't work out together. Shirley's given me the address of a retreat for married couples that we could go on. She says . . .'

Still the same old Trevor, she thought, as he rambled on, pretending that there was an easy alternative to the dreadful suggestion she had made. He was still prepared to live with his head jammed into the sand. 'Trevor,' she said firmly, watching him reach for the teapot from the draining-board, 'please listen to me. I meant every word of what I said last night. It may have been very wrong of me to tell you in front of the group and, believe me, I never intended it to happen that way. In fact I never intended it to happen at all, but it really is the way I feel. It's what I want. What I need to do.'

He stopped fiddling with the teapot, raised his eyes to her for a fraction of a second, then lowered his gaze back to the small brown teapot in his hand and stared at it as if he wasn't quite sure what it was or how it had got there. Then he threw it across the kitchen. It smashed against the back door, the pieces scattering all over the floor. Only the spout and handle remained intact.

At last, she thought, a genuine emotion. She waited for his verbal outburst to follow suit. Almost hoped that it would. But he didn't even raise his voice. Bizarrely he reached for another teapot from the cupboard to the right of the kettle, which was boiling fiercely, sending a cloud of steam into the cold kitchen.

'And just how did you intend to tell me that you wanted to end our marriage?'

'I never intended to. I thought . . . I thought I could go on.'

'Go on?' he repeated. 'You make it sound as if it was a trial. An ordeal.'

She lowered her eyes from his bewildered face. How could she tell him the truth? That every day for her had been a trial. 'I'm sorry,' she said, knowing that it wasn't enough. An apology was never going to undo the harm she'd caused. 'I never meant to hurt you,' she added.

'But you have, Sarah. You and Ali.' He turned his back to her and made the tea that she knew she wouldn't drink. She wanted to make him stop what he was doing, but knew that he needed to occupy himself with something while they were having this unthinkable conversation. At last he swung round to look at her again and said, 'Sarah, I'm prepared to forgive you if you promise me that you'll seek help. This isn't the first time you've behaved irrationally and I'm sure that there's a perfectly reasonable explanation for what's triggered this madness. Shirley says it's probably an early menopause. Apparently lots of women go through similar episodes of confusion.'

Her heart sank. He was never going to face the truth. His make-believe world, which was way up there on some surreal plane, didn't have the foundations for such a weight of concrete reality. 'And what would you say was a reasonable

493

explanation for Ali's behaviour?' she asked scathingly. 'Was that merely an episode of hormonal confusion too?'

His face hardened. 'That woman is totally beyond my comprehension. And if we're to make a go of our marriage, you would have to promise me that you wouldn't have anything more to do with her.'

'I'm afraid that's not possible, Trevor.'

'That sounds as though you're prepared to choose Ali over me.'

'Trevor,' she said in exasperation, 'listen to me, please. I'm leaving you because I don't love you. Not because I prefer Ali's friendship or because I'm having a funny hormonal turn. Is that clear enough for you?'

'And what about my rights? Don't I, as your husband, have a say in what happens to our marriage?'

'You deserve the right to be free of me, to live a life that's free of lies and guilt.'

'But you're my wife. Your duty is—'

'Trevor, if you so much as dare to quote a piece of scripture at me I shall leave without another word.'

But that was exactly what he did do. And, just as she'd warned him, she turned on her heel and went up to the spare bedroom. A few minutes later she came down the stairs carrying her sewing-machine and several rolls of fabric. She went out to Ali's car, dumped them in the boot, and returned to the house where she proceeded to stuff a selection of clothes and other personal possessions into carrier-bags. Trevor didn't try to stop her. He stayed in the kitchen, at the table, his head in his hands, murmuring to himself. He was praying. Other women might have been moved by the sight of a man beseeching God to save his marriage, but all it did to Sarah was confirm her conviction that if Trevor had spent less time chatting to God and more time talking to her their marriage might not have needed saving.

With the last of the bags in the car, she went back into the house and gave Trevor a final parting shot of honesty. She told him that Ali hadn't seduced him that night at the mill. She wanted to believe that her motive for telling him the truth was an honourable one, that she didn't want him to go through the rest of his life thinking that he'd committed a terrible sin – but she was more inclined to think less of herself: she suspected that she wanted to deflate that well-disguised bit of his male ego that was indubitably proud that he'd slept with an attractive woman like Ali. That he couldn't recall having done so was immaterial – no doubt even his slow-working, virtuous brain could fill in the gaps for him.

His final words were, 'May God forgive you. You and Ali.'

It was not so much the bestowing of a benediction as a snarled, fist-clenched threat. It pained Sarah that they should part so acrimoniously, but as Ali had said during the drive back to the mill, 'Sarah, there's no reasoning with a fanatic when he starts wielding his beliefs as a weapon.'

Realising that there was little chance of her getting back to sleep, Sarah slipped out of bed, pulled on her dressing-gown, and went downstairs to join Ali in her nocturnal potterings. She found her in the sitting room, curled up on the sofa beneath the quilt Sarah had made for her last Christmas. She was fast asleep and could easily have been mistaken for a small child. The image was further enhanced by the poignant sight of Mr Squeezy's head poking out from the quilt. Quietly retracing her steps, Sarah went back upstairs to her bedroom.

Once again she lay in the darkness and, unable to sleep, her thoughts turned to Hannah.

Since that brief phone call and the letter she had sent her, Hannah had phoned almost every day. After each conversation Sarah had felt sufficiently encouraged to hope that her daughter's understanding and acceptance of the situation were increasing. It was generally acknowledged that children were extraordinarily selfish, and while Hannah's relationship with her father this past year had not been as happy as in previous years, it was clear that she didn't want the status quo changed; neither did she relish being saddled with the stigma of coming from a broken family.

'Your mind's obviously made up,' she said to Sarah during one conversation. 'There's nothing I can say to make you reconsider, is there?'

'Nothing at all,' she'd said.

'What will you do?'

'I don't know exactly.'

'God, Mum, don't you think you've been a bit hasty? You should at least have put a plan together.'

'Something will come up, I'm sure.'

It was strange to experience the sensation of their roles having been reversed. Suddenly Hannah was the questioning I-know-better adult and Sarah was the shoulder-shrugging teenager.

Hannah was also in regular contact with Trevor. 'How is he?' Sarah had asked only yesterday.

'He seems okay. The Worthies are rallying round him like bees to a honey-pot. He says he's going on a retreat for Christmas. It'll be some retreat – he's going with the entire Slipper Gang! Just imagine, if it's one of those places where you have to keep your gob shut the whole time they'll explode, the lot of them. By the way, Jamie's coming across from Bristol to give me a lift home. That okay with you?'

The fact that Hannah was able so soon, and so easily, to flit in and out of the unpleasant subject of her parents' broken marriage, gave Sarah further cause to hope that eventually all would be well.

Ali left for work just after eight, leaving Sarah wondering how much longer her friend could go on as she was. She hadn't touched the bowl of cereal Sarah had set out for her, or the piece of peanut-butter toast she'd hoped would tempt her. Ali had taken no more than a few sips of her tea before she'd reached for her briefcase and said, 'I'll be off now.'

Maybe once she's got this day over with she'll start to pick up, Sarah told herself, as she watched Ali's car headlamps pick out the frosty hedgerow as she disappeared down the dark lane. But she knew that it wasn't just Isaac's death that was causing Ali so much misery.

Most of her heartache was caused by Elliot.

Poor Ali, she had banked on him getting in touch with her after she'd had lunch with Sam, but there hadn't been a single word from him.

Sarah cleared away Ali's untouched breakfast, then went upstairs to sort out the room on the top floor of the mill. It was Ali's study, but over the Christmas holiday it was to be Hannah's bedroom. In a genuine and sincere attempt not to be partisan, Sarah had said that maybe Hannah ought to stay with her father for a few days before he went off on his retreat with the Slipper Gang. Her suggestion had been met with an indifferent 'Yeah, maybe.' She had not tried to justify her lack of enthusiasm for the idea and Sarah had not enquired why.

Thinking about it now as she made up the camp bed, Sarah concluded that Hannah was very much her own woman and carried a lot less self-doubt on her shoulders than Sarah had at that age. She wondered if this was a trait inherited from her biological father. Certainly he'd never had a problem with self-doubt. In all the years she'd carried the guilty secret of his presence in her life, she had rarely given him much thought. Through the necessity of trying to forget what she'd done, she had been, for the most part, successful in blocking him out. Occasionally, though, she had pondered on the scenario of accidentally bumping into him and imagining the conversation they would have. But the scene always ran along the same lines: he couldn't remember who she was, let alone recall ever having gone to bed with her. But it was also true that she could scarcely bring his face to mind. Vague recollections told her that he'd been blond with blue eyes and a strong jaw, but other than that she had little to work on when trying to think if Hannah bore any physical resemblance to him.

She had never been angry or bitter with John for getting her pregnant – how could she be when she had such a lovely daughter? – but that day last week in Chester when she'd come across the lad who was using his strength to dominate the girl at his feet, an explosion of suppressed anger had erupted within her. It had reminded her all too sharply of how she had got herself into a situation that had led to her being pregnant. She had thought herself totally in control of what was going on – after all, she knew what John's reputation was – but vanity had got the better of her. She'd allowed herself to go along with his notorious easy charm and naturally flirtatious manner. It won't go any further, she'd told herself, as he'd brushed her cheek with his lips. I'll stop him before anything happens, she thought, as she shivered at the touch of his fingers on her neck. But when he'd slipped his hand inside her dress she'd realised her mistake. She'd tried to wriggle out of his grasp but he'd pulled her to him and started to part her legs. Part of her – the part that was dizzy with desire – wanted him to carry on with what he was doing but the other part wanted to run. She didn't want this. Not this way. Not with a man she didn't love. She tried again to free herself but he smiled his bewitching smile and said, 'I won't hurt you, Sarah. It'll be okay. I promise you everything will be all right.'

Stupid girl that she was, she had believed him. The very next day she had heard him boasting in the college library to a fellow American how easy she'd been. 'Ten points for a virgin,' he'd laughed, 'and another five because she's prettier than the usual ones.'

She smoothed out the duvet on the camp bed, then went and stood at the window. It was light now and a bright sun shone down on the surrounding fields, which were white with frost. In the distance she could see the row of terraced cottages where Ali's cleaner, Lizzie, lived. A thin trail of smoke rose from one of the chimneys and Sarah thought how snug and cosy the little houses looked. The other morning Lizzie had mentioned that the tenant of the middle cottage was thinking of moving out in the next few months, and that the owner would be keen to find a new tenant. 'It's a bit grotty,' Lizzie had said, 'only two bedrooms and the kitchen is minute, barely room to swing a mouse, never mind a cat. But the rent's dirt cheap.' And, although she was more than happy to stay here with Ali, Sarah knew that there would come a time when she would have to stand on her own two feet . . . and that little cottage would be just perfect for her.

When she had told Hannah she didn't have a plan for her future, it wasn't strictly true. She had vague ideas of setting herself up in business. Why keep slogging away for a shop, which determined her work and wages, when she could be mistress of her own destiny? The only difference would be that she would have to seek out her customers – but the money she could earn would be so much more than she was currently being paid. It was worth a try. What did she have to lose?

Gazing out across the fields, and watching a crow flap its broad, languid wings as it swooped from one telegraph pole to another, she thought with satisfaction that she had come a long way in just a week.

'And who would have thought that possible?' she said aloud. Eight days ago she had been trying to hold together a life that seemed intent on falling apart. She had tried so hard to keep everything neat and tidy, safe and secure. She realised now how wearing it had been. 'Fighting the inevitable is a futile and profoundly exhausting occupation,' Grace had told her on the phone, when she'd called to see how she was getting on. 'We never understand what a heavy burden it is that we're carrying until we let go of it.'

It didn't seem right to describe her marriage as a burden, but in essence that was exactly what it had become. She felt sorry for Trevor and would probably always feel guilty that she had used him as she had, but as she stared into the empty blue sky, she had the strongest feeling that from the death of her old life a new and better one would emerge.

For Trevor too.

She hoped that God wouldn't mind if she took a break from religion. 'It's nothing personal,' she said, addressing the perfect canopy of blue, 'only I think I need to take stock of what it all really means.'

Just then the telephone rang. She moved away from the window and picked up the receiver from the extension on the desk. She was surprised to hear Daniel's voice.

'Hello, Sarah,' he said. 'I hope you believe in miracles, because this is the best. I've just had a call from Elliot.'

Later that afternoon, Ali left her car outside the post office in Great Budworth and made her way towards the sandstone church. She followed the path round to the furthest side of the churchyard and thought how inappropriate and insensitive it was that, on a day such as this, the sun was shining. But although it was indecently bright, there was no warmth to it and the air was cold and raw. She hurried on briskly, passing *Robert Ashworth* along with *Amy and Joseph Riley* and didn't slow her pace until she was at the foot of Isaac's small grave. She stooped to the frozen ground and laid out her offering of white roses. 'Oh, Isaac,' she murmured, 'thank goodness you're not here to see how much I've hurt your father. I've been so careless with him.'

She pulled off her gloves and tugged at the weeds to ward off her misery. But it didn't work and, without being able to stop it, she felt herself dragged down into the dark depths of her grief and anguish. All she could think of was the overwhelming need to hold her child. 'Just to hold you once more,' she whispered, 'just once would do it.' She closed her eyes and pictured herself cradling Isaac, breathing in his sweet baby smell, touching his soft silky cheek, stroking his fine blond hair. The illusion felt so very real to her that the poignancy of it ripped through her. She lost every ounce of control and wept helplessly.

Blinded by the tears streaming down her face, she thought, for the craziest of moments, that Isaac was near her . . . that he had just touched her. She held her breath, squeezed her eyes shut and allowed herself to think that he *was* there. But when she felt the pressure on her shoulder increase, she opened her eyes and saw that she wasn't alone. Elliot was crouching beside her.

'How long have you been there?' she mumbled, through her choking sobs, too weak to stand or move away from him.

'Long enough,' he answered, his own voice thick with emotion. Carefully he added his flowers to hers, and then, with extreme gentleness, lifted her to her feet. He led her to a nearby bench and sat her down beside him. Then, removing a handkerchief from his coat pocket, he raised her face to his and wiped away the tears from the ash grey arcs under her tired eyes. It was the most loving act and made her cry all the more.

'Stop, please,' she said, taking the handkerchief from him and pressing it to her face. 'You're making it worse.'

Distressed to see how changed she was since he last saw her, he said, 'I've made a lot of things worse, haven't I?'

With eyes that were so terribly sad, she met the intensity of his gaze. 'We both have,' she said. And then: 'Why didn't you ring me, Elliot? After I had lunch with Sam, I waited every day for you to call. Every day.'

'I'm sorry, but I was still cross with you. It was petty, I know, but I was angry because you had put your friendship for Sarah before your love for me.'

She hardly dared to ask the next question for fear of being rejected again, but she forced herself. 'And do you still feel that way?'

'No. That enormously influential lateral thinker, and your great advocate, Sam, put me straight last night. He said that

I'd got it all wrong and that what you'd actually done was put Sarah's happiness before your own.'

'He's right, that's exactly what I did . . . I just didn't realise how big a sacrifice it would be. Or how painful.'

He took her icy hand in his and raised it to his lips. 'You're a woman of extraordinary conviction, Ali, and I love you for it. But promise me one thing. Promise you'll never do anything as unwise or as reckless as that again.'

She nodded and blinked away the threat of fresh tears. 'I promise.'

'Good.'

'Does that mean you're giving me another chance to get it right between us?'

He shook his head. 'No. I'm giving us both a chance to get it right.'

'But you deserve better, Elliot.'

'Anyone else would bore me. I need the challenge of you.'

She almost smiled. 'I can't think why.'

He drew her closer to him, held her cold face in his hands and kissed her slowly and deeply. 'But I can,' he said at last, tilting his head back to look into her eyes, 'and that's all that matters.'

'But is it enough?'

'Oh, I think so.'

He kissed her again. Then, leaning tranquilly into each other, they stared in silence at the view beyond the church-yard, to the frost-whitened fields that were criss-crossed with stark, wintry hedges and trees. A skein of birds flew overhead, their formation as precise and perfect as the blue of the sky. With not a word passing between them, they each lowered their gaze to the grave of their son a few yards from where they were sitting.

Elliot said, 'We won't ever get over his death, Ali, not fully, but together we might learn to live with it.'

'I hope you're right,' she said faintly, then with a small smile, she added, 'You usually are.'

He squeezed her hand. 'Not always.'

She sighed and gave a little shiver. 'I hate it here,' she said, with heartfelt sadness. 'I wish I could derive some comfort from it but I can't. I doubt I ever will.'

'I'm hoping that after today you might feel differently.' He rose from the bench and held out a hand to her. 'I hope you approve of what I've done. I wanted to give you a happy memory of this place. It was the best I could do at such short notice.'

She looked at him quizzically.

'Come on,' he said, and pulled her to her feet. He led her back up the path towards the church. But as they neared the lych-gate, Ali stopped in her tracks. There, in front of the churchyard wall, was Sarah. Daniel was there too. So was Richard. And, with a grin that was stretched from ear to ear, so was Sam. He looked at Elliot and said, 'Well, Romeo, is it all sorted? Did you kiss and make up? Are we on for a celebratory drink?'

One of his rare-as-gold-dust smiles flickered across Elliot's face and, after exchanging an intimate glance of tenderness with Ali, he put his arm around her and said, 'Oh, aye, Dad, about as sorted as it's ever likely to be.'

Sam laughed heartily. 'Well, thank God for that!'